MY SOUL TO KEEP

MY SOUL TO KEEP

Jackie Sonnenberg

4 Horsemen
Publications, Inc.

Original nursery rhyme, often called "The Lord's Prayer"

"Now I lay me down to sleep
I pray the lord my soul to keep.
And if I die before I wake,
I pray the lord my soul to take."

~18th century children's bedtime nursery rhyme~

CONTENTS

Chapter 1 1
Chapter 2 10
Chapter 3 17
Chapter 4 24
Chapter 5 36
Chapter 6 46
Chapter 7 56
Chapter 8 65
Chapter 9 73
Chapter 10 85
Chapter 11. 96
Chapter 12 117
Chapter 13 131
Chapter 14 143
Chapter 15 160
Chapter 16 168
Chapter 17. 177
Chapter 18 187
Chapter 19 191
Chapter 20 196
Chapter 21 203
Chapter 22 211
Chapter 23 220
Chapter 24 229

Chapter 25 235
Chapter 26 243
Chapter 27 251
Chapter 28 255
Chapter 29 258
Chapter 30 269
Chapter 31 276
Chapter 32 283
Chapter 33 289
Chapter 34 299
Chapter 35 308
Chapter 36 318
Chapter 37 351
Chapter 38 357
Chapter 39 366
Chapter 40 372

Book Club Questions 375
Author Bio 377
Author's Note 379

CHAPTER 1

September 2012

I was only at school for five minutes and already I was seeing ghosts.

I saw someone—or something—flicker along the sides of the building and in between trees, and then disappear. The overbearing sunlight caused me to blink repeatedly; one, two, three times, and each time, it was like the flashes of a camera bringing people in and out of focus until they were gone.

People say that seeing is believing ... or is it believing is seeing? Truth is, I never knew if I believed in spirits before I had a reason to.

Spirits were all I obsessed over after my own brush with death.

In my grief, I started looking for him everywhere, trying in vain to see if there was a part of him that still floated around, to see if anything still floated around. My mom took me to different doctors: the kind that gave you medicine and the kind you had to sit and talk to. I spent my time alone when I wasn't in school. Except, of course, for these doctor sessions.

"I have the poem you wrote in school," the lady said gently. She held the unfolded notebook sheet in her hand, spread out against a clipboard with my name, grade, date, and teacher's name scribbled in the top left corner. "Can you tell me what was on your mind when you wrote it?"

"I don't know," I said.

"It's a very morbid poem for a sweet girl like you," she said, handing the clipboard over to me. "Will you read it to me?"

I looked back at what I wrote for class, the one that made the teacher cross her brow at me worriedly and call home, as though any single thing I did meant I was emotionally unstable.

"'Now I lay me down to sleep, I pray the lord my soul to keep. And if I die before I wake, I pray the lord my soul to take.'"

The doctor just nodded, holding the tip of her pen to her chin.

"Is it about wanting to be protected, no matter what happens to you?"

"My dad will protect me," I said.

"He will always be with you," the woman said.

"He is with me right now."

"Yes, in spirit he is."

"No," I said. "I think he's in the chair next to me."

I wished everyone would just leave me alone. Anyone that asked me how I was doing, I said I was getting some peace and recovery. My friends understood and tried to treat me normally. I got the classic response: "If there is anything I can do, just let me know!" Which, everyone knows is just an empty line to tell a grieving party that you care. No one actually needs anything, and no one is going to do anything about it. It is such a stupid thing to say.

I almost jumped when something brushed my hair and, turning around, I saw my mother's still-concerned face.

"Sky? Are you all right?"

"Yeah," I said right away.

She and my younger brother and sister came out of the building behind us. My mother carried most of the stuff: the blue information folder and packet we got for Orientation, including a map of the campus and my assigned dorm. There were too many buildings at this place for me to keep track of. Some were academic and others were residencies, and according to the snobby brochure, it said Applewhite Preparatory Boarding School would "plant the seeds of success into young, barren minds." My mom fell for it, thinking it would be the best thing for me, and packed me up for it barely after my thirteenth birthday. Just like that, my next life was already set out for me.

"Did you take your meds?"

I sighed. "Come on, Mom."

"You know how important that is. The school is going to make sure you are taken care of, but you still need to take care of yourself."

I nodded and dared to look around to see if I could still see ... whatever I saw.

"Honey, you're going to be just fine," my mother continued. "The lady we talked to was really nice, wasn't she? You are going to have everything you need here. This is such a good place for you, and much better than the public school!"

I fought the urge to groan. She squeezed my shoulder while my brother and sister just stood there and stared at nothing. I knew they stared at nothing. They weren't looking to see anything, but I was.

"Remember honey, don't talk about ghost stuff here."

I stiffened.

"Skyler, remember what we talked about. It's part of counseling. It's part of moving on. We are all doing the same thing. This place will help you get you back on your feet."

"He's here," I said.

My family just looked at me, expressionless and numb.

"He is *always* here..." my mom said, choking on her words.

And with that, it was time for them to leave me. We hugged and promised to keep in touch, everybody leaking out tears but me. I had none left. They left and made their way towards the visitor parking lot, where other families headed after abandoning their children.

There were some surviving droplets on the concrete steps from that morning's rain, which meant mud puddles to avoid. Using my map, I made my way back to my dorm, where an exciting day of unpacking awaited me. The sun managed to break away from a horde of clouds in spurts, revealing the aged brick on the buildings.

I saw a girl walking across the street, and I stopped to watch her. It could have been the glaze of the sun, or the fog of the morning, but somehow something made her seem transparent.

A boy sat on a bench behind me, facing forward and not saying anything. I thought I saw the girl walking, and the next cloud that passed over the sun revealed that there was no one there at all.

"Did you see that?"

He looked at me, almost startled to see that not only was I standing there, but I witnessed the same thing he did.

"See ... what?"

"That girl disappear."

He smiled. "You think she disappeared?"

"Well," I answered. "It looked like it."

"She was just finding some peace: taking a nice walk and clearing her mind of stress."

I didn't realize it, but I blurted out that I wish I could, too.

"I know how you can."

"Yeah, how?"

"If you find the right outlets, you can find your inner strength."

"I've heard that before," I said.

"I know how you can heal yourself."

I paused and turned to look at him as I realized he was giving me a flyer.

"Oh, thanks," I said, taking the lime green sheet. It was the same thing I already had in my Orientation folder, just printed on different paper to stand out on its own. The boy smiled at me, his curls falling into his eyes. They were almost the same color, and it was strange I couldn't figure out what. It was too light to be brown but too dark to be blonde.

"Student Activities event soon. Hope to see you there," he said. "Please come by and check out our booth. I hope that you find happiness, peace, and guidance on your journey to greatness."

I looked at him, slightly dazed. Before I could stop myself, I let out a snicker.

"Are they seriously making all of you recite that to the incoming newbies?"

It was so cheesy I couldn't help but laugh, but I stopped immediately since this guy had not cracked a smile.

"No," he said, looking at me quizzically. "Why would anyone make me say that? Shouldn't we all want happiness for one another?"

I didn't know what to say to this, really. "No, I don't mean it like that. I just didn't expect that, that's all."

I noticed he wore a black t-shirt with a yellow logo on the right, similar to the one on the flyer. The letters were "G.O.L" inside of a rectangle shape. A cage? A lantern.

"It is important for new students, and anyone for that matter, to know the right way to live a life of fulfillment. You think you do, but you really don't. There is so much darkness and not enough light. I am with an organization that will help you find your way. We are here to spread the message to find the Light. We hope you have the strength in your heart to come and see what we're all about and make the choice to be the one in control of your life."

I just stood there, clutching the flyer, eyes wandering from it to the boy.

"Look for us," he said with a smile. "We're the Guardians of Light, and we're here to shine a beacon of knowledge for a better world."

"Okay, that's nice. Thanks," I said. I neatly put the flyer in my packet and then I headed to my dorm like I was in a hurry, but really, I did not want more word vomit. It made me cringe the way he just preached to me like a television evangelist. And although it seemed rehearsed, I knew that he believed every word he said to me.

I opened my door to reveal my bedding and boxes of stuff still lying around from that morning. My mom and I came in, dumped off my stuff, and headed off to Orientation. I was happy that my new roommate Deanna was still out and about because what I was about to do required me to be alone. Alone—but not completely.

I rummaged through my backpack to find it wrapped up in a T-shirt to prevent my mom from seeing it. The title alone won my attention once I set foot in that "special" bookstore: *Contacting the Deceased: Making a Connection to the Spiritual Channels.* I held the leather-covered book for a moment, even getting a slight chill from the Gothic lettering. It reminded me of when I was at a sleepover in 4th grade and we watched *The Craft*. It freaked me out then, but it did not freak me out now. They were able to make things happen, and they made things happen by making spiritual connections. I learned that it was possible—only if you believed in it.

I killed the lights and closed the curtains, allowing only a thin line of light in the room so I could see. I moved a desk chair out of the way to make more room, and then I got the piece of chalk out of my backpack. I sat down with that book and drew a circle on the floor around me, light enough so that I could clean it off later. I also wrote down his name, underlined three times. Next, I lit two little tea light candles and put those very close to the edge, but not over. I opened it to the page that I folded down into a little triangle I could find when needed and took a deep breath.

"I call you," I chanted. "I call you ... Jeff Monroe ... to enter my circle. Enter my circle, Jeff Monroe, and come to me. Come to me."

I placed one hand on the three lines as I continued this phrase, holding the book in the other hand. I closed my eyes and concentrated on his face, just as the book instructed. I changed my breathing rhythm from slow to slower.

"Come to this circle. Come to me."

Both my hands rested on the lines, like the home row of a keyboard. I exhaled as slowly as someone letting the air out of a balloon, little by little until my lungs were deflated enough to refill. I didn't open my eyes or stop concentrating, even when I heard my door push.

It moved in the doorframe gently at first ... then it graduated to a full-force shove. I jumped and opened my eyes, smearing some of the chalk lines. The door moved again, consistently jamming in the doorframe. I shuffled around on the floor, slowly backing up but not quite leaving the circle I made. Somehow, I thought I should stay inside of it.

"Hello?" I asked pitifully.

The door pushed again, forcefully.

"Hello, who's there?" I asked again, a little louder.

The door suddenly slammed, and I grabbed my shaking knees as something at the bottom frightened and confused me: My room was starting to flood. The pools were small at first but took no time getting bigger and spreading down my entire floor. I got up and jumped on my bed as I realized the water was well on its way to kill the candles and the circle. The chalk was erased on the rippling wood.

"Anybody there?" I cried. "Anybody?"

I looked down when I realized that spellbook was still there and the pages were drowning. My back against the wall, at that moment, I knew the book was the last thing in the world I wanted to touch. I yelled out again and suddenly the door burst open, causing me to jump and grab my blanket.

My roommate tiptoed in, iPod hanging from her ears and kicking an empty water jug. She looked up at me bashfully, taking out an earbud.

"Oh my God, hi. I am so sorry! My key got stuck and wasn't working and I dropped that stupid jug and now the whole place is wet! I have towels, though. Can you help me get them?"

She threw the other bags she was carrying to her bed and got out some beach towels to lay on the floor. I needed my body temperature to go down to somewhat normal before I could spring into action. I got down off my bed, thankful I was still wearing shoes, and lay down some more towels. My roommate mentioned something about getting paper towels or a mop and left the room. As soon as she was gone, I went back to my backpack to get something else. I took some big gulps from my own water bottle and swallowed two of my pills.

CHAPTER 2

The mirror had to be playing a practical joke on me. This wasn't me. This was *never* something I would be caught dead wearing, but here I was, and here it would stay. It was the entire dorky package of prim and proper cardigan, blouse, and pleated skirt, complete with the knee-high socks and those strap Mary Jane shoes. Some guys are into the schoolgirl thing and this only made it worse. I was going to be a walking fetish for any perverted janitor. I grabbed my backpack off my bed and set out for the first day of torture, suddenly thinking that I would have a series of strict teachers at this place.

My first class was Music Appreciation and History, and thanks to the Orientation paper the buildings and room numbers were all color-coded and highlighted. I felt it would be easy to have a no-brainer elective class first thing in the morning.

Applewhite Prep was almost like a tiny college; the academic buildings were grouped together along with common buildings like the library and athletic center. Dorm houses were scattered according to age: 7th grade to 12th. I read that some houses were for individual student groups, too. As I made my way down the sidewalk and passed said buildings, I saw several of the student masses trickling out all going to different classes but all at the same time. Everyone in the navy cardigans and pants and gray pleated skirts all packing together like sardines—like the parts of one big controlled brain.

I got to class and immediately sat down in the first empty seat on the right, not wanting to draw any attention to myself. I realized it was a stupid thought, as everyone looked exactly the same, and even though this elective was mixed of both 7th and 8th grade, I could not tell who was who. That was, except, for the three girls seated at the back.

I turned around to loop my backpack around the chair and almost dropped it. I only saw the uniform skirts and stocking legs underneath the desk, but seated at the desk were three black hooded cloaks, long and disguising. Their heads were bent down so I couldn't see their faces, but they were talking softly and they made me feel creeped out. They looked like three Ghosts of Christmas Yet to Come ... waiting to point a ghostly finger to someone's doom.

I turned around as soon as the teacher walked in and announced "Good morning!"

My first teacher looked like any other teacher: A middle-aged woman dressed business-like with her hair neatly tied back. I didn't know what I was expecting, a nun? It didn't mean that the teachers here would be any better or worse than a regular school. I soon discovered what she made of the three girls.

"Ladies in the back," the teacher said folding her arms. "I don't believe those things you are wearing are uniform. You need to take those off."

"We can wear them," one of the girls said defiantly. She looked at the teacher as though she had no control over what she could do.

"No Iris, you *cannot*. They are not uniform."

"Mitchell says we can," the one named Iris stuck her nose up, and for a moment she and the teacher had a stare-down.

"*Mr. Books*. We do not call teachers by their first names!"

"Mitchell wants to be called Mitchell, he's different and cool. And these cloaks *are* uniform because they are a part of a student group. It's for spiritual reasons. Our faith is offended if we can't wear them."

I saw the teacher struggle with this internally and then throw her hands up in defeat. "I will talk with him about this."

She turned her back and proceeded to write some things on the chalkboard. I turned slightly to look at the girls, and I regretted it. The one named Iris looked straight at me in another attempted stare-down.

My next class was the one to really make me feel the intimidation of the teacher. He was a middle-aged man with graying hair and of short stature, but he held the class's attention. He was not doing anything at the desk at the front of the room except watching everybody come in. His look alone told you that he was, in fact, in charge of the classroom and you'd better pay attention.

I suppose class officially began when he decided to get up and stand before the class.

"Welcome to English."

He walked to the front of the room where he could see and be seen by all, observing each one of us.

"I am Mr. Brooks, but I prefer being called Mitchell. While I will be doing a considerable amount of talking in this class, you will too."

Mitchell made a point to pace and make steady eye contact.

"This is 7th Grade English and Composition, not only will you spend class time writing essays but you will also work on presentation and public speaking. The way to successful writing and speaking is to be confident and know your subject well. How well? Well enough," he shrugged. "Of course, it needs to be well enough so that your audience takes in every word you say. Make yourself believable. And the only way to do this is the most important part: confidence. If you don't have confidence, you don't have an audience. Who is going to take you seriously if you can't take yourself seriously?"

The teacher walked back to his desk and pulled out a book.

"*Steps To a More Successful You*. I wrote this in my early years as a motivational speaker and teacher. Step One is finding that confidence and grasping it tight."

Here, he slowly curled his fingers into a fist.

"Grab it, hold it, and do not let it go. Be confident in yourself and an audience will never intimidate you. It should be the other way around. You are in control of the audience by having a powerful presence. In this class, we will work on getting you to that confident level and then some."

Then, I guessed we were starting right then and there. Each of us was to come to the front of the class and state our names and what activities we were interested in. I for one had a massive wedgie and felt only a little insecure about standing there not being able to do anything about it, and if it wasn't for that I probably would have looked much more confident. Still, Mitchell eyed me curiously, and I hoped it had nothing to do with my wrong choice of underwear that day.

"My name is Sky Monroe, and I guess I don't really know what I want to do yet. I've ... I've been wanting to be in touch with my spiritual side lately. I guess I've been trying to find myself internally."

I knew how dumb that sounded to some people, but I did notice how the teacher reacted to that. He seemed to be very interested in what I said.

After classes, Deanna and I worked on homework at our desks. We were both annoyed that we got so much of it only after the first day.

"This place is going to be the death of me," Deanna complained. You could say we were funny foils: She was the tall, golden blonde, and beauty queen type, and I was the average-size, dirty blonde, four-eyed geek. She was the type that developed breasts as soon as she hit double digits and skipped the rest of childhood. "I wish my parents would have let me go to a normal school!"

I bit my tongue. I knew there was a reason each one of us was at Applewhite Prep. We were made up of delinquent and troubled kids, and exceptional and rich kids. Whatever the reason was, there was one, and if you weren't born and bred to go to an Ivy League college, you were there because you were broken and needed to be fixed. I'll bet Deanna and I were both secretly wondering what the other was here for.

We eventually went to the mess hall for dinner, doing more eating than talking and more people watching than socializing. I had not realized Deanna actually made friends already when some girls came up to our table and invited Deanna to play basketball after dinner.

"Sure!" she cried right away before looking at me awkwardly. "Oh, did you want to come?" There was an obligated invite if I ever saw one.

"Oh, no thanks," I said shaking my head. Horrors of gym class replayed in my head that I never wanted to relive.

"Okay, see you later, then!" Deanna carried up her food tray and left with the girls while I played with leftover croutons in my salad.

As I walked back to my dorm alone, shivering a bit from the evening chill, something familiar caught my eye. They were on the sidewalk across the street and their long black cloaks dragged on the ground gracefully. Instead of three girls, it was two guys, and they were carrying glowing candles that illuminated the space around them. A couple more hooded people trickled out of dorm houses and joined those guys on their path. They all carried candles, too, carrying into the night like a bunch of fireflies. None of them said one word. It made me trip over my feet and stop from going any further down my path to my dorm room. I saw all the candles and black hoods walking further and further in unison and before I could stop myself, I started walking on that same path. Would any of them notice if someone was following them? I did not run to catch up to them for fear I would be seen. So, I walked, purposely hiding behind other students.

The hooded figures walked on, slightly turning to the right to go off-path and head for the grassy area by some trees. I snuck around one of the buildings, feeling like a spy and any snap of a twig under my feet would betray my position. The figures gathered together to make them look like bristles on a brush and then arranged themselves to sit in a circle on the ground. They held their candles in their laps and bowed their heads. I leaned my head in as far as I dared to. They appeared to be chanting something together.

"Come together," I heard. "Come together Guardians of Light. Of present and past."

Their bodies did not move but the flames on the candles did, wavering in the wind like hands beckoning something forward.

"Guardians of Light. Protect the lights. Are you here with us, spirits? Are you here with us?"

I got on my hands and knees and crawled closer so I could peer through a bush.

"We know you are here, spirits. Come to us. Give us a sign you are with us. Give us a sign."

My body was paralyzed by the activity I witnessed. Slowly yet all together the black hooded figures seemed to get higher, like they were all standing up, only when I saw the bottoms of those robes I also saw their legs were still folded. They floated ... They rose ... until they were almost lined up with the higher tree branches. I nearly lost my balance, my open mouth dry and silent.

"We will be with you in a higher level," the kids chanted again. "Soon we will connect on the same level. We are with you, spirits. You are with us, spirits."

CHAPTER 3

I never closed my eyes.

Deanna wheezed peacefully in slumber, but I wrapped myself in blankets in the event I would be lifted off and flown out my window.

The scene I witnessed never left my head, but the more I replayed it the more I wanted to grasp it and keep the memory for myself. It was real. Those cloaked kids made contact, and they did it with almost no effort. It was real. I stared at the dark, knowing there was a way, and there were so many people I could prove wrong: My family, my friends from my other school, and my therapist. I could prove it. The only time my eyes left the ceiling was when I saw the first amber light of dawn. And then, I remembered what that day was.

It was the Student Activities event, and originally I was not planning on going, but the name that wrapped itself around all the folds in my brain caused me to change my plans. The name I heard last night was the same one on the flyer that boy gave me on orientation, and I knew it was the one. Guardians of Light.

After classes I went to dinner alone, Deanna running off with some already-established clique. Once I got my tray of potatoes, grilled chicken sandwich, and fruit cup,

I scanned the mostly filled tables to find one standing out with only one occupant—and I was surprised to see who it was.

I remember playing with him on the playground, bending to tie his loosened shoelaces, and even receiving noogies from his older brother. He was in my class last year and we were even partners for a lab in science and always got A's on everything when we worked together. We used to trade snacks at lunchtime, especially when our mothers gave us healthy crap. His favorite was the vanilla and chocolate swirl pudding cups and those I had to work extra hard to trade for. I'd say, "Trade you for a swirl?" and he would only do it if I had something really good, like fruit gushers or Twizzlers. I had to laugh a little, seeing he was only in school for a day and already he busted out the Gummi worms.

"Need some company, Damien?"

He looked up. "Sky? Hey!" His brown hair was very flat on his head like he spent all day wearing a baseball hat and finally decided to let his hair breathe for a while.

"I totally forgot you were coming here," I said having a seat and—of course—taking a worm.

He laughed. "Ha, well, I forgot you were coming here too."

"So I guess that makes us even."

Finding a familiar face put us both at ease, and instantly we bonded over this reunion. For a moment I forgot my isolation and latched on to something that I knew I would need: A friend. I swished around the last bit of water in my glass and crunched the leftover ice chunks.

"So, what do you have going on now?"

"Homework?" Damien answered with a very lack of enthusiasm.

"Well, I was thinking about going to that Student Activities thing. What about you?"

"Yeah, I was planning on that. I want to see if they have a chess club."

"There is this one group I want to check out," I admitted. "It seems like it would be something I could use right now … it's like a spiritual group."

Damien raised his brow. "A spiritual group?"

"From the sounds of it. I mean, it seems like it would be good for me."

I was sure Damien remembered what happened to me last spring. There was a beat of silence as we both slurped the last of our drinks through our straws.

"I actually took yoga once."

This made me look straight at him.

"Really?"

"Yeah, I just never told a soul. My life would be hell if I did."

I didn't say anything else, just waited for him to continue.

"It's very peaceful … you know? A good de-stresser. Really clears your mind."

"It's cool," I said. "Could be worth checking out."

"Is there one here?"

"Probably, but I was thinking about this spiritual group."

He shrugged. "Sure, why not?"

"I found out about it walking back from Orientation. One of the group members gave me a flyer and was all formal and practically preaching to me. He was so serious and so into it … it was completely genuine."

"People are more serious here."

"Yeah, I guess."

"So, I'll see you tonight at that thing?"

"Yup. Sounds good."

I—of course—left out everything else.

What they don't tell you about any Student Activities event is that it is just an excuse to eat pizza and walk around and socialize. I could tell many people couldn't care less about organizations and activities. Free pizza was practically the only way to get bodies into the multi-purpose room and even send some wandering eyes to the tables.

I caught up with my roommate here, but she did not acknowledge me much. She hopped around to a few tables, chatting with a bunch of people.

I shook my head, wondering how anyone could show up at a new school and just instantly make so many friends. That was always something other people could do that I couldn't. It was like you had to be born with it like it was a type of flower that had the right pollen all the bees were attracted to. Before long, I bumped into the one and only familiar face I knew.

"Geez, how many times a day do you eat?"

I rolled my eyes, folding up the grease-soaked flyers. "I don't know. I eat when I'm bored."

"I'm still full from the pulled pork, and I didn't even eat all the cole slaw. And here you are eating pizza." Damien considered me for a minute. "Is it good?"

"It's not bad. I got it over there."

"I am still looking at stuff."

"Me too."

We saw sports teams, AV club, and choir.

"Did you find that spiritual group?"

"No," I said, both disappointed and surprised. "I actually didn't."

"I didn't find yoga either," Damien added, "or chess."

I never really understood the expression "speak of the devil," but I said it anyway as I peered at the table at the end of the row.

"What?" Damien asked, looking down the row.

"I think that's it," I stated confidently. I recognized the yellow symbol on the flyer and that boy's t-shirt, and also because I recognized that boy.

The table was small with one of those lame poster boards like everyone else's, but instead of students wearing jerseys, there were pictures of group prayer. I was a little hesitant about approaching them, knowing exactly what they were capable of ... but I walked to the booth, knowing perfectly well I wanted that terrifying power. Damien walked with me. The students there all wore these same T-shirts. They smiled warmly.

"Do you carry Light?" one of the girls asked. I looked at the poster board, at the logo of the lantern and the fire inside. "Do you have the Light inside of you?"

"I'd like to think so," I replied. I didn't see the girls from my class. The boy I first met recognized me and came over.

"Hi again! So glad you could come!"

I took a closer look at the pictures of this group, and it was clear they all had a special bond with a special purpose. They stood in circles linking their arms, heads bowed down in love and loyalty. They were together at barbeques, around campfires, and at a beautiful, picturesque scene at a park. The sun hit them perfectly so that every surface of their faces glowed, and the grass was too green to be real. It could have been a painting or photoshopped.

I faced the boy again and returned his smile.

"So, what exactly do you guys do?" I chose my words carefully.

"I'm sorry. I realized I never properly introduced myself to you. I'm Seth."

To the surprise of both Damien and I, he reached out to shake hands. I didn't think students did that with other students, but his class was impressive. He was a little older than us, I would say at least 10th grade.

"I'm Skyler Monroe, but most people call me Sky. This is my friend Damien."

Damien gave a shy wave.

"So good to meet you!" Seth continued. "Well, Guardians of Light is a spiritual group. We are more like a family than anything. We are people who are in touch with our inner Light, our inner spirits, and our goal is to go around and spread this Light for others to follow. That is our goal and objective. We get together to talk about how we can lead rich, fulfilling lives and how we can inspire others and spread this message."

Seth pointed out other stuff on the board, including testimonials of members saying they "found their Light" and were able to find peace.

"We get together and have a good time and just want to spread happiness and positivity. We are actually having an introductory meeting Tuesday evening at eight at our house, which we call 'The Manor'."

"Wait, this house?" asked Damien, peering at the pictures. "This awesome log cabin?"

"Yep, that it is!"

We both stared at the photo of the mini-mansion built out of logs. It truly was one of the coolest-looking houses I've ever seen, surrounded by a fence with—I couldn't believe it—lanterns tied to the planks giving it a mysteriously beautiful glow. It looked like a Thomas Kincaid painting.

"Wow," was all I could say.

"You should see it in person when it's nighttime and all lit up," Seth continued. "It is our home, all right."

"So if we join, we get to live there?" asked Damien, which I admit excited me as well.

"Well, not at first. What year are you guys?"

"Seventh," we both answered.

"There is a wait list that we have reserved for upper-classmen. Usually never for seventh or eighth graders because it gives you time to become more active. Once you are more active, you'll be spending more time there being a part of everything. But people are over all the time anyway, and it does not matter that much. We are a family."

Seth took two notecards from a stack on the table next to the pens and bowl of mints. "This tells you where we are on the map as well as the time and date for the meeting, and phone number. We're kind of hidden but not that hard to find, if you know where to look. We urge you to come and check us out."

"Thanks," I said, pocketing it.

"It could be worth checking out," Damien finally spoke up. "Just to see that house is real."

CHAPTER 4

"**N**o way! I did not! Nuh-uh!"

I didn't need to open the door all the way to know that Deanna was home and on the phone. Practically the whole floor knew when she was around, and if they didn't, her laugh gave it away for sure. She gave a big appreciative one just as I turned the knob. She smiled and waved a finger in greeting as I tossed my backpack to my bed. It put a big dent in the blankets from the book weight.

"Well, whatever, we'll just have to see about that!" Deanna continued to pace in front of her desk with a smirk growing on her face.

"Yeah, sure, I'll totally beat you next time we play. It's a deal! Okay, I guess I'll see you later! Bye!"

She hung up but continued talking.

"God, he is so *cute*."

I smiled as I checked my emails and helped myself to a piece of gum.

"Is this the Chad guy you were playing basketball with?"

"Yup, and he's such a sore loser. But he's adorable, so that makes up for it."

Deanna sat down at her desk.

"That's awesome," I said. "I knew he was into you."

"You doing anything for dinner?"

"Not yet, but actually I have something going on later tonight at eight with my friend Damien. We got invited to this organization open house thing at their house, and it's this really awesome and huge log cabin!"

In the middle of my description, Deanna's eyes popped.

"Wait, *shut up*. A club already invited you to their open house meeting?"

"Yeah, it's this one," I said, showing her the flyer.

Deanna took a brief look and crossed her brow a little. "Well, whatever it is, it's so cool you got invited somewhere already. So, what is it?"

"It's like a religious group," I said.

"Like, what kind of religion?"

"Oh, I don't think it's a specific one. What I should say is that it's a spiritual group. Spiritual, not religious. I mean, they're not preaching about Jesus or anything, just about how to find inner peace. They talk about inner strength and spreading a message about how to find your inner light."

She shrugged indifferently.

"I think it could be something good to have."

Deanna looked at the flyer again. "Whoa, is that the house?"

"Yeah! Isn't it awesome?"

"None of the other houses here look like that. It looks like my aunt's summer house on the lake."

"I think it's one of the older ones built. I can't wait to check it out. We're going tonight if you want to come with."

"No thanks," Deanna said. "But tell me about it later."

"I will."

Deanna sat at her desk, which was on the right side of our room, by her bed. The left side was my side, with my desk closer to the window, next to the couch that looked like it's been there since the school opened. I went over to mine to finish reading emails. I saw that I had a new message from my mom.

> Hi Sky! How are you? How are classes so far? How is your roommate? She seems really nice! I hope you are joining organizations and activities and making some new friends!
>
> Did you meet with your counselor yet? I know it's early and you probably want to wait until you get more settled, but you should be going. I know it won't be the same as your other counselor, but you know how much better you feel when you speak your thoughts. Be open and know that help is available. Your sister and brother and I know that you're strong and will have a good time. You can call us at home anytime you want and your room will be waiting for you whenever you want to visit! Taylor and Jordan say "hi" and hope you're adjusting well.
>
> Hope to talk soon! <3 Mom

I already hit "reply."

> Hey Mom! Classes are pretty okay so far. I am just getting more homework, but I guess any Jr. High would. I will look into counseling, but not just yet. Like you said, I want to be comfortable, and really, the busier I am, the easier it will be to move on and sort of get back to normal. It's funny you mentioned getting involved in organizations because I think I found the PERFECT one!

It's a spiritual group and I think it's exactly what I need. They are all about healing your soul and meditation and stuff. I went to this student activities information event, and I got invited to their meeting. They are in this log cabin house and I can't wait to see it! We're going there tonight, so I'll be able to tell you all about it soon. Say "hi" to Taylor and Jordan! Tell Tay to stay out of my room! Ha ha ha. Take care of yourselves and we'll talk again soon!

Sending my love,
Sky

I hit "send," not saying that someone would send his love from the grave soon.

About a quarter to, I walked outside of my dorm building to look for Damien. He told me in an email that he already went exploring during the day and found the house; it was a little walk away from the furthest academic building in a little woodsy-type area. I paced back and forth for a bit, awaiting him to get here soon so we could get on with it. It was an understatement to say that I was excited, really. I certainly believed they would make things happen for me.

Before I knew it, Damien appeared on the sidewalk and I joined him on our walk.

"It really is as big as it looks, Sky," he said to me as we walked on the sidewalk.

"That's so great you found it. I was worried I never would. They didn't really tell us where it was."

"It's the only residential house out there by the woods. Apparently, they were planning on building more residential places out there but The Manor was the only one they finished and had the budget for, so it sort of just stays on its own. Seth told me that."

"That is actually awesome. Did you see inside yet?"

"No, not yet. No one was around, but I saw it from afar in the woods. There's a bridge over there too with a small pond, and then I saw the areas in the pictures where they have their campfires, so it had to be the place."

I heard the enthusiasm in Damien's voice, knowing that it echoed mine. I exhaled and cleared my head, beginning to see how my new life was about to unfold as it should.

Soon, after passing the academic buildings and even the place where Student Orientation was near the library, we crossed through the parking lot near the end of campus.

"This is going to suck coming back at night when it's dark … the street lamps stopped before the parking lot."

"Right, and navigating through the woods won't be easy."

As soon as Damien said, "woods," we approached the wooded area and saw the bridge. The "pond" underneath it was more like a shallow stream whose flow was interrupted by empty water bottles, pop cans, and cigarettes. We would have walked across if I hadn't stopped short and tugged on Damien's shirt.

"Look," I said. "What was that?"

Damien looked in the direction I was pointing at. I felt stupid because I was pretty sure his answer would have been "a student walking? So what?" But the expression on his face changed as soon as he realized that it was not exactly a student … but more like the figure of one … as this student did not seem to be all there. He looked at me.

"It's gone."

"So you saw it too?"

"Yeah ... it was a person or shadow of a person. And it didn't look ... normal."

"Right. I see them all the time."

Damien's eyes slightly twitched. "See ... what?"

We stood there before the bridge, not crossing over just yet.

"Do you believe in ghosts?" I asked him.

"Yeah," he said. "I do."

"Really? You do too?"

"It does kind of freak me out," Damien admitted. "But I'm also kind of interested, you know?"

His answer lifted my mood. "I am too, you know, I believe in it. Not a lot of people do and no one understands me. I know these people will."

Damien and I crossed the bridge into the wooded area, the wood, leaves, and twigs on the ground multiplying as we went. We turned a corner around a small hill and then that house came into view. The majestic being greeted us at the top as the keeper of the woods. We quickened our pace and approached it head-on until we stood right in front of it, almost waiting for it to give us permission to enter.

It was huge. Big enough to house a large student body and hold group activities and events. We were aching to get in to see the inside, but at the same time we could not stop staring at it like it was one of those fake backdrops people use for photo shoots, and if we got any closer, it would sway and wrinkle. But the house, and whatever was going on inside had a gravitational pull of its own, and lingering was not necessary. We got up to the front door without a moment's waste. Damien eyed me curiously.

"Should we knock?"

I crossed my brow, not thinking it through.

"Are we supposed to? I don't even see a doorbell anywhere."

As I looked all over the place, I finally saw a piece of paper that answered our question.

"Welcome to the Guardians of Light headquarters," I read aloud. "If you are seeking the Light, please come on in and join us in the lounge to the left of the hall."

I waved it at Damien.

"See? There ya go. They should have put more tape on here."

I stuck the sign back on the door and opened it.

It was a small hallway, and we followed the left as per the sign. As promised, it led us to a big lounge area out to our right. To our left was a kitchen area where someone burned strong sticks of incense. We suddenly saw the smoke trailing into long, tight streams in front of our faces. It tickled and almost made me sneeze, but I welcomed it.

Damien and I turned our attention to the lounge area, where everyone sat on couches around a lit fireplace in a horseshoe. A girl with a big smile stood near us. She had to be at least a 10th or 11th grader.

"Welcome!" she exclaimed. "Please sign our guest book and then come join us."

We had absolutely no idea just how many people were actual members or incoming newbies like us. We just signed our names in the book as well as our email, dorm, extension, year—who cared?

Damien and I went to find empty seats on the couches and we were greeted instantly by everyone.

"So, what are your names?" the girl asked us.

"Sky."

"Damien."

"I'm Kimberly. What can I get you guys to drink? We have water and some soft drinks."

"Hey Kim, Josh is already in the kitchen getting the snacks and stuff to bring out, so don't worry about it," said a guy near the back.

"Oh, all right. We'll just hang out and get to know each other before the snacks come out and the meeting starts."

I eyeballed the hell out of the room, which I realized was bigger than I thought. Around what I thought was the ceiling was actually another floor with a balcony and more seated areas, and two beautifully curling staircases leading up to it. The log cabin definitely lived up to its appearance: Everything about the structure of the balconies and stairs looked like freshly shaven Lincoln logs finished with a gloss. Behind those balconies I could see the lines of students descending them, all wearing those membership T-shirts. I recognized Seth, and then I recognized someone else.

It seemed to feel colder in the room for some reason when she came down.

No doubt it was the girl in my class, but this time I saw what she really looked like without the cloak as a shield. She had long, dark hair which hung down her back and as she came downstairs, she looked at us, all of us, and sized out the newcomers. Her bright eyes picked Damien and me out already—and she recognized me, too. She smiled as she sat down with the others, but didn't say anything.

"Come on in," Kimberly said to the three, four, and five new people who just walked in. While they were taking their turn at the guest book, a guy came out with a cooler, followed by a woman carrying a tray of cookies. I could tell they were freshly made because of #1: the uncooked dough still sticking to the sides and #2: the smell. Oh God, the smell.

"Hi there," the woman said with a smile. She had "school lunch lady" written all over her, but instead of a fat bun hiding behind a hairnet, she allowed her blonde locks to run free. She put down the cookie tray and rolled her sleeves up.

"I'm Carol," she introduced herself. "I work with housekeeping and campus catering, but I was converted to come to The Manor full time as of the resident faculty. This place is like a family."

"I'm Sky," I answered.

She pointed to the tray. "Help yourself. I've got to go help out."

Others brought out more goodies on the table, and I had to smile. I was starting to believe I could be quite comfortable, but I felt something else. The walls, the ceiling, every nook and cranny of the house, I could feel that something was there. It was like an overwhelming sense of being; it was a force field that would keep me within its walls. Weirdly enough, it was what I felt when I witnessed that group ceremony. Their presence meant something, and I know it meant she came from this place.

As some more people trickled into the room, we were given the official green light to swarm the food table. Carol put out the napkins while I got a plate of veggies and dip, a few cookies, and a Pepsi.

"Hi, Sky and Damien!"

"Hi, Seth," I greeted as I popped open the tab and took a swig. Damien waved, already chewing a mouthful.

"So happy you could make it."

"The house is awesome!" I said.

Out of the corner of my eye, someone crossed behind some couches and made their way to the front of the fireplace.

"Are we ready to begin?"

I turned to the familiar voice and saw none other than my English teacher. Instead of the student-clad T-shirt, he wore a black polo bearing the logo and freshly ironed khaki pants.

"Hello all, and welcome to 'The Manor' as we like to call it."

As soon as he began to speak all the members came into the lounge immediately to sit down.

"I'm Mitchell Brooks, but in here and everywhere, I am just Mitchell. This is a family, and we all act like a family. We encourage everyone to relax and learn to be comfortable with one another."

Then, suddenly, I felt like I was back in class as Mr. Brooks—Mitchell—started to do his pacing thing.

"We are the Guardians of Light, and we have this group and this house as a place of haven. Our mission is simple: to spread the Light. We—you—all of us have Light on the inside. We just have to find it and shine that light on the darkest parts of the world and on those who need it the most. We bring knowledge and understanding to all we encounter. Our house is a place of sanctuary, and when we are together, we are helping build that sanctuary."

During his spiel, some members came over, bringing a small table with a laptop. As he continued to preach, a screen began to descend behind him.

"We have a lot of fun here, too. We host a lot of student-run activities that everyone enjoys. This should tell you a bit more about us."

It took a few seconds for a video to start playing with the instrumental elevator music to go along with it. I felt like it was one of those cheesy training videos for Walmart or something where different people are telling the camera sugar-filled testimonials. The only difference is here, I actually liked it.

"Guardians of Light changed me for the better!" boasted a brace-faced girl on screen, while pictures flashed by of this girl working at a nursing home. We saw student members clad in their group hoodies as more testimonials played.

"I needed something to help me find myself, and Guardians of Light did just that," said a boy at a group prayer service.

We saw all those members during meditation ceremonies, the lights all out, sans the glow of about a thousand candles. It was this picture that drove me the most: From the candles, the only thing visible was the faces of the holders. The black clothes concealed them in the dark, showing their heads floating all by themselves. It was eerie, and it got under my skin … but I was in love with it.

Mitchell shut off the film and proceeded to tell us that we were all blessed and we were capable of inspiring others and doing great things. We just needed to believe it for ourselves. The introductory meeting ended not too long after that, with a few students sticking around and answering questions.

"I'd like to leave you with one other thing," Mitchell said. "That, if you are interested in coming, we are having a barbeque and spiritual retreat on Labor Day. It is a time to break from studies and cleanse your souls with a walk through the woods, followed by a meditation and reflection session. It will be a rewarding time for all, and we hope you can come."

After Damien and I were stuffed full of food and socializing, we decided to go back to our dorms.

The minute we opened the door to the outside, we confirmed our concerns from earlier. The area of the woods was considerably dark, with nothing but the moon peeking through the trees.

"Um…" I started.

"Keep going," Damien said.

We descended the stairs, but before I took out my phone as a flashlight, Damien pointed at the glowing orbs appearing as we turned on the path. Strategically placed around the fence and even on trees were those little lanterns, solar-charged and fired up, showing us the way. Of course. I remembered them from the pictures.

"That was nice." Damien broke the ice as we comfortably walked down the path.

"I know," I agreed.

Damien sideways looked at me as we followed the solar lanterns down, left, and onward.

"I feel like they … accept me."

It was my turn to look at him. "Why wouldn't anyone accept you?"

He shrugged. "I just had a hard time fitting in school. I could never join any groups because none of them were for me. But I was talking to some people there and they seem really cool, like I could actually fit in with them."

"That explains why I never saw you after school."

"Well, we're in Jr. High now, and there are more things available here. We're not little kids anymore."

"I feel good about them, too. They could help me. I feel like there is more to them … and more that is there."

"So … you felt it too?"

His answer made my heart flutter with joy. So, it was true, and I was not the only one who knew it. I didn't need to ask him to know what he was talking about. Stepping foot in that house only proved it.

"I did. Yeah, it was like … a presence. I definitely feel like there is something behind this group."

CHAPTER 5

I was in the middle of studying for science when Deanna came in.

"Girl, *guess what!*" she said finishing her Styrofoam cup of what smelled like coffee.

"What?"

"I got invited to a party!"

"Nice."

Deanna came over and sat on her bed across the room, still staring at me in shock.

"No, no, you don't understand. A *real* party. Like, this girl who lives just a couple of houses down who is a freaking *ninth grader* and that means the best part: There's going to be a ton of guys there!"

"Well, that's good." I wanted to pay more attention to animal classifications than that conversation, as I did not like where it was headed.

"It's tonight!"

Before I could come up with another supportive, yet passive, remark, Deanna went for the throat.

"You're coming with!"

I shook my head immediately.

"No, no, I'm not."

"Yes, you are! Come on, it will be fun!"

"I don't know..."

"Sky, you're cool, and you need to embrace that about yourself and branch out a bit. You're not having any fun just sitting in the dorm."

"I just don't think I'm the 'party' type person," I explained this with the finger quotes and all, but Deanna still didn't buy it.

"The only way you're going to make any friends is if you actually leave your room. Don't you want to fit in and have a social life?"

I paused, and I knew that gave my answer away.

"Of course you do," Deanna answered for me. "It is the most important thing about junior high and high school. So, you're in, right?"

I surrendered.

"Yeah, what the heck."

"Great!"

It was cold out and I buttoned that stupid little cardigan as far as it would go. It wasn't considered "cool" to button them all the way to the top, but I didn't even care.

"So Chad invited me," Deanna said. "I see him and Bryan and Jen and some other people at the gym and pool and stuff. They seem cool. Do you think you'll play any sports?"

"Nah," I said, hugging my arms.

We turned a corner up the sidewalk to this dorm house. Deanna immediately knocked, and a moment later, a girl answered the door wearing about three Hawaiian leis. We were brought in out of the cold and not two steps in when, lo-and-behold, two other girls passed us holding some official red plastic cups. It shocked me since I could prob-ably guess what was in them.

"I guess we're in the right place," I remarked as we fol-lowed them down the hall. It was mainly High School kids, and I saw that, immediately feeling like the stupid baby 7th grader I was. It was weird no one seemed to care, especially with Deanna, because Deanna obviously didn't seem like a stupid baby 7th grader, so maybe they didn't know. What I really wanted to know was where the residential adult was. It was a Friday, and I guess a lot of them left for the weekend, but still…

"Here we are," Deanna said, as though we couldn't already figure it out. The music was vibrating the entire house.

People were dancing and having hors d'oeuvres in the lounge room, and someone strung white party lights all around the pillars. They could have been Christmas lights someone busted out months early. Some guy in an obnox-ious Hawaiian shirt greeted us.

"Hey, you made it!"

"Sure did!" Deanna replied, and I know I just met her eye candy.

"Chad, this is my roommate, Sky. Sky, Chad."

Chad took a swig of whatever was in his red cup of importance.

"Why don't you ladies go help yourselves to some drinks? They're in Mikala's room."

Deanna headed to that room and, like a dumb puppy, I followed, the paranoia hitting me at full blast. This was no doubt unsupervised, and there were a lot of people there. We then saw an assortment of bottles on the dresser, some with fancy names and different colored liquids. Deanna shrugged at me.

"Best to keep it simple," she stated as she took the rum and brought it over to a Coke bottle.

"Wait, I don't know about this."

"It's totally cool," Deanna said. "Everyone drinks. It's not a big deal."

"I don't think we should. We could get in big trouble for this."

"It's just fun!" Deanna said. "It's not going to kill anyone, and no one is going to know."

Deanna made herself something while I just poured a Sprite. After a while, we joined in the dancing, and when I say dancing, I mean I nodded my head along to the music and Deanna rubbed her hips on her Chad friend, whose eyes were red and swimming from the start. Deanna laughed and almost tripped over a sweatshirt in a heap on the ground. I'd see her dancing and then leave to get another drink, and then come back, and then leave again. At one point she came back all excited.

"Sky! Come on, we're doing shots!"

I was grabbed and dragged over to the kitchen where other people were holding shots, and although they spilled all over the place, they managed to stay in the glasses.

I didn't know what it was, but I took it anyway. It was strong; it made me a little sick, but it wasn't bad. It was even a little fruity. Deanna grinned from ear to ear as she took another drink.

"What's that?" I asked.

"I have no idea! Chad made it. Wanna try?"

"No," I said immediately. "And you know you shouldn't take drinks from guys you don't know."

"Oh, pshh! It's really good!"

I tried it anyway, and almost immediately I wanted to hurl up the shot, the Sprite, and the burger I ate for dinner.

"Oh my God, what is that? It tastes like nail polish remover!"

"I don't know, girl, but I'm getting really shit-faced. Let's go dance!"

I could not take this, any of this. Deanna, on the other hand, felt that she had a high alcohol tolerance, not to mention the four stomach chambers of a cow. It was not possible for her eyes to get any more bloodshot and cloudy. When her dancing started to look more and more like dry humping followed by spasm attacks, the tingle in my stomach turned from Code Yellow to Code Red.

"Hey, Deanna?" I had to shout. "We need to head back. It is getting pretty late!"

"What?"

I repeated it. My throat hurt.

"No!" she cried back and danced with Chad again. Those two continued in their humping spasm dance, and I use the term "dance" lightly as they rubbed against each other and Chad's hands trailed lower and lower on Deanna's body. I tried my best to ignore it, but when other red, swimming-eyed guys came by me and thought they could repeat this same scene, I started to get more annoyed. Deanna and Chad continued to go at it and then I had the sudden thought she forgot I was there.

"God, I have to pee!" Deanna shouted. Chad guided her through the crowd as she stumbled around and I couldn't shake that tight feeling that I had to follow. I got through a crowd—and then another one—before I lost them both. I looked around but all I could see were bodies slamming up against each other, so I shoved my way through and asked the first person that made eye contact with me.

"Where's the bathroom?"

"What?" he shouted.

"*Where's the bathroom?*"

Why did that music have to be so *loud?*

"THE BATHROOM!"

"Right down there!"

I went down the hall and saw the bathroom door wide open, no one in there, and the stalls empty. Now, the panic started to grow.

"Deanna? Deanna?" I yelled, walking down the hall. "Deanna?"

My heart started to thump faster, and I found it hard to think over the music. The panic fluttered slightly when I heard that stupid laugh and followed it to that Mikala girl's room. Deanna sat on a bed surrounded by some people and they were all laughing.

"Sky, heyyyy. There you are!" Deanna slurred.

"Geez, Dee, I couldn't find you. You just sort of wandered off."

"It's cool," she said. The girl next to her had some little thing I didn't recognize. It looked like a colorful sculpture.

"What are you doing?" I asked, stepping into the room, and then a strong smell hit me and I almost gagged. It was like a combination of Earth and a dead skunk. Like a skunk got run over by a lawnmower just as it was cutting grass. It was disgusting, and I was coughing uncontrollably.

"What is that?" I shouted in between coughs.

"Is she cool?" asked some girl behind Deanna. Although drunk, Deanna was quick to respond.

"Yeah, yeah, she's cool." She looked over at me and her eyes—it was possible, after all—were ten times redder and swimming. "It's weed, Sky."

I fought back the urge to hack.

"All right ... well ... I'm going to ... um ... go that way."

I turned on my heels and left that room just as Deanna reached for that little thing and lit a Zippo lighter underneath it.

In the lounge I knew I couldn't do anything at all, trying to calm my stomach enough so I could think, even though the music was still playing at full max volume. I was surprised it wasn't bothering people whose heads were already pulsating from all the drinks and other things. I drank my Sprite and then saw something blonde dash to the bathroom.

Whether or not I wanted to see, I went to the bathroom anyway, just as Deanna lifted up the toilet seat and pushed her head into it. Out of reaction, I grabbed her hair as she made the most God-awful noises and projected liquids—and maybe even some solids—into the bowl. She hurled some more, and I buried my face in my cardigan.

"Deanna," I said. "We're going to leave now."

She leaned back from the toilet, now remembering how to breathe.

"I feel better now."

"No, you don't," I said forcefully. "Just how much of what did you have tonight?"

"I don't know," she answered weakly. "A little bit of everything."

"Why did you do that? You had alcohol and then you smoked?"

That triggered her to go back to the toilet, and me to the inside of my shirt.

Right on time, Lover Boy decided to show his face.

"Hey, is she okay?"

"She's throwing her guts up, man. What do you think?"

The next time Deanna emerged, I patted her back and tried to get her to sit up. She did, almost reluctantly.

"Come on," I said.

She rubbed her head but did not outright object, which I took to be progress.

"Where's my sweatshirt?" she asked weakly.

I practically leaped up, taking this as a cue.

"I think you left it on the couch when we were dancing. I'll go get it."

I let Deanna rest for a minute while I swam my way back through the crowds. By the time I did find the wrinkled black thing on the couch and made my way back, Deanna was gone. I cursed myself. Why did I think that was a good idea to leave her alone for five seconds? I knew to check Mikala's room, but somehow I didn't think there would be different activity.

The door, now, was slightly ajar, and I heard some quick breaths. I pushed it with my knee and saw Deanna and Chad playing tonsil hockey, her hands on his neck and his moving up her shirt. I didn't move, and they didn't make any indication that they saw me or that they cared.

"Okay, ready?" I said, holding up her sweatshirt. "I found it."

They broke it off quickly and stood there awkwardly as I stood there even more awkwardly.

Deanna could hardly stand straight, so I took her arm.

"Let's go."

"Bye Chad, I'll call you," Deanna managed to say.

The only good part of the evening? Deanna didn't stop to puke on our way back. She did gush about Chad the whole way, which made me want to.

"Thank God it was Saturday," was all I could say. I slept until about eleven, made a cheese sandwich, and enjoyed that with a Snapple while I waited for Deanna to come back from the bathroom. She woke up about twenty minutes before I did and immediately headed off there. Our door opened and in she came, still looking tired with some of her eye makeup still on.

"Hey," she said softly.

"How's it going?"

"I feel like shit."

"Yeah, well, you were drunk last night."

Deanna climbed back on her bed while I took a big gulp of Snapple.

"You were all over the place ... I didn't even know what you were going to do," I said.

"Yeah, I guess."

She laid down, and I continued eating, trying to think of what to say next.

"I do not plan on leaving my bed today," she finally said.

"Do you even remember anything from last night?"

She managed to shrug. "Kind of."

"Well," I said frankly. "It was bad, Deanna. You were out of control. I was getting worried about you. You drank a lot and then smoked and then got sick, and you and that Chad guy were all over each other and almost ... yeah."

She slightly perked up, but still cringed a little. "Oh."

I looked at her. "You were going too far."

"Sorry, I was *sooo* drunk."

"Yeah, well, you didn't have the best judgment."

"Sorry, okay? Are you mad?"

"Well, there was a lot going on at once, and I felt like I had to watch you. You could have been in serious trouble and probably wouldn't have made it home last night if it weren't for me! What would you have done if I wasn't there?

This party was a bad idea and if anybody knew about it, we would all be in serious trouble. You completely lost control."

She got quiet. "I'm so sorry Sky."

I tried not to think about what actually *would* have happened if I wasn't there. It was clear that Deanna's kind would be in juvie if they weren't here. Although my frustration was still fresh, I felt a sense of pride in how I handled the situation and took care of her. I swooped right in and got out of a situation and didn't let common young adulthood vices tempt me at all. I was smarter, and I was stronger. I made positive decisions. I thought of Guardians of Light. They would probably have done the same, wouldn't they?

CHAPTER 6

I brushed my hair one last time, although it was a lost cause and wasn't going to change. I was so happy weekends allowed us to be out of uniform for once, even though I couldn't do any better than jeans and a T-shirt. I shook my head and swung my bag around my shoulder. It was time to leave.

I knew that Damien was going to meet me there, so I didn't linger while walking past his dorm. It seemed like everyone was doing something for Labor Day weekend as more cars drove down the street and more people were out walking around, especially some parents. My mom tried to convince me to come home a while back for the weekend. I already explained to her that I had plans with this new student group I was involved in, and instead of being disappointed, my mother was ecstatic.

"Oh, that is great! You're fitting in already! I hope you have fun!" she said. "We'll have you come down another next weekend so we can go shopping or something!"

I felt good after hanging up.

I was already getting a better grasp of the campus as I approached the picnic area, no doubt reserved ahead of time for our group. It was behind a few athletic fields which were usually crammed with people, but today, it was empty sans those in the black shirts. I smiled as I walked through the fields and saw the familiar banner fluttering against the gazebo. All the picnic tables in the park area were covered in yellow tablecloths, decorated in ribbon, and filled with people.

I saw Damien right away standing by the cooler, watching Carol set up the grill. He looked so awkward like he wanted to offer help but was not sure what to do. I smiled as I finally made my way into the scene.

"Hi, Sky."

"Hey."

I noticed some of the others too, some I knew their faces but not their names yet. The exception was Iris, who could clear a path in the room with her stare. People moved chairs to a firepit area and played volleyball with their pants rolled up to their shins, kicking up sand in every step. Damien and I recognized Kimberly from our first meeting, pulling out bags of hot dog and burger buns.

"There you are!" she called out, her voice upbeat and high-pitched. "Can you guys get those cups for me from over there?"

We got them and started to help set up tables. Iris came over with some chairs, smiling at me but smiling even more at Damien.

It was mostly aimless mingling and meeting everyone. The upperclassmen were very welcoming. Even the 12th graders treated us like people instead of stupid little 7th graders like they would at any other school. They made us feel as though we already belonged to the group. I guess according to them, if we showed up, we automatically were. It didn't take long for Mitchell Brooks to show his face and make his rounds.

We sat around the picnic tables eating and talking. Mitchell told us we were to have a little meditation after dinner. I sat up anxiously.

Suddenly I saw something white move out of the corner of my eye. I jerked my eyes towards the trees, but whatever it was, it was gone. I continued to stare at the area, not quite sure what it was, but something was telling me it was not just my imagination. Whatever I saw earlier—whatever I kept seeing on this campus was here. It had to be. I looked around at the others at the tables to see if they noticed anything, too. Everyone continued to talk and eat. I looked again.

"What is it?" asked Damien.

"I thought I saw something," I said lamely.

"Like what?"

A rustle in the bushes answered for me. I saw flashes of white and then it burst out into the open.

"Well, there you are, baby!" cooed Mitchell. "We didn't think you'd miss our party today!"

The cat—covered head to toe in a thick white coat—scampered over to Mitchell and rubbed against his legs. He got up from his table and picked it up.

"This, everyone, is our own little mascot and a longtime companion of mine, Ad Astra. She lives at the house and can be seen wandering campus from time to time. She comes and goes as she pleases like she owns the place!"

He laughed and rubbed the cat behind her ears. For a minute she looked at me and I saw the bright gold ornaments that were her eyes. Purring, she closed them in bliss. Once we finished eating, Mitchell stood up and asked for our attention.

"We'd like to begin our little after-meal meditation to help us relax, gather our thoughts, and let the food we just ate feed our souls, charge our bodies, and charge our lights so they continue to shine their brightest. After big meals, we like to do meditations like these, but especially since this is our first meal of the year and we have so many new members to our family, we want to welcome them officially and help their spirits find their home!"

Some of the older members put out the last of the blankets on the open grass area, held down by various rocks. Ad Astra, at one point, felt it was important to walk on every single one of them, as though by blessing or even by security. Mitchell held our attention.

"Now, for all of you 7th grade and new members, I first want to tell you that we do not enforce any organized religion here. This is not a religion. This is just life, although I do believe in a higher power. What is life? What is the very thing that rests behind your ribcage? It is the powerful source of energy that is your soul, and your soul is nursed by your body your whole life ... before the time comes for it to be set free into the universe. They say that when you die, you see a glorious white light that shows you the way. Who has heard of this? This is what Guardians of Light is founded by and believes to be true. The White Light is the most powerful being in the universe. It is both a mother and a father. It watches over us, right now, as we hone our spirits. Open your mind and your soul to The White Light and you will be rewarded."

I was grounded. What that teacher said had to be the most captivating and beautiful thing I had ever heard.

"Now, let us gather on the blankets and allow ourselves to relax."

Seth was the only one who stayed behind, fumbling with a music player he set on a tree stub. Then the mood music set in: the soothing kind that you hear at a spa and you're being told to close your eyes and relax. Mitchell was asking us to do the same.

Damien and I knew that day that in this type of community, it was normal to just let go, so we did so at ease. As the music played, and our eyes were closed, we heard less of other people moving around on blankets and more of our inner thoughts.

It was funny, too, the way it suddenly got warmer outside as we were getting lost in our inner thoughts. The hoodie I brought with sat lifelessly by my side and I wondered why I even brought it as my chest heated up. We were in an open area with a big wide field stretched before us, and my thoughts seemed to take me further into that meadow. My breathing became rhythmic and I no longer had to concentrate on it, as I soon didn't even feel the rest of my body. It was as though I leaped out of it and now walked through the open grass.

The picnic area, the baseball fields, the buildings, the people, and even the trees were all gone. It just seemed to stretch into a never-ending patch of green that I could see going on for miles. I could not see where it stopped ... or even where it began. The only other thing I knew was that the sun was directly above me. It had to be—the way the sweat ran down my neck and dampened my armpits. In my mind, I was not running; I was not even walking fast. How did it get so hot all of a sudden? I regretted not wearing sunblock, picturing my nose cooking to roast. But the warmth was pleasant. Very pleasant. It was the most peaceful I felt in what seemed like a long time. I walked in my vision, and although the only thing I could do for a while was feel, I started to see. I started to see a figure ahead of me.

It was blurred by the still-burning sun and barely a shape on the mounds of the grass field, but I somehow knew it was a person. Although my eyes were shut, I was able to squint them as the figure appeared to be moving toward me.

My shirt stuck to my chest and drops of sweat rolled down my face. My breathing quickened. The figure, the person, got closer until his form and face came into view, and suddenly sweat wasn't the only thing dripping down my face.

"Sky," he said, as clear as though he were sitting right next to me.

I gasped out of my meditation, eyes popped wide open, and I breathed in and out heavily.

I was back at the park, on my blanket, and now everyone was staring at me. I wiped off my tears and tried to hold back those little sobs escaping from my throat. Out of the corner of my eye, I saw Damien's concerned expression and tried very hard not to look at him.

"Skyler," said Mitchell, appearing out of nowhere. "Are you all right? You must have experienced a very deep and moving meditation session. What did you see?"

I honestly did not know how to answer this. Everyone continued to stare at me while I tried to think of what to say.

"I ... I don't know," I said lamely. "I just felt ... something." I composed myself and sat upright on the blanket, although I wanted nothing more than to pull it over my head.

"Skyler is in touch with her Light," Mitchell said again. "She must be in a peaceful state."

"I need to get some water," I said.

I grabbed my hoodie and got up to get a drink while the others listened to Mitchell lead them through another session. I chugged the first water bottle I grabbed from the table and leaned my back up against a tree. I let a few more tears roll down, making sure they did not turn into full-blown sobs.

I saw him.

I did it.
I made contact.
This was real, and they could make it real.

After classes, I decided to go back to The Manor right away. As I left the academic building, I checked out my surroundings obsessively, almost as though I expected a spirit to pop out of nowhere and start talking to me. Students walked past in groups as they were on their way back to the dorms. I sidestepped everyone and quickened my pace on the sidewalk, feeling the chaos lift as I passed the academic buildings and reached the more deserted parts of campus. As soon as I crossed the parking lot, I reached the grassy knolls and wooded area. I was alone. I was alone, but I did not feel alone anymore.

I looked around at all the trees around me, watching their branches sway in the wind a bit, as though they were waving me to come closer. I stepped on a few leaves that crunched, but through the crunching, I heard something else. I stopped in mid-step and jerked my head to the trees behind me and to my left. I turned around and looked to my right. As I stepped on more leaves, I heard it again, this time closer. I dismissed the idea that it was the wind because the wind didn't whisper like that.

They were whispers.

What were they saying?

I heard them again closer to The Manor, so I quickened my pace on that pathway. I walked so fast that I could see the flashes of things that passed in between the trees, and I couldn't tell if something was moving or not. I tried to listen again for the voices, for anything. I didn't hear anything else but caught more of those flashes in the trees. One tree, in particular, looked like something passed right through it. I turned completely in the direction of that tree, staring at it and staring at the leaves. The shadow moved and I could make out something else, something shimmery, like fog or smoke. That's what it could have been, but it was too humanoid for fog or smoke.

I kept walking and passed that tree, turning my head in all directions until I saw someone standing between two tree trunks in the corner of my eye. I ducked under some branches to make my way over there, only to stop midway to find myself staring at three identical trees. No, there were only two. The one in the middle had no branches. When I looked at it from where I was before, it had arms.

I stopped dead in my tracks, confused but mostly disappointed. I knew what I saw.

I got to the house, once again alone in the woods. I put my backpack on one of the chairs in the upper lounge and stretched my arms, Kimberly looking up at me from her book.

"Hi, Skyler," she said.

"I saw a ghost."

Kimberly showed almost no reaction.

"Oh, just now?"

I crossed my brow at her. "Yeah."

Kimberly seemed very calm, as though we were discussing the weather. "The Manor is a very special place."

"Tell me more!" I stared at her.

"Calm down, it's okay, really!"

"I just told you I saw a ghost. You act like I just told you I saw a squirrel."

"Was it a ghost squirrel?"

I sighed.

"Good lord."

"Sky, Sky. It's okay. I'm sorry. I didn't think you would be scared."

"I'm NOT scared," I said, sitting down in the chair my backpack was on. "Why are you acting like it's not a big deal?"

She put her book down. "The thing is, we are actually in touch with things no one else is."

"I knew it," I said, my heart growing a pair of wings and fluttering away.

"What we don't tell everyone at Orientation is that this house is something special. We have ... other occupants. It's something that true members not only accept but believe in their hearts. You do believe in it, don't you?"

"Yes I do," I said. "I believe in ghosts—I mean, well, spirits."

"They are around, and they make themselves known in different ways."

"How so?"

"Some choose different ways to communicate, some make things happen."

I fought the urge to look behind me ... or look anywhere, for that matter.

"What do you mean 'make things happen?' What do they want?"

Kimberly smiled genuinely. "Want? Well, it's us who are supposed to be doing the wanting. They are like our guides. That's why they're here. They watch over us in our mission to spread the word of the Light and protect the house."

Any other people would be afraid and in disbelief. I was not. I nodded along, looking at her carefully. She kept smiling at me.

"I am so glad that you understand. So many people wouldn't. It's sad, really, how people are so closed-minded and think their way is right because it's the only way they know."

"Yeah. I believe that. I believe in this group and I want to be a part of because I believe I have those connections, too."

She smiled again. "And you can and will be a part of it. You think you are connected to the spiritual world?"

"Yes," I said seriously. "Yes, I am. At the Labor Day event, when we meditated, I had a vision. Do you remember that?"

She sat up. "Yeah. You went to a deep place. Mitchell talked about it afterward. He said you were the only one in touch with yourself."

"It wasn't me I saw. It was almost like I was walking in heaven. I made my own connection. I encountered someone who passed away recently. I saw him. I heard him. I talked to him."

"Who?"

"My dad."

CHAPTER 7

I checked my phone again to be sure I didn't get any texts or calls from Damien. He did mention he was running a little late, but I didn't care so much about that. That obviously wasn't making me so anxious.

Damien finally came over to my table.

"Hi. Do you want to get some food first?"

"Yeah, sounds good, then you can tell me what absolutely couldn't wait another minute."

"Okay," I said, trying not to make anything seem too urgent. When I talked to Damien on the phone last night, I first told him I wanted to meet at lunch tomorrow. Then I said I couldn't finish our conversation and I would explain later.

"Your roommate?" he guessed. "You don't want to talk about it in front of her?"

"Or anyone."

He agreed to meet me for lunch at the sandwich and coffee shop. So, we sat down with our bagel sandwiches, chips, and coffee.

"What do you think of Guardians of Light?" I asked.

"I like it," he said honestly. "I think it's refreshing."

"So you're joining?"

"Definitely. Are you?"

"Yeah."

"Cool."

I took a sip of my coffee to wash down my bite.

"Damien, this is a very special group. There is something I have to tell you I learned about them ... and how personal it is."

"What is it?" he asked, digging into his own lunch.

"Okay, you remember when we thought we saw things?"

"....Yeah?"

"The Guardians of Light can talk to the dead. The Manor ... has spirits there."

Damien's jaw twitched, but he kept eye contact. "Really?"

"There are spirits around that place, Damien. I believe I've had a few encounters with them. Including my own from the meditation at Labor Day."

"What happened?"

"I made contact with my dad."

Damien slowed down his chewing.

"I saw him in my vision, and that was what made me get so emotional. It was really him, and this group has the power to contact the afterlife. I went back to The Manor after school and I swore I heard and saw something by the trees, but I didn't get to see it too close or anything and it was gone, but something was there."

"A ghost?"

"Yeah. And I went in the house and talked to Kimberly. She told me that they watch over us, you know? It's like we have guardian angels at this place. My dad is my guardian angel."

"Whoa," Damien said, keeping his eyes on me. They never left.

"I knew they would be people who would understand me."

"I understand you."

During a beat of silence, I took a sip from my cup, and out of the corner of my eye, I looked at the empty table next to me.

I believe in you, I said mentally to whoever was sitting in the chair.

Deanna came home in an almost mad rush.

"Hey, come on, we have to go."

"Go where?" I asked.

Deanna was already halfway out the door. I grabbed my hot chocolate, still hot, and followed Deanna out of our room as she locked the door.

"What's all this about?" I asked, taking a careful sip.

"Homecoming, for sure! Where have you been? Oh yeah, your worship group. You missed the last few dorm floor meetings."

"I did? Did I miss much?"

"Well, not really. We'll bring you up to date."

The rest of our floor gathered in the common room. I've become used to these gatherings at school. It was about community. It was comfortable. It made sense. However, meetings with my dorm did not quite go the same as meetings with GOL did. As I looked around the room, I realized I didn't recognize the faces or know the names of any of the girls. From the looks of people, I could tell they weren't that familiar with me, either.

"Okay, everyone!" Our dorm mother, Stephanie, said with a bounce. She was fresh out of college and ready to be someone's mommy. "Your vote results are in and our Homecoming theme is ... VEGAS!"

Several people cheered and clapped. I smiled, pretending like I knew what was going on.

"So, as you know, we are going to need a decorating committee, like a group of about five or six, to get decorations. Go nuts, think everything Las Vegas! We'll need stuff in the windows, common room, the door, and, of course, the front bulletin board. We have to win! Our biggest competition is the second floor, whose theme is the Renaissance, so let's do our best to beat them and get that party!"

I drank my hot chocolate and listened to Deanna talk to some of our neighbors.

"I wouldn't know the first thing about decorating," she said. "I would probably make those lame construction paper rings first graders put on a Christmas tree. Vegas, huh? I wish that meant we could have slot machines in here."

Stephanie picked up a large poster board, already shot with glitter and poor drawings of playing cards. "Here's the sign-up list! If you're interested in signing up, put your name, room number, and extension. Once we have our Homecoming committee, we'll get together with creative plans. I'm going to put this up on the hallway bulletin board."

I assumed the meeting ended once Stephanie said that and went off to the board. People went off into little groups to chat.

"I guess I have missed a lot, huh?" I asked Deanna.

"Well, not really. It's okay. I was going to ask what you're doing for Homecoming, anyway."

"Not sure. No doubt we'll be doing something at GOL, anyway."

"Well, I'm going to go back and finish my paper on *Huck Finn*."

I shrugged and followed her back, not seeing any point of sticking around there. On the way, I already saw a few people had made their way to the bulletin board.

"We could make it *look* like a casino, maybe get a few tables and make them blackjack and poker and stuff," one of the girls was saying.

"But we can't have random tables with cards and chips just sitting there. People will probably steal them, and then it will just be a table sitting there once the judges come around."

"Lame."

I walked by the bulletin on my way to our room with Deanna already gone. Before I could stop myself, I blurted out, "What about if you decorate using the themes of all the resorts?"

All three of them looked at me. "How?" asked the tallest girl.

"Well, it's pretty easy if you use your imagination," I replied. "I mean, there's Treasure Island, MGM, The Venetian, The Mirage. You can, like, dedicate an area to that theme."

"That's good," someone else said.

"Yeah," said another girl. "Are you signing up?"

I don't know what came over me, but I nodded and then did just that. It was so spontaneous, but it made me feel really good. I saw the three other names on there: Kristen, Katie, and Lindsay. I didn't know who was who, but I had to pretend like I did.

"Awesome!" one of the girls said as soon as I was done.

"You must be Deanna's roommate," piped up another.

"I am," I said.

"Well, thanks for your help..." The girl made a point to look at the sheet. "Skyler. We'll call you later."

"Okay."

I went back to my room with my lukewarm hot chocolate.

"Hey Deanna, guess who's on the decorating committee?"

Deanna's face brightened without taking her eyes off her computer screen.

"Really? Cool! That is a good idea for you to make friends here."

I sat at my desk to check my email. "Yeah, why not? Could be fun."

Deanna typed away while I opened up my inbox. I ignored the flow of campus-wide emails and those pointless forwards from friends until I came to one from the GOL group base. This I, of course, opened immediately.

"Come back to The Manor Thursday at six-thirty for important information about our next event, plus new baking recipes and discussions for community service and movie nights! Please also bring in $25 for new hoodie orders. All new members are encouraged to get one as we wear these at many events. Our next event is the Guardians of Light Day of Silence, where we take a vow of silence for a day in honor of those without Light. Join us to learn more about this special day to spread Light and find our voices!"

There was a picture included that looked like a picture of the woods, but it was blurry and hard to tell. What was that supposed to be? The longer I stared at it, the more the picture actually came into focus and revealed what those trees really were: people. People wearing those black cloaks, all standing together, legs and arms almost perfectly straight down their sides. This picture was creepy as hell to look at, but it was the most beautiful thing I ever saw. I knew what it really was: It was very deep symbolism. These people were standing together and were standing for something. There was a beautiful mystery about it—because looking at them told you they all knew something you did not.

The beef sandwiches at The Manor were by far the best ones I had ever eaten in my whole life. I was at the point where I no longer wanted to go to the caf' or the food court. I didn't need to. I had my own meal source. Someone was always cooking something, baking something, and it wouldn't be a lie at all to call it home cooking. The beef juice dribbled down my chin as I bit and positioned the paper plate under my mouth.

"Don't forget, guys!" announced Kimberly, coming into the room we were all in. We actually had our own mess hall, long tables, and everything. It felt just like *Harry Potter.*

Kimberly held up a can labeled "Food Fund."

"Please continue to donate if you want to have more food days! We'd like to do a pancake breakfast here soon, so we need to save up!"

I tossed in what was in my pocket, a grand total of seventy-seven cents. I—along with everyone else—continued to stuff my face with beef and salad and fresh fruit until I actually had to unbuckle my skirt, and that was saying something. It's a tired cliché used in old cartoons, but here I was doing the same thing. I didn't even care, since it hid well under my shirt. A moment later, Mitchell announced to us to gather in the upper lounge and we would clean our plates afterwards.

We got to the lounge and relaxed. I almost felt too full to want to move ever again. Mitchell and the older members assembled near the front of the fireplace.

"It looks like everyone got the email, and I am pleased to see some returning new faces!" started Mitchell. "We would like to give you a little backstory on our Day of Silence. It is a tradition that started almost as when Guardians of Light did some years ago. It is a day that we all take a vow of silence. That's right." Mitchell looked around the room for dramatic effect. "For a full day, from the moment you wake up and go to your classes and go out for lunch until you rest your heads on your dorm room pillows, we challenge you to not speak for an entire day. It is a challenge, but it is a rewarding one. We do this in honor of those who have no voice, who therefore have no Light. We call this forward to be recognized, for everyone to think about who has no Light in this world: those who are lost, those who make bad decisions, those without family, friends, or purpose in life. Our Day of Silence will be next week and we urge you all to participate. It is your duty to make this statement. We will be making T-shirts and have handouts for you to carry with you throughout your day."

He held up a shirt, black with dark yellow lettering on it outlined in white:

"I have taken a vow of silence for those who have no voice and no Light, and I work to help spread this Light and let it shine!"

On the back was the GOL logo.

"We have some extra for new members, so see Kimberly for sizes. If you can do it, if you can give yourself the discipline to not talk for a full day, you will help spread our message."

Mitchell motioned to a pile of handouts by the fireplace.

"We have a day print-out of the agenda. It's nothing complicated at all. During the day, you will go about your regular schedules and classes, of course. In case you're concerned, we will be sending out a campus-wide email alerting everyone what is going on. This is mainly for teachers so that they don't call on you in class, and for students to gain interest. Later in the evening, we will be having a candle lighting ceremony, meditation, dinner, and midnight party, where the day and vow will be over and we can talk about our days. Does anyone have any questions?"

As though the vows started already, everyone was silent. It was eerie, really, as though there was a gravitational pull on the group to keep us grounded. I was grounded all right— and enthralled.

CHAPTER 8

My uniform shirt was crumpled on my closet floor. I wore a long, black long-sleeved shirt under my T-shirt and let it go, untucked, over my skirt. I took my backpack over my shoulder and started out.

"See you later, Sky."

I gave Deanna a short nod, and she crossed her brow.

"Oh," she realized. "That's today, right? Well, good luck."

I smiled and waved, and walked out the door, not forgetting my electric candle.

I felt relief like today was going to be like no other because I felt like I'd just been given a get-out-of-jail card. It meant for one day, teachers wouldn't call on me in class and I didn't have to answer to anyone. I could get away scot-free. But also, I was drawing attention to GOL and spreading their message.

I looked at all the students I passed on the way to class. I felt like I had a mission to spread an important message, something to influence people to better themselves. I had to make this my purpose. So, I did it. My classes went by, and I didn't say one word, and it was like our teachers already knew to respect our vow, and everywhere I went, I felt recognized as part of a group. This, of course, I felt was the best part. I sat up straighter that day, knowing that I stood out

for a reason and the reason I stood for. As far as the other students went, I did notice that they were singling me out, too. I got a couple—if not many—funny looks as I passed people in the buildings, outside, and in between classes. I also noticed several who were just avoiding eye contact. Was I imagining it? I didn't look any different. I was just in a T-shirt over my uniform, carrying an electric candlestick and a small bundle of flyers.

Some people I passed took the time to read my shirt, and I handed out as many flyers as I could. Most acknowledged it for a minute and then threw it away. From those I did see I saw something they all had in common: They didn't get it. I saw the raised brows, the curled lips that read "How lame!" It bugged me. Didn't people want to lead better lives? Of course, all the other GOL members were getting the same reactions. I didn't care, and I was certain they didn't either.

I would see other members that day, and even if they were people I didn't know that well, it was like there was all the communication in the world among us. We would pass by one another, and I would feel a charge of energy. It was an understanding; it was an agreement, and even if we didn't take a vow of silence, we did not need words, anyway. I'd look at other members, and they'd look at me, and I don't know how this happened, but we were all going to the cafeteria for lunch at 12:30. I knew this. I passed Seth and Kimberly, and all we did was lock eyes, and it was settled. We had the power within ourselves. We were so strong that we could communicate without words. Could we?

Was it just a feeling? Was it just that people met in the caf' every day for lunch and we assumed that because this was a special day, we would go?

I made my way towards the caf' at the supposed lunchtime and saw the flock of black shirts settle on one table like ants at our own picnic. I got in line, picking up some chicken quesadillas and rice. The cafeteria was loud and boisterous, as usual, but we still held that silence around us as a protective shield. I only smiled at people I knew as I went over to join the rest of the group. My smile faded as soon as I saw how other people were staring at our table.

I recognized that stare. It was the way white people stared at black people when integration started. Now they stared at those with black shirts. It was an ugly stare, a look to purposely put down and alienate, and instead of feeling alienated, I felt irritated.

What were we doing wrong? Nothing! We were an organization wearing T-shirts and not speaking. What was wrong with that? If those popular athletic kids did the same thing, no one would blink an eyelash. I guess junior high and high school were the same no matter what school you went to.

I found Damien right away, as there was conveniently a spot saved for me right across from him. I sat down and we acknowledged each other, and then ate.

I admit it was very weird being in the loud and busy cafeteria and all of us sitting together with no one talking. It was surreal, really, like we were in our own bubble. After a while, I took out my phone and started punching keys.

The soft hum in Damien's pants went off, and he pulled his own phone out and looked at me curiously.

[Would this be considered cheating?] read the message on his screen.

A moment later,

[Probably not] appeared on mine.

I looked around at the others at the table, making sure they weren't giving us disproving looks. No one cared or noticed. Damien and I continued to "talk" for the first time all day.

[How's it going?]

[Okay! Kinda weird, though. I was texting people all day lol! What about you?]

[It's not that hard at all. But I don't talk to that many people, anyway.]

[Me neither, even though I've been meaning to hang out with the guys on the track team, but I think they think I'm a dork.]

[Lol why?]

[I dunno, but I want to try out for it and I want them to like me.]

[I volunteered to decorate our floor for Homecoming Spirit Week. Not sure what to do about it just yet, since I don't know if we're doing anything at The Manor.]

[I'm sure they'll tell us.]

[Yeah.]

A moment passed as we continued to eat our lunch, then my phone lit up again.

[Do you know about tonight?]

[No, what?]

[We're supposed to write our experiences down at the pri-vate meditations before the midnight ceremony tonight.]

[Really? I didn't know that. Was there a new email? I didn't check mine.]

[No, actually. I don't know how I know. I just do. It sounds weird, but it popped in my head...]

I put the phone down and nodded at him, letting him know I understood. It popped in mine, too.

We were not meeting at the caf' again for dinner, as we would be having a midnight feast at The Manor, anyway. We were on our own to eat somewhere between then. I made some ramen in my room along with a cup of coffee. I was excited about the evening's activities. Our own meditations could take place at any time, I guessed. I had no idea when Deanna would come back to the room, but I decided to take advantage of alone time while I had it.

I got out a sheet of paper and cleared my desk, opening up iTunes for some relaxing music on my playlist. I allowed myself to relax and take a few breaths, then shut the lights off and turned a candle on. It was the only light I had sans my laptop monitor. I guessed that we were supposed to reflect on the day and what it meant to us, as we spent all day turning inward. It was supposed to be easy.

While I jotted some notes down, I noticed the door opened. In the reflection of my computer, I saw Deanna come in, see me, and then automatically leave. I don't know why, but I kept watching the door through the screen, expecting her to come back. Once she did, I turned around.

"Sorry, I didn't know you were … you know, doing something. Is it private? Do you want me to leave?"

I shrugged and shook my head.

"That's okay, that's cool. I'm going to go talk to Kristen about something, anyway."

She left, and I got back on track. After a while, I got up to go to the bathroom. Kristen's room was near it, and on the way back I could not help but stop by the door. I could overhear their voices.

"She's just so *weird!*"

"I know!"

"Is she like, into witchcraft and spells and stuff?"

"She definitely is. Seriously, she creeps me out sometimes."

I walked slower until I was close enough to stop.

"Me too. Her and her creepy friends acted like walking zombies all day. It was hard not to stare."

"You should see when she does weird séance stuff in our room. I don't know what to do! But it's like I can't talk to her anyway because she's not supposed to talk until tomorrow."

"Well, whenever you need somewhere to hang that's normal, my door is always open."

"Thanks."

My skin prickling, I went back to my room with more to add to that essay.

At midnight we all gathered in the lower lounge, and with us, about a hundred lit candles positioned on set tables, the mantle place, windowpanes, and all down the stairs. We held our own but turned off. New kids, like myself, wore regular black GOL T-shirts while upper members had on the hooded cloaks. They were long and Gothic, very decorative with subtle hints of color but still black, the back pieces sweeping the floor as they walked. They were so elegant I was envious that I would have to wait a semester to get my own.

We were all stuffed from the pancake dinner, or breakfast, technically. I think it was supposed to be seen as breakfast, as the ceremony was considered a beginning.

The second hand officially declared it midnight, but I noticed everyone still abided by the vow of silence, which I didn't understand. Mitchell stayed mute as well, and somehow it was like we knew we had to wait for his official cue. We watched him when he left his spot at one of the long tables and headed towards the front. What happened next was so quick that anyone could have missed it.

A piece of his cloak passed over a windowsill over a burning candle. I held my breath, instantly thinking it would catch fire. The flame did not wander or even flicker as he passed, but as soon as a loose thread got caught on the candlestick, it quickly tipped in his direction.

I jumped up. *Watch out!*

I said it. I know I did, but no sound came out of me. Maybe it was the shock, or maybe it was the fact that the candle didn't fall. A guy near Mitchell grabbed the thread just in time. Mitchell simply nodded a thank you to him and walked on, with no accidents.

Mitchell went up to the front carrying his own candle and held it up before us. Music turned on while all the lights shut off. He stared at us and the candle lit up his face. He turned on his electric candle while other members joined him and did the same. One by one we did the same, at the same time as though through a joint reaction. We held our candles up above our heads. They glowed on, the fire candles around us glowed on, and we stood still.

Mitchell lowered his candle, and we all followed, looking at all of us and smiling.

"Let your Lights shine."

CHAPTER 9

I heard voices in the common room as I climbed the stairs to my floor, but as soon as I entered, the voices stopped and they stared at me. Well, for a minute they stared, and then they pretended to be invested in their homework and ignored me. I didn't care so much; it just got uncomfortable every time I was around. The girls quietly discussed homework until I left the room, and then out of the corner of my eye, I saw one of them eyeball me.

"Why are they so weird?" I asked Deanna while flipping off my shoes.

"Who?"

"You know who, The Three Musketeers clique of the floor, who are always together and whispering."

Deanna shrugged, and it irritated me.

"So how come Kristen, Katie, and Lindsey talk to you and no one else?"

Deanna shrugged again, and I waited for her dumb excuse.

"It's not that they don't talk to anyone else. We go to lunch and sometimes hang out in each other's rooms, like when we have floor movie nights."

"Floor movie nights?"

"Yeah, you're never around for those."

I went to my computer so it could hide my face, as I knew I was scowling by then. I missed out on everything, and apparently, it made all the difference.

"Hey, by the way, we had another meeting about the floor decorating."

"Oh! I missed it again. How come I never know when this stuff is?"

Deanna just shrugged. "You're obviously involved in something else ... but I want to be the one to tell you, you're not on it anymore."

I wasn't mad, exactly. I just felt like I had the wool pulled over my eyes.

"Well, I guess I'll find out."

The three girls were still in the common room. I had to get this over with. Kristen, Katie, and Lindsey were chatting and didn't stop when I walked in.

"Hi," I said, casually approaching their table. They gave small smiles and greeted me back. All right, this was a start.

"Just wanted to ask what was going on with Homecoming decorations."

They looked at each other, and that look was all it took. My stomach tightened, but I tried to ignore it. Kristen looked to Lindsey, who looked to Katie, who looked back. Their brows rose, and they bit their lips.

"Mmmmmmm," was all Katie said. I just stood there, looking from one to another.

"Actually, we kind of already did it."

"Yeah, we mostly got everything done."

"Oh," was all I said.

"Yeah, I mean, there isn't a whole lot to do," Kristen said. "We got most of the stuff from the dollar store and all we have to do is put it up and everything. There really isn't much to do. So I'm sorry, but we don't need you."

"Oh."

They all were avoiding eye contact for the most part.

"Sorry," added Lindsey.

"No, whatever," I said right away. "It's fine."

Snobs.

Back in my room, I just did my homework and tuned the world out until my mom called.

"How are you doing?"

"I'm good. How are you?" I replied.

"We're doing fine! We went by Grandma and Grandpa the other night for dinner. You know they're into yoga now! They're taking classes at the Park District and are really enjoying it!"

"That's great," I said, closing my math book on my desk. "What about you and Taylor and Jordan?"

"The usual. Taylor joined the academic bowl, and Jordan is still doing swimming. We still have to find a weekend where we can visit, but we've all been busy over here."

"I know. Me too."

"How's it going with classes and that club you're in?"

"Classes are good, not too hard. This group focuses on spirituality without any forced religion. It is so nice, Mom! These people actually care about cleansing your soul. It's really special. Trust me. It actually is making me get better."

I glanced over at Deanna at her computer. Her headphones were on and she was not even listening to me.

"What do you do there?" my mom asked.

"We do a lot of things and every day it feels like a better day. We hold group meditations and affirmations and just do positive things in general to spread a good message. It is good discipline for the soul, too. Like the other day, we had a day where we took a vow of silence."

"That is so good. I'm glad you found something you enjoy that makes you happy. So, do they talk to you?"

"Well, yeah."

"I mean, is there a teacher?"

"Yeah."

"Do they have counseling sessions?"

"Well ... well not exactly."

At this point, I walked out and wandered into the lounge, which was empty. I shut the door to the hallway.

"Sky, did you even go to the campus counseling yet?"

"No," I hesitated saying.

I heard my mom sigh and I could just see her face now, her disappointed eyes closing.

"You need that."

"I don't really need it anymore!"

"Honey, I'm proud of you that you found this group and it will help you, but you still need to see a counselor. It will be good for you to continue to talk to someone. We still go."

"I know, Mom. I will. This is pretty therapeutic on its own. I guess I'll talk about it when I'm ready. I'm not sure when that will be, but honestly, I feel pretty good right now."

"Good."

"Yeah."

"Okay, well, I better let you go, just wanted to catch up!"

"Sounds good. Send me an email or something."

"I will, honey. Love you!"

"Love you too!"

I went back to my room and was startled to see Kristen come out of it. She didn't see me as she left.

"What did Kristen want?" I asked Deanna.

"Nothing much," Deanna replied, playing with her hair.

"Look," I sat down in my chair next to the couch. "I'm not stupid. She and those other girls are acting weird around me. Are they talking about me?"

Deanna cringes. "Actually, yeah. They are."

"Why?" I demanded

"I'm so sorry Sky. I ... I didn't want to be the one to hurt your feelings. Basically ... they think you're weird."

"*I'm* weird?"

"Yeah, just with that group you're in."

"Guardians of Light? Why? What's so weird about it? We don't do anything except spread a positive message! What, is that too cheesy for some people?"

"Sky, I don't know. I'm sorry, but it just creeps everyone out."

I raised my eyebrows. "Everyone?"

Deanna got very quiet.

"Everyone on this floor ... like... thinks you're a Satanist."

"That's RIDICULOUS!"

"I know it is, but I just thought you should know. You do all these rituals and stuff. But people feel that way about stuff that is different."

I sighed, exasperated, and Deanna stared at the floor.

"Don't think anything of it," she said.

"Well, kind of hard to when people hate me for no real reason."

"It's really stupid. I wouldn't even worry about it. They say stupid things like you worship the devil and you do creepy ceremonies with witchcraft and stuff."

"Oh, my GOD!"

"I know!" Deanna said. She looked at me funny.

"You don't believe in that stuff, do you?"

"Of course not."

"Good, see? I told you it was crazy. Don't let them bother you!"

I just shook my head, too annoyed and too confused to say anything else.

That night, once Deanna was asleep, I stretched out on my bed over the covers and started whispering. I did not want her to hear me, but I wanted others to.

"Guide me, spirits. Give me a sign. Give me a sign that you are here."

My fingertips shook a little at my sides, but they stayed there. I repeated the phrase.

"Lift me ... come on ... lift me ..."

I shivered out of my blankets, but that was all the movement I had. Nothing happened, and I sighed, getting back in and rolling on my side. I heard Deanna roll on her side too, and she might have lifted her head to hear if I was talking.

It was a Friday, and the only thing I could think about was the Burning of the Burdens activity at The Manor. I was looking forward to it, but at the same time, I was really nervous. We were to have a ceremony where we'd write down the things that upset and bothered us, share them openly, and then put them in a fire.

I realized my moment had come, and it was making me crazy to have to share something so personal with people I still did not know very well. I guess the time had to come eventually. It was time for us to bond. It was another step towards my personal healing, and it might have been the step I was waiting for.

Damien and I walked over there right away, a little before six. As we headed on, I couldn't help but notice Damien was in just as much of an anxious state as I was, if not a bit more. We were both pretty quiet on our way to The Manor. The only thing we could hear was the rustling of the leaves as, one by one, they detached themselves and floated to the ground in piles. It could have been the burden that Damien still carried, the one he was to purge tonight, along with the others. I was going to find out sooner or later. The entrance to The Manor was lit up, as it usually was, the lanterns all in a line of light in the evening dusk.

The evening started with a spaghetti dinner in our mess hall, which had to add another table to accommodate new members. The food, of course, was the best I'd ever eaten. I slurped those noodles and didn't care when I got red sauce speckled on my chin. We, for a fact, had the best bread on campus. It was hot and fresh like someone actually made it from scratch, but we never knew since we were never around when it was being made. We dipped it into our plates and scooped up the masses to devour in mouthfuls.

And then, I suddenly got very tired. I slumped in my seat and chugged the rest of my Pepsi in a vain attempt for a caffeine boost. Next to me, Damien yawned and even loosened the belt around his pants. I didn't need to look around to know that everyone else was just as satisfied as we were. It was like one big secret everyone was in on. We got the royal treatment at this place. The Manor was an island from the rest of the campus. We were the special ones. After all, if we were the only ones who knew what it took to better our lives, why shouldn't we be given the royal treatment?

Mitchell stood up and cleared his throat.

"I think this lovely pasta dinner put us all in a nice, relaxing mood! Perfect for tonight's activities. We'd like you all to start filing out and fill up the cushion seats by row in the lower lounge. And, as you walk, consider the ceremony started. No talking whatsoever. Now is the time to gather your thoughts."

We did so, exiting the mess hall area, and I got the chills. It wasn't the cold kind, but I did suddenly feel colder. True, I was slightly anxious about this unmasking event we were having. My body seemed to be feeling that pressure.

The basement door was already propped open by the angel statue that seemed to be staring into our minds and judging us as we passed. I avoided eye contact. A few people already in the lower lounge were seated in rows of horseshoes on the floor. At the front, at the fireplace, was a table with a single large candle burning a tiny bored flame. Someone played music somewhere. It was slow and instrumental, but loud, and it echoed in the walls as though the symphony were playing live on the upper level. It enchanted our legs to move in synch down the stairs and over to neighboring cushions on the floor. We folded our legs in unison and stared at the candle until the whole lounge was filled. My body began to feel heavy, and from the neck down, I didn't move anything. When parts of your body fall asleep, most notably appendages, your veins get prickling sensations of blood re-flowing and waking your body back to life. That would be the case if I even thought to wiggle a toe or shuffle a leg, but I didn't. As far as I was concerned, I was a stone paperweight, and the cushion below me flattened of any fluff.

Mitchell entered the scene, donning a large black cloak bearing our group's logo. He opened his arms in address.

"Lights, we begin the Burning of the Burdens. But in order to do so, you must first confront your burdens. Bring them out into the open. Look under your seats for notebooks and pencils and begin your reflections."

And my body reanimated enough to do so, getting that spiral notebook and a small pencil, which was the kind you find in board games and end up breaking. I wasn't sure how much to write or how much detail to go into, so I just started pouring it out. Over the repetitive, instrumental solos of our current soundtrack were the scratches of those pencils, running together in a similar motion, some so quickly and passionately they sounded like hurried whispers. And soon enough, I realized I was having a hard time seeing my paper. Somewhere down the line we little by little started to lose light in the room. The lone candle at the front of the lounge burned brighter as the only light source. Looking up at the ceiling, I saw the top light bulbs off and out of use, but the chandelier itself seemed to sway a little, only a little. I saw the world around me go blacker. If none of the lights in the room were on, how could it be getting darker? Older members lit smaller candles and put them on the stairs of the lounge, and I could only see their faces against their cloaks, floating in midair.

I broke my paper from the notebook, my hands shaking, for as soon as the room got darker the chills came back as well. Soon, we were to go up in front of everyone and share our vulnerabilities. I started shaking so much I was sure my glasses were throbbing on my nose. The floating faces gathered near the front by the candle and Mitchell, who now held a glass container. He motioned to one of the members holding a cloth pouch at her side.

"Now is the time for us to confront our burdens. We confront them with strength and determination that they will not run our lives."

The girl flung something into the fireplace, and a huge cloud of green exploded from the ashes and rumbled the walls. I jumped at the sparks that flew out, especially at the loud emerald and yellow flames that now took residence in the fireplace. Even the walls around it looked green.

"We cast them away in this fire, a symbol of our brightness and richness in character. And as we cast away our troubles, our weaknesses, we must remember to honor and protect our flames."

Mitchell put the glass cover over the little candle, which never even flickered against the green monster.

"Let the Burning of the Burdens begin."

The music filled our ears as we were left alone with our thoughts. The upperclassmen at the front were already in a line formation, the girl who started the green fire up first. She held up her paper and faced the crowd, staring at a spot on the back wall.

"My burden is that I struggle with independence. I grew up as an only child to a wealthy family, and as an only child, my parents always spoiled me and I grew up getting everything I ever asked for. I worry that I won't be able to take care of myself and money will be the only thing to raise me."

She crumpled the paper and tossed it in the fire. The embers hissed, the flames immediately eating it up with yellow crinkly teeth.

And so, one by one, we went, row by row, as each member said their thing. I noticed that many people's burdens were common. Most worried about relationships, getting good grades, and getting a good job, which made me a little more worried about my own. A few had some more severity, such as a serious addiction and someone who got arrested for shoplifting. I would be going up there before Damien, so everyone would know my baggage before knowing his. I couldn't figure out if his was as serious as stealing or doing drugs, but somehow I knew mine would stand out from anyone else's.

I knew my legs had fallen asleep, but instead of feeling prickly, they were in their stone marble state. I didn't even know when my legs started to move until they did so for me, without my even knowing it as the person to my left came and sat back down.

Mitchell's eyes turned to me. The fireplace was urging me to the front with the hastily written piece of paper I held. As I got closer to the front, I could hear that green fire crackling in different extremes, like a witch's laughter, waiting for me to feed it another snack.

I stood at the front and found myself staring at the same point on the back wall, knowing how difficult it was to make any eye contact with people you were sharing your deep, personal secrets with. I didn't even want to look at Damien. I opened my mouth and thought if I gave them the basics, it would be all over and I could sit back down.

"Around April, I lost my dad. He was shot and killed by gang members in the street in downtown Chicago."

Well, there was no way I could stop there. If I ran back to sit down after that, everyone's stares would burn holes through my head.

"It was back when we lived in the city. He was walking home from the train station. It was a typical night; that was how he got home every night."

I was talking faster because the angry, hateful chunks were starting to rise in my throat already.

"There were gang members out and fighting with each other. One of them was running away from someone else. He had a gun on him and ran through the streets and was looking for rival members and eventually found them. They fired at each other and one of them came around the corner and fired and missed. They got my dad instead. Right in the throat."

The tears were flowing faster and faster and my face started to scrunch up as I could no longer compose myself.

"He was doing *nothing*! He was minding his own business! He did nothing! But criminals decided that they were going to make their business other people's business and my dad died because of it! He didn't last long. Someone called 911, but it was too late. The best part? They didn't even catch whoever did it, cause some gang members were found dead too, so no one could be punished."

My sleeve was damp with each wipe, and by this time, I stopped staring at the wall and turned my face down to the candle, imploring it: *Give me strength, give me strength.*

"No matter what happens, there will always be criminals. I want to get past the hate I have, the hate I have for the law not taking control of violence in the streets. I want to be strong and know that he is always with me, my family, and for us to find peace and healing. This past couple of months, I ... I've been trying to forgive the world, but I just can't. I want more strength to get through this."

I already had the paper crumbled in a sweaty wad in my palm, but I tried to make it tighter. I turned and tossed it in the fire with great relief, even the tiniest explosion seeming much bigger. I stayed up there just to watch it burn and melt into nothing, just to be sure. I sniffed and composed myself, taking a deep breath. I didn't walk back to my seat. I almost floated—my head on a cloud and my eyes washed clean—to the back bathroom.

CHAPTER 10

My iPod was rolled up to a pretty high volume, but I still heard the knock on the door.

"Yeah, come on in."

Damien opened the door and smiled at me.

"Hey," we both said simultaneously.

"What are you up to?" he asked, sidestepping around a pair of my jeans on the floor—or they could have been Deanna's.

"Nothing, really," I answered, shrugging.

I took my iPod off from around my neck and set it on my desk.

"Just hanging out, I guess. Glad you came by, though. I was bored."

"Me too," he said. "I felt like getting out for a while."

"Your dorm pretty quiet too?"

"Yeah. They all usually are on weekends."

"Hey, did you ever hear anything about getting in that trackhouse?"

"No, actually. I don't know anything about that yet."

Damien came over and sat on the couch. I got up to go to the fridge on the other side.

"Want anything?"

"Sure."

We opened up Dr. Peppers and took sips. It was quiet for a second while I closed out of my email window. I was definitely feeling Damien's gravitational pull. I turned in my chair while taking another big gulp.

"So, how are you?" he said.

"I'm fine," I answered. "I feel kind of bad, though. I didn't stick around to hear your burden."

"No, don't worry about it," he said immediately. "It's okay. It's nothing compared to yours. No one's was, really. I would have excused myself too, after that. I mean, that was tough. No one blamed you."

"I couldn't help myself. I was such a wreck."

"It's okay, Sky. What you went through, I mean, I remembered, in school when that happened to you, but I didn't really get to hear the details until then. And you weren't even gone that long, anyway."

"I did feel like I was in the bathroom forever."

At that point, I thought that I cried out all the tears in me. I was wrong. I put my pop can down as I started to sniff uncontrollably.

"It was just ... so hard to say all that in front of everyone."

Damien leaned forward, also momentarily abandoning his drink.

"It's something that is just never going away."

"Hey, it's okay," Damien soothed my stupid hiccups.

He put an arm around me, awkwardly half-off the couch.

"Sky, seriously, that was so brave of you to tell everyone that," Damien continued, giving my back a little rub.

"You had to get it out in the open and off your chest. That's what that whole ceremony was about. For us to let go of our burdens."

I wiped my face and hugged him back, allowing myself to be half off the chair.

We separated for a minute so I could get up to get a tissue.

"I know I told you before, but I am so sorry about your dad."

"Thanks," I managed to say behind the tissue.

"And those asshole gangs, that is just terrible."

"Yeah. Go figure. That happens all the time, and no one does anything about it. Why not?"

I went back to my desk but didn't sit down, taking another drink.

"Truth is, shit happens, especially in ghetto city areas. It just happens. There are bad things in certain areas and innocent people suffer from it."

There was a very inviting area on the couch next to Damien, and we were both willing me to sit down. Damien reached his arm out when I sat down and draped it over my shoulders, and the next thing I knew, I found myself in the cozy nook that was his chest. It was like how I felt after the ceremony relieved, comforted, better. I turned sideways and allowed myself to hug him back, to hold him, and I closed my eyes.

"I think about him every day. And I know he is with me."

He pulled me in tighter and even stroked my arm a bit with his thumb.

"My family and I ...we're ... we're getting by. But it's still hard."

"And he'll always be with you. You're a strong person, Sky. Look how far you've come. He's proud of you."

I wiped my face enough so that I wouldn't get my tears all over Damien's T-shirt, seeing how thin it was. It was so thin I could smell his freshly showered stomach ... whatever manly soap guys used.

Our stomachs pressed against one another as we breathed, and soon we adapted the same breathing patterns, so we inhaled and exhaled in one rhythmic motion. He once in a while stroked my arm with his thumb and I rested my hand on his other arm, doing the same.

"Oh, God. I'm sorry. I didn't even ask you about your burden."

I looked up at him, which was kind of awkward, given that I was right into the bottom profile of his face.

"I'm sorry I missed it."

"No, it's okay," he answered. "Mine is dumb anyway."

"No, come on," I said, resting my head back on his stomach. "Tell me, it's only fair."

Damien moved some of my hair down by my ear. It must have been tickling his chin.

"My burden was that I'm not perfect like my brother and sister. My whole life, that is what it's been like. I was never like Ally or Neil. They are academic all-stars, you know the kind: The straight-A honor students, star athletes, and star musicians, and student body president, and blah blah blah. Perfect at everything. And, I'm not. I can't play an instrument, I couldn't play football or chess and my grades were just so-so. My parents must hate me. 'Why can't you be more like your brother and sister?' Do you know how old that gets?"

I shrugged. "Yeah."

"Do you know how frustrating it is to grow up with two perfect siblings that you just can't measure up to, no matter what you do? I would study for weeks for a test and get a B, and that was never good enough! So, they sent me off to a boarding school that would set me straight."

He let out a heavy sigh.

"Yeah, I could imagine. But you're a different person. It doesn't mean you're not good at anything, it just means you're good at other things."

"Like what?"

"Well," I said. "I hope I get to see that side of you. It makes you mysterious."

He stroked my hair again, and I smiled. I didn't need to look at him to know that he was smiling, too.

For the rest of the night, we sat like that. I didn't know how much time had passed until Deanna came home. All I knew was that it was much later because it was darker. As soon as I heard the doorknob turn, my first reaction was to blush and get off of Damien, but I couldn't. Deanna apparently was in no condition to notice or care.

She stumbled in with her zip-up sweatshirt barely draped on her shoulders ... and her eyes were all squinty.

"Heyy, yooo. What's up, everybody?!"

"Where were you tonight?" I asked, trying to sound casual instead of a disgusted parent.

"I was with Chad at a party."

She laughed as she finger-combed through her hair.

"I am sooo tired, I just wanna lay down. So, what did you two do tonight?" She smiled at us teasingly.

"Nothing," I said truthfully.

Damien yawned and started to lift his arm.

"Don't worry about me Damien," Deanna stated as she flip-kicked her shoes into the closet. "You can stay or whatever. I'm just going to go pass out."

"Actually, I should get going," Damien replied as he started to get up, prompting me to do the same. It was the first time we were actually facing each other in what seemed like hours, now face-to-face instead of side by side, and I wasn't sure what to do.

"Thanks, Damien," I finally said. *Should I hug him, or was that already one long hug?*

"Yeah, no problem, thanks to you too," he said, smiling. "Bye, Deanna."

"See ya."

As soon as he was gone, Deanna didn't take long to get in her bed with her face propped up on her elbow, grinning at me.

"Soooo. You and Damien, huh?"

I turned around, praying I wasn't blushing.

"Yeah, I don't know," I mumbled as I picked up my long-forgotten Dr. Pepper can, now lukewarm. "We're just really good friends."

Classes were boring, but I knew it was only because I was looking forward to going to The Manor again tonight. I saw Seth and another girl, Holly, already ahead of me down the path as I stepped outside. They had their heads lowered, and they seemed to be walking solemnly, not even talking. Tonight was described as a cleansing ceremony, which, unlike Burning of the Burdens, was to be more relaxing, although still a release. People in the group took it very seriously, and it was a message that the rest of us should as well.

Damien met me outside my dorm, and we walked together, as usual.

"We're not on Daylight Savings time yet, are we?"

I looked at him, confused. "Um no, why?"

Damien looked to the sky, and all around campus, from the buildings to those outside.

"Doesn't it seem darker to you?"

I took a look around myself, and it could have been that I had a lot on my mind that I didn't notice, but he was right. How did I not notice that I couldn't see anything until now?

The sun set way past the last academic building and the trees were nothing but silhouettes in the navy sky. I completely lost sight of Seth and Holly and could swear I saw a firefly or two in the far-off distance.

"What the?" I objected, not even seeing my own shadow.

"Right?" said Damien. "What time is it?"

"Barely six-thirty, isn't it?"

"I guess so, but it feels more like nine."

"It is fall, after all. Maybe it just gets darker in Wisconsin."

He didn't say much else, and I became slightly uneasy. Did the sun set so far behind us on campus that we actually left it behind? We were walking in pure darkness now as the trees formed an umbrella over our heads. The only light we had was the solar lanterns giving us our path to the house, which, there it was, all lit up. It seemed like every light was on in that place, almost expecting darkness to swallow up everything around it except for the house itself. It was glowing a comforting orange; warm and inviting. I was only more excited to get in there for … for … I don't know … protection? I couldn't figure out why.

Iris greeted us at the door, donning her black cloak that made her look like Morticia Adams.

"May the Light always guide you and keep you safe from darkness," she said, opening the door for us.

"Are we meeting downstairs?" I asked.

"We are. Take some paper and markers with you."

Damien and I got some from the kitchen counter.

"I hope it's not another Burning of the Burdens."

"No, don't worry, Sky," Damien said confidently as we passed through the hallway with the bookcases. I meant it to be a joke.

The bookcases creaked as we passed them like the books themselves were talking to us. I realized I never took the time to enjoy this little library, and I should sit and read sometime.

At this point, we already got used to the candles on the stairs; we didn't have to worry about kicking them over. They, for some reason, were always safe.

Mitchell was waiting in the lower lounge with other members already seated. Instead of a colorful, roaring fire this time, we were all looking at a large punch bowl on a little table he stood behind. "Welcome, my children," he greeted.

We got settled and soon the older kids came downstairs in a line formation, ushering lower-classmen to their seats. Iris came down last, carrying a pitcher.

"Tonight, we celebrate our purity," Mitchell began. "Pure soul and pure heart. Last time we met, we had a wonderful Burning of the Burdens ceremony where we took our troubles and cast them away, destroying them. Now we are free of these troubles and we must continue to nourish our souls with a cleansing. Row by row, you'll come up here and be washed with purifying water, and then you'll use the paper to write affirmations. Write uplifting messages that you want to spread around campus, and then go do so. Take your affirmations to your dorms, classrooms, the cafeteria, library, bathroom mirrors, and wherever you can think of. Spread the message of Light in hopes of saving a lost soul from the dark."

Mitchell gave a small wave, and Kimberly came over with the pitcher. No one could see what was inside until she poured it into the bowl. When the water hit the bowl, an enormous cloud of smoke came out and rolled on the top. Some people had alarmed yet curious looks, especially since after Iris poured it all, the smoke stayed there, a witch's frothy brew. It looked like it was just water, but it obviously wasn't. It couldn't be.

Everyone lined up before the bowl to set an example. Mitchell dipped a little cup and poured a small morsel over Kimberly's head. I don't know what I was expecting, but nothing happened. Nothing happened when it was my turn, either. I got water poured on my head, which dripped down my neck and down my sweatshirt, but that was it.

I sat down and wrote my affirmations, which turned out to be a couple. Mine said things like "Be proud of your Light" and "A pure soul is a happy soul" and "Dirty souls make dirty actions—come clean." I felt happy. I knew where these would go, and it made me even happier. That night I taped them all in my dorm bathroom. Maybe, just maybe, I could inspire others.

I came back to my room, confused and annoyed. Deanna saw the look on my face and answered my question.

"It was me."

I stared at her. "What?"

Deanna looked down for a second. "I'm the one who took them down. All day people were reading those signs and laughing, and making fun of them."

"Why?"

Deanna looked right back up at me as though she couldn't believe her ears. "I already told you. Remember? About how people think of you on this floor?"

"So?"

"So, it was embarrassing. I put them by your desk, though. I didn't throw them out."

"What's the big deal?" I stammered. "Why did you take them down? What exactly is so bad about it?"

"I told you. Because people make fun of you, Sky! They knew it had to be you, saying you're like preachy and you need to get a life. So sometime after they had their laugh and left, I got out of my stall and took the signs down."

I sat down hard on my bed across from Deanna's.

"What the hell is everyone's problem? They think I'm weird because of the things I believe in? They have a huge problem with me wanting to be a better person? What's wrong with that? What's wrong with sending out positive messages to the world, given that some people actually need that?"

I turned to my left to see that my signs were indeed on my desk.

"I mean, other GOL members are posting these all over too, so it's not like anybody can shut me up."

I got up, realizing I still had my backpack on my shoulders.

"I'm going to grab a coffee and go do homework with some people at The Manor."

Deanna just nodded. "Sure, okay. See ya. And... And... I'm sorry."

I shrugged it off and took my signs as I left.

Down the hallway, I passed some of the girls, who saw what I was holding and suppressed smiles. I passed the floor lounge with more people in it, and they definitely noticed me walking through. I walked faster, knowing that there was only one place I was accepted.

I was happy when I got to The Manor, just as happy when I saw other Affirmation signs posted around campus. I had to keep reminding myself that I was not alone, and the more I repeated this in my head, the more I believed it.

I was able to relax and do some homework in the upper lounge with some others. Damien wasn't there, but I got to hang out with another member, Holly, for a bit.

I sat down in one of the big chairs with my backpack and didn't notice right away that Holly was there, but only there physically. She sat in a yoga pretzel position with her arms facing up over her legs. Her eyes closed. The only noise she made was the gentle whistling as she breathed in and out of her teeth. I, myself, tried not to make any noise and for a minute considered that I would be disturbing her and should go somewhere else. Before I could lean forward to get up, she opened her eyes and looked at me.

"Sorry," I said right away.

"Oh no, don't worry about it! I wasn't very successful, anyway. I am just having a hard time concentrating today, I guess. Have... Have... Have you ever tried to leave your body?"

I let my backpack slip off and didn't bother picking it up. "What?"

"You know, have an out-of-body experience. Some of the others mentioned it once, and I guess I was curious."

"No, I never even thought of that before. Is that even possible?"

She unfolded her legs. "It might be. I think it would be really awesome. Iris claimed she does it all the time."

"Somehow I believe that."

"Me too. Iris seems like she can ... connect."

I nodded. "Yeah. I definitely believe that. That is something I am actually trying to do."

Holly looked uncertain for a minute. "I want to, but at the same time, I don't. Every time I walk around here and get a shiver up my spine, I don't think that could be anything good."

CHAPTER 11

Deanna burst into the room just as I was reading my GOL email. "Check this out!" she squealed enthusiastically.

I turned around to witness a huge poster, black and orange writing, and, of course, pumpkins and taffy apple doodles.

"So, Student Council is hosting this HUGE party for Halloween!" she gushed. "Chad's going to be there, obviously. He's one of the hosts. It's going to be rad!"

"Neat," I replied, forcing a smile. *Sure, an excuse for every girl to dress slutty.*

Deanna made sure she put the poster down where we both could see it. "Hell yeah! I need to start planning an outfit! Amy and Kristen and Ashley are talking about going as nurses. Amy has these really cute white shoes. Anyway, if you have nothing planned, you should come!"

I turned back to my GOL email, the newest one with the subject line "All Hallows Eve Gathering."

"Well, it looks like GOL is doing something, too."

"Yeah, that's cool, but you should come by at least for a little bit and then go to your thing afterward. Or just come by afterward, whatever works. I mean, it's fun to meet new people. Maybe you should take a break from all that spiritual stuff. I mean, doesn't it get tiring? You really need to let loose and go somewhere just to have a good time."

"It doesn't get tiring," I said, trying not to be too defensive. "And we do have fun. I mean, we don't party, but we just have our own fun. We play games, we do things for our minds, we do things as a group. That's all."

"That's cool. You can do whatever. It's just ... you just ... you should get to know other people and let other people get to know you and show that you can do other cool things. I mean, you're supposed to jump around to different groups and do different things."

"Maybe," I said, not turning around this time. I was an embarrassment to her. I was probably making her look bad because she lived with me and had to deal with what others said about me. I knew that, but I couldn't say it.

Satisfied with that answer, Deanna slid her book bag off her back and sat at her own desk. She played music softly, and I returned to my email.

Gather with us on All Hallow's Eve for a night of celebration you will not forget. This will be an open party to anyone who wishes to join us in our ceremony to separate ourselves from the darkness. We will first have our own feast before the party starts. Special for Halloween, we will have our own costuming party. We ask that you dress in your own visual interpretation of darkness. What is darkness? What is it that consumes our lives and prevents us from living to our fullest? What is evil? We not only want to see your visual interpretation, but we want to feel it. We want to see the evil on your face and your body.

All this week, GOL members will be getting together to work on any costumes and help new members with theirs. Halloween is NOT about putting on a costume and getting candy, it allows us to have a special occasion with "the other side". It is about fear and learning not to fear the after-life and death. This will be a very special occasion, and we urge you to pass this message along to others who want a different experience.

Our ceremony will continue with the theme of the darkness, that while darkness may consume us on the outside, it will never touch us on the inside. We ask that you also bring with you a change of clothes and they are to be all WHITE. At midnight on Halloween night, once it is officially over and November first, we will change from our Darkness costumes into our white clothes to symbolize our casting away of it and revealing our inner lights. We will have a short tea ceremony for cleansing and then you will wear the same clothes during the day to further continue this theme.

A costume, huh? I somehow knew the regular clothes I had around my closet wouldn't do so well. But I would rather put the effort into something like this than in that popular kids' club Deanna was obsessed with. I even shuddered a little. Either way, I decided that maybe I should head on over to The Manor to see if people were already there planning it.

Seth greeted me at the door, and I was a little confused to see that he was wearing a blindfold.

"Uh, Seth?"

"Greetings, Sister Skyler."

"Whatever. Why are you blindfolded?"

"It's perfect for Halloween. Darkness being something that blinds us, part of the outfit I want to put together."

"Well, you're not going to walk around like that all day, are you? How will you see?"

I let myself in and he smiled. "I don't need to. I feel around me. It's like echolocation."

"Uh-huh." I walked past him and noticed that he seemed to be watching me as though he could actually see through the blindfold.

I reached the kitchen area, and some members were there having lemonade and chips and doing homework. I greeted everyone and got settled, and a minute later Damien came out of the bathroom in the hall. He seemed almost surprised to see me.

"Hey, Sky,"

"Hi," I answered. "Where have you been?"

"Here, mostly. I started to work on my Scrabble skills." He had a big smile that changed when he looked at Iris in the lounge room, sprawled on a sofa chair. She eyed him and then went back to the book she was reading. Without a word, Damien walked over to the table and poured a large glass of lemonade. Instead of sitting down at the table, he walked right over to Iris and handed it over. She took it without even looking at him and he came back to the table.

I looked from Iris to Damien, who grabbed a cookie and silently munched on it. No one else seemed to notice or care and continued talking.

"What was that all about?"

Damien looked at me. "Oh, nothing. Iris asked me to get her some lemonade, that's all."

"No, she didn't."

"Well, yeah she did."

"Oh," I thought, thinking that conversation took place before I got here.

"So what are you going to do for Halloween?" he asked me.

"I don't know yet!" I replied. "I was hoping to get some ideas. Could be cool. I was hoping we were doing something here, anyway. Deanna invited me to another popular-people party."

"Really?" said Damien, and I could tell he was as disgusted as me.

"I don't get what is so unbelievably awesome about them, anyway."

At this point, one of the girls at our table looked at me, a junior, I believe. "That's why you belong here, Skyler," she said with a smile. "You're special and have a good mindset."

"Thanks," I said.

Mitchell walked in holding Ad Astra, whose eyes were closed in bliss while he rubbed behind her ears.

"Hello, everyone."

Seth came into the room but then stopped suddenly and started feeling his way down the other hallway. No one really noticed him; it seemed, except for me. Ad Astra purred loudly.

"We are going to have a wonderful Halloween tradition," Mitchell said to us at the table. Iris looked up for a minute and grinned. "Some of the members are already making flyers to go around campus, and it's so important for you all to pass them around and tell your friends about."

"We'll do what we can," said a girl at the table.

Mitchell went into the kitchen to get a treat for Ad Astra and then left again. The girl looked at Damien and me curiously.

"So are you guys 7th grade?"

"Yeah," Damien answered.

"Oh. I thought you were higher since you seemed like you lived here."

Something warm spread in my stomach. I wasn't sure if Damien had the same thought I did, but if he did, he didn't show it. "Live here? I actually forgot about that. I thought it was only for upperclassmen." I said.

"It's mostly just for upperclassmen to live here. The rooms upstairs? I mean, there's not a huge amount of rooms or even spare rooms, but older members take priority."

"That is awesome. What does it take to live here?"

"Like I said, it's mostly for high school level and there is usually a waiting list. It's for dedicated members. But I hear it's awesome."

My costume was kind of lame. But, it really didn't matter as long as the point was across, even though I still didn't really know what that was. I had a long black cape that I cut up a bit and distressed to make it look jagged and sharp. My theme was violence, and violence is in itself jagged and sharp, so there you go. The rest of my outfit was just black baggy Capri pants, and this wicked jacket-vest I found with a lot of buckles and zippers. I was impressed with what I found in the GOL clothing trunk. My makeup was another story. I actually admit I had too much fun practicing different looks in my room. I had some cheap Party City-type black and white stuff and was practicing making sharp-blade-type things on my face. Deanna, at one point, came home and peered at me curiously.

"What are you doing?"

"Trying different makeup stuff for Halloween."

"Oh, what are you going to be?"

"Well, our theme is darkness and whatever we think is a symbol for darkness, and my theme is violence, so I'm going for anything sharp ... ish."

She nodded like she was understanding instead of approving. I tried not to look at her as I wiped some of the black away from my eyes with my wet washcloth to fix it. I didn't care, really. I knew it was only a week away, and I was still very excited. Even if a part of it was scaring me a little bit.

Leaves fell on the ground that seemed to pick up in a mini tornado and followed us everywhere we went. That could have been one more reason people on campus stared at us, other than the fact they always did and that we all looked like the offspring of The Addams Family. I got used to ignoring the stares by now. I was on the lookout for the random things we were supposed to collect during the day, even though I couldn't see past how cheesy and downright fictional it was. Mitchell made the "official list" in an email to us earlier in the week to start looking for things we were going to use at our ceremony. The only thing I had that was of any significance was a never-burned candle, still in my pocket.

"Personify that darkness," Mitchell had told us consistently. "Cast it out; believe that it is leaving you."

The forecast for Halloween was supposed to be partly cloudy. The picture even showed the little sun peeking out, but today was nowhere near a peeking sun. I could have sworn the sun never came up at all, and the only light we relied on to tell us it was daylight was the leftover cast from the moon. The sky was actually still gray.

On campus, I felt confident every time I saw fellow GOL members in their black ensembles and painted faces.

We were a community; we were a team, a family, and it became an unspoken bond every time we did something to set us apart on campus. I was not the only Gothic fashion statement in my classes as I realized our number seemed to grow since I joined them at the beginning of the year. It was strange that I didn't seem to notice any new members before.

At one point I spotted Ad Astra stalking along the trees, a little white blob cast down from the clouds. She disappeared and reappeared between the trees without revealing a purpose or objective, and it seemed like I was the only one who noticed her. She stopped in mid-step and stared, not at me, but what was whatever directly next to me with soft, focused eyes. Her paw was still slightly raised, but she did not move and she did not blink. The fur on her body stood up, and she scattered away. How that cat got around was beyond me, but she always made it back to The Manor.

What little light we had did not last long. It was only my third period, but it felt and looked like evening, and soon it was almost like it was completely night. Our windows led to nothing.

"Is there going to be a tornado?" asked a paranoid girl in my class dressed like a zombie cheerleader. Or, I guess that was what she was supposed to be. I'm no expert, but I don't think that zombies—even cheerleader zombies—have sparkly red blood daintily sprinkled on their chins.

"No, I don't think so," the teacher said, cautiously peering out the window and holding herself as though cold. "It's just forecast, that's all. Kind of spooky."

As though on cue, the light bulbs above started to flicker, but that wasn't the only thing. The set of computers near the front of the room hummed dangerously at a high pitch, and at the same time, everything died out. The lights from the monitors and the lights above went out, and all across the hall, we heard cries of surprise, frustration, and small cheers.

"Power outage," said our teacher in annoyance. She left the room for whatever reason, and everyone in my class either celebrated or cowered.

"Oh my God, it is a storm," Zombie Cheerleader said again.

"No, it's not," said another girl in a purple wig and leather jacket. "It means we get out of class!"

"Yeah, maybe it's ghosts telling us to screw the rest of the day," said a guy in a plain T-shirt.

It really was getting darker out, and I knew it was too soon for Daylight Savings or anything to do with it. "It's just a power outage," our teacher said, coming back into the room. "And there's nothing really we can do about it right now. Just carry on until the lights come back on."

That was all right for an afternoon when it was merely grayish outside, but that gray got darker and darker until it was almost black, and I knew nighttime had come early. An announcement came on over the PA, and I know the same one was being said over all the other buildings:

"Attention teachers and students, due to the power outage that is affecting the whole campus without finding a source or a solution to the problem, we are going to cancel the rest of the day's classes. Everyone go back to your dorms, find some flashlights, and stay safe tonight."

There were some shouts of victory, but only some did not join in. That selection of students looked out the window, knowing. We knew that something was happening, and we could all feel it. It was too strong and too weird to be happy about canceled classes for Halloween night. We looked to one another, the GOL members and I. We said nothing.

Everyone left their classrooms, and the first thought that popped into my head was to go to The Manor. It was my haven. We had flashlights and candles there. It would be good to get those ready before we had our Halloween celebration that night.

I stepped outside and almost didn't know where I was. The light from the sky was being sucked away slowly, and I actually thought we might have a tornado from the way that sky looked. It was a threatening maelstrom of grays and blacks. I couldn't see the sun. I couldn't even see the moon. It was the timeframe of when they were both on opposite ends of the earth with no hope of showing themselves, and we were stuck in the lightless in-between ... for who knew how long? I adjusted my backpack on my shoulder and waved my own hand in front of me. I could still see that, but the buildings around me have downsized to silhouettes. I thought there were birds, but they turned out to be just trees. I looked down to my surprise to see that I couldn't even see the sidewalk ... it seemed like a part of the sky fell down here, too. I realized it was a thick fog that was rapidly taking over the ground.

I got walking, carefully but quickly. If it got darker and the fog grew, I would have no chance of finding my way out of there or anywhere. Students everywhere called out to each other as they disappeared into the misty masses. Some used their cell phones as lights. I was dumb enough to leave mine charging in my room. I reached my hand out and found a tree in the fog and used it to guide myself along the rest of the path. I had a horrible feeling that if this was bad, the path to The Manor in the heavily wooded area was going to be much worse.

It swallowed me. The weird part was, I actually felt it. I felt it without feeling the teeth, lips, or tongue of the fog creature, but I knew I was inside it. Not even our campus street lights were on. I could now barely make out the trees or the buildings. I saw nothing but dark gray smoke.

I couldn't panic as my fingers idly groped for another tree, a lamppost, a car, anything. I managed to find a garbage bin my hip slammed into. I bent over to rub it, cringing in pain, forcing myself to keep going. I wasn't alone out there and tried to listen to voices I knew. GOL members. Holly. Seth. Iris. Damien. Where was Damien? He was a bigger sissy about the dark than I was.

I was right about not being alone, but it wasn't what I thought. I saw something moving in the fog that was not supposed to be a part of it. It moved quickly towards me and I wasn't sure if it was something I could touch or not. To my pleasant surprise, it meowed.

"Ad Astra! Come here, girl!"

The cat appeared out of the fog, a radiant white creature with eyes of gold. The fog lifted away from her immaculately as she appeared from behind the garbage bin and approached me, looking either bored or irritated, or both.

"Meow."

I reached down and petted her on the head. She understood.

Turning around, she lifted her tail in the air and stalked the fog swirls ahead of her. Then, she began to walk very slowly. I trailed behind her, straining my eyes, her tail shifting poses from a question mark to a straight exclamation mark. She scuttled and bit and walked a little faster, before stopping completely and turning around to look at me.

"Right behind ya."

Satisfied, she continued walking through the fog as a little white beacon piercing through the dark. I followed her the whole way to The Manor, and I knew we were getting close when I could no longer hear the shouts of students trying to find each other. I knew we were away from the most civilized parts of campus when I felt wood shavings under my shoes.

Ad Astra stopped for a minute at the first solar lantern, very, very dim, but still glowing. She sat down and began to clean the back of her leg.

"Well, thanks," I said.

She ignored me and kept licking herself.

"So, are you going to be awhile? Or should I just take it from here, or...?"

She looked up at me, and I swear, if she could roll her eyes, she would have done so right then and there.

Her head suddenly jerked to her left, her leg still in midair. She stared at something in the trees.

I looked too, even though every time that cat stared out into space she was staring at nothing, but this time I did see something. It was something whitish hanging around the tree, and it had some sort of figure to it I couldn't make out. But it was there all right, and soon I saw it wasn't the only thing there. There were actually about two or three near the tree ... and they were hovering.

Ad Astra was still frozen as she watched these things, not really scared of them, more like curious, or just aware of them in general. She wasn't scared, but I sure was. Soon those forms looked like they were taking human shape.

The humanoid things moved around the tree. They moved about so much that they actually disappeared back into the fog. Ad Astra's tail twitched, and she got up. I started to walk, trying to see the dim lanterns. She walked as well as usual and did not look back. I kept looking back, but then decided that was dumb and only tried to walk faster. That was just the fog, that was just the fog, that was just the fog.

We got to the house, and I opened the door. Ad Astra busted in through the door crack when it was barely a sliver and disappeared somewhere. The first thing that went through my mind was to feel for a light switch, but then about a hundred lit candles told me that was pointless. They were everywhere, from tables to windowsills to nestled in people's shoes. I could make out the rest of the hallway and even a little of the kitchen. I tried to listen for voices to find out where the other members were, but I didn't need to do this either.

Hands touched my elbows and made me jump a foot into the air. Seth's voice was behind me.

"Sorry Sky! Didn't mean to startle you!"

"Well, everything is startling right now!"

"I know it is."

When Seth turned to be in front of me, I saw that he was still wearing his blindfold.

"Um, do you still think that's necessary?" I blurted out. I pointed to the handkerchief without being sure of whether he could see me. By the way he walked and carried himself, it was like he could see just fine.

"Don't worry about me, Sky."

"Is everyone here? Did you see outside and what's going on?"

"Power outage and darkness, yeah, I know. There's nothing to worry about."

The tone in his voice started to creep me out and only started to.

"Let's go downstairs," he said.

The path of candles on the stairs ensured we would find our way, but it was almost as though we didn't even need them. We knew the way around The Manor by heart and not by sight. Everyone gathered together; their costumes were the same but relatively different. We all wore our costumes to represent the Darkness in us we were trying to banish away. They were all different forms of black in different outfits and accessories. Some wore veils and some painted various designs on their faces. With so much black from our clothing, and so much orange from the glow of thousands of candles surrounding us, we *were* walking presentations of Halloween.

By the glow of a dozen candles lined up in rows, I saw the others were writing on their hands and up their arms, and lining up other members to do the same. Someone held a book of Latin phrases and carefully copied from this book. Iris eyed me and beckoned for me to approach her.

"Come here, Sky. It's your turn."

I went up to her and automatically rolled up my sleeves.

"This won't take long and we use washable marker, but consider this a deep symbol to bring what's printed on the outside to the inside."

So then, from fingertips to mid-elbows, I was a walking notepad. The black letters blurred together as Iris wrote all up and down my skin, leaving no room for flesh anywhere and turning my fingers into moving black squiggles. I looked at the book on the table and back and forth to translate the phrases Iris wrote on me:

"De fumo en flammam"—Out of the smoke into the flame.

"De pilo pendet"—It hangs by a hair.

"Cras credemus hodie nihil"—Tomorrow we believe, but not today.

"Ipsa scientia potestas est"—Knowledge itself is power.

"Aut viam invenium aut faciam"—I'll either find a way or make one.

"Credite posteri"—Believe it, future generations.

"Crede quod habes, et habes"—Believe that you have it, and you do.

"Credo ut intelligem"—I believe so that I understand.

"Fallaces sunt rerum species"—The appearances of things are deceptive.

"Flat justitia ruat coelom"—Let justice be done through the heavens fall.

"Legum servi sumus ut liberi esse possimus"—We are slaves of the law in order that we may be able to be free.

"Mutantur Omnia nos et mutamur in illis"—All things change, and we change with them.

"Memento mori"—Remember that you will die.

"Next," Iris simply announced.

I walked away and took my own candle to join the others and my arms felt ... heavy. Heavy like the time I was in my mother's room and tried on as many bracelets as I could until they couldn't fit up my arms. I could lift my arms, but it felt like I had to with effort.

"Guardians of Light," Mitchell proclaimed, holding up a box. "Darkness has swallowed our world we call home and left everybody alone and without a way. The time has come for us to shine that light and show them the way. Show them the way of the Light!"

He picked out a torch from the box and barely touched it before it had its own orange glow. "Come and get your light. And know ... that you are not alone in the darkness. May you find your way and yourself."

As he talked, the glow from the torch went from a deep orange to a lighter gold.

Hordes of black gathered at the front to obtain our own, our jackets and dresses and capes swishing on the ground like we were witches. It made it all the more exciting, and I felt a power rush in my stomach as I stood up.

"Bring the Light," Mitchell said. "Bring the Light."

"Bring the Light," echoed those around me. "Bring the Light." It became a chant.

We filtered out. A hundred torches went from dim to bright in a matter of seconds as we climbed the stairs, moved through The Manor, and exited to the dark woods. The outside welcomed us, but we welcomed it more. We moved together, a giant flickering paramecium in the night.

We broke apart, each torch and light running and disappearing among the trees. Shouts were called out, names were called out, chants were chanted, and we were all separate.

"Bring the light," I muttered under my breath. "Bring the light."

Would this really work? If I had any doubts before, they were gone now. I became so into it, so into the moment, and so into today and the spirit of Halloween that I barely noticed it. I was a full believer now, actually thinking our little torches could solve the blackout. But what could it do, really?

The power was still gone; I could tell by the way the campus streetlights were still out. Our Manor lanterns and candles were the only survivors. I had no idea what the time was, but it was well past dusk. I shivered as I looked to the sky, and I couldn't tell the difference in the horizon between the sky and the ground. I couldn't see the line where one ended and one began. I raised my torch to the sky. No. The moon itself had been frightened behind the clouds.

My torch lit up with a funny light. I couldn't tell if it was real fire or a light bulb. It seemed to waver between the two. I almost dared myself to touch it, but it suddenly made me very afraid. I couldn't touch it, I couldn't look at it, so the only thing left to do was trust it. And trust it, I did.

I know we were to walk the campus. The whole campus. It was counting on us. I could make out where the other Guardians were … in the distance, further away, all along the borders. I felt safe. I felt good.

I walked along the wooded area among the trees, trying to concentrate. Out of the corner of my eye, I saw something move. It was a student who didn't have a torch and was not a GOL member. It was a girl standing nearby, holding herself as though cold and trying to look around campus.

"Hey," I called out to her. "Are you all right?"

I approached her, holding out my torch. "Come on, I'll walk you back to campus."

She made no response, but I walked up to her, anyway. Her hoodie was gray which made it difficult to see in the dark and fog. Her hair was red and curly, but those curls seemed to have lost their bounce and hung heavily by her shoulders. I couldn't make out her face.

"Are you lost? Where do you live?"

The girl turned to look at me and her face came into full view. It was pale—almost too pale. She had giant eye circles under her eyes that gave her entire face a sunk-in feature.

"Hey. Are you okay?"

The girl just looked at me. "I'm lost," she said softly.

"Okay, you can walk with me," I said.

I started on our normal path out of the wooded area. I heard some screams which made me stop. I raised my torch to look. Some people in dumb Party City costumes were running around. I couldn't tell if they were goofing or legitimately scared, but I decided not to bother myself with them. I kept reminding myself that we were there to protect.

We came across another student idly hanging out by one of the benches. He had on a black T-shirt and looked cold, too. I got closer to him.

"Hey. Need to find your way back to your dorm? Which one is it?"

He looked at me too with that same lost, solemn look the girl had. He did not answer me, just continued to stare at nothing. I shook my head. *Was everyone out tonight just getting high or something?*

"I don't know where I am," the guy said solemnly.

"I'll take you," I said. "Come on."

As I walked with my newly found party, I heard another scream.

"Get away from me!" someone shouted. "I can't see! Help!"

I waved my torch, saw other torches nearby, and knew that other GOL members were present. I wondered if other students thought to have flashlights on them, or at least their cell phones. The people that were now with me had neither, and were quiet and distant, like being outside during a campus-wide blackout was truly scaring them into helplessness.

We continued down the sidewalk as I strained to make out the campus building outlines in the darkness. All around, I still heard screams and shouts. I saw shadows running; I saw people appear and then disappear. I thought to myself that people were truly freaked out by darkness and nothing else, and it was the thrill of Halloween making the students anxious. Then I heard another scream that didn't sound playful and got a cold feeling that maybe there was something out here that was dangerous.

I waved my torch around and kept my eyes forward. "Let's go up this way," I said to my followers. I turned to them, only to my first real shock of the day that they were gone.

I turned around quickly, jerking my light around here and there. *Where did they go?*

I couldn't worry about other students at that time. Up ahead on the rest of campus, I saw more lights and gravitated towards them. There were more students, standing around, hanging around. They looked like they had nowhere to go, and they looked like they did not care. I wasn't sure what to make of them, but they all walked idly on their own and didn't acknowledge anyone. They were fuzzy in the dark.

"Let the light come forth! Let the light come back!" I heard some shouting up ahead, and then I joined in.

Other students ran off—or tried to—in the dark. Most of the campus was still blacked out. I didn't even know where anyone was. Were people just hiding in their dorms with illegal candles and the light from their phones? Were they at parties huddled together, waiting pathetically for the lights to come back on? Were faculty and staff having their own battles with the circuit breakers and power boxes? It just seemed to me, blindly walking along in nothing but pitch black, that we were the only ones who were trying to do something about it. Even though us walking about with torches didn't seem like it would do anything. Why would it? For some reason we all walked around with the only light source on campus like we had the power, like we knew the power was ours and it was ours to take away ... and then give back. The thought suddenly popped into my head ... and I believed it.

"Bring the Light!" someone yelled. "Show your Light!"

"Make the darkness leave us!"

I ran up the sidewalk, waving my torch in every direction I could. I could still see some people roaming around, but I had a hard time catching up to them. Other lights waved up ahead. I knew that at some point I was in between the last dorm buildings.

"Sky."

I jumped about ten feet. His voice I only heard in my visions, but then I was wide awake and heard it right next to me.

"Dad!"

"Sky," this time the voice was further away.

So what did I do? Like a panicked idiot, I ran in the dark, my feet hitting the pavement, a few leaves, and some campus garbage.

"Dad!" I called out to him. "Can you hear me?"

"Sky, don't..."

I paused, frantically shining my light in different directions. I couldn't see him anywhere.

"Dad? DAD?"

I ran up ahead, stopping once every few steps, and waved my torch around. For some reason, I knew that he was gone from the area, and he only could show himself briefly. I couldn't make up my mind whether I was frustrated or flattered. At least he stopped just appearing in visions, but why now? Why couldn't I see him? What was this going to do?

I strained my eyesight in the dark, trying desperately to see the spirit of my father. I walked along the sidewalk by a parking lot at the end of campus. "I know you're here," I said calmly. "I know you're here with me. Help us bring the light back. Help us bring the light back."

Something told me to raise my torch in the air, which I did, and then I saw stretching out all around me the different torches of other GOL members. We were scattered;

we were quiet, and we were alone. The campus currently belonged to us. Somehow, I knew where we were all supposed to go.

We walked through the first parking lot that greeted people on campus, crossed the grass on the other side, and climbed the hill towards the back of the property. Soon, the hill was dominated by all the members. The torches came together as one, and we raised them all up in the air. We created the sun that lit the hill; we could see ourselves, we could see each other, in the distance, although still foggy.

"Bring the Light," Mitchell, coming out of nowhere, stated.

"Bring the Light," we echoed. "Bring the Light."

If I told you our torches shone brighter, you would think I was exaggerating or being overdramatic. I was being neither. Our torches shone brighter. We were making the sun. I know this to be a fact because the night around us faded away.

It was so bright it seemed like the night already turned to day, but that's exactly what it was. Day.

We brought our torches down and looked at each other, looked at the new blue sky and all around us at the scene that appeared out of nowhere. Mitchell was more towards the middle of our huddle, and he smiled in triumph.

"Children, we have done it."

All we could do was stare at him. Did what? Magically fast forward the night into day? Or were we really out here all night for the time to pass and the sun to come up?

CHAPTER 12

Officially November 1st, it meant fall was now showing its ugly side with the harsher biting winds. It also meant that it was time for the uniform pants: crisp navy blue corduroys. They still felt stiff when I put them on, barely breaking out of their fold lines, but they were still better than that stupid skirt.

After class, we all gathered in the lower lounge once again. After Mitchell dismissed us to get some rest, he reminded us that we needed to be back after classes to finish the after-Halloween part of the event. We all had to continue the session by wearing white robes to foil our black costumes from the night before. I walked back across campus retracing some of my steps. We were powerful last night because we also had a power among us ... and we used it to bring the light back to the campus. The spirits were there. I believed they were since I was convinced I saw several of them. I knew there was some sort of connection between these spirits and the Guardians of Light, and I was determined to find out.

As we started our meditation session, I put my hood up over my head and felt like a monk about to do some sacred ritual. It sure felt ritualistic as always, but that time it felt a little more with last night's activities and paranormal encounters. I lost myself in that meditation as a true believer.

"Channel your Lights," Mitchell called above the music. "You have found your lights easily before, so you can do it again. Relax your Guardians and look inside your Lights. Find yourselves."

We breathed in and out slowly and concentrated. I found myself in a dream. I saw my dorm common room in my thoughts for some reason, the last place I would want to be. It was empty, and that was the only reason I felt comfortable being there. It was not too bright but not too dark. I walked alone and knew I was alone, but the curtains in the window moved. I walked around in it even though I didn't know where I was walking or why. I could see something right away. At first, it was just a shadow that moved across the floor, but then it rose up into the shape of a person. I felt a lump grow in my throat. Even though the light was long gone from his eyes, it was like it was still there, but now it was all over him. The shadow disappeared, and he came out in full view.

"Dad."

"Sky."

His voice was so soft I could barely hear it.

"Dad, is that really you?"

"Sky ... you have to get out of here."

His form floated higher by the ceiling like he was in a rush to be somewhere.

"What? Wait, come back!"

"Sky ... get out."

I jolted awake, and the vision was gone. I closed my eyes again tightly in desperation to get it back. To get him back. "Dad, Dad, Dad, Dad," I whispered frantically. A hand on my shoulder made me open my eyes again and Mitchell was standing over me.

"Skyler, take it easy," he said quietly. The others seemed to be too deep in their trances to notice me this time. "Are you all right?"

"Yeah, yeah, I'm fine," I said.

After the session ended, everyone was herded upstairs to leave. Mitchell asked me to see me while people trickled out of the lounge. I wasn't all that surprised, knowing it had something to do with my outburst so I approached him with as much courage as I could muster.

"Skyler, I wanted to make sure you were all right."

I paused, wanting to show nothing but strength. We both stood idly by the staircase, me leaning against it casually.

"Yeah, I'm fine."

"This is the second time this happened to you, and I and some of the others are concerned about you. There seems to be something stirring inside you that is disturbing your light."

"It's just that ... in my visions, I've been seeing my Dad. And I feel like he is trying to tell me something. The last meditation he told me I had to 'get out,' and I can't figure out what it means."

He stared at me, but I knew he believed me. He really believed me.

"That is powerful. Your dad's Light lives on and is trying to help you with yours. What do you think he wants to tell you?"

"It might have something to do with my dorm. That was where I saw him. I was in our common room and he was there, telling me I needed to get out."

"I see. Your dorm is not the right place for you. They do not have light there, or they are ignoring it."

"Right," I said. "A little of both."

"Then you must help them see their lights, Skyler. Perhaps your dad is telling you to get out of the darkness of your dorm."

"I don't know," I said. "But I know he is with me."

"He is," Mitchell said with a smile. "The dead are not *really* dead, you know. Those that are important to us in life remain important to us forever. Even in the afterlife. They will find a way to reconnect. So know that you are never alone, even when you feel that way. You are not. You are surrounded by people who care."

"I believe in that," I said. "Thanks."

"Anytime. Just remember you have the power to spread the Light to others."

I believed Mitchell didn't just mean that as a metaphor.

The next day's classes made me feel more alert than my usual grande coffee. I didn't even need it. All day I thought about going back to The Manor. I needed to know more about the spirits that were a part of the house, the woods, and more...

After leaving my last class, I made my way back there. I didn't see too many familiar faces hanging out. Damien must have rushed off to his next class so I couldn't get his thoughts. My own thoughts, however, focused on the walls in this very house.

I walked down a corridor, walking a little slower than usual. I had the courage to explore the parts of the house I had never seen before, including the upstairs area. It was quiet, quiet even with resident students chatting in adjacent rooms, but something made me want to touch the wall. The gothic floral wallpaper flattened a bit under my hand, one flower's petals closely resembling a broken heart. Did the wall move? I pressed my hand against it, almost feeling it move. Up a bit, and then down a bit. I took my hand away slowly, not reacting, even though the thought that ran through my head was that the wall was breathing.

I continued down the hall. At first, I was just wandering aimlessly, wandering to get to know this house and what exactly was in it. I saw a room near the end of the hallway with the door left open just a tad. I knew this only because of the triangle the light made on the floor. As I walked closer, I realized I needed to be quieter. There was someone in there whispering.

I got up to the triangle, careful not to cast a shadow, and leaned my ear to the door opening.

"Where are you?" someone whispered, very very softly. "Are you here?"

I badly wanted to see, wanted to see if that voice was even attached to a body. I leaned in a little more.

"If you are here, give me a sign. Are you here?"

I poked my face in and saw a girl standing with her back turned in the middle of the room. Her short and very spiky hair cast a freaky profile. I almost thought they were horns.

"Are you here?"

I didn't mean to, but I answered her question. My shadow moved on the floor and a slight movement on the door made it squeak louder than my thumping heart. The girl jumped a mile in the air as I put my hands up in defense.

"I'm sorry! I'm sorry!" I stammered. "I didn't mean to scare you or … interrupt."

The girl turned to me, her face and mouth still in a wide oval. She let out a sigh and then sat down on the bed that was in the room. I came in all the way this time, realizing that this room was not hers. In fact, I could tell this room was very much unoccupied. There was nothing in there except for the bed and a dresser, and the bed itself had blankets on it that looked like they never were made up. The bed creaked as she sat down, rubbing her temples.

"Again, really sorry."

"No, no," the girl looked up at me and smiled a little. "It's okay. I shouldn't be in here anyway. Is this your room?"

"No," I said confused. "I thought it was yours?"

"No," she said again shaking her head. "I don't think anyone lives in here. I just wanted to come in because … well…"

The girl started playing with the drawstrings on her sweatshirt, which was as thin as she was.

"I thought there was a ghost."

I looked around the room.

"Really? Did you hear or see something?" I asked.

"Yeah, I thought so," the girl said seriously. "I thought I heard voices around here. But it was only for a second. You're Sky, right? Are you in 7th?"

"Yep to both," I said.

"I'm Becky. And I am both, too. I actually just joined GOL, like, a week ago. So … you've felt some of the paranormal things around here, huh?"

I took this as my invitation to come into the room completely and sit on the bed.

"Yeah," I said enthusiastically. "I did. I've heard voices, and generally felt things lingering around, especially on Halloween."

"So did I!" Becky interrupted. "I thought those were just students, but they didn't seem to be at all. The only time I see or hear anything it is associated with this place and this group. It is definitely haunted."

"Yeah, it is," I answered. "But I don't think it's in a spooky and threatening way, you know? Kimberly told me the spirits that are in this place watch over it. And watch over us. Like they believe in the same things we do, or they want us to believe in the same things they do."

Becky looked up at all four corners of the ceiling. "I don't know about this," she said.

"I don't think it's anything to be afraid of," I assured her. "If you think about it, it's kind of cool. You know, my dad's a ghost. He's around here too."

"Oh, that's cool. I just ... I don't know. It is a little freaky. I thought maybe there was a spirit around here a while ago. I thought maybe I could see it or something. But I didn't see or hear anything else."

"I saw some walking around that disappeared, and then the other day I thought I saw something walking along by the trees. It could have been a trick of the light or just the shadows from the leaves or something. I couldn't tell ya."

"That is pretty cool," Becky said. "But if only we could find out more about them. Why are they here? Doesn't that mean spirits have unfinished business if they are here? Something that makes them stick around?"

I shrugged. "Sometimes. I guess so. I don't really know."

"I don't know either. But I want to know."

"Me too," I replied.

Becky pulled her sleeve back and cursed at her watch.

"I should go, I have math tutoring."

She got up and smiled at me.

"It was cool to meet you though. I've had a hard time finding people to talk to. I don't know everyone here that well enough yet. Being away at school like this is a big deal for me."

"It's nice to meet you, too. My friend Damien is here too, I'll introduce you when we get a chance. We've been coming back here a lot."

"Cool. See you later, Sky."

"Bye, Becky!"

Becky turned the corner and left the room, and I replayed our conversation back in my head. I was surrounded by believers, and that could only mean one thing: I was getting closer to the truth, and closer to something that was bigger than me and the world I lived in.

It was my turn to look around the room, and up at the four corners of the ceiling.

Are you here? I asked in my head.

The latest email from GOL stated that we would have another potluck dinner that night, as it was supposed to be another informational meeting for new members. From what I could tell we only had a few more, and lately, Mitchell had been pushing us for more. I was reading responses as to what people were going to bring and trying to think of what I could bring from my collection of ramen and Easy Mac when Deanna came home.

"Hi, I'm starving. Want to grab some food or what?"

"I can't," I replied. "Dinner at The Manor. Hey!" I brightened up. "It's like another informational meeting, and anybody can go! Want to come? It's free food!"

Deanna made a face. "Mmmm, no thanks."

"Oh, come on. You might actually like it if you give it a chance! You'll meet some of my friends."

"It's okay Sky, really."

"I mean all it is, is an inspirational group. That's all we do is inspire people and promote good values and spread a good message."

"No, I don't doubt that."

"Yeah, it is really good and you should come. After all, you keep trying to get me to go to places with you, so why not go somewhere with me? You know, it could do good for you."

Deanna seemed to twitch a little. "What do you mean?"

"It's a good thing to have. To be involved in a group that promotes morals."

She gave a little shake. "Sky, I don't know what that means."

I paused, trying to read her. "Huh?"

"What are you saying?"

"What am I saying what?"

"That I need morals, and it could do good for me." Her voice started to sound higher. "Like, you think I need it?"

"No," I said right away. "I didn't say that."

She sighed. "No, but you implied it."

"I did not."

"Look, Sky, I get it. I'm not squeaky clean and I like to have fun. There's nothing wrong with that. Having fun doesn't mean I'm a bad person."

"I didn't say that! All I said was it's a good group and *anyone* could benefit from it. Seriously."

"Well, whatever," she mumbled. "I don't need a Jesus-loving cult to make me a good person."

"It's *not* a Jesus-loving cult!" I practically shouted. "See? You don't even know what it's about and you're judging."

"I'm not judging. I'm going by what I see and what I hear."

"Well, don't listen to anything you hear! You see? That's judgment. That's ignorance. You don't even know us. And people who say things don't know us either."

"They just say you're all so weird and creepy."

"Judgment!" I exclaimed again.

"Just ... whatever, Skyler. You can have fun with your group and whatever it is you do." She stood up and took

her shower tote and some clothes. "I'm going to get in the shower and then go get some dinner with people."

I was out of there before Deanna came back, fuming mad and disgusted with the rest of the world. I let my thoughts gather on my way to the wooded area and tried to form them into one collective thought: I just thought differently than most others did. I had to keep telling myself that this was okay and that I was not wrong. Of course, I was not wrong.

I was ridiculously early for our next shindig but welcomed the downtime to do nothing for a while. I made myself some hot chocolate and just sat at the kitchen counter to ... wait.

As I blew across the chocolate froth threatening to ooze over the rim of my cup, I heard footsteps on the floor above me. They made their way down the stairs and to the kitchen area. I noticed that it was Seth, but even more so I noticed that his footsteps, and mannerisms in general, were with caution.

"Seth?"

Seth stood by the kitchen, turning his head and blinking. He rubbed his eyes and looked in my general direction ... just not directly at me. My stomach flipped.

"Hi."

"Seth ... you okay?"

Seth's hand found the chair.

"I'm ... going through a change."

Seth pulled the chair out and sat in it carefully, his face still unfocused and not making eye contact.

"I knew it was going to happen. I had a dream of something or someone telling me that I was going to look inward from now on, and then a couple days after that I was starting to lose my eyesight. I went to the doctor a couple of times and they told me it was true. Little by little, I have been going blind."

"God, that's awful!" I said.

He nodded. "I think someone from the other side was trying to tell me that so I could prepare for it. Ever since then, I have accepted it and have learned to look inward. I have to be strong."

"That is intense ... like it was a warning. Is that why you were wearing a blindfold on Halloween? Did you know who it was?"

"Yes and ... no," he answered. "I couldn't see them. It might have been The White Light itself. That is what Mitchell believes, and that is why he hasn't left my side since. He's treating me like some sort of holy icon now that needs to be taken care of."

Seth rubbed his eyes, not quite the same color as his hair anymore, now having almost no color at all.

I could not make out too many new members at our informational meeting. The ones that were there only looked curious and skeptical and were not really all that interested. As a member now, I felt it was my duty to represent the group. At one point, I felt like we were all crowding the guests. They stood around awkwardly by the refreshments table in the upper lounge and kitchen area. For us, it was just another social gathering, but we did not feel like we reached any new people that evening.

Once the informational part was over and the perspective students left, Mitchell asked the rest of us to gather in the lower lounge.

"Everyone," Mitchell announced. "The White Light appeared to me in my dream."

The whole lower lounge was quiet and paying close, undivided attention. I could tell the older members especially did not even blink. I saw Iris put her hand over her mouth but did not move.

"It told me my message is strong and all my Guardians of Light shine true, but our numbers are too small. We did not reach as many people tonight as we would have liked. Tonight, it is crucial for us all to think about other people we know on this campus who need the Light. Concentrate on them, see them ... and allow your Lights to travel."

Mitchell motioned toward Iris, who picked up a goblet at her feet and brought it to him. He blew over it, causing smoke to pour out of the sides as he placed it on the table. I am not sure what the smell was once it went up my nose. Citronella? He led us in a chant as we closed our eyes and got comfortable.

"We are Lights. We are Lights. We are Lights..."

I breathed in that something-scented smoke as it covered my face, traveled up my nostrils, and down my windpipe. It would have covered my eyes if I opened them. Instead of suffocating, the smoke actually felt cleansing, like it was opening up my pores and I was able to breathe out of all of them. My eyes stayed closed as we focused on our breathing exercises, but I felt the room we were in was much, much bigger.

As far as I was concerned, I was no longer in the room. Instead, I felt as though I were floating high above the sky at a rapid speed. I could no longer see or hear, except for glimpses of brightness here and there in flashes. I couldn't really feel anything at all in my deep trance.

I suddenly saw my dorm. I was walking along the hallway on my floor, seeing everything from the pimples on the concrete walls to the notes on everyone's door dry-erase boards.

One door was slightly ajar, and it was the exact door I would want to visit. I heard music playing softly: I actually heard it. Or was I imagining it that strongly? Why was I meditating on this so strongly? Then, I realized why when I saw Kristen lying down on her bed about to go to sleep that she had been on my mind. Well, not just her, but basically everyone in my dorm. This was where my meditating was taking me. I go to The Manor to meditate to get away from it, and here was exactly where it took me back. The minute I "saw" Kristen in my vision, I got annoyed. I wanted to go somewhere else. I wanted to meditate on something more pleasant, but she moved a bit and saw me.

I moved in closer. For some reason, I wanted to approach her. I suddenly felt it in me that I could change her; I could warp her mind into exactly what I wanted to. I concentrated on it and moved closer to her bed, and yet she still just stared out in the dark, not moving. What could this mean? It was my own vision, and I didn't understand it.

"What ... what are you doing?" Kristen finally stammered. "Get out! Get out!"

I stopped, and then I was out of the room. What was that? What was it supposed to mean? Of course, it meant that I couldn't change people.

The meditation session ended, and I shook out of it, sighing and regaining the feeling back in my legs.

Well, the next few meditation sessions were much more pleasant. In many, I found myself in this serene jungle. There were so many different colored plants of so many shapes and sizes; I couldn't even tell what they were. Even so, I felt like it was more like a garden than a jungle. Jungles are deep, dark, and dangerous; gardens are welcoming, beautiful, and peaceful.

I found myself walking along a copper pathway, my very own yellow brick road of sorts. Only, they were not bricks at all but tiny droplets. I had to look closer to see what they were, and to my surprise, I found that they were hundreds of pennies all glued down on the ground. Instead of chucked into a fountain, they were spread on the path for all to wish on at once: Hundreds—thousands of little Abraham Lincoln heads. I ran through them, letting all the leaves of the plants brush my hair and face. They were long, short, fat, thin, smooth, and prickly, and I felt them all at once. I felt them, and saw the colors, and smelled the flowers, and even heard the fountain. I knew where it was. I walked down the path and felt the air get cooler. The fountain was just a tiny trickle down a trough, but it got the message across the same. It was a meditation. It was only a meditation, but I sat down on the fountain and felt the loose droplets sprinkle my back. I sighed in my meditation. Such a strong one. Lately, those have been the most vivid and have helped me escape from the stress of school.

I found myself making frequent mental trips to this garden, this jungle, whatever it was, as part of a routine. Afterward, I awoke, taking a minute to blink out all the green and take in the brown of the lower lounge to get back to reality. I reached to feel the back of my neck and part of my back, feeling the dampness seeping through my clothes.

CHAPTER 13

In science class, I found out that we were going on a field trip. This gave me one reason to look forward to class the next day ... to an extent. Katie was in this class, but I would do my best to avoid the awkwardness of her ignoring me and only acknowledging me with raised eyebrows. The last time I tried to post GOL flyers on our dorm floor bulletin board, I got only one raised eyebrow, and then the giggling with her little squeaky friends after I left. Other than that, I was pretty much left alone.

My class got one of those tour buses and went to some conservatory about thirty minutes away. The minute the bus rolled over the rocky pavement, my teacher, Mr. Egle, immediately received a phone call.

"What?" A rather monotone man, Mr. Egle's bald head shone brighter than his personality, but even here I could make out traces of hesitation and discomfort in his voice. He sat a few seats ahead of me and I could see his brow was crossed.

"What do you mean? We're already almost there. This is absolutely ridiculous!"

Around me, my classmates and I eyed each other.

"Is it canceled?" some girl asked.

"I hope not," I answered. "I don't feel like having a lecture today."

Mr. Egle put his hand up as though the person on the other end could see it. "Let me assure you, the students won't go for that stuff and frankly, I don't either. You might as well forget that because we just pulled in. Yes, we're outside right now. Yes, I'm sure! Really, with all this superstitious mumbo-jumbo..."

Mr. Egle hung up, continuing to mumble to himself.

"Everyone, listen," he said, standing up. "We're still going in, but I wanted to give you a head's up. Someone from the staff called me, all spooked out."

"Say what?" some guy asked.

"The lady just called to tell me, and this is word for word, that we should consider canceling because for the past couple of days, the conservatory has been haunted."

Some snickered, and some remained silent.

"They probably heard the wind through the cracks or something. Nothing to worry about. Jesus, people will be spooked about anything. Well, let's go on in, shall we?"

So, we exited the bus, not exactly in a rush, not sure what to think. It was mostly silent except for the stones under our shoes.

A lady let us in, although reluctantly, and barely even looked at us as she propped the door open.

"The conservatory is this way," she said, smiling weakly as we shuffled along. I noticed there were some other workers there wearing galoshes and wading in some marshy areas. It seemed as though they were less looking for something and more trying to hide from something else. One man pretended to give something plant food as he ducked behind a leaf as thick as his head.

The greenhouse we walked into smelled like rain. It seemed nice and didn't creep us out at all. It was a quarter to ten in the morning and instead of going back to bed, I wanted to take a hammock and set it up between the two sausage fruit trees.

All right, so we were supposed to draw pictures of different kinds of plants and label the different parts. My drawing skills were far from majestic, so I saw a challenge. The rest of the class scattered throughout the greenhouse. One small group huddled with the lady who let us in. She was shaking her head and speaking in hushed whispers. Mr. Egle just shrugged and walked over to another area. I decided to get closer.

"So, you really saw a ghost?" asked a guy near the front.

"Yes," the lady said seriously. "It's been wandering around here and in the fountain room. Never talks, just walks around and then always disappear into thin air. I've seen it!"

"It doesn't speak it all?"

"No, and I'm too afraid to talk to it! Everyone is, too."

I edged a bit closer.

"What does it look like?" someone asked.

"It's the ghost of a girl," the lady answered.

Then suddenly, she shrieked. Everyone, including the teacher, jumped and looked around. The lady stared behind us with all the white in her eyes.

"What? Do you see it?"

"Where is it?"

The lady took a small step backward and pointed with a trembling hand. We all looked behind us, but we saw nothing. I sort of sidestepped away from the opening, feeling more than a little terrified.

"There!" she cried. "She's right there!"

It took everyone a minute, but it took less for me. My blood froze in acknowledgment. She was pointing and staring directly at me.

"Her!" she cried again. "There she is!"

Everyone—all my classmates, the teacher, the greenhouse workers, even the butterflies on the plants—stared at me with confusion.

"Skyler?" Mr. Egle said. "Now that is ridiculous. She's a student."

"I'm telling you, it's her!" the woman cried again, clearly not wanting to be within ten feet of me. "I've seen her before wandering around here. Same hair, same eyes, same face!"

"Um..." I said lamely. "I'm not a ghost."

"Well ... maybe you were sleepwalking or something!" The woman stated, and she went from being only scared to scared and angry. "You probably have a sleepwalking condition that makes you wander to places. I don't know. But no doubt in my mind it is *you*."

Everyone still stared at me, and it wasn't long before the other staff members decided to leave the room. My classmates, of course, couldn't go anywhere, and that made all the staring worse. I didn't know what to say or do.

"I don't sleepwalk! And I've never even been here before!"

My awkward eyes darted everywhere. I looked down at my feet—anywhere but up—and I almost couldn't believe what I saw. The ground, the pathway, was covered and made up of hundreds of pennies.

That was the most uncomfortable and tense bus ride I'd ever been on, much worse than the time I threw up in the second grade and had to ride home up front with a bucket between my legs. I would take that day again instead of this.

All right, so I was shocked beyond belief to see the penny-graved pathway and to just know where the fountain in the greenhouse was. Of course, I was. I was so scared I froze up and only kept denying it, which made them even more afraid of me. My class ended up being kicked out of the conservatory because of the "stunt I pulled." I was given heavy advice to get on strong medication and see a shrink.

How—everyone wanted to know—did I not only manage to sleepwalk all the way over here on foot, but how did I get into the building without anyone seeing me? I just shook my head. I told them of course I didn't sleepwalk and the woman just spooked herself and blamed it on me. They didn't know what to believe. I kept thinking back to my meditations. What did this mean? How was it possible that I saw this place in a dream, only to visit the exact place in person? All I knew was my dreams, my meditations, had been getting stronger, and this was the biggest indicator. The last place I wanted to go was my dorm, especially after this field trip. No doubt Katie already told them all about the newest freaky thing that I did.

I went to The Manor with my backpack full of books, not exactly wanting to dive into studying. To my surprise, it was relatively empty, save a few people hanging out outside.

I helped myself to a glass of lemonade and sat down at the counter, taking a few gulps. As soon as I put the glass down, I almost choked it back up, seeing Iris five feet away from me in the kitchen. I didn't even hear her come in.

"Jesus, you scared me," I stated.

"Sorry," she replied, starting to come around the counter. I ran my fingers through my hair and exhaled while she helped herself to a glass.

"Rough day?"

I shrugged. "Well, not exactly rough. Weird, more like. And ... I don't really know what just happened and what's going on anymore."

"Maybe I can help," Iris said. She sat down on one of the stools next to me.

"Actually, I think you could," I said, looking at her. "This seems like the sort of thing only a GOL member would be able to understand and explain."

She leaned in, clearly interested. "Did something happen?"

"Yeah ... this is going to sound really weird and I don't know how to explain this to you so it doesn't."

I had the chills and it might have been from the lemonade. Might have been.

"Okay, so you know our meditation sessions? Well, mine have been really strong lately, and I guess I didn't know just *how* strong because ... they became more of a reality. I've been doing sessions where I'm walking through this greenhouse, and I hear and see all the details, right down to the pennies that are glued down on the pathway. My class takes a field trip to this conservatory and lo-and-behold it is the *exact* one from my vision, right down to those pennies and the sausage fruit! It gets better; the lady there at first said we couldn't go because it was haunted and then she freaks out when she sees me because she says that *I* am the ghost that everyone saw!"

Iris studied me without the reaction of horror I was expecting, or even confusion or disbelief.

"That is amazing."

"Amazing?" I looked at her. "That's freaky as hell. The lady then said that I must have been sleepwalking, after I, you know, told her that I wasn't a ghost. How the hell could I have sleepwalked from my dorm, on foot, all the way out to somewhere I've never even been before? It just doesn't make sense!"

I took a sip to cool my running mouth off.

"Sky," Iris said. "You didn't sleepwalk."

It was how she said it, so simply, something that I knew all along but could not begin to believe.

"You just had a wonderful experience that only people with true spiritual strength have. This is what makes a true Guardian of Light. You know your spirit is a living thing inside of you, and your body is just the shell that protects it. You can now leave your body."

The sip did nothing. My mouth felt like it was full of cotton balls and I couldn't form the right words.

"I can?"

"It's true," she said, forming a coy smile on her face. "Everyone here can do it."

"They can?"

"Mostly everyone. Upperclassmen who are advanced members. 7th graders and new people are just awkward and haven't found themselves yet, but *you*. Mitchell is going to be so impressed."

"So wait a minute ... I *was* a ghost?"

"Well, in a way. It was your spirit. You have seen those of the other members before, right?"

"The others?" I asked. Then, the penny dropped. "I have! Wandering campus. I did think they were ghosts. They would just come and go in the blink of an eye—"

"That's right," Iris said, smiling.

"So ... that's what that was," I said. What else could I say?

"You just relax," Iris replied. "Stick around here, gather your thoughts. The first time is hard for everyone. Soon, it will be like second nature."

I nodded and drank some more.

"Iris."

"Hmm?"

"It's not *always* the other students, is it?"

She smiled. "Of course not. If you sense something, but do not see it, then it is the spirits that guard the woods and our house. But those you can't see."

"They made themselves seen one time," I blurted out.

Iris nodded. "So they have. They say all spirits make themselves seen on All Hallow's Eve, that is what it is for. The rest of the time, they make themselves known in other ways. They are kindred spirits, ambassadors of The White Light, so to speak."

Right. I understood. I decided that was all I needed to know. I took long chugs of my lemonade and noticed the whole time Iris had not touched hers.

"Just you wait and see," she continued. "Things are going to be better for you now."

"How so?"

"You're stronger now."

"Yeah. Yeah, I am."

"Good," she said, still smiling.

I didn't get back to my dorm until after a small dinner at the food court. Of course, I put it off as long as I could. The aftermath of my field trip fiasco still greeted me as soon as I turned the doorknob and barely stuck a foot inside.

"Sky, holy crap! What happened?"

I sighed and tried not to look at Deanna.

"It was really weird. I honestly don't know."

Deanna just stood there with her arms crossed.

"You were sleepwalking? I have never seen you sleepwalk."

"No," I said quickly. "No, I don't know what that lady was talking about. I was there, just for something else. That lady is just crazy."

"Um, okay, that's not what Katie said."

"Well, what *did* Katie say?" My voice rose without my meaning it to. "Do you always listen to everything she says or what?"

"No ... she said that she believes it because ... because Kristen said she *saw* you sleepwalking."

"What?" I stammered. "When?"

"This one night Kristen said she was lying in bed, and you just appeared out of nowhere. It looked like you were in a daze or trance, so you had to have been sleepwalking. You went right in her room and walked right up to her bed like you were going to do something to her, and she yelled at you to go away and you wouldn't listen and you just kept coming closer—"

I turned away from Deanna to act like I was disgusted, when, in reality, I didn't want her to see the recognition in my face.

"I was there when Kristen and Katie were talking about that and then Katie brought up the field trip and now the whole floor is afraid of you."

I still said nothing and put together a poker face.

"Sky ... I think you have a problem."

"I don't," I said. "It was an accident; that never happens to me. I must have been really stressed out or something, or I don't know, maybe I actually got drunk!" I laughed a little, hoping to turn it into a joke. "Just ... I don't know, don't worry about it. I didn't mean to freak Kristen out. I just wanted to see if she was awake to ask her something. Not important."

"Ooo-kay," Deanna said in that annoyingly stupid sing-song voice. I hate that voice. It's so patronizing. "Everyone is just freaked out by you."

"Great, thanks," I said sarcastically. "Just what I needed."

"I just thought you should know. I mean, if you have a serious problem, you should get help."

"I'm *fine*," I snapped. "Geez, if anyone needs help, it's the delinquent kids who do nothing but party and mess around with alcohol. If they weren't here, they'd be in jail."

I regretted it as soon as I said it. Deanna's eyes were so wide she could have been in anime.

"What?"

"Dee, sorry."

"Look, that was an accident! Excuse me for being human, and excuse me for being normal and wanting to experience life! That's what you do! Lighten up."

"Lighten *up*?" My voice got higher and louder and I didn't care anymore how mad I was. "Lighten *up? Me?* I'm the only person in this dorm who actually has any sense. I am the only person who is a part of something that actually means something."

"Oh, sure!" Deanna chuckled, which infuriated me even more. "You do weird cult rituals and brainwash people. You are *so* brainwashed!"

"That is not true!"

"Yes, you are, Sky. Everyone always talks about how you try to shove your newfound holier-than-thou beliefs down everyone's throats. No one cares, okay?"

"You're just being negative," I stated. "You're in a negative environment, so you're just blinded to the truth."

"Oh, gimme a *break.*"

I was about to retort when I heard something outside our room and realized I didn't shut the door all the way.

"Skyler's really losing it," came a hushed voice.

"Oh, my God," came another.

Oh, they thought I was losing it?

Before Deanna could say or do anything, I stormed over and pulled the door open to reveal none other than the gossiping clique itself.

"You got something to say to me? Say it." I stared them down, challenging their shocked faces, and realized even I was a little shocked at my confrontation. I was too fired up to care.

They just stood there looking awkward. Finally, Kristen spoke up.

"Um, just think that maybe you have some problems. And we think you need help."

"And we don't care or believe in your cult stuff."

"Well, maybe *I* believe in my 'cult stuff,'" I declared, actually making the finger quotes for dramatic effect. "Because it actually promotes good morals and spirituality, and you just passed judgment before even knowing what it was."

"Whatever, Skyler. Whatever."

They walked away to their rooms, and I actually questioned whether I should follow them out and yell at them some more, but even in my anger, I held myself back. I turned to Deanna, who just lifted her hands to me in defense and went to her computer in silence. I felt the steam come out of my ears as I grabbed my hoodie off the door coat rack and hastily made my way out of the dorm. The evening sky was dimming, the sun, almost already gone, took more of the heat away, but my own burning insides kept me warm. I power walked down the sidewalks, past the buildings, and away from the populous parts of campus. I approached the wooded area and, with it, the completed twilight. The solar lanterns lighting up The Manor pathway greeted me as they always did. I charged right between them, wondering why I even took a hoodie in a warm jog. I walked up this Manor pathway and, for some reason, I didn't care or pay too much attention to the solar lamps going out two by two as I passed them all up to the house and to the door.

CHAPTER 14

I didn't even know what I was going to say or do as soon as I got inside. It was funny. With all the rage I had, it seemed to drain from me with every inch I took in that house. It was only a few hours ago I was at that same counter talking to Iris, and little did I know I would be back here again, still feeling distraught. I seemed to freeze a bit as I walked in and saw a group of people hanging out in the lounge. Much to my surprise, Damien was in there, too.

"Hey, Sky," he said, waving me over to the couches.

I sat down, just giving everyone a general greeting. Iris sat in one of the armchairs with Ad Astra, and both of them were looking at me with interest.

Damien pushed some of his homework out of the way on the couch to make room for me. "What's up?" he asked.

And that was the point when I didn't know where to begin. Damien didn't say anything, but Holly, Becky, Iris, Seth, and others had funny looks on their faces. Iris put a book on the coffee table. Ad Astra seemed like she wanted to come and sit on my lap, but Iris's very light hold on the small of her back said she would not. Her eyes closed as Iris pet her and finally said something.

"Something's up with you again."

So, as though it were the cue I was waiting for, I blurted out the whole story. I started with just feeling ostracized by the dorm in general and ended with the sleepwalking incidents.

"There's more on that, actually. It was something I talked to Iris about today."

Iris held up a finger. "Hold that thought. Mitchell! He's here, Sky. I told him. Mitchell, can you come in here? Skyler just got here."

Lo-and-behold, Mitchell came out of nowhere. He approached me immediately, looking like he wanted to hand me a major award or something.

"Skyler, I heard all about it," he said, sitting on the edge of the coffee table so he could be right in front of me. The instant he did, Ad Astra leaped off of Iris and sat between his legs. He smiled at me like his own flesh and blood did something he was so proud of. "You've been having out-of-body experiences."

The others around us, Holly, Becky, and Seth included, smiled, which indicated that they all shared this knowledge. Damien was the only one who was hearing this for the first time.

"A what?" he asked.

Mitchell made a small nod.

"Our Skyler here, through meditation, was able to leave her body and let her spirit roam freely."

Damien's eyes rose to me, but it was not out of disbelief.

"I ... I guess," I answered. "I didn't mean to, because I didn't even know I was doing it. Someone said they saw a ghost, and it was me, and everyone at the dorm thinks I have a sleepwalking problem and that I'm a freak."

Mitchell nodded. "Iris has told me you are having a hard time fitting in at your dorm. They are not receiving you well."

Part of me felt angry with Iris for putting her nose where it didn't belong, but the larger part of me was grateful. I was surrounded by people who cared about me and understood me, and I knew right then and there that something was going to change.

"You see, Skyler," Mitchell continued. "You are a very special person. You are only in 7th grade, but I have seen such amazing things from you already. You know how to connect, you know how to look inside yourself and broadcast your light. I applaud you for reaching out to those people in your dorm. You are strong. They don't receive you well because they, obviously, are the weak ones."

Everyone started nodding.

"That being said, you may or may not know this, but there are housing opportunities for GOL students here at The Manor."

I was so happy hearing this; I wanted to cry.

"Now, this is usually reserved for upperclassmen, only because of commitment and space. We only make exceptions for exceptional underclassmen, and that would be you. Skyler, I officially invite you to live in The Manor. Your real home."

It happened almost instantly. Or, rather, it happened a lot quicker than I thought. Usually you have to wait until the next semester to change living arrangements, but Mitchell was able to pull some strings. He made some phone calls to whoever was in charge of Housing on campus, and the next thing I knew I had a weekend where I was leaving the dorm for the last time.

It went smoothly, to my surprise. I remember packing up my room, but I don't really remember the details. I was on auto-pilot with no independent thoughts or actions. I just did it. It was like all the tension I felt being there was leaving me forever and I never would have to worry about it again. I was so happy.

Deanna was actually cool about it. As far as the others were concerned, they pretty much ignored me and stayed out of my way, no doubt happy about my leaving. Deanna seemed to be happy about it too, but not in the way I expected. She wasn't exactly happy to get rid of me, but she actually acted like she was happy for me, and even felt a little sympathetic. We didn't say much about it, either. It became an unspoken agreement.

Walking through that door to The Manor felt like I was coming home for the first time, no matter how many times I entered. This time felt for real.

My new room was a tad smaller than my old room, but I didn't care. It didn't matter now, since it was my own room. I didn't have to share with anybody. For that reason, it seemed bigger. I opened the door and noticed that it already had new pillows, blankets, and sheets. And something else. I wasn't alone. I was, but I wasn't.

I sat down on the bed, stretched out on it, and felt the whole room welcome me. It did so in such a subtle way, but I noticed. I received an invisible hug. I thought to myself that the GOL spirits, whoever they were, were fully aware of my presence. The door opened a crack and began to creek. It waited a minute, then creaked open some more. I saw in the hallway that no one was there. The door stayed that way and I didn't look at it again as I shut my eyes and allowed myself to relax. I didn't need to look up to know that it closed on its own, too.

On my first night living in The Manor, the whispering in my head jolted me out of my dream. My eyes flew open as quickly as window shades and then I couldn't remember my dream. Instead, I just strained my ears around my room.

I didn't hear any more whispers, but the more my ears woke up and tuned in around me, the more they started to pick up other things. Steps. Creaking. Maybe a door or two opening. Something moving. What gave me any reason to think it wasn't other students?

As I strained my ears to listen, I also strained my eyes to see. I saw nothing but black in my room. I knew my desk and dresser were in two corners, but I couldn't even make out their hazy shapes. As I turned my head, I thought I heard a whisper from the other end of the room. I jerked my head back. It was too close to be coming from any of the rooms next to mine. I slowly and carefully sat up to try to see the hazy dresser, thinking that something had to be perched on top of it and watching me.

In an instant, I grabbed my cell from inside my pillow-case and flashed it across the room. The small beam picked up on my clothes sticking out of the drawers, the loose change on top, and my books on the floor, but nothing else. Outside, I heard the floor creaking again. Someone was awake. My phone told me it was four in the morning: too late to still be up and too early to get up. My stomach felt a little heavy, but it flat-out jumped as soon as I heard my door creak.

I aimed the phone light at the door. It was barely open a crack, but one more push opened it a little more. I tensed up in my blankets and became perfectly still. No one was in the darkness of the hallway. I knew instantly that whatever haunted these halls was out and about ... this very moment.

I got out of bed and grabbed my glasses. Taking deep and steady breaths, I prepared myself for anything I was about to encounter. I wouldn't allow myself to be afraid. Holding my phone flashlight as steady as I could, I left my room and shut the door. A wind blew through the walls, rattled the ceiling light fixtures, and fluttered the window curtains. Both windows on both sides of the hallway were shut.

I didn't exactly know where I was going; my feet just took me down the stairs and into the corridor. I walked, moving my light from left to right in a sweep of my surroundings. I came across the bookcases, stopping instantly at the scene before me. There was a single book sticking out of a bookshelf, no doubt just lazily put back by a student. As I approached that book, I realized just how far it was sticking out, so far that it was not even on the shelf at all—but levitating on its own.

I paused and kept my light on it, sitting there in mid-air only inches—inches—away from the shelf. Was it really just floating there? I couldn't go closer, thinking I wanted to watch it. Nothing moved. Nothing, that is, except for what came around the corner.

I jumped a little—only a little—to see two eyes brighter than my phone light. I brought my phone down as the face shot through the light and stared right at me, arching her whole body back and raising her head a little.

"It's okay," I whispered. "It's only me."

She lurched forward a bit, only acknowledging me for a minute; then she turned her attention to something by the bookshelves.

I dared to look where the cat looked and saw that the levitating book was now just sticking out of the shelf. I walked closer, needing to be sure. Yep, it was on the shelf, just poking out like someone wanted to see the front and then just didn't push it back in. It was on the shelf all right, not floating out in mid-air. I just stood there, bewildered. It was floating before. It *was*.

Ad Astra emitted a low growling noise from her throat. She was still staring intensely at whatever she was staring at. I sidestepped a little, not sure what to think or do.

"What is it?" I asked. "What do you see?"

She continued to stare, lowering herself to the ground more and more until she was almost touching it. Her tail brushed a little and her whiskers rose up and down. Finally, she started to crawl away and gave me a good long look as she passed me. I shone my light around a bit ... then something told me I had to follow the cat.

She waited until I caught up with her, then walked down the corridor. I felt ... safer, somehow. We came to the staircase leading downstairs to the lower lounge and my knees started to shake. Ad Astra meowed softly at the door.

"What's going on down there?"

The cat looked up at me with her golden eyes. I turned the knob carefully so as not to make any noise. Ad Astra took a few steps down, waited for me, and we descended.

Instantly, I heard hushed and whispered voices. I got low enough on the stairs to try to see anything on the lounge floor. It sounded like there were huffing and puffing noises coming from the fireplace. As I got down the stairs, I focused my phone light on that fireplace, watching dust particles blow out every few minutes in clouds of smoke. I didn't know what was causing the noise, but it sure sounded like the fireplace was snoring. I needed my phone light to look around the room, but Ad Astra didn't. She walked right on past the fireplace and the open space of the lounge to the private sitting rooms in the back. One of them was opened a crack, and there was a light on inside.

I hid my phone underneath my shirt and tried to listen before peering in. I heard whispering that stopped as soon as I approached and cast a shadow. I dared to peek in. Before I could see anything at all, the door flung open and Iris stood in the doorway. She was dressed in a T-shirt and jeans. I had no idea if she woke up early or if she had yet to go to bed. Her bright eyes were very alert, nowhere near tired, and they focused on me. She smiled annoyingly—if that was even possible.

"Ill met by moonlight, proud Titania?"

I blinked. "Midsummer Night's Dream."

"You know your Shakespeare, very good."

Iris opened the door up all the way to reveal a boy sitting in one of the plush chairs.

"What are you doing up?" Iris asked accusingly, even though I was set to ask her the same question.

"Me? I heard noises and couldn't sleep, and … and…"

Honestly, my tongue was tied about the voices, the doors, and the floating book.

"That was his problem." She jerked her head to the boy in the room. He looked up at me, and I saw a look that said he had been awake this whole time.

"You have nothing to worry about," Iris said to him. "Nothing is wrong. Go back to sleep."

In an instant, he got up, left the room, and climbed the stairs out of the lower lounge. By that time, the soft blue dawn was fading the darkness in the room.

"You couldn't sleep either? Were you hearing things?"

"No," Iris said. "I just saw him wandering around and being freaked out and I had to calm him down. It gets to people, you know, the first time. It's something you will get used to. No one is alone."

I didn't feel much different the next morning, and when I opened my eyes and looked around the room, everything was still. Nothing creaked, nothing moved, nothing echoed in the walls. I didn't hear whispering, but what I did hear were dishes clanging together and that meant one thing: My first Manor breakfast. I pushed the covers back, noting the time: 9:45. The bathroom for my floor was right across the hall from my room, which made it even better.

People already gathered downstairs when I got there, and for the first time, I got to see just which members were living residents. They were mainly upperclassmen, not to my surprise. I joined the table seating Seth, Kimberly, Iris, and some others. They smiled and greeted me, Iris waving me over to a seat next to her.

"Sit down and relax, Sky. You are one of us now. I mean, for real now."

She seemed happy to see me, but not as happy as she was to see her friend from last night. The boy came down and looked a little lost, but of course, as soon as he saw the other empty seat next to Iris, he flocked to it immediately. Iris grinned and stroked the back of his head adoringly. I resisted the urge to laugh or gag ... or both. It was the way she did it that bothered me—like he was her pet. As weird as it was, I had to shake it off. I also needed to get used to the fact that it was a co-ed house, even though the boys were on separate floors. I couldn't care, because I belonged here, and not in the dorms with those other people.

Plates of bagels and cream cheese and a pitcher of juice sat before us. We dug in as, almost to my surprise, Mitchell appeared in a sweat suit.

"Good morning, my children," he greeted pleasantly.

"Morning, Mitchell," everyone said, almost in unison.

Of course, it would make sense that he also lived at The Manor. He didn't come from the upstairs rooms, so I guessed he had his own private room on the first floor.

"And hello to you, Skyler," he said immediately. "How did you sleep your first night in The Manor?"

"It was nice," I responded, avoiding looking at Iris and her puppy.

"Good. You'll find that this was the best choice for you. We're so happy to have you as your Light grows stronger."

After breakfast, and helping Carol with dishes, it honestly felt like an extended version of the dorms. Everyone cleaned up after themselves and worked together to clean up common areas, except this time I wouldn't be washing my plate and cup in the bathroom sink. The Manor had a dishwasher which we loaded after doing a formation of rinsing. Carol ran the washer after putting the food away and went around doing whatever other work she did. And after that, it was just regular school. I went to my classes and went to lunch at the caf', only this time I wasn't walking back to the dorms with everyone else. It felt so strange at first, but I didn't miss it a single bit. I did think of Deanna, though. I wondered if she thought of me, and what she thought of me. She was actually nice to me, at times. Of course, now that I was gone, those girls probably had more to freedom to talk about me. Let them. Since I wasn't there anymore, they would eventually run out of things to say, and now I could do my own thing in peace. They were no longer my problem.

When I got back to The Manor—home—I got to unwind a bit in the upper lounge. I started some homework, at once noticing how more pleasant it was than the dorm common rooms. Maybe it was as though The Manor knew. It understood, and it silenced itself to respect our study time. I knew that living here would also have its perks of being ahead of other members. Later in the evening, Mitchell stepped into the lounge to address us there.

"Everyone, I will be sending out an email soon about another meeting. It will be this Sunday night. Come back here around 8 P.M, all right?"

Turned out the email itself was just as vague as his announcement. It sounded like it was going to be another deeply spiritual session; we were probably going to talk about what our souls were made of or something to that extent. The only thing I knew was before Sunday came, I had to do something spiritual of my own.

I hid in my room for the most part on Saturday, working on homework, barely noticing the numbers change on the digital clock. I felt a little nervous about exploring again, even though nothing really happened, but I knew if I ever wanted to find what I wanted, I had to go looking myself.

So, I found myself needing to take a "water break" and going downstairs at a reasonably late hour. Some people were in bed already. Some were scattered, so I wasn't completely alone. I wasn't sure if this would still work, regardless.

I walked back around the corridor and back into the hallway area with the bookcases. I paused and slowed my pace. Just what was I expecting to see? Nothing floated, for one. The cat wasn't around. Nothing felt out of the ordinary. Still, I couldn't help myself.

"Are you here?" I whispered. Nothing answered, of course.

"It's me," I tried again. "Are you here?"

I looked around, and the room and the bookshelves remained normal. I stayed there though, thinking something would come if I stayed patient. As if on some strange clockwork routine, Iris walked out from the back hallway carrying a book.

"Well, hi again," she said, coming into the room.

"Hi," I answered, feeling a little on-the-spot. *Did this girl ever sleep?*

She put her book back into the empty slot on the shelf.

"You looking for something? Some extra books from classes are here, as well as just ones to read."

"No," I said. "That wasn't what I was looking for, exactly."

That same look formed on Iris's face—the look she got when you were talking about something that interested her. She smirked a bit.

"You were looking for something last night too, weren't you?"

"Well ... not really. I just ... wanted to get to know this place better. Get to know ... all the residents. Not just the living ones."

Iris nodded casually. "Yeah. Yeah, you've got the right idea here, don't you? Well, they are here. They are around, filtering in and out whenever they feel like it. They're not here to scare you or bother you. They're our Guardian spirits."

"I'm not scared," I said quickly. "I believe in the spirits. I just wanted to see if a particular one was here."

Something flickered in Iris's eyes. A realization.

"Your dad."

I looked at the bookcases, the floor, and the windows.

Iris came a little closer to me. "You know Sky, that was very touching that you were able to connect with him in your dreams. What a moving experience for you ... and for all of us. You made believers out of people. Your dad is with you ... but he is only with you."

"What do you mean?" I said, puzzled.

Iris shrugged. "Well, I'm not a spirit expert, but I don't think his spirit would be hanging around here."

"Why not?"

"Well, was he ever here in life? Does he know this place? He doesn't, so I don't think you will see his spirit around." She said those words carefully, but they still stung.

"I ... I don't know. I wasn't expecting to see him, or anything. I just wanted ... a connection. Like I did in the visions."

"You *have* had connections. And you always will. He is with you. No one else. Just you. That is unbelievably sacred, Sky. You don't need to go looking for something that is within you. You just need to continue to be in touch with your own spirit," she smiled sincerely, and I knew that she understood.

"So I can only see him in my visions?"

"I would think so, yeah. But why complain about something so special like that? He's here to help guide you down the right path, just like the rest of us."

Another perk of living at The Manor: I didn't have to walk from the dorms in the dark to any meeting. I was already there. All I had to do was go downstairs.

We residents got first pick of seating as we waited for the others to show up. We gathered on the cushions in the lower lounge, not exactly sure if this would be a meditation or journaling session or whatever. Kimberly and I got to chat a little, her asking me how my room was and how I enjoyed living there now.

"Everything I wanted," I said confidently.

"Good," she said. "It is such a rare privilege for a 7th grader, the only other one has been me in 8th! I learned so much! I am a better person being here."

As people trickled in, I instantly noticed Damien. I waved him over, realizing I have not seen him since my move.

"Hey, man!"

"Hey Sky! How's it going?"

"Great," I said honestly.

He sat down next to me. "You like living here, huh?"

"It's so much better. I feel so much freer. What have you been up to?"

"Trying to pep myself for swim tryouts."

"That's cool."

I noticed he seemed a little stressed, but I didn't probe.

Soon, Mitchell came downstairs. He looked out at the room, at all of us cuddled on blankets on the lower lounge floor. He handed out blank journals and pens for this exercise, and he had a pretty serious look on his face, more so than usual.

"Everyone, we've talked briefly about the afterlife ... what happens after we die. But we have not yet had the opportunity to explore this further. Now is the time I want you all to do your own reflective journaling. Where do you envision going after you die ... your body dies ... and your Light is set free for the next life?"

I paused, taking in the seriousness that had just filtered through the room. I had no idea how to answer that question. Some people had thoughtful looks on their faces, others just looked outright scared. It wasn't something people thought about often ... or even at all. Mitchell cleared his throat again.

"We, Guardians of Light, believe that our time on earth is only the beginning. It is a training ground for the next life ...

the true life we have after passing on this earth, commonly known as dying."

Older members watched him and smiled, having the same kind of pride on their faces.

"It is not us who die," Mitchell continued, and I noted his voice got lower and slower, giving us time to process his words. "Just our bodies. Our spirits ... the true part of ourselves ... our Lights ... are protected by our bodies. Our bodies are the Guardians of this Light that nourish us until our time comes."

As Mitchell paced in front of the fireplace, I noticed the candles on the mantel behind him were all lit. Seconds before, I could have sworn they were not.

"Now, my children of Light. Reflect on your spirits. Reflect on the next world. What do you think it is? Where is it? Well, we don't know where or what. But, it is our destiny and we will all be happier and more intelligent beings, without sin and crime. Journal now on this place and what it means to you."

I ended up staring at blank pages for a while; this came as a bit of a surprise. No doubt GOL had beliefs of some sort, and here they were, and I didn't know what to make of them. It intrigued me, of course. It poked at places in the back of my brain that I never used and struggled to know.

Going off of Mitchell's prompt, I just wrote down the things he mentioned: Our souls moving on to a better world, the next phase and whatnot. I imagined that wherever it was, it was meant to be a profound experience. Ideas of the afterlife? I started to scribble away, and soon I couldn't stop myself from writing two to three pages.

"The concept of the afterlife and general 'what next?' has always fascinated me. Where do we go after this? Our bodies die, but our spirits do not. Our spirits are the lights that live inside of our bodies. Where do we take them from here? Do they ever take on another form? I thought we could have a short group meditation, then go around and share what we saw. Take this time, do your breathing exercises, and concentrate on looking to the not-too-far-distant future."

Mitchell took a seat on the lone cushion in front of the fireplace. Ad Astra came over and climbed in his lap, purring. As soon as his eyes were closed, hers closed too and her tail swished back and forth over his folded legs.

The first thought that came to my mind was the general idea of Heaven: Sunlight and a bunch of white clouds surrounding a set of pearly gates. I didn't want to think about this at all, so instead I started thinking about ... I don't know ... the beyond. I imagined outer space, endless stars stretched out against a black nothing that went on infinitely. And other planets ... other planets that may or may not have life on them, and other galaxies and other planets. Is that where we went when we were done with Earth? Another lifetime ... another galaxy ... another world?

When Mitchell said our time was up, we looked up from writing.

"Now let's go around the room. What did you see?"

An 11th grade guy sat nearest to him. "Lots of trees," he said. "Not like the woods, just enough outside, and a wide open field."

Some people had other similar answers; one girl saw trees too, but palm trees on a beach. More beaches, oceans. Some imagined cloud paradises and unicorns and other weird fantasy things. Is this what everyone's interpretation of Heaven was? It had to be, especially since some imagined mountains made out of chocolate, living in a million dollar mansions, and driving flying cars.

My turn came, and I shrugged and told the truth. "I didn't think about dying and going to Heaven. I actually thought about another life after death."

Some were looking at me curiously, but everyone had interest, especially the upperclassman and Mitchell himself.

"Interesting. Tell us more!"

"Like, I envisioned floating in space and that there is a whole new planet with a whole new life that's supposed to be a better one, and after life, we go there and start a new one."

Mitchell was beaming at this and some of the others were too.

"Very well done, Sky. You actually see the truth of it all; you envisioned another life after this one. A better one, no doubt. You, actually, are the only one who has the right idea here."

I do?

CHAPTER 15

We were told to keep our journals in our rooms from then on and write in them whenever we felt inspired. Mitchell enforced private time and told us to have personal reflections. We were to think about things like what our strengths were and how to use them and what our weaknesses were and how to change them. But, more than anything, we thought about our spirits floating free after death. I didn't know about the others, but I definitely thought about the spirits that were floating free right then and there. This was because now that I lived at The Manor, I started to know their existence more and more.

It started when I left my room to head to class, or rather, grab breakfast and then head to class, but like it mattered. I don't even know which started first: the bursts of freezing cold air down the hallway or the whispers that echoed in the walls.

I stepped outside my door with my backpack over my shoulders, and instantly I felt like I needed a heavier coat. It couldn't have been cold enough for snow already. The previous day was only a little chilly, so this overnight frost bothered me. It bothered me more once I got a look out the window and saw no frost, no snow, so the cold was not the weather at all.

I walked on, hugging myself and wondering if someone in The Manor accidentally turned on the air conditioning instead of the heat. I stopped suddenly when I heard a whisper almost right in my ear.

I looked behind me, to my left and right, and all around me. No one was there. I heard it again, and it sounded like it was very close, if not right next to me. Every time I turned, I saw nothing but the walls. I braced myself, trying to stay calm as I walked downstairs. *They're not here to hurt you,* I reminded myself. The tip of my nose froze over—like something touched it—and I retreated. It didn't matter if nothing was going to hurt me; it was enough to make anyone scared. I only felt a flutter of relief when I saw other members hanging out and making their way to class. I also saw Ad Astra rubbing against the table leg in the kitchen when she suddenly diverted her attention to her left. The other students were almost all gone by now, and as the last person left, she looked at me and meowed.

"What?" I stupidly asked.

She stood up, still staring to her left, and stalked in that direction. I watched her walk toward some of the rooms by the downstairs corridor, some storage rooms, a bathroom, and an office. I jerked my head behind me, clear as day, hearing a voice somewhere around me. When I looked back, I saw the cat was doing the same thing. She stared for a minute or so, seeming nonplussed, then continued walking along the corridor hall. I heard a small thump from one of the rooms. It was subtle at first, but then I heard it again and it was louder. It could have been a student rummaging around, it could have been Carol doing something, but she was working at the caf' today. The closer I walked down the hallway, the less I thought it was someone moving something. It sounded like someone pounding on something.

Ad Astra stayed by the wall, stopping before the room with the closed door. It could have been a storage room. I had no idea since I never saw the inside, but I knew that someone or something had to be in it.

I almost called out to see who was in there, but something in me decided against it. Something pounded again. This time, it seemed more human and more urgent. I thought I heard a voice again hidden in between the pounds.

"H—hello?" I tried.

More pounds hit at the walls, and then some hit at the door.

"Hello?" I asked again, louder. "Is someone in there?"

Ad Astra stood by the wall, tail swaying, staring at the door. She made no other movements or noises. When I heard the pounding again, I lifted my shaking hand to the doorknob and turned in.

I heard hushes in the room, more whispers. I couldn't make them out as words even though they sounded like they could be words. I felt so cold that my limbs and clothes were stiff, that even if I could breathe at that moment, I would see my breath. I turned the knob and practically jumped back.

The cat moved slightly behind me so she could come next to me. I opened the door and shrieked as a bunch of old boxes and newspapers fell at my feet. Back issues of a newspaper spread out on the floor. And that was it. I looked all the way inside even though I knew it was completely filled wall to wall with these boxes, folding tables and chairs and other things. There was no real room to get in and out. Even if someone wanted to, they would have to move things out to get in. There was no one in the room and the room, I could tell, was a very small one.

I exhaled a big sigh and saw that I could not see my breath. It actually did not feel cold anymore. Ad Astra walked in front of me and through the open door, the old paper covers crinkling under her paws.

"Hey—move," I said, pulling myself together and cleaning up the papers. I didn't care about making it look too neat or pretty at all. I shoved it all back into the storage room and shut the door, using all of my strength to push it and maintain a hold on my psyche. I did not hear someone's fists pounding on the wall and door. It was a bunch of boxes that just fell over. Maybe a rat or something got in there and—

I shook that thought off as that did not make sense nor did it help. Ad Astra started to turn around and walk back the way we came and I went with her, power-walking out the front door and on the way to my daily routine.

A yogurt parfait and a large coffee later, I was taking notes in class when the thought *no, those were fists pounding,* sounded in my head. It didn't scare me this time. Instead, it made me intrigued. It was a final and definite thought, like that was that.

I got back to The Manor immediately after classes, part looking forward to it and part not. A small comfort was that there were other people there ... who most likely heard that kind of stuff all the time. I walked through the front door and into the kitchen, which I thought to be empty until I saw Becky sitting at the table by herself. She sipped a cup of something hot while the rest of her engaged in a book. When I came into the room, I saw that she was not completely engaged.

"Hi," she greeted me almost immediately.

"Hey," I said in return, taking a seat. "How's it going?"

"All right."

Becky put the book down and took a sip of whatever she was drinking. I caught a whiff of herbs and declared it to be tea. She cocked her head slightly to the left, listening, and that was when the penny dropped.

"Did you…" I started.

"Hear something?"

"No, not just now. But I did before. Earlier today."

"I did too."

I knew it. I leaned forward, also looking in Becky's direction. "I heard some whispering down that hallway, and it sounded like someone was banging on the walls."

"Yeah," Becky nodded. "Yeah, so did I. I couldn't tell where it was coming from at first."

"Well, I went down that hallway and I heard more of it coming from one of those doors," I started. "But I opened it and it was a storage closet with nothing in it but boxes of newspapers and junk. And then I didn't hear it again after that."

"I heard it only a couple of times, but I didn't exactly go investigating. I asked some people here if they heard that and they didn't, and then someone said someone might be moving things in their room, so I left it at that. But I was not convinced."

We both were silent for a minute, but just a minute.

"I followed the cat down the hallway. She heard it too."

Becky's eyes widened. "Really?"

"Yeah. But that was it. Nothing else."

Becky sipped her tea, and I stared at nothing. At the time, it didn't click that we were happy to be alone.

"I feel funny talking to the others about it, especially any of the upperclassmen. They're true believers, and I don't want to sound stupid. Especially since—well—I don't want them to try to scare me."

"They won't. What makes you think that?"

"I don't know. Some of them kind of freak me out, like they want to be in charge of everyone and watch our every move."

I snickered. "I guess that's what being a 7th grader feels like."

"Eh, who knows?" Becky smiled. "Mitchell says I need to find myself. I need to look inside more. But I think we need to figure out what else is going on around here..."

Becky and I stayed there for a while, mostly in silence, listening for any other kind of activity.

The empty food jar on the table meant that we were having another Manor meal, so I was looking forward to dinner no matter what it was. I finished homework in my room and went downstairs early.

Mitchell gathered some things in the kitchen with Carol and disappeared in the back, no doubt working on the meal already. The TV was on in the upper lounge and a bunch of people were hanging out, and to my pleasant surprise, Damien was among them. I went over to join him when my smile momentarily faded. I saw Iris sitting next to him, leaning in very close and telling him something in his ear. Some sort of electric volt passed through my veins, but it subsided as soon as she got up and left the room. I rushed over and plopped down in that now available seat.

"Hi. Long time no see!"

I was happy to see him return my smile with his own.

"Yeah, I know. Classes have been kinda kicking my ass lately," he answered.

"A lot of homework?"

"Yeah, papers and tests. Most of it just seems like busy work. Sorry I couldn't go to the caf' with you the other day."

"No, that's all right. I knew I'd see you, eventually. So … what was Iris telling you?"

"Huh? Oh … nothing really. She was saying something about one of the other members she didn't want anyone to hear."

"Oh. Kay."

"Yeah, one of the guys was saying something dumb, and she told me that he's an idiot and not to listen to him."

"Mmm."

A loud scream from the TV startled me so much that I actually jumped. I didn't even see what was on until now. It was a horror movie of some kind. Damien actually laughed when I jumped.

"Whoa, okay there, tiger?"

"I wasn't even watching!"

"You're not usually this jumpy."

"No, but things have been interesting lately."

He eyebrowed me.

"I'll tell you later," I promised, even though it bothered me I didn't know when this "later" would come.

At dinner, we all gathered in our mess hall/dining area to homemade cream of broccoli soup and bread, the perfect thing to have as the real November started to show its face. It was hot enough to heat our insides, but not too hot to scald our tongues. I stirred my bowl a little, noticing at once a strange pattern to the mass.

I took my spoon away and saw a large lining near the middle, making an oval shape, soup ripples wavering in and out. Two chunks of broccoli at the top looked like eyes … and the ripples were starting to form a mouth. I wasn't even stirring anymore. I saw a different kind of face now.

These eyes and mouth molded tightly in the soup, along with eyelids, eyelashes, lips, nose, and cheekbones. It was right off of a painting, flushed with broccoli and cream and cheddar as the media. It wasn't a recognizable face. It was just a face, and the longer I stared at it, the more it formed. The broccoli bits that marked the eyes now became pupils without blinking.

My soup was staring at me.

I shot my head up and looked around me at everyone else. Most, if not all of them, were eating normally and talking to each other. Did they know they were eating faces? Or was I the only one? I looked at the guy next to me. I was positive his bowl had a nose in it before he dipped his bread in and made it disappear.

My own soup still sat there facing me. Literally. I couldn't eat this. I sat back, watching it, almost expecting it to start to speak to me. I kept looking around at the others as well in hopes of them finding the same thing. I did not want it to be just me. Why would it be just me?

The second I looked back at my bowl, the face started to fade away. I stirred it again, watching the wavy mouth shrink in protest and the eyes swirl together into nothing. I imagined the whole thing. I must have. I dipped my bread in the soup and ate it just as I did before, feeling that same warming comfort as I did before. After all, it was soup and nothing else. A month ago, upon seeing this, I would have screamed louder than the horror movie. Now, it was something that just gave me a little scare but mostly, made me think. It was just another thing to add to the list.

CHAPTER 16

Mitchell mentioned in an email that morning that we should get our own poster boards, which were only like 99 cents in the bookstore. They would have markers at The Manor for our activity tonight. I was a little annoyed that he told us this last minute, but it was just a stop after school. My heart burst in relief when I walked into the bookstore and saw Damien standing in line.

"Dude."

He turned around, taking out an iPod earbud.

"Yo."

I joined him in line, as he was there for the same reason I was.

"He said just one, right?" he asked me.

"Yeah, I guess."

"I am not too sure about my artistic ability, but we'll find out."

We held our posters as we moved up in line.

"So," I started. "What did you think of the soup the other night?"

"It was awesome."

"Yeah, it was … even though I saw a face in it."

He turned to me. "What?"

"Yep. I saw an actual face in my soup. But that's not the weirdest thing that happened this week. Hearing voices and someone pounding on the door to a storage room with no one in it was pretty off the wall, too."

Damien paused. "Huh."

"Indeed," I answered.

We walked out of the store together after paying, and I knew that I was waiting for too long to talk to him.

"I have had quite the share of paranormal encounters around the house."

Damien listened as we walked outside, slowing our steps and moving close together.

"You have?"

"Someone was clearly whispering to me in the room in the middle of the night, someone was clearly pounding on the walls in a room in the corridor. When I opened the door, all this junk fell out. It was filled up. No one was in there. And a face, clear as day, appeared in my soup the other night. It was like a camera developed in broccoli bits and cheese."

"That's ... intense," Damien replied, clearly struggling with the right words.

I shrugged. "I feel like I want to know more about the ... spirits in the house. This girl Becky has had some encounters, too. Have you met her? She usually keeps to herself, but we have been talking a lot. We want to learn more about them, you know? Like who they are and what they're doing there."

I knew Damien was listening, but he said nothing else.

"Are you freaked out now?"

"Well, kind of, but I am interested, too," he answered. "I was just wondering if you were doing okay living there."

"It is actually great. Aside from living there being great, it seems like the spirits are with us rather than against us or anything like that."

"I think that's a beautiful thing," Damien said. "Spirits, anyway. I want to know them and respect them."

This was why I loved talking to him.

"You need to come to The Manor more often," I stated.

"I'll try. But, anyway, I'll see you later for this thing," he said, holding the poster.

"See ya."

The lower lounge wasn't as decked out in candles or tablecloths as it usually was, so I guessed it wasn't going to be a real serious meeting or activity. We were actually gathering in the mess hall this time, which made sense since we needed the tables. The tables themselves were ready for us with a bunch of markers and colored pencils spread out on each one. Mitchell had everyone take a seat, the upperclassmen of course crowding him at the front.

"Everyone, I asked you all to bring a poster board. If you didn't get a chance to get one, we have just a few extras. Now, tonight we are going to express ourselves and our messages of Light through art. Now, now, it doesn't matter how great of an artist you are or if you think you have no artistic talents at all. The point of this exercise is to continue to spread our message in a new way. Come up with your own artistic vision of our new destiny in The Next Life. It is through your visions you will make something visually beautiful to inspire in someone else to come and seek out their own Lights. It can be anything you personally believe is the next world that awaits us: any kind of paradise you imagine and believe. As long as somewhere, anywhere, you incorporate the GOL logo as the focus. Inspire others! Let us decorate the campus with our knowledge!"

We were left alone with soft music and our thoughts. I looked at my blank poster board, and it didn't take long for a picture to pop in my head.

I instantly grabbed some green colored pencils of various shades to draw the fields. I drew green lines from the bottom edges up and curved them smaller towards the top to appear stretched out very far. I made mounds and little lines for grass. The rest of the poster would obviously be the sky. I made three of the clouds spell out a wavy "GOL." I spent the time shading and coloring it a little better, and that was it. In my mind, and in my mind only, the edge of the field at the top of the page wasn't empty. Someone stood there, but I did not draw him in. Only I could see him. In my mind was where he stayed.

Well, I was no amazing artist. I didn't care.

After having a cup of tea, I was surprised to find out that we would be going around campus to hang our posters up—tonight. Most people had their GOL hoodies on as of habit.

"If you don't have your hoodie today, we have extras also. It is quite chilly out there," said Mitchell. Seth stood at the end of the table with a couple of rolls of duct tape on his arms. Mitchell stood by him and lovingly put his hand on his back. "Seth here will give you tape while you all go out, and we will take care of The Manor for you until you get back."

A smile formed on Seth's lips, and I couldn't help but think how creepy that made him look now.

Everyone seemed happy with the impromptu campus roaming. I caught up with Damien and we shyly showed our pictures. His was a picture of an androgynous angel in a bright sky.

"I just picture myself being able to fly, like an angel. I know it's cheesy." Damien was actually trying to hide his poster by his legs. I never saw him this bashful before. It was adorable.

"No, it's great," I assured him.

We found Becky and Holly once we stepped outside, and I felt really good about introducing Becky to my friends. She was just an awkward outsider. Like I was at the dorms.

"Let's see your pictures!" I prompted, putting my coat on over my hoodie. Holly's was modest; a bunch of multi-colored candlesticks with black shading in the background, but Becky's was the coolest. It was an abstract of weird shapes and it was in the shape of Earth, or something that could be Earth, with people and objects making up the continents. So many different things made up North and South America, Africa, Europe, that you had to look twice and closer in order to see what the objects were. It wasn't sure what to think except that Becky had to be an art major.

"Whoa. That is *wicked*," I couldn't help but say. "That is seriously freaking awesome."

Becky sort of shrugged it off. "Thanks! I'm really happy we get to hang these up. I love art."

"Come on, guys." Kimberly came out of nowhere, walking down the wooded path. "Let's not spend all night out here."

Not even sure where to go, we just walked down the campus sidewalks, casually chatting. Our coats bundled up and our hoods pulled over our heads. We mostly hid our faces in the fall-almost-winter night. We dispersed a bit to roam potential areas to hang up our artwork. We saw that some people put their posters on trees, around posts, on building windows and walls and even on fences. I managed to get mine on the side of a building along with many others. Damien taped his to one of the athletic buildings.

We watched other members walk up and down campus in the darkness, and saw Holly at one point standing alone across the street. She held her poster by her side, looking both ways and not making much effort to move. She eventually eyed the trash can, and we figured out where she intended to put it. Iris sauntered down that sidewalk and stepped in front of the trash can with a tight look on her face.

"I don't think people are going to look in the garbage to find enlightenment," she said bluntly.

Holly just shrugged. She might even have been a little embarrassed. Iris continued to stare at her until she came up with an answer.

"Well, I just don't think mine is very good," she said.

"Well, what you are throwing away is a symbol of your spirit and your mind. Is that what you think of yourself? That you aren't very good? You don't really want to do that, do you?"

Holly didn't get a chance to answer.

"Because then that is a symbol of weakness. You don't want to be a symbol of weakness, do you?"

"No, I just—"

"Strong people care about spreading their messages. Weak people care too much about the opinions of others and over think. Are you weak, Holly?"

Holly stared at the sidewalk. "No."

"Good. Then go and find a place to put your poster. Don't be a disappointment to Mitchell or The White Light."

Iris left her to catch up with some other members up ahead. Damien, Becky, and I pretended to be talking to each other. As dumb as that was, I saw that Iris legitimately made Holly feel uncomfortable. All about a poster. I thought it was unlike Holly to care so much about a drawing, but it was Iris's attitude that rubbed me the wrong way. The three of us started to walk back, pretending we didn't see her.

Seth greeted us at the door, having opened it all the way, and stood there waiting for all the cattle to come back into the barn.

"Come on in the kitchen," he said, hearing us come up the path. "Carol's baking something."

He probably had no idea who he was talking to. He just heard the mumbles and the footsteps coming up the path to the house and probably just gave every mystery group the same lines. I couldn't help it. I felt profoundly sorry for Seth. What a horrible fate to just come out of nowhere like that, and how he came to accept it.

We gathered where everyone else was around the tables and Mitchell, at once, raised his head and inhaled the new aroma lingering in the air.

"I can't wait to see what Carol's got for us this time," he said happily. "We'll have a nice treat to go along with our meditation session tonight! That does smell delightful, doesn't it?"

Carol came out with the finished product and set it on the kitchen counter.

"What kind is it?" someone asked.

"Oatmeal raisin, with walnuts!"

I had to admit I was disappointed. Damien and I eyed each other. We had our hearts set on the chocolate chip ones we had at our first meeting. We politely took cookies as Carol gave them to us all and walked to the upper lounge.

"I don't like oatmeal raisin," I admitted.

"Yeah, and I don't like nuts," Damien added.

"So," I said to him, a twinkle in my eye. "What do you have?"

He returned the twinkle with a smile. "I got a box of Girl Scout cookies in my backpack."

"Shut up! Where did you get them?"

He laughed. "They were selling them at the caf'. Didn't you know that?"

"No. What kind?"

"Thin Mints."

"Oh, man. You're the best."

We looked around sneakily with this great secret we didn't want anyone else to know about, and I followed Damien to a corner in the lounge. He pulled his backpack off a couch and revealed the green box of Heaven. We snuck those thin mints, and would have eaten the whole box if Mitchell didn't announce to gather downstairs.

The lower lounge was all decked out with candles lining every edge of the windows. We settled on the floor cushions, Damien taking up the one on my left and letting his jacket sit between us. The whole time during our session, I felt it on my arm and leg and I wondered: If he and I were touching, would we share the same vision?

I can't say I remember the graphic details of that session. Truth was, I was having a hard time connecting with anything at all. It wasn't the vision itself that was out of the ordinary, but how I felt. My head hurt for some reason, and I knew it had something to do with the lack of vision I had. I couldn't see anything in the meditation and the more I tried, the more it hurt. It bothered me since I thought I had a pretty clear mind. Why couldn't I imagine anything? Better yet—did this mean that my spirit didn't go anywhere?

I struggled to focus during this session, to see or hear anything at all. Mostly, it looked like a bunch of gray swirls in my head. Was this the source of my massive headache? My head throbbed with every swirl that passed through my brain pores and, for once, I wanted a meditation session to be over. It was only a few minutes that passed, but it seemed like much longer. I longed for the sound of Mitchell's voice to wake us out of our reveries, still scrunching my eyes and forehead in discomfort. What was wrong with me? When neither the brain swirls nor the pounding ceased, I felt like I had to opt out. I opened my eyes and rubbed my temples. All the other members were still in meditation mode, so I didn't feel the need to say or do anything. I excused myself and quietly went up into the kitchen. In the top counter drawer, we kept stuff like painkillers and Band-Aids. I popped a pill and took it with a glass of water, with a shudder. I should have been used to taking pills, but instead, it made me feel like I wanted to throw up.

After several satisfying gulps, I honestly didn't know if I wanted to go back downstairs. I paced the area to kill time, around the kitchen and lounge and even to the laundry area in the back. I was actually in the laundry room when I saw Ad Astra's pipe cleaner tail sticking out from behind the washing machine. I knew it was funny I hadn't seen her all night, but there she was, hiding out for some reason.

I knew the session was over by the voices coming back upstairs. I met with Damien, and our conversation turned out to be mutual.

"Did you do anything?"

"No."

"Me neither."

"I couldn't get into anything."

"I couldn't either. It was so weird. I felt like I couldn't connect."

"Same here, but for some reason I still have a headache."

"Me too. I'm going to go call it a night. See you later."

"Yeah, later."

Once Damien left, I went to my room, feeling like I was balancing on the tip of a pin. Why was I so dizzy?

CHAPTER 17

Dreaming might have made that worse. My head was spinning. I could almost feel the fluids in my brain sloshing inside my ears. I could have been dreaming—yet I didn't, or couldn't—open my eyes. Things could have flown outside the window: leaves, mailboxes, boxes, cars, just like in *The Wizard of Oz*. The fumbling and shaking I felt was a strange comfort like it was rocking me in my bed and keeping me asleep.

Whatever it was, the headache and chaos were gone the second I opened my eyes. From the general feeling I had waking up, there was a good possibility of it coming back.

There was a very pale light coming from my window. The light was not the usual color of daytime. It looked like a very sickly yellow-green, not the bright and happy kind. It looked like the sun came up briefly, vomited, and then went back down. It wasn't that early, but it was still morning. It was early enough, and something was going on. I got out of bed and grabbed my glasses. People in the rooms adjacent to me were coming out and talking.

"What's going on?" I asked.

"There was a storm or something!" Holly exclaimed. "It's windy as hell. There were a couple of trees that snapped and fell over already and hit things."

"Jeez."

"We have to go downstairs," another girl said calmly. "Mitchell wants us all to gather together."

We all went downstairs, all of us. All the residents were awake and making their way down, and the pit of my stomach also went down.

"Where's Mitchell?" someone asked.

"He's downstairs. He wants us all to go down there immediately," a 12th grade guy said, trying to move to group along. He made us all gather at the base of the stairs and waited until everyone was downstairs.

"A tornado touched down on campus last night."

"What?"

"Holy shit."

"Where?"

"It's gone now, but it was on this morning's news. Come on now, Mitchell will explain everything."

Everyone in their pajamas gathered in the upper lounge. Mitchell stood at the front in a long blue robe, like a bit like a younger Hugh Hefner. I would have found it funny if I didn't see what was next to him. He had on the news segment on the television, which played the live news segment of a reporter walking around a pile of bricks. She talked about the severe building damage done by the tornado that struck last night. The more the cameras showed the buildings with the giant, brick-less holes, the more they looked familiar.

"Oh my god," someone next to me said. "That's Gander Hall!"

We all watched in frozen silence as the news showed more buildings and the severity of the tornado's work. Fallen trees and loose branches laid on the ground along with many roof shingles and wall pieces stripped from the top. The reporter came on to explain the details.

"The tornado at Applewhite Prep has unfortunately taken out more residential buildings on this side. It appears Cattail Hall, Gander Hall, and Birch Hall have some severe damage to the building, but none suffered more than the Egret Hall, which practically lost its entire roof."

I stopped breathing when the cameras passed over and I saw for myself. It barely was a building anymore. It barely balanced on its foundation. Almost the entire thing was smashed in and the roof had ripped pieces sticking out all over like a bad hair day.

"Thankfully, none of the students were hurt. They were all able to retreat into the basement, where they stayed safe until the tornado passed. Residential supervisors were able to ensure the safety of everyone. Unfortunately, with the mess of Egret Hall, it looks like the students will need to take up other forms of housing. They will be in the process of temporarily moving to a hotel the school has arranged, providing also transportation vans to and from class. It's going to take a major constructional turnaround for Applewhite Prep to get its campus back to how it used to be, but everyone turned out okay."

I dashed away from the group, fumbling with my phone. I didn't care how early it was: I called him, pacing with every ring I heard on my side.

"'Lo." I heard a tired voice.

"Shit, Damien, it's all over the news! You're okay, right?"

"Yeah, yeah I'm fine. Just can't sleep."

"Sorry—we all just woke up and put the news on and saw the whole thing. Where are you?"

"At the Best Western. Gonna be here awhile. It was so fucking scary, Sky. Like, we heard the roof pieces fly off and all those trees and shit go flying and hit things and—are you okay?"

"Yeah!" I said. "We're fine. I mean, nothing happened here. We didn't even hear anything."

"Really? Good, I'm so glad."

"Okay, well, you get some sleep. I'm so glad you're okay. Call me later."

"I will. Thanks for calling."

"G'night."

"Later."

I hung up, relieved, and returned to the group where people still watched the details of the incident. It was something Damien said that triggered something else that bothered me.

"The tornado didn't even come over here, did it?" I asked.

"No," Mitchell said. "The Manor was not harmed. The tornado only reached the other side of campus and came up to the buildings before it left, and then stopped. My children—we are all safe, strong souls in this house. Let us take the time to be grateful for who we are. We are strong. We shall have a breakfast feast today!"

I only brushed my teeth and threw clothes on before going outside with some others. We were curious and had to see it for ourselves. In the upper lounge, Mitchell kept the TV on to campus news for updates. A lot of people were on the phone or on their laptops, emailing and communicating with friends and family members. I called my mom once I got outside and sat on the bench; the metal chilling me through my jeans.

"So wait, this tornado just missed that cabin of yours?!" my mom exclaimed.

"I gather!" I answered. "But Egret Hall is all torn up. The president got a deal with the hotel that's down the street and sent people there to live. It sucks."

"I'm so happy nothing happened to you!"

"Me too."

As I talked with my mom, I saw Becky wandering around the yard, and out a bit towards the trees. She just stood there and stared out at nothing, no doubt looking to see if anything happened out here. I saw nothing, even from where I sat. Becky, at one point, leaned against a tree and stayed there for a while. She was still there even after I finished talking with Mom. I got up from the porch to see what was on her mind, but then Kimberly opened the door to call everyone in.

"Hey, breakfast!"

No one said anything, but I knew we all felt a little weird about our little feast. Why were we celebrating not being blown away when the rest of the campus was? Or was it just a comforting meal that we were lucky? I didn't know and couldn't really think about it too much. I just ate waffles.

The tornado didn't hit us, but in a way, it still did. The whole campus was torn up. GOL members saw firsthand when we went to our regular class routines. It was strange walking around there, in a place of utter ruin that was hardly recognizable. Remains of trees and pieces of buildings and debris spread past the campus grounds and onto the main roads. The flotsam and jetsam that littered the streets and campus grounds ranged from garbage to garbage cans to posts to streets signs, tires, and bikes. Not an inch of the sidewalk or street was untouched, and campus maintenance was already out trying to clean up the mess while the rest of us stepped over obstacles on our way to classes.

I walked past a car flipped over on its side; the doors flung right open and leaves and dirt all over it. I walked over tree branches—and even a few whole trees. Maintenance workers had a section of the street blocked off because it was apparently too much for anyone to try to climb over. I walked among the buildings, hulk-punched and shaven of their own layers of bricks. The tornado ripped the campus apart, and our home was the only one untouched. For some reason, this made me feel guilty, but the feeling turned into mass confusion a moment later: Everywhere I stepped, everywhere I looked, I saw that every one of our GOL posters was perfectly intact.

Our teachers updated us with campus cleanup and the like, and the school even issued a special notice in the Applewhite Press paper. I found out what I needed to, but part of me was numb to everything else. I couldn't get those posters out of my head. Everywhere I turned, one was there to stare me in the face and remind me that we were, in fact, untouched and unharmed. I didn't know what it meant at all, but it made me feel so uncomfortable I almost couldn't look at them. This feeling was a seed that was planted when I first surveyed the campus, and it only started to grow more as the day progressed. It took me until the end of the day to talk to and see the most important person of all. We bumped into each other between buildings on the lightly dusted sidewalk.

"Damien!"

"Hi!"

We sidestepped rubble on the ground, our shoes already scrapped with dirt.

"How's it going?" I asked.

"Um, it sucks," he said, not even sugar-coating it. "I mean, the hotel is cool. It's a hotel. We have someone to make our beds and stuff, but we still have to go through the shit rubble at the dorm to look for our stuff. Most of my clothes have brick dust all over there and I had to get them washed."

"That is so horrible, man," I said, the guilt seed well on its way to a watermelon. "You're so lucky you weren't hurt, and you all got out okay. It freaked me out."

"Freaked me out, too! You should have been there. We heard all the high winds and then our dorm leaders came out and knocked on the doors and told us to stay calm but to get down to the basement as soon as possible. Everyone did, and we were able to hear the tornado through the walls."

As Damien talked, we walked away from the main sidewalk. It became a habit to walk to The Manor after the school day was done, even for him.

"It was horrifying. We thought the walls were going to crash in on us. It passed through pretty fast, though. Fast and violent."

"I can't believe it."

"I can't believe it missed you at The Manor!"

Cue the guilt growth.

"Yeah," I said. "Yeah, we were the only place it didn't hit."

"Well, it sort of makes sense. It's the only place that's by itself and sort of away from the rest of campus."

"Okay, well, guess what doesn't make sense? Did you notice what else wasn't touched by the tornado?"

"No?"

"All our posters."

"Our *posters*?"

"Yeah."

"How is that possible? That's some serious duct tape."

Soon Damien saw The Manor for himself once we crossed the parking lot and to the wooded area, the only part of campus where all the trees still stood. We opened the door and went about a normal routine of hanging our coats in the hall closet and helping ourselves to hot tea. Of course, everyone flooded Damien once he was there.

"Dude, that is terrible," Holly said first.

"We saw it on the news!"

"Yeah Damien, you got the worst of it. We're so glad you're okay!"

Damien smiled at the attention. "Thanks guys. I'm glad you are too."

Seth felt his way into the kitchen with his new walking stick clanging on the table and chair legs and sitting down at it.

"Hi Damien," he said from a couple of feet away. "We're so happy to have your strong spirit with us. Nothing can knock you down."

Damien smiled, even though Seth couldn't see him.

"Thanks, man."

I watched Seth for a minute as he took some devices out of his backpack. As Damien and the others went back to chatting, I realized Seth probably didn't think he was being watched, but I still did so privately. He fingered the buttons on the device and actually pressed down on it several times like it was a keyboard. He opened up another device, and I saw that it had enlarged letters along with enlarged dots. My heart sank. Everyone thought a tornado destroying the campus was a tragedy, but the real tragedy was right here at our kitchen table. Seth's fingers studied the letters and the braille components carefully before moving on to—what I figured out—class textbooks that were converted to braille. Studying was nothing when you already knew how to read. Seth's clouded stare stayed unfocused while the rest of him concentrated. I stared at his eyes, how milky and gray they were now. I thought back to when I first met him, not too long ago at all, when he greeted me on my way out from Orientation. His eyes matched his hair: Honey-colored and full of life. What were they full of now?

Iris came into the kitchen area but then stepped out. She reappeared a moment later with Mitchell in tow. They both looked very happy to see Damien among everyone drinking tea and snacking on pretzels.

"Damien!" Mitchell exclaimed brightly.

Damien turned his attention away for a minute as Mitchell came around the kitchen corner.

"We are so happy you are all right."

"Thanks, Mitchell."

"Come with me a minute, won't you? I want to talk to you."

Iris grinned as Damien put his tea down and started to follow him.

Chatter continued as normal. At one point, I noticed Becky put her head in a book pretending to study, but she hadn't turned a page since she sat down. I took my cup and joined her.

"Hey, Becky."

I saw she looked at me only by slightly moving her eyes and actually just looking at my elbows.

"Hi."

"Studying hard?"

"No, not really. Big test this week. But can you ... I mean, meet me later? I want to like ... talk to you about something."

"Oh," I replied, not sure where this was going. "Sure."

I didn't know what to do after that, and then Damien came back with Mitchell and his face was beaming.

"I'm moving into The Manor!" he cried.

Happiness fluttered all the way down to my legs. He got a mixture of congratulations to jealous looks. It only took me a half a second to get up and give him a hug.

"That's great!"

"I know!" he said. "Mitchell said that GOL members belong at The Manor and my dorm being destroyed only means that I belong here, and it came at a good time. I have to go to Housing, and he is going to call them now to help with the arrangements. Then I get to get my stuff!"

"I'm so happy we get to be here together now!"

"Hell yeah, we are."

"Looks like everything happens for a reason, huh?"

I saw Becky jerk her head up and give me a look. I didn't see it too well, but I knew it was not a good one. She closed her book and left the room without a word.

CHAPTER 18

I didn't see Becky for the rest of the day. Damien left a while back to take care of his housing stuff, so I spend it finishing homework and watching TV with some others. There had been no new updates about the weather, of course, but the campus was going to take a while to clean up. We watched a few movies, and then just made some sandwiches for dinner, not wanting to go through the obstacles on the way to the caf'. It was a quiet evening, as those of us there felt drained of energy and really did not want to do anything. I almost expected to have another meditation session, but we did not. Everyone spent time by themselves that evening.

Around a quarter to midnight, or maybe even after midnight, I had the desire to spend the rest of the night alone in my room. I had a book upstairs I barely started reading and thought putting a dent in it was a good idea. I went up the stairs to my room and was shocked to see who was waiting for me, although I was a little bit not surprised. She sat on my bed with a nervous smile.

"Hi Sky."

"Hi Becky."

"I'm sorry. I didn't mean to invade. I actually just got there and was hoping I'd catch you eventually, since I wanted to make sure I got to talk to you privately."

"Yeah, I remember that," I said, not feeling invaded as much since I saw the look on her face. She fidgeted a bit, anxious in her seat, like whatever words were in her brain crawled all over and tickled her. I felt more like nervous.

"Could you..?" she motioned toward the door.

"Of course," I said, shutting it. My stomach started to harden.

"I don't want anyone overhearing, but I checked out other people's rooms and I think they're all asleep, anyway."

I sat down next to her and nodded, giving her the cue.

"Sky, did you feel ... funny the other night when we had our last meditation session? The one right before the tornado?"

"Not really," I admitted. "But I got a headache."

Becky nodded, watching me carefully. "Your head hurt. And you felt dizzy? Like you were spinning?"

"Yeah," I said again. "A little bit. Why?"

"I did too, and I think we all did... Did you see anything? In your vision?"

"No, actually, I didn't see anything at all. I couldn't get into it."

"Was everything blurry?" Becky asked, her voice almost increasing each time she answered me. "Blurry like it was moving really, really fast? Right? Right?"

I just stared at her.

"Like ... a tornado?"

My lips dried up. "Huh? Are you talking about how we meditated during the tornado?"

"Sky!" Becky exclaimed. "We *were* the tornado!"

"What are you talking about?" I stammered.

"It was us, Sky. All of us. Our spirits merged together, and we made a natural disaster. Didn't you see it? Didn't you see nothing but spinning clouds? Didn't you feel dizzy? I felt so dizzy I wanted to puke."

"Wait a minute, wait a *minute*. Instead of our spirits just, you know, leaving our bodies and going to a different plane, they all made a tornado?"

"Yes!"

"How?!"

"I don't know how. But it did. I saw it. I didn't mean to do it. I felt like I was out of control."

"I didn't see or feel anything!"

"I thought you did, actually, because of what you said to Damien."

"Oh—no. No, no, I didn't... I couldn't have. You think I did that to make him come here?" I've heard everything now.

"I thought so at first. But this is a relief."

"Who else did you talk to? This is unreal. Someone needs to tell Mitchell."

"No! You know as well as I that these walls especially have ears. You can't say anything to anyone. *Especially* Mitchell!"

"Why not?"

She practically rolled her eyes. "Don't you get it?! They started it. They knew what they were doing. Mitchell and the upperclassmen. They just pulled us along with it."

"You're saying they did that on purpose."

"They did. I heard Mitchell saying something about wanting to test our power ... test the strength of our souls or something like that."

"What?"

"I don't know. I don't know what to say or do. I have no idea we were capable of something like that. What else are we capable of?"

We sat in silence for a moment, almost grateful to have that silence.

"I have to tell Damien."

Becky cringed. "Well, okay, just him. But this can't get out to anyone else. This place is different, Sky. And it's made us different. It's like it's the gateway to a supernatural realm or something. It's definitely more than we thought it was."

We let another moment pass while I processed everything. I did believe Becky, but part of me did not want to. Still, an uneasy annoyance stuck around. I was a part of a tornado. A tornado that attacked the campus. How the hell did I do that?

"I better get going. It's late."

"Yeah, you have to go all the way back to the dorms."

"I can call security for a ride. I just need to lay down for a while. I mean, even with everything that happened ... it's all very supernatural. Isn't it?"

"Yeah ... I just ... I just want to make sense of it all."

"Me too."

We left it at that, and Becky got off my bed.

"At least I have you, Sky. Someone to help make sense of it all."

She left, giving the campus security a buzz on her phone. I stretched out on my back, my fingers scrunching sheets and pillowcase above my head. Closing my eyes, I asked over and over: *What happened?* Almost expecting an answer, I drifted off into a much-needed, headache-free sleep.

CHAPTER 19

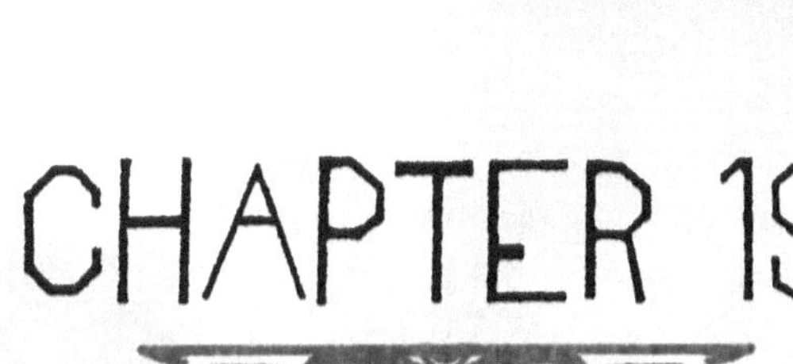

"That's … impossible."

Even though he said so, I could tell a part of Damien did believe it. He dropped the cardboard box he held to the floor.

"I don't know where Becky came up with this, but what's weirder is that Mitchell wanted that to happen on purpose. I certainly didn't go into the session with that in mind."

"No one did! This is unbelievable."

"Except for Mitchell. And probably the upperclassmen. They seem to be in control of everything. That's what Becky was saying. And it does make sense, even though it doesn't feel right."

Damien stacked some more boxes on top of one another. One easy thing about moving, again, was the very little to no packing you got to do.

"It left parts of the campus in ruin. *We* left parts of the campus in ruin. Did we want to do that?"

"No," I said, looking at him seriously. "But you know what I want to know? How come we're the only ones who weren't in on it?"

"We couldn't be."

"I don't know," I said, frustrated, and looked at the floor. Damien managed to get cookie crumbs all over the carpet, and he was there a grand total of two nights. At least the Best Western staff would vacuum that, but at The Manor, we took better care of our rooms and didn't leave everything to Carol.

"I mean, I'm still coming," Damien broke the ice. "Of course I'm still coming. I mean, supernatural abilities and out-of-body experiences and stuff ... It sounds crazy that I want to go there, but I do. I want to learn more. I want to find out more about this group and ... this power."

"That is why I'm staying."

"Me too. More than ever, I want to know what is going on with this group. I'm scared, but I'm interested."

"That is how I feel. Exactly how I feel."

We made sure more of his boxes were full and taped up. Then, for the first time that night, Damien and I locked eyes and spoke without words. He was ready to go.

Damien's move happened quickly and smoothly, and I was happy when that moving van showed up. He perfectly planned it on a boring Sunday afternoon, where the sun was buried behind threatening frosted clouds but no snow fell, not yet. The trees outside were stiff from cold, but the creek's waters still ran unharmed. Friends helped us carry Damien's stuff to his room, which was a floor above mine on the third floor. Now that Damien was a part of the house, it changed for me, and I mean, it made it better. When I went to sleep, I knew he was right above me, and it made me happy. It made me feel not so alone.

I was having Ramen noodles when Damien finally came downstairs, smiling at the regulars—the residents.

"All done?" I asked him.

"Yep," he said, joining me at the table. I slurped some noodles while Iris and Kimberly came into the kitchen to get drinks. They shut the fridge and smiled at us, Iris's smile especially daunting and maybe a little flirtatious towards Damien. I swallowed those noodles without chewing.

"What's with them?" Damien whispered once they left.

"Natural disaster went to their heads," I replied, also whispering. "Iris, though. She ... seems a little weird sometimes."

Damien shrugged.

"Hello my special children!" announced Mitchell as he walked into the kitchen, and he was quite the beam of sunshine. His smile was so big it looked like it was hooked on to each ear.

"Dinner is on me tonight!" he cried. "We're having a pizza night!"

Of course, everyone loved that.

"We are celebrating how strong our spirits got since the start of the term. Not only are we strong in mind, but we are strong in spirit, and not just as individuals, but as a whole group. The White Light gave us a beautiful day as a reward. And as my reward, I am ordering pizzas tonight, so don't make any plans!"

Mitchell disappeared a moment after that, off to find other groups of students to repeat his message, Ad Astra trailing behind him.

"How's that for going to someone's head?" Damien jerked his chin behind him, once again making sure only I heard it.

"I guess we'll find out exactly what is going through it."

Of course, Mitchell sent out a group email about the pizza party, because the entire student group showed up that night. There had to be at least ten to twelve of those wonderful square boxes waiting on the tables for us. The pizza tasted even better for me knowing as a resident, I got dibs on leftovers.

"Everyone," Mitchell called out once we slowed down. "Everyone, tonight we are having this treat as a token of pride, and not to mention gratitude. We stand strong together, and you all have grown so much since the beginning of the year. I am so proud of all of you and your abilities to look inside yourselves and cast such strong Lights. We feast in celebration of that, but also, there is more."

We figured out by now that when Mitchell paced, he demanded attention, and attention was always what he got, whether voluntarily or not.

"I understand there is some buzz going around among some of you regarding recent events."

My veins prickled, and I was certain Damien's and Becky's did as well.

"Let me assure you, you have nothing to worry about. There is nothing to be concerned about and you have nothing to fear. No harm will come to you. You are special. You cannot be touched."

Yeah. We were special, all right. The prickles in my veins got replaced with heat. We were special. Our spirits were like ... The Chosen Ones. Or something like that. Weren't they?

Well, us "Chosen Ones" finished our pizza feast happily. Mitchell waited until we were done eating and chatting idly to speak up again.

"I will send out another email, but we will be having another Open House night, complete with our very own recipe for hot chocolate! You see, it is fate that our posters still hang on campus. They stand strong. Our message is meant to be heard. We must grow our numbers if we want to be stronger, especially in the events to come..."

Some people murmured but then quieted down immediately.

"We were tested, no doubt. The White Light is counting on us. We have to be prepared for everything and anything. We will have flyers printed up for you shortly, my Lights. But until then, we will enjoy the rest of the evening with some homemade cookies and movies in the upper lounge!"

Damien, Becky and I, we all just relaxed that evening. Chocolate chunk cookies were passed around and we gobbled those up and forgot about everything else. Mitchell told us not to be afraid. He said we were special, and we would be taken care of. And when Mitchell told us not to be afraid, we weren't.

CHAPTER 20

I was so glad I busted out my hat, scarf, and gloves. Jack Frost skipped the nipping stage and went straight to chomping. I bundled up so much I could pass for Randy from *A Christmas Story* with his multiple layers. All the students looked this ridiculous, of course, when our means of transportation was on foot.

The stack of yellow flyers fluttered in my arms in between classes. I found random places to put them, mostly in groups so I could be rid of the stack. Mitchell pushed us to get the Open House & Hot Chocolate invites out as soon as possible, and this excited a spark in all of us. What was he planning? What were we going to do next? Once I got back to The Manor at the end of the day, I released the scarf from my face, finally able to breathe properly. Becky and Damien were by themselves watching TV.

"Hey," I greeted them.

Becky looked at me, chewing on her lower lip as Damien nodded in my general direction.

"Sky will tell you," she said to him.

"Tell him what?"

Damien sat up on the sofa. "Becky has been telling me about some ... encounters she had around the house."

"Yeah," Becky interrupted. "The ones she had too, only this time I heard more fists banging on all the walls. I heard a bunch of them today, all over. I heard more voices, too. I could swear I heard them."

I sat down, unzipping my coat and tossing it aside for the time being.

"I heard that too."

"I haven't heard anything yet," Damien replied. "I mean, I've heard voices and stuff on my floor but I assume it's the people in the other rooms. I think."

"They're here, all right," I said. "You'll see, eventually. I can't figure out who they are or what they want."

"Do you think we could find a way to talk to them?"

Silence answered Becky's question, as we let that sink in, the idea was more than a little frightening. During this time Ad Astra dashed through the kitchen and down the stairs to the lower lounge.

"She's an indicator," I said.

"Who?" said Damien looking up.

"The cat. She just ran downstairs."

"Maybe she was chasing something."

"Yeah. Something we can't see."

"I saw her come out when I was checking out those noises."

"What did you find, Becky?" I asked her.

"I don't really know, but it sounded like someone was in pain or angry, or both. I tried to look around, but then they were gone."

We all heard the familiar tapping of Seth's stick at the front door. He came in, removed his coat, and placed it on the coat hook before entering the house. For some reason, all three of us became quiet when he did. It was like some unspoken agreement that we all wanted to watch him privately, trying to make sense of his life. He made his way through the halls and to the stairs to the dormitories—making very little to no use of his stick at all. He knew The Manor intimately by now—and it knew him. Protecting, watching, and guiding. It was what The Manor did.

I got my homework done at a decent time, even though I couldn't stop thinking about what Becky told us. We retreated to our own rooms to do homework before the hot chocolate party. We didn't even know how many prospect members would show up, but we didn't care. I sat in my room, almost thinking for a second I would have my own meditation session then and go somewhere else for a while. I did that sometimes when I felt stressed out, but it was rare. It felt more rewarding and protective to do it with the group. Besides, I actually didn't want to go somewhere else. I wanted to stay right there, right among those walls, to get a better idea of what was in them.

So, I listened.

I sat on my bed, not really looking at anything and not really thinking anything. I listened, opening up my mind to my surroundings. I saw Ad Astra saunter by as my door was left open. She looked in my room and at me and then stared at something by my window. In seconds, she took off like a flash. I looked immediately at that window. Saw nothing, heard nothing, felt nothing.

"Are you here?" I whispered. I knew something had to be. Someone … or something … had to know. "Is … anyone here?"

I got an answer, but it wasn't one I expected. Damien showed up at my doorway.

"Hey," he said casually. "Iris asked to come help out downstairs."

He came in, reading the look on my face and the yoga position I was in. He looked all over the room and up at the ceiling.

"Are you ... connecting with something?"

"No luck."

"Is it your dad?"

"Somewhere, but I don't think he can come here. Something about complications with spiritual planes."

He smiled at me, and I actually hopped off the bed. "I'll come help," I offered.

Geez. Mitchell went so far as to have yellow balloons tied to everything, from the stair banister to the bathroom doorknob to the fence outside the house. I didn't even remember seeing them anywhere until the Open House Party, but there they were, floating everywhere like an obnoxious birthday or engagement party. I saw a line of GOL members pass by, all decked out in cloaks. As soon as I got downstairs, Kimberly had one for me.

"Here, Sky!" she said, draping one over my shoulders. "We had to iron these."

"Oh, thanks," I replied, slipping my head through, but leaving the hood on my back for the time being. I was certain she gave me a large instead of a medium and I was facing tripping over it all night long. Before I could say anything, she left down the hallway in a hurry. I thought I would at least deal with it. It would be the least of my problems that night.

Our new friends stood in the kitchen and lounge area. There were about nine of them, bunched together like awkward sardines among the black cloaks. Everyone talked together and ate chips and dip while the pot on the stove bubbled the hot chocolate. It was my understanding we would eat and drink and mingle with the potential newcomers, and then bring them downstairs for a "simple" group meditation and spiritual discussion. We were not to have traveling spirits, Mitchell warned. We were to keep our spirits intact and focus on our new friends. Only the true members should know the power.

Despite the smug attitude Mitchell had that night, it was actually kind of pleasant. The hot chocolate had to be the best I've ever tasted in my life. It wasn't just that powdered stuff you added to water or milk; it was like someone made the perfect chocolate candy bar and then melted it. It was not too rich, not too hot, and it was actually borderline chug-able. I forgot everything when I went for that second cupful. Damien, Becky, and I had no problem showing those new people the ropes, and the best house on campus. We all were having fun talking, and it made them have fun and talk as well. They made themselves right at home, and GOL gained those nine new members without a spoken word. My veins running chocolate, my pores sweating chocolate, I almost thought someone had spiked it, and I actually did not care.

"Time for some relaxing reflections, everyone!" Mitchell announced. The upperclassmen led everyone downstairs, and we waited for the cue from Mitchell. Once he followed us down, he stood at the front and admired his growing group.

"Here at Guardians of Light, we do a lot of spiritual awareness, spiritual cleansing, and spiritual growth. I invite you—I invite us all—to do some inner reflections. Concentrate on what you want in yourself to be stronger. What about yourself do you want to change? How do you want to be better?"

I relaxed, but I didn't reflect much. I don't know. I actually felt like I didn't need it for once. I felt fine just the way I was. The new people, though, had some catching up to do if they were going to be with us. The only thing I felt was sleepy. I admit that staying up late and having morning classes always did me in. That was my excuse. I couldn't understand what made everyone else feel the same. The minute Mitchell said we could open our eyes, we complained and cringed that the light hurt our eyes, although it was pretty dim. Some students rubbed their eyes very hard, and some even yawned.

"Stay with me children, don't fall asleep!" scolded Mitchell with a chuckle. "Now, to our new friends, what did you reflect on? Don't be shy, share with us. We are a family."

All the new kids sat together, of course, and shared their thoughts down the row. They wanted to have more confidence, get better grades, all the usual stuff.

"And you *can* be!" Mitchell enthusiastically declared. "You can have stronger spirits. You are well on your way already, and it started with the decision to be a part of this group."

I was so glad when the evening ended. I was already getting bored. I might have almost bored myself to sleep because I had a hard time getting up. My bed was calling me, and I was actually annoyed it couldn't just float downstairs and come and get me itself. Everyone took their time getting upstairs.

"I'm afraid we've kept you past your bedtime," Mitchell said to the new people. "I will arrange a security ride back to the dorms. Can't have anything happen to you on your first night, now."

GOL members dragged themselves upstairs, however difficult. Who knew that such a short meditation could make everyone so sluggish? We felt and looked weak. Before the newbies left, they were given some handouts and small bags of cookies.

"Go on and tell your friends about us!" Mitchell said to them. "Please bring some more friends with you to our next meeting!"

We were left with cleanup and leftover snacks. No one really felt like cleaning up, but we gathered trash and dishes like clockwork and didn't stop until all the dirty hot chocolate mugs were rinsed out and all the soiled paper plates were thrown away.

"Good work, my children," said Mitchell, appearing out of nowhere. "Now, off to bed."

That was an easy thing to do.

CHAPTER 21

I woke up feeling like my body was just a burlap bag full of rocks, stiff and hard, and an effort with every move. I rubbed my hands down my arms and legs to wake them up, startled that my brain was awake while the rest of me was still asleep. I tried to remember any dreams that I had, with no success. I could not remember anything I even meditated about.

After class, Damien and I went back to The Manor and the first person we saw was Becky, and what she was doing made us both stop short and stare. Her back turned, Becky had one ear pressed against the wall in a corridor. She mumbled a little, crawling her fingers up the wall like itsy bitsy spiders.

"If you can hear me, make a noise..." I heard her whisper.

Neither of us moved, afraid of interrupting, but also afraid of her getting a response. Some other people came through the front door and interrupted that moment of silence, causing Becky to turn around. The others made their way to their rooms to do homework, and Becky approached us.

"Did you guys feel funny today?"

"I guess so," I answered. "I definitely did this morning."

"I did too," Damien said. "I am not really sure why."

"I want to talk to you," she said. "About ... something I think I figured out."

Becky led us down the corridor toward the lower lounge, where we found an empty room. She shut the door behind her and pressed her ear against it and looked at us. Her face was almost as gray as the plaid in the uniform skirt.

"I think the ghosts can possess us."

My stomach curled as I stared at the expression on her face.

"What?"

"Don't you see? Anytime we meditate, something happens. We feel tired or dizzy and we don't remember anything. And then there's a tornado or something. Don't you think that's weird?"

"Well, yeah but—"

"I think they can control us," she interrupted me. "I think they are controlling us and everything we do ... and everything we think."

My head shook, but just a little.

"I don't know how, but they are. The walls have ears, and they can hear us and see us and they can control our spirits whenever we meditate!"

We didn't know what to say but hearing Mitchell's voice made us all perk up. We left the room and went into the kitchen, where he asked everyone to contribute to the food fund for another meal.

"Now everyone, go do your homework!" Mitchell said cheerily, making sure to look at each of us individually as we put our spare change in the can. We started to walk away, but only turned slightly because we thought Mitchell was still talking to us. I watched him leave the kitchen, especially how he had his head titled to the side, as though raising a listening ear. "Yes, my children," I heard him mumble. What in the world was that about?

The Manor did not feel any different that evening. Students studying and hanging out like normal. No one showed any signs of ... anything ... out of the ordinary. Except for Becky.

She sat on the couch with two other people, talking in hushed tones. I immediately went over to join them. One looked dubious, the other looked concerned.

"Ask Sky if you don't believe me!" Becky exclaimed in a whisper as I sat down. I didn't need any other cue.

"There are things happening here that are out of our control," I said to the two girls. "And our minds are being messed with."

"I don't think so," one girl said.

"Yeah, I mean ... they couldn't."

"They *can* control us," Becky said. "They are controlling our spirits."

"What in the world are you talking about?"

The looks on their faces alone said they weren't biting.

"No, it's true," she tried to nudge. "Didn't you feel ... anything? Like you were doing something you didn't mean to? They are controlling us and making us do things ... turn into tornadoes and destroy the campus and send our spirits to place to haunt people."

At that point, the hallway bathroom door opened and Iris stepped out. She walked past and eyed us.

"Hi."

"Hey," we said as casually as possible.

She smirked, especially at Becky. I did not like the look she gave us on the way out.

Damien's homecoming at least made me relieved, if not a little anxious. I just sat on the couch like a zombie watching TV. Nothing else happened. I wasn't exactly sure what to expect anymore, anyway.

"Hi," Damien said.

"Hi," I returned.

He sat down next to me. "So … anything going on?"

"No," I answered. "Nothing. No one acted weird or even said anything. Becky was talking to these girls, but they didn't seem to buy it."

And speaking of the devil.

She came in while some others were trailing behind her. She noticed us right away and came to sit in the lounge.

"Hi guys," she said sort of casually. "What's … happening?"

"Nothing," I answered first.

Damien wiped his hair out of his face. "No one listens or wants to."

Out of nowhere, Mitchell came out of his office and made his way to the kitchen. "Hello, everyone," he greeted us. We mumbled greetings, and it appeared as though he was going in the fridge for a drink but stopped once he saw the three of us.

"Becky," he said. "Becky, I've heard from some other members that you have things troubling you."

She turned around, but Damien and I couldn't.

"Come with me, my dear, and we can talk about it."

No Becky, don't! I mentally urged as the goosebumps formed up and down my legs, but she went willingly without saying another word. Damien and I did nothing but pretend to be watching TV. I saw, in the reflection of the TV screen, Becky walk to Mitchell's open arms. He led her back to his office, and we heard the door shut. Damien and I eyed each other, but we didn't make any sudden movements or any movements at all. When she came back out, we turned our heads.

"Hey guys."

We practically jumped up, and she came over and sat down on the couch again.

"What happened in there?"

"What did Mitchell say?"

"Nothing, nothing!" said Becky pleasantly. "He told me he heard what I was saying to the others, and that I had it all wrong, and I shouldn't be spreading lies like that. The hot chocolate was just hot chocolate, and we were all tired because it was our bodies' way of telling us we were well rested. Nobody is controlling anything, that is just ridiculous. And that is all!"

Damien and I looked at each other, lips opened in small 'o's.

"Um, really?" I asked.

"What about everything you were telling us?" Damien chimed in.

Becky shook her head. "Nothing to worry about! As far as the spirits go, they will not harm us. I was wrong! All wrong."

"What's with you?" I asked Becky, who appeared to be chewing her face.

"Nothing. My tongue itches."

Becky smiled at us, scratching her tongue with her teeth. My forehead tensed, but neither I nor Damien could come up with anything else to say. She was quite the alarmist before. Now she sat with us watching sitcoms like nothing ever happened. What did happen? Where did she come up with her ideas in the first place?

Was I supposed to sleep better that night? Because, of course, I couldn't.

My head swam with the thoughts of the group and everything that happened recently. Part of me did want to believe what Becky told us about the tornado and the students and the meditations, but I wasn't so sure. It was a new feeling I had that I couldn't shake. Why would Becky say one thing and then say the opposite? As I tossed and turned, I felt like even my own pillow and blankets were suffocating me. I heard the swishing of the sheets and the electric static of the wool blanket making tiny firecrackers in my bed, seeing the sparks run across my pant legs.

Some voices echoed in the halls, here and there, barely whispers. Whatever was living in the walls tonight was out and active. Then I heard a cry that was much closer.

I pushed the blankets from my face and sat up. The cries came again, but these were very close and very human. They were cries of fear or pain or both. I kicked away the rest of the bedding and flew out of bed. I opened my door and struggled to see in the darkness, still too dark to put on my glasses. I heard the cry again, and this time it was closer and more persistent. As I ran down the hallway, I noticed two other doors open and Kimberly and Holly rushed out.

"Who is that?" Holly asked.

"I don't know!" I answered. "I think it's someone on this floor."

"This way," Kimberly said. "It's got to be someone down here."

The three of us strode down the hallway following more outbursts. They were painful cries, and they were getting louder. And more familiar.

"It's Becky," I whispered anxiously.

Without even knocking, Kimberly opened her door, and we filtered right in.

"Becky!" she cried. "Becky, what is it?"

Holly turned on the lamp on the nightstand and we crowded the bed, where she lay with her mouth wide open and never-ending tears streaming down her face. She alternated trying to shove her pillow in her mouth and screaming.

"Becky!" Kimberly yelled again. "Are you awake? Wake up!" She gave her a shake as Becky crammed one of the pillow corners in her mouth and sobbed in the fluff. Becky's eyes opened, and she stared at all of us, her eyes wide and white. It was all we saw as she chewed ferociously on the pillow and screamed into it.

"What the ... what's wrong with her?" stammered Holly. I sat on her bed and tried to take the pillow.

"Becky! Becky, what happened? Are you hurt?" I asked. "Give me the pillow."

Becky loosened her grip weakly, still making hysterical animal noises. Once the pillow revealed her face, we all fell back in gasps.

We saw the blackened corner, dripping the horrifying black liquid that soaked all the way through. Becky's mouth dripped black blood down her chin and she opened her mouth in a painful cry. Her tongue bubbled actively, black with a greenish froth oozing on top, and bubbled faster and faster as though it were boiling. Becky let out a powerful cry as we saw her tongue curl, and then shrink shorter and shorter. Before our eyes, her tongue dissolved away thinner and thinner until it was as thin as a pencil.

"Holy shit!" I exclaimed. "Go get Carol! Hurry!"

Kimberly and Holly took off in a flash while I help-lessly stayed behind with Becky, grabbing a towel from her hamper and putting it over her mouth.

"It's okay, we're getting you help!" I told her, her eyes so pathetically big and moist. "We're going to get you to a hospital!"

She opened her mouth, nothing more than a bowl of this tar-like acid. It spilled over her lips as she moved her mouth in an attempt to talk.

"What?" I started. "What is it?"

Becky struggled to make words ... any kind of words. Her eyes moved animatedly, as though she were trying to talk to me through them.

"What are you trying to say?"

Becky cried again in frustration, her eyes crying tears and her mouth crying black in defeat.

CHAPTER 22

With Becky at the hospital most, if not all of the morning and afternoon, I sat in a quiet reverie, replaying the night in my head. Carol came in and we were able to rush Becky to the hospital, where she stayed the night so doctors could perform tests on her to find out what happened. It was not the hot chocolate this time. I don't even know if it was something she consumed at all. Now, I was really scared.

Of course, it didn't take long at all for this news to spread through The Manor. Some were awake in the night once Becky was off to the hospital and saw the whole thing, whereas others just heard about it.

"You should have seen it," started Holly among a table of people. "It was like she had the bubonic plaque in her mouth! It was absolutely horrible!"

"It was melting!" I added in. "We don't even know anything about it or how it started because she couldn't tell us. She looked like she was in so much pain and we couldn't do anything about it."

"Shit," I heard a voice behind me. I turned to see Damien coming into the lounge with some others. "What the hell happened?" He asked.

"I don't know!" I answered. "We still don't know!"

While Damien and I were in close proximity, we couldn't exactly talk about it. By my body language I tried to tell him I wanted to talk more, and by his I knew he wanted to do the same.

The other members around us expressed alarm and questions, but we didn't hear back all day, and the longer it took, the harder it was to accept that Becky was okay. Before the sun even set for the evening and before anyone could make any dinner plans, Mitchell sent out an email calling a meeting that night for any and all members who might have ventured across campus for dinner. "Mandatory Meeting in the Lower Lounge tonight, 8 P.M." I put my phone down in frustration. Whatever was going on, we were going to have to wait to find out Becky's fate, if that was even what it was about. But if Mitchell knew, then wouldn't he have told us by now? What was going on? But this was now my chance.

"Damien, want to head to the caf'?"

No, we weren't hungry.

"Yeah," he said.

It wasn't safe to talk until we got out of the woods area. Although the trees covered our heads in protection, it still felt somewhat suffocating, closing in on us.

"I can't even begin to tell you how fucked up that was."

"Her tongue shriveled up and melted off?!"

"Yes. It dissolved away into nothing! Her entire mouth was burning like her saliva turned into acid. It came out of nowhere and it turned into this black, green boiling stuff that ate away in her mouth."

"Holy shit. And no one knows what the hell happened to her?"

"No! She couldn't talk, obviously, and now we are forced to just wait."

"Do you think Mitchell knows?"

"Yeah, but Damien…" I looked around campus as we walked, burying my face in my scarf a little, although not too many people were around. "Damien, I think that someone did this to her."

"How?"

"I don't know how, or even who. But I can't shake it. I can't shake anything she said."

"I can't either. First Seth, then the tornado, then our ghosts free roaming, now this. Who or what is behind this? Is it us?"

"It has something to do with The Manor. It is. It has to be. It's got everything to do with the spirits that haunt the place. They're evil spirits."

"The spirits," Damien repeated, a hint of alarm in his voice.

"They may be manipulating or controlling us and making things happen," I suggested.

"And Mitchell is the ringleader."

"He has to be. Unless he's being controlled, too. And maybe the upperclassmen."

"Definitely. Do they even know they're being controlled?"

"Doubt it, but one thing's for certain. We need to figure out how to fight the spirits and save everyone. Look, it's not safe to talk, Damien. Look what happened to Becky. Something might happen to us if we are not careful."

"What are we supposed to do?"

We were past the caf' at this point. Walking into the building, we instead made our way to a set of couches underneath a flight of stairs.

"Well," I started. "We find out what is going on, what is causing it. We need to get in touch with … friendly spirits, if any."

"How?" asked Damien. "If the spirits are all evil, they'll try to stop us."

"Yeah," I said. "We practically have nothing. But we have to look."

I looked at him, knowing how tired we both were. "There is something going on here, and the only way to reveal it and stop it is to stick around and ... I hate to say it ... play along and pretend to play dumb, so nothing happens to us."

"Well, we are kind of involved now, anyway. As soon as something happens, I'm out of here and back at Best Western. How can we report this to the school?"

"Oh yeah, right. Like they'll believe campus ghost story crap."

"Well, we'll need proof."

"A hell of a lot of proof," I agreed. "Worst-case scenario, I'll join you at the Best Western. But first, we get to the bottom of this ... you in?"

"Yeah," he said, giving me his brave face. "I'm in."

"We can't talk there. We have to play dumb and act like one of the drones."

A set of students walked down the stairs and went outside without even noticing us. I looked at my watch and back at Damien. "Do you want to eat?"

After dinner, the walk back to The Manor seemed like a suicide mission. Even though we had something to fear, we had worse to fear if we tried to rebel. We needed to keep a low profile for a while, and keep a strong hold on ourselves. Doing anything to stand out could cost us ... everything. Damien stuck by me and kept his word.

Once we got back, Mitchell led everyone downstairs, all alert yet slightly nervous. There were no special candles, no beverages or snacks, mood music or black cloaks. This was not a ceremony; this was a talk.

"My children, thank you for being so strong! I know you are all worried about one of our sisters, Becky. I received word that she is doing all right! As you know, she suffered a terrible fate. She was in the hospital all day and night being treated for a mystery disease. Doctors did everything they could for her. They saved her life, but they could not save her tongue or speech, which is now gone."

Some small gasps came from the group, but no one said anything.

"Doctors do not know what happened. It is a form of a rare tongue disease, possibly a serious infection, but it is not contagious. Becky lost her tongue. Now she can no longer speak. No one knows how this happened. It must have been in her for a long time and finally showed its ugly face. Perhaps it is an indication of Becky's sins that she must now pay for ... as she had a sharp and wandering tongue. Perhaps this is what happens when one tells lies and doesn't listen to their Lights. Becky lost the gift of speech, now she has to rely on the power of her Light to do the speaking for her. Becky is strong, she has been born again, and she is coming back home to us tonight ... coming back to live as a resident so she can be with her family. Let us welcome this strong spirit who overcame a deadly tongue!"

Mitchell's cell phone rang, and he answered it, staying pleasant and calm. "Oh, wonderful! We've been so worried about her. Yes, bring her on in. We are all here waiting to welcome her home." The minute he put his phone away and looked at all of us, a slight cold breeze came through the air vents. That was what it felt like, but that wasn't what it was.

"Come, everyone. Let's welcome back our sister, who has suffered so much and, like a phoenix, rose from the ashes."

We all rushed upstairs, myself going a bit faster than the others and Iris leading Seth with a smirk on her face. I kept my head down and avoided her gaze. I knew that she told Mitchell something about Becky, somehow, and she believed that Becky was a sinner who deserved to be punished. I stayed cool, more anxious to see how Becky was now. Carol led her in, and both were smiling pleasantly. We all greeted her, her closer friends hugging her and Carol keeping her hands on her shoulders. "Becky went through hell," Carol said. "But she made it out and now she's okay!"

I ran up to Becky and squeezed her, dying to explode in the words running through my mind.

"Are you okay? Does it hurt?" I asked her.

Becky smiled a ghostly smile and shook her head, her eyes twinkling. I stared into them, hoping they would give me an answer or any answer at all. "Your ... your tongue."

Becky opened her mouth slightly, just enough for me and only me to see the empty void where it used to be. She shut it immediately and touched her mouth.

"Oh, my God."

Becky shook her head and put her hands on my shoulders, her eyes increasing in a glossy twinkle. "Okay," she mouthed. "Okay. I am okay."

I found that very hard to believe, and when I heard his voice behind me, I jumped.

"Becky! My child, my Light!"

Mitchell came over to her and embraced her. "You must get some rest. We have arranged your bed for you upstairs, and Carol will bring you some nice broth. We are going to take care of all your dietary needs from now on. Anything to make it easy for you."

He led Becky upstairs, some of the others following along. I stayed behind with Damien, where we both did our own wordless communication. His face was chalky white, and I didn't blame him. I pressed down on my own lips, terrified if I even said the wrong thing, I would wake up tomorrow with my tongue melted in magical acid. We didn't need to stay anything to know that we were both going to check on Becky on our own time. It would have to be late.

Around one in the morning, Damien came to my room.

"Hey. Is she asleep?" he whispered.

"I don't know," I answered. "But does it matter if we wake her up? Getting her alone is the only time we can talk … sort of. Did you bring it?"

He held up a notebook under his arm, a clicky pen snug in the spiral binder.

"Good. She'll write down everything and then we'll have written proof."

"Unless someone finds it … or she doesn't talk."

"There's only one way to find out, okay? Come on, before anyone sees us."

Damien and I walked down the hallway as quietly as we could. Becky's door was, of course, closed, and we didn't see the line of light underneath the door. It was very likely she was sleeping. I touched the doorknob and opened it carefully, nervous about any creek that could give us away. Once Damien and I were in, I turned on the lamp on the dresser and shut the door.

Becky slept on her side, one arm over her head and the other hanging off the bed. I walked right up to her and gave her a gentle shake. She awoke, startled, of course, but I noticed she might have been relieved that it was us.

"Becky, hey, sorry to wake you. We didn't mean to scare you," I said. Becky rubbed her eyes and sat up.

"We needed to see you without anyone else around," I continued. Damien came over with the notebook.

"Here, Becky," he started. "It's okay, we're here for you. Okay? We need you to tell us everything. Tell us what happened to you."

"We're going to help you," I added. "Not sure how, but we will. We know that someone did this to you. Tell us who!"

Becky took the notebook and pen and wrote something down. She did so in such a calm and demure manner that seemed out of place. Nowhere near the frantic victim she used to be, or actually was. She held up the notebook where Damien and I read:

The White Light.

We stared at it, all the blood draining from our heads, and stared back at Becky, whose face never changed expression.

"What do you mean 'The White Light'?" I asked.

She continued, and I definitely did not like where this was going.

The White Light decided that my tongue was evil. It spoke slander, of untrue words, and it needed to be punished. I am now rid of that evil that made me spread the untruth. My Light now shines brighter than before without it and I can truly express myself the way I am supposed to.

Damien and I exchanged glances with Becky, smiling peacefully, in such a dreamlike state. She might still have been half-asleep, or her engine was running, but someone else was behind the wheel. Not waiting for us, she wrote again.

I am at peace without the evil in my mouth. I may be silent now, but I have not been silenced. My Light works in other ways, my Light can communicate in action. I can seek out the weak.

I read her last line at least three times. Looking at Becky, I mentally tried to appeal to her. *Becky, I know the real you is in there somewhere.*

I can seek out the weak.

I can seek out the weak.

I can seek out the weak.

CHAPTER 23

Our friend acted as she normally would, going to classes, participating in GOL activities, having dinner...

But her dinner was not the same. It was mashed up or put in a blender. She drank her dinner. She drank her dinner the same way she drank her own conscience: down the tubes and then out the other end to be flushed away.

We were all told that Becky surmounted a physical trauma, a true test to see if her spirit was stronger than her body. She was seen as a living miracle, just like Seth was. Mitchell told us over and over that The White Light can test us, and we needed to be prepared. We all believed him.

One evening, as we sat around in preparation for another meditation, Mitchell said something that should have scared us all to call our parents to take us out of school.

"My Lights ... as you are all my children and we are a family, that means you are *my* children, and I would like the pleasure of having you all for Thanksgiving. I am planning a Thanksgiving retreat for when everyone else gets out of school, we get to stay here."

Some, if not all, protested.

"Mitchell, my family is going to my aunt and uncle's."

"My parents want me home."

"Mine too."

"I haven't been home since summer!"

"Everyone." Mitchell didn't need to shout. Mitchell never shouted and never felt the need to. No one said anything else. "Everyone, please. Consider the day of giving thanks with your GOL family to be much more worthwhile. We are being thankful for the Lights we have. Aren't we? Aren't we thankful that we have the strongest spirits in the world? I want you all to think about it. This is what our session will be about today. Think about how thankful you are to be a part of this family. It will be our own Thanksgiving retreat, a time to stay at The Manor where we are not burdened with classes and tests and studying. We will allow our spirits to have a restful ... staycation."

If my hair were any shorter, it would be standing up on all ends. He was keeping us for Thanksgiving? Could he really do that? We couldn't go home? Would the school allow that? I ignored the ringing in my ears. I needed to figure out how to get out of this. Somehow, this did not sound good.

"A Thanksgiving Retreat," Mitchell repeated, annunciating the words as though they were delicious to say. "You will all strengthen your minds and your souls, with no one around to bother you. We will have nothing but great feasts and great fun! We'll have team-building exercises and games."

I kept my head down, trying to hide the concerned look on my face. Out of the corner of my eye, I saw Mitchell wave his hand over the whole congregation.

"Meditate, my children."

I closed my eyes, at once deciding I had to rely on the power of my spirit to do the escaping for me. I flew high and soared above The Manor, above the trees and sky itself. I left my body behind as well as my rapidly beating heart—and suddenly everything slowed down. I was away from The Manor, away from campus, but who knew where. The air was cool, but it was way too warm for November. Clouds covered my face and went through my nose, down my lungs, and into the pit of my stomach, calming all my acidic nerves.

As I inhaled and exhaled those cloud fumes, they cleared my sight and I saw a large open field. As it cleared away more and more, I could make out what dominated the background: the largest, layered mountain ranges I had ever seen in person. The cloud fumes stopped there, gathering at the top and mingling into the blue and green and brown speckled in the mountain rocks. I heard a loud rushing behind me, and turning around, an enormous waterfall greeted me. It splashed on the rocks and some hit me in the face, droplets that reflected every color of the rainbow in glorious prisms.

I had no clue where I was. How could I know? And yet, as I walked along the fields and let the waterfall reflect in my eyes, I knew it was a very real, very foreign place. I tried to look around for the others. I could hear them, but I couldn't see them.

"Hello?" I tried asking. "Hello? Where are you? Where are we?"

I tensed up momentarily, coming to the conclusion that I was not the only ... spirit ... in this place. The presence I felt was not a familiar one at all. I walked through the fields and stared at the mountains because I saw something move near them. Some things were moving, and they looked like they were moving in order to join together. Shadows were starting to blend into the mountains and moved as one, and then broke apart as individuals. Pieces of them broke off and turned into arms, wiggling wavy fingers that beckoned me to come forward. I walked in that direction without thinking about it.

They had faces, but they were unrecognizable. Out of the corner of my eyes, I saw that all these spirits ran down the fields, all along the horizon, and surrounded the entire area. Several flew right past me. Were we all here together? What was this place?

"Do you see it?"

I heard Mitchell's voice clear and strong, as though this world were a covered dome with a PA system.

"Do you ... all see it?"

Yes. We were all in the same vision. Our spirits all went to the same place this time, although I don't know how this was arranged. As I looked out past the mountain ranges, I could see that this place stretched out for miles and miles. We were only in a small section of a great, wide field and whatever else lay beyond. There was plenty more, and I was dying to see it, but for some reason, we could go no further. The spirits—the ones gathered by the vast mountain ranges—joined wavy arms in a people rope. As far as myself went ... my spiritual self, I couldn't move. Not at all.

"My Lights," Mitchell's voice boomed again. "You all see before you ... a paradise waits. A potential one ... for a potential future home. Are you worthy of it? Are you ready for it? Do you see what could be yours only if you continue to believe in The White Light?"

We opened our eyes. All of us. I didn't want to, but I did, and the vision was now gone.

"You can be worthy of such a paradise," Mitchell said, standing before us and bringing us all back to Earth. "Our time here is short. Remember that. We will die here, and then where will we go? Consider this and more in the time that we have. This Thanksgiving Retreat will allow us special time for that reflection. Do you now see how important that is? Do not let your spirits down."

The fireplace heaved in, sighed out, and then sneezed out a cloud of smoke. All the candles in the lounge went out.

I paced my room with my phone to my ear, hoping it would go smoothly.

"Well…" I said. "That's what I wanted to talk to you about. We're actually having Thanksgiving here."

"You are?" my mom asked, her voice ending on a higher, disappointed note. "What do you mean? You're not coming home?"

"I'm sorry, Mom, don't take it personally. Mitchell is making a really big thing out of it, and he got permission from the school for us all to stay here and have an entire retreat from classes and such. It's supposed to be a special thing where we reflect on our lives and stuff."

"Well, all right honey," she said. "If that's what you want, that sounds like a great time. We're going by Grandma and Grandpa, and I don't even think your cousins are around, anyway. This sounds like it will be a lot of fun."

"Yeah, it's going to be great."

"This group is really doing wonders for you, isn't it?"

"Yeah, it sure is."

I still paced my room, only part of me believing what I just said.

Well, our last day of classes and the beginning of this "retreat" were, of course, wonderful. Not like I expected it to go any differently. Everyone was in the most amazing spirits, like Christmas had come early. Even Becky. Especially Becky.

I came downstairs for breakfast, and the first thing she did was grab me in an enormous embrace.

"Hey Becky … how are you feeling? How…" I motioned to her mouth. It, after everything it had been through, still managed to smile. "Does it still hurt?"

Becky shook her head, then patted her mouth and patted her chest. She shrugged it off like it was nothing. She motioned across the room, still keeping her hand across her chest.

"You're … you're at peace," I guessed.

She nodded and then led me to the kitchen, where I helped myself to some cereal and just tried not to talk or think about it anymore.

It was the last day of classes before the weekend, and then the following Monday would officially start the retreat. The mood in the manner was very uplifting and exciting. I thought to myself that I only had one more day of classes. At first I thought it was the only time I could get out so I could escape The Manor … but now I thought it was the last time I had to go so I could escape classes.

I actually couldn't believe I thought we were being held hostage or trapped there. Really. What was I thinking? I wanted to stay there. I wanted fulfillment, and most importantly, I wanted to make more spiritual connections around the house. The thing was, I didn't exactly have a plan of how to get in touch with them. Damien and I agreed to be low-key and keep an eye on everything to see when and if there would be an opportunity for us to explore … or to give us a clue on something. So far, no such events topped the tornado and Becky's sudden tongue horror. We also had a hard time connecting the two to anything. We were getting nowhere, basically. We only knew that somehow, something was going to happen during this Thanksgiving Retreat, and we had no idea what it would be until it happened.

The evening and the night went—normally. Mitchell didn't have any big speeches prepared or anything. The only thing we had to do was make sure to pitch in the Food Fund jar that would take care of us for the week, as the campus eateries would be closed. Carol and Mitchell would get food supplies periodically, and that was basically it.

Damien and I stayed up late and talked a little, doing homework together or pretending to. After a while, he gave me a tired look. We both knew what that meant. There was nothing to do but to call it a night. He went to sleep, but I for some reason stayed downstairs staring at the one paragraph in my textbook for the longest time. I wasn't even sure I read it at all.

Ad Astra broke my trance, weaving in and out of table and chair legs. Her whiskers twitched, and she sat down on the kitchen floor, cleaning herself behind her leg. She got into her own trance at one point, acknowledging me sitting at the table but mostly just staring at something down the hallway. I kept my eye on her, not sure if I should stick around or go to bed. It seemed liked déjà vu, this scene we played for the second time. I stood up and walked over to her, looking in the direction she was looking at. She obviously heard it before me.

The thumps were quiet at first, almost obscured by the noises in the heater, but they were recognizable. The cat got up; her tail a solid sword of protection behind her, behind us. She stalked, and I followed, following the thumps as they got louder down the hallway. The doors to the rooms were all shut; the noise could have been coming from any of them. They persisted and soon turned into an entirely different beat of pounding. They were almost knocking. The cat shuffled down the hallway quickly with me right behind her, and I held my breath. She never took her eyes off of whatever was in front of us, whatever she could see and I could not.

I had a feeling this time, I truly did. Ad Astra crawled towards the same storage closet I discovered days ago. The knocking got louder and more spaced apart. She emitted a low growl and pointed her tail right at the door, keeping very low. I knew this was my cue.

I reached for the doorknob with little hesitation this time and turned it all the way, almost jumping back. I expected something to fall out on me again or even jump out, but nothing did. I opened the door and the only thing that hit me was a cold breeze, dust mites blowing away in escape at my feet. The room was too dark to see anything in it, too dark to even make out all the crap that I had found there previously. I held the door wide open and listened, almost thinking the pounding stopped, but it did not. It was actually coming closer.

Ad Astra's ears twitched and folded back. I wished I had my phone so I could poke a light around in the dark. I leaned in and my heart jumped to my throat when I heard a pound a few feet away from me. I swear that no matter how many times I tried to swallow my stomach down, it stayed there. I stared a few feet away from me because I could also swear that there was a box on the ground was hopping towards me like a rabbit.

I saw the box near the corner of the storage room entrance, not quite out of the room. I reached towards it and grabbed the box. Ad Astra poked her nose at it and waved her whiskers in curiosity, caution, or both. As soon as I touched the box, it stopped thumping. I got it out and shut the door, putting the box on the ground.

"Well," I said stupidly. "Here goes nothing."

Ad Astra watched me open the box, not leaving me. I pushed back those flaps and peered in to see what was inside.

Part of me wanted to scream, part of me wanted to laugh, because it felt like Jumanji. But of course, it wasn't Jumanji. It was a freaking Ouija board.

CHAPTER 24

It wasn't even in a regular game box, the kind you usually get from the toy section at Target. It was older ... a box with intricate wooden designs featuring stars and moons and clouds. I took that game up to my room and put it under my desk. I spent most of the night staring at it from my bed from behind the spaces in my fingers. What was I expecting? It wasn't going to float in the air and fly in my face, and it didn't. It never thumped again. I understood that it wanted attention, and it got mine. The next step was to get a partner to use it, and I knew exactly who to ask.

I gazed at the digital clock on my nightstand, my dripping eyes failing to see the exact numbers. I was so tired I didn't even know what time it was. It would have been dumb to wake up Damien now, anyway. So I slept, that game under my desk watching me all night.

The next day marked the first day of our Thanksgiving retreat. It was the day that everyone was supposed to go home. Everyone, of course, except for us. Mitchell got away with it and got the school's approval on the grounds that it was a sacred and spiritual reason. Nobody can say anything or ask any questions when it comes to faith. That "religious reason" card lets you get away will almost everything. That being said, the first day that we had the campus to ourselves, so everyone was in unbelievably high spirits. Not to mention we got a break from wearing uniforms and could just wear jeans and our own sweatshirts all week. Everyone, of course, loved that, even though when we put on our special cloaks, we were still in a different kind of uniform.

"Good morning to you, my Lights!" Mitchell greeted us as we came downstairs for breakfast. Carol was already whipping up batches of pancakes. I could smell them from the stairs. They were made with blueberries and strawberries and someone already opened the maple syrup. Everyone gathered in the mess hall. We weren't fooling around. We were starting these festivities as soon as possible. Mitchell started us off with, of course, his usual great speech.

"The campus is all gone," he said with a big smile. "Everyone went home for Thanksgiving break, and we are home for Thanksgiving. We get to have our own break ... together as a family. The world is ours and we get our time to ourselves."

Carol and some others brought out plates of pancakes, but that wasn't the first thing I smelled. It was incense, and it was incredibly strong.

"I am so happy to have you, all of you, and you will not regret your decision as a member of this family."

I turned my head this way and that way to pick up all the different scents in the room, but there was something else that was different. Our numbers did grow, at one point. When did we get so many new members? Not to mention ... new residents. The same kids that were here for the last meeting lived here as well. They were still in their pajamas. As I looked around the room, I realized how much of this was true. The entire congregation now lived at The Manor. We were all here. Did we really have that many people? Did The Manor really have that much room? I never noticed that before, and I never noticed when we got all the GOL members out of the dorm houses. Even 7th and 8th grade. That last thought fluttered in my stomach. How could I have been so oblivious?

Breakfast turned out to be no less than incredible. Warmth ran down my throat and mixed with my fluttering stomach. Our meal was so big we would be full until dinner, until the next grand feast. I felt like relaxing, but now was not the time to relax. Now was the time for games. Or, also called "team-building exercises," such as a grown-up version of "the floor is lava."

Our floor cushions were strewn all over the lower lounge. We all lined up on the far end of the room and had to all "safely" cross the room without touching the floor, moving one row at a time and sharing cushion space and helping out friends. It was a fun-filled day; afterwards we relaxed on pillows and blankets while Mitchell rolled the projector and played movies.

I finally carried myself up to my room, and it was only when I opened my door that all the fun energy suddenly drained out of me and sucked into the ground. I stared at the Ouija board under my desk, sitting there so patiently for the whole day. I leaned my elbow on the doorknob, not even wanting to go in. I couldn't believe I forgot all about it. How was that possible? Something—or someone—wanted me to find that Ouija board and I did, and I hadn't opened it yet. I flipped open my phone and browsed through my contacts. What better time than the present?

I didn't move from my room doorway, so I saw Damien once he came.

"What's up?" He asked, already thinking or knowing that something was going on.

"Come in here," I said, and his eyes widened. I didn't mean to sound so creepy, but I did.

"Sky, you okay? What happened?"

I shut the door.

"Well, I found something last night during another little paranormal episode of mine and somehow completely forgot about it all day until now."

I could tell Damien looked a bit hesitant to be in my room, so I sat on the bed, prompting him to do the same.

"Like what?"

"Okay," I said, bringing my voice down to a hush. "Remember when Becky and I were talking about hearing pounding in the walls? And then I found that storage closet with nothing in it?"

"Yeah?"

I walked over to my desk and picked it up.

"I heard the same thing last night, and the pounding was coming from this."

Damien eyed it. "Ohhhhhhh. Oh, man."

"Yeah. Yeah. This ... something was messing with it. I think something wants to talk."

Damien pulled at his hair and rubbed his cheeks as though they were clay.

"Jesus Sky. Those things always freaked me out a little."

I pressed my lips. "I need your help."

He nodded, probably knowing all along he would do anything to figure out the mysteries of The Manor and to help me.

"What—what do we do?"

"Well," I said, still holding the box. "I guess there is only one way to find out."

We both decided on sitting on the floor, the navy blue carpet bringing us out to sea without any life preservers. We really didn't know what we were getting ourselves into.

Damien and I sat across from each other with the board in between us. I placed the hand piece near the top of the letters, right over Ouija, then looked at him.

"Okay, now we both have to touch it and ask it a question."

We placed our fingertips on the hand piece delicately.

"Let's move it around a little, so they know we're here."

We led the planchette around in a couple of circles, carefully positioning it back over the title name.

"Are we looking for someone in particular?"

"No. I don't know. We should ask it something."

Damien leaned forward, aware of the "no" and "yes" on the board.

"Is there a spirit present?" he asked.

We steadied our hands, arranged in triangles with fingertips barely touching. Suddenly the planchette began to move. I exhaled extremely carefully, afraid that a stray puff of air would interfere.

Yes.

"Are you here because you ... need something?" I tried.

The piece moved again. *Yes.*

"Do you want to tell us something?"

Yes.

Damien and I looked at each other.

The hand piece moved down the board to the alphabet. I stayed as steady as possible. We never took our eyes off the board as it moved around, stopping on a letter for a few seconds before moving on.

"J."

"O."

"I."

"N."

"U."

"S."

We looked up. "Join us?"

"Holy shit."

"Where?" I asked them. "What do you mean?"

The piece moved down the alphabet again.

"Get."

"Out."

"Of."

"The."

"Dark."

The piece stayed at the letter "k." Damien and I looked at each other, our hands shaking.

"What the hell does that mean?" He asked me.

"I don't know."

We took our hands away, clasping them together.

After a minute, Damien reached out and took my hands and put them on the piece.

"What do we do?" he asked.

"Look."

"In."

"The."

"Woods."

"The woods?"

The planchette moved all the way down to the board.

Goodbye.

CHAPTER 25

Damien and I stayed up for a while and talked, obviously in no mood to curl up in the dark and try to go to sleep. The Ouija board was safely tucked away in its box under the desk. We left it alone as we tried to come up with a plan. Our little retreat schedule had some allotted free time in the afternoon in between meals and activities, so we knew that would be the best time to explore the woods area to see whatever we could find. It could be tricky, as we didn't know what we should say or do if anyone asked us.

Eventually, we called it a night, Damien sluggishly pulling himself out of my room and myself hiding under my covers. The Ouija board itself didn't scare me, really. I guess you could say it made me more alert.

We were encouraged to journal or be in groups during our free time. Damien and I had cups of tea after breakfast and pretended to watch a card game. Then, once our cups were empty, we were up. We got our coats and bundled up, no one really paying attention to us. I wrapped my scarf around my head and stepped out.

"Okay, so..."

Damien and I looked out into the vast, never-ending scene of trees. Obviously, our spirit friend last night didn't specify anything. We walked around The Manor, around the bushes with the solar lamps, and past the tree that had a homemade bird feeder with frozen peanut butter. We both looked in the backyard area of The Manor, the path of trees that did not lead to campus.

"That might be the best bet," I said, a little uneasy.

"Right," Damien said, stepping over some rocks.

We set out, mostly looking at nothing. Every once in a while I turned to look at The Manor behind us to make sure that we never lost sight of it, and our way back. I turned back around to see Damien staring at something.

"Um, Sky?"

"What?" I asked, looking.

It was a circle of trees, literally, as though someone planted them using a compass. We walked in it and saw these trees had something else in common. A big white "x" was painted on each one of them, or maybe it was supposed to be a cross. I could not tell. We moved some branches and thorns out of the way to get a better look. Smack dab in the middle was an arrangement of stones. They almost looked like kitchen tile, diagonal lines connecting each tree trunk. Damien and I stopped right there, the wind blowing through our coats, somehow knowing we were not to step foot inside this circle.

"Whoa," was all I could say.

"What the hell is this?" Damien asked.

"I don't know, but whatever it is, we found it."

We leaned on other trees, not the marked ones. We didn't touch them. We didn't dare.

"This is sacred ground," I observed. "Obviously, something happened here. A ritual of some sort."

"Do you think anyone knows about it?"

I faced him. "I don't think we should tell anyone."

"Why not?"

"It's obviously private. Maybe it belongs to the spirits and they don't want their space invaded?"

"Then how come the spirit from the Ouija board told us to come out here in the first place?"

We paused, looking at the tree markings and the stones. Nothing about the scene revealed anything other than it had not been touched for years.

"Well, they obviously wanted us to see it. Maybe we should ask it."

Damien was freaked out. I was freaked out. But we agreed.

We headed back to The Manor, the wind whistling in our ears. It could have been whistling words in particular, but I couldn't make it out.

"Game time in the lower lounge! Come, my children!"

Damien and I were just putting our coats away, the outside cold disappearing from our bodies except for the very tips of our noses. Everybody was going downstairs in anticipation of the next game, and we found ourselves swimming with the current. We couldn't go missing.

"This is the game of truths," Mitchell announced to the congregation. "This is where we will learn more about ourselves by admitting things that are true. They can be good truths, and they can be bad truths. What we are going to do is line up all the way to the wall. I will make a statement, and you will move accordingly. If it is a positive truth, you step forward. If it is a negative truth, you step backwards. This exercise is important in our retreat for the weeks to come."

Mitchell motioned to the back wall on the other side of the lounge, where we all herded like cattle. From here, he looked so small. He looked really far away. For a moment, I was scared I wouldn't make it so far. I told myself that I had to get to the other wall in this game. I had to.

"First statement is an easy one to get you all off the wall. After all, you are *well* past that first step. I am a Guardian of Light."

Like soldiers, we all took one step forward.

"I believe my spirit is strong."

Step forward.

"I believe in the afterlife, and after my time is done on Earth, I will be in a better place."

Step forward.

"Now, if any of these statements are true, step backwards. I am afraid of dying."

Some stepped back. I thought of it, but I was not.

"I wish l could live on Earth forever."

A few stepped back.

"Positive. I am happy with the time I spent on Earth."

Some stepped forward, some did not. This bothered me because it seemed like a trick question. Was I happy with life so far? What about my future? It wasn't over yet. At least ... I didn't believe so. But I knew Mitchell did. I kept my eyes down, one foot shuffling in front of me. Did I take a half-step?

More statements, more steps. At one point, I was surprised to see that I was far ahead of Damien. What had he said no to? I didn't understand.

"I believe in the spirits of The Manor."

Step forward, definitely. Most did as well, and that made me happy.

"I believe the spirits of The Manor are here to support us and will be our guides as we pass to the Next Life."

Step forward. I knew they were. They had to be. I just didn't understand the mysteries of it all. What exactly was on our side?

"I believe my Light will move on ... move on to the Next Life where I will be one of the strongest beings in the new world because of the generous prep time I was given on Earth."

Everyone stepped forward. Mitchell's enormous grin could be seen by everyone in the room.

"Very good," he cooed. "I am so proud of all of you."

Several people reached the wall. I got pretty far. Holly, Kimberly, Becky, and Seth, with a little help, all touched the wall and looked at the rest of the members who still lingered in the middle of the lounge. Becky's face was glowing. It was like a different version of herself like she was born again. Damien, however, remained a few spaces back. I couldn't shake that small sting of annoyance.

"Our upperclassmen proved themselves worthy of their rank," Mitchell indicated them standing at the wall. "And some of our younger brothers and sisters ... they have certainly come a long way." Seth kept one hand on the wall and waved a dumb queen wave, where Iris smiled at everyone like a spider would smile at flies. I avoided her glance.

"Why don't we all have a short meditation session? After dinner tonight, we'll have a fun movie marathon!"

So, of course, Damien and I couldn't consult the Ouija board until much later. I did not want anyone to see us using it or know that we were trying to communicate with the spirits of the house. I was not sure what the reaction would be, and I did not want to find out. We both knew this somehow but still managed to forget about it and enjoy the evening.

At one point during some free time upstairs, Iris sat next to Damien and talked with him privately. I was with Holly and Becky. Becky's never-ending sunshine was contagious to everyone and made me a combination of curious and suspicious, but this made me feel worse. Iris kept leaning in to Damien's ear and whispering. I saw him mumble something, and she petted him up and down his arm. I saw red, and I could almost feel my eyes burn.

She didn't sit with him during dinner, as he was with me and the others.

"What was Iris talking to you about?" I blurted out.

"Nothing," he answered, scooping a mouthful of potatoes. He caught my look.

"She was just telling me she could be my spiritual mentor ... or something."

I shrugged.

It still bothered me all night, but I didn't bring it up again. Students filtered in and out of the movie sessions in the lower lounge, the fireplace flickering warmth in the room. Informal setting, it seemed like a good time.

Now? I texted him.

My phone jingled. *Yeah.*

We went upstairs and shut the bedroom door.

"Okay, let's see what we can find out..."

I opened the Ouija board from its case, unclasped the top, and brushed the deeply carved designs in the wood.

We sat down and pushed the planchette in gentle circles around the board.

"Ready?"

"Yeah."

"Okay," I said, trying to concentrate. "Those trees in the woods … with the stones and markings, is that what we were supposed to find?"

The planchette started to move, practically gliding.

Yes.

"What exactly is it?" I asked again.

The hand piece went down to the alphabet.

"D."

"E."

"A."

"T."

"H."

Damien and I almost took our hands off the piece. They were barely touching and shaking.

We heard people talking in the hallway and froze, both afraid someone would knock or come in and interrupt our session. The voices came closer and stopped a few feet from my door. Damien and I stayed quiet, but then the planchette started to take us around the board.

"How can we know what happened?" I managed to say.

"The."

"Office."

"Office…" Damien's brow crossed.

"Does that mean Mitchell's office?"

Just then, a knock sounded on my door, prompting Damien and me to jerk our hands back and look up.

"Yeah?" I asked.

The door opened and Kimberly stuck her head in.

"Hey," she said. "Oh, no, I'm sorry. I … didn't realize you were having a private, spiritual moment. I'm so sorry. It's just that we made hot chocolate again! And we're going to start a Harry Potter marathon. Anyway, uh, so sorry again." That time, Kimberly looked at the ceiling when she apologized.

"Um, bring that downstairs when you're done!" she said. "I'm sure others would want a turn with it!"

She shut my door all the way and Damien and I sighed.

"Now what?" he asked.

I looked down at the board. "Look."

The planchette, all on its own, already moved down and parked on *Goodbye*.

CHAPTER 26

Now, our new goal was impossible. How were we going to sneak into Mitchell's office? The idea itself was insane. I was actually afraid to find out what was in there. Damien and I struggled with this idea and how to find an opening—any opening—but this opportunity didn't show itself. Everyone was out and about until very late that night—blame Harry Potter. Still, we sat together, keeping our eyes and ears peeled. At one point, Damien suggested checking it out when everyone went to bed. I instantly axed that, knowing that was an even greater risk. Mitchell's office was right next to, or even directly attached to the room he slept in. I had never been in there before, but it seemed likely. We had no choice but to wait this one out, and it was killing us.

The following day, we woke up and were pleasantly surprised to see that it was a laid-back morning. Some made coffee and were watching something on TV when I came downstairs, Damien trailing right behind me. It became our habit to poke our heads in the residential floors to see who was up first. Damien spotted me just as I came out of the bathroom, and we traveled downstairs together to see what the day would bring us.

We had ourselves a modest breakfast of orange juice and toast and didn't do much else until Mitchell himself came into the room, waking both Damien and me out of our post-slumber.

"Carol and I are going to run some errands," he announced, shaking The Manor Food Fund can. "Get some groceries for you lot, as well as kitty food and treats for my baby. Be back soon."

Both Mitchell and Carol put on their coats and went out the door, leaving Damien and I stared at each other from across cup rims. We didn't say anything, we both just got up.

Mitchell's office and room were down another hallway, near the bathroom, but of course, further in the back.

"Wait," I whispered as soon as we were in the hallway. "One of us is going to have to keep watch. What if Iris or Kimberly come down here and ask us what we're doing?"

"Right," Damien agreed. "How about I keep watch?"

I didn't argue. "Okay. Just keep anyone from going in his office, which I don't think anyone does, anyway. But give me a signal if someone tries to or is coming too close."

"Like what?"

"I don't know, but it has to be loud enough for me to hear it and be able to hide or something."

"Okay."

"I'll let you know when I want to come out."

"Got it."

We walked down the hallway like we were going to uncover a secret lair, but in a way, it was true. We had absolutely no idea what was in Mitchell's office, and it honestly scared us. I put my hand on the doorknob, nodded to Damien, and turned it. Once the inside was big enough, I slid into the room and shut the door, leaving Damien in the hallway.

I didn't know what I was expecting to see, but it was an office. It had a cherry mahogany desk, a leather swivel chair, and a desktop computer with silver-white picture frames lined up right next to it. I knew I was going to have to do more searching, and I didn't know how much time I had until Mitchell got back.

I peered to my left, a closet with two jackets in it and a couple of pairs of shoes in piles as though they were always just kicked off. I peered to my right. An adjoining bedroom that looked like it also had its own bath. Of course, Mitchell would have a master suite. I didn't dare go into the bedroom, anyway. I walked closer to the desk and opened file cabinets and desk drawers, looked inside notebooks, and looked in boxes. A thought occurred to me that something was in the computer itself, but I immediately crossed that off my list. What in the world was I supposed to be looking for, anyway? Files on séances and how to brainwash a bunch of kids? That actually didn't sound too far off.

Class notes, lecture notes, pamphlets, blah blah blah. Old GOL flyers, a book of games, and activities for large groups. I wasn't getting anywhere. I looked on the desk and saw that the silver picture frames were not full of a wife and kids on vacation or during Christmas. No, these were all full of Mitchell with Ad Astra. The one on the end was just her sitting on a windowsill on a sunny day. The biggest picture in the middle had Mitchell decked out in his most formal of prep school teacher wear, complete with sweater vest and pipe in one hand, the other petting the cat on his lap. I choked back a laugh. At first, it reminded me of the Austin Powers villain, Dr. Evil. I couldn't laugh at all, because it was one of the creepiest photos I'd ever seen. It had to be the look on the teacher's face. All the light was gone except for his eyes. They were yellowish, almost like the photographer messed up the lighting and made him look weird. He looked possessed. I had to look away.

I heard a voice in the hallway, and I froze under Mitchell's photographic eye.

Shit.

I immediately ducked under the desk and brought my knees to my chest as I heard the mumblings of Damien and someone else, some girl.

"No no, actually, Mitchell went to the store!" Damien said, or rather, yelled. "Yeah, he'll be back soon. He told everyone to go do journaling or something."

"Why are you shouting?" asked some girl.

"Oh, I don't know. I was playing my iPod really loud today."

They stopped talking, and I heard nothing else.

Good Damien.

I slowly started to climb out from under the desk, wondering what to do next, and then I felt it. I jumped about a foot in the air and bumped my head on the desk, but wasn't really caring about my head. Something tugged on my ear.

No, it wasn't an itch. I didn't brush up against something. *Something actually tugged on my frickin' ear.* I almost lost my balance crawling out from under the desk, but I stayed still, trying not to look next to me even though I knew nothing was there. My ear tugged again, and this time it didn't scare me as much.

"What?" I said to whatever was there.

It was like it was tugging downward, trying to get my attention to something below me. I put my hands on the bottom right desk drawer and it stopped. I pulled open that drawer and found a folder of newspaper clippings. They were so old the edges were pale yellow and the paper was soft enough to be toilet paper. The headline at the top of one of them made my arms break out in goosebumps:

Six Found Dead in Local Wood

The picture underneath it was the very same circle of trees Damien and I found. I shoved those clipping back into the folder and shut the desk drawer. As soon as I stood up, I froze dead in my tracks and clamped my hand over my mouth. I didn't even hear voices outside. I didn't hear the door open, but he was standing there, and he was staring right at me.

Or, he was just staring, because he couldn't see.

But still, Seth's eyes were dead set on me anyway, like he could see me. I kept my hand over my mouth, nervous that he could probably hear my breathing. I made no other moment. Seth kept his hands on the door frame and started to make his way into the office, feeling out in front of him zombie-like.

"Hello?" he asked.

I sidestepped, once. Maybe if I could duck into the bedroom or something ... *where the hell was Damien?*

Seth came further into the room, feeling around for the desk until he found it. I barely breathed, knowing that one wrong movement could really screw me up. I sidestepped again, careful not to crash into the desk chair that I pushed back.

"Is someone there?" Seth asked again. His hands moved around the desk and I jumped when they accidentally knocked over Mitchell's picture frames. I could get past the desk chair and make a run for it, but Seth was close. Very close. He could hear me or reach out and touch me.

"Hey! Seth, what are you doing?"

I could have killed him.

Seth turned his head. "Hi Damien."

My trusty watchman came into the room and put his hands on Seth's shoulders, careful to not look at me and keep his face towards him when he talked.

"Er, did you mean to come into Mitchell's office?"

"What? Oh, no," said Seth, acting embarrassed. "Is that where I am? I was looking for that other storage room."

"Well, all right, let's get you out of here, shall we? Mitchell will be back soon and you know he wouldn't want anyone in his office."

"Right, of course."

Damien and Seth left, leaving me clutching the folder so tightly I could feel my pulse in my fingertips. I counted to ten before I made my way out myself, shutting the door carefully behind me.

I had the folder in my sweatshirt as I crept through the hallway like a criminal, but what else was I to do? Damien obviously got Seth out of the way, but now I had to find him and get out of sight.

Damien waited by the bathroom.

"All right, did ... did you find something?" he asked, eyeing my sweatshirt. "Okay, yeah, that was close. Let's go."

He put his arm around me and we went to my room since it was closer, surprised we didn't bump into anyone on the way there. We shut the door, and I pulled that folder out to let it breathe.

"I'm sorry!" he said right away. "He seriously came out of nowhere. He's like a ninja the way he sneaks around, and I didn't see him!"

"Well, it's a good thing it was him and no one else."

I knew we could have argued on, but I still had that folder, and Damien was burning a hole through it.

"What is that?"

I pulled out the newspaper clippings carefully so they wouldn't spill out.

"I found these in one of the desk drawers ... and not by accident. I was under there hiding and ... I felt something tug on my ear. I swear to God. It tugged me towards the bottom drawer where I found this. It was like someone wanted me to find it."

"Whoa," he exhaled.

I sorted through the articles, not wanting to talk about it anymore.

"Look," I said. "*Six Found Dead.* It's the spot!"

We both read over articles and scanned some more similar headlines. This much was clear; they all had the same pictures.

"They were not that much older than us," I said.

"Look at the date," Damien said. "1992. Damn. This is all before Applewhite even became a school."

"Yeah, but you'd think it wouldn't be a detail they'd miss when looking for a spot to build!"

"Not to mention building The Manor right next to the death site!"

"Why the hell does Mitchell have all of this?"

I picked up another article with a picture that made me stare at it the longest. It only took me a minute to get it.

"Oh my God, Damien..."

"What."

I showed him the picture of the girl. Her curls were springy here and full of life, not like they were the last time I saw her in person. If he reacted the same way I did, then my thoughts were confirmed. He picked up the paper and looked from the picture to me.

"Does she look familiar to you?"

"I don't know. Who is she?"

"Damien, let me just ask you something. On Halloween night, when we did ritual in the dark, did you see some creepy-looking students you never saw before?"

"I don't know, why?"

"The ghosts of these people never left," I stated. "We saw them. That's why Mitchell has these. They're *here*."

CHAPTER 27

The first thing we did was go back downstairs to find that Ouija board.

We tried not to look too frantic going into the kitchen and lower lounge area, as many people were there. I spotted Kimberly right away.

"Hey, Kim. Where was that Ouija board we had the other day?"

"Oh," she poked her head over the couch at me and thought about it. "I'm sorry, I have no clue. Did you ask Carol? She probably put it away somewhere."

Before we could say or do anything else, Mitchell came back into the lounge. Who knew just how long he had been back? We didn't even know how much time we spent upstairs.

"Hello my Lights!" he called. "Come, come, we're going to have a meditation session before dinner and our games tonight. We've got to keep those spirits strong, now don't we?"

Iris got up and brought Seth with her like a puppy on a leash to the lower lounge. The angel statue's head stared at us as we walked down.

I found that, for some reason, we were getting less and less freedom with even the meditation sessions. It was like

our spirits were being blocked off from roaming too far. I took that to mean that they wanted us to be more focused. Not that I complained about the lush, purple paradise we were all in. There must have been blueberry trees/plants somewhere because I could almost taste them. Still, the roam in paradise once again did its job. I was relaxed, a limp wet noodle, like how you'd feel after hours in the hot tub.

Mitchell smiled at us at the front of the lounge, bent in a pretzel yoga position.

"We are all calm and focused now."

We ate dinner, still feeling sluggish and wondering how we could have the energy for another game tonight. I certainly wasn't feeling it. I wanted to find that Ouija board again, figure out if I was in fact talking to a dead former member of the Guardians of Light, and if they had answers for me. It drove me crazy that it was missing. I only thought about it once, and then somehow forgot about it for the rest of the evening.

For our downtime, we all just watched TV after dinner, waiting for Mitchell to give us an itinerary. Once he came in, we knew something had changed. He just came from his office, and there was a dark shadow cast over his face.

"Everyone. Lounge time. There is something the time has come for me to discuss with you."

We went down and sat before Mitchell as he slowly paced in front of the fireplace, which was turned on and heating up against the November chill.

"Firstly, it has come to my attention," he started. "That some of you are ... curious. I don't blame you, of course. Everyone has doubts from time to time and is in a dire state of desperation, of wanting to have faith and have all their questions answered. But that does not give anyone the permission to snoop around in my office."

Something stabbed my stomach. I tried very hard not to look at Damien and not let Mitchell see the shock on my face. I swallowed and waited.

"I was looking for something when I noticed I had a folder missing in one of my drawers. This folder had important newspaper clippings in it that I hold dear. Now, it is gone. I am not going to ask who took it, and for what reason, but I would like it returned. I will leave my office door open tonight and look the other way. I don't care who took it, really. But the more I think about it, the more I know that whoever took it has questions ... so... I guess that means I must provide some answers."

I sat up straight while Mitchell paced.

"In the early 90s, before Applewhite Prep was established, this area used to be an apartment complex where I would go and visit a small group of young adults. They came to one of my motivational speeches panels once and I stayed in touch with them. We would meet frequently. They were very sad. They were not strong. They had no faith. Their spirits were weak. What happened was they became weakened by life on Earth. They knew, in their hearts, that there was a better place for them. What they did was decide to end their time on Earth sooner. They decided it as a group, and their Guardian bodies were found in the woods days later."

I barely breathed.

"They were weak," he continued. "The White Light must have inspired them, but they did not have enough faith and they did not hone their souls. They were not ready. They were unable to pass on to the Next Life because of this."

Everyone had their attention on Mitchell, barely shuffling in their seats.

"Now, my Lights," he continued. "You know that these spirits are here with us now in this very house, near the very place where they ended their lives. We can all find the right path to paradise together. They need our help. As you all know, The White Light appeared to me in a dream. We need to spread The White Light's message and help guide all the lost souls of this world. Our time is short. We must continue to ready ourselves for this time, and since it is sooner than we think, I am glad to have this discussion with you. Do not be afraid."

CHAPTER 28

You could hear nothing except for the occasional shuffle of legs, crack of candle flames, or steps Mitchell took as he paced the room. The energy that he had directed at the room was not an inspiring one it usually was, but rather like a strong grasp on all of us to keep our attention. It was working. The very presence of the spirits always held us. Learning their origin was another, but nothing compared to the next bit of news our leader bestowed upon us.

"I am proud of all of you, the progress you've made, and how strong you have all become. You are an inspiration, and you are ready to become leaders in the Next Life, which may come sooner than we think."

My entire body was numb, and I could not move it. I did not even try.

"There has been talk about a Mayan prophecy, which I am sure you have all heard of: the prophecy that the world will come to an end on December 21st, 2012. Of course, many people are skeptical about this and do not believe it. But why not believe it? This is a sign, and we should treat it as one. We do not know exactly what will happen, but if Earth is indeed going to end, are you ready to go?"

He paused, scanning our faces.

"The White Light appeared in my dream to warn me of this prophecy. It reminded me of this, over and over, and I knew that it was my duty to not only prepare you but inform you as soon as I felt ready. The time has come to tell you. It is November, and this time is upon us. That is why we need to use this time crucially. Treat these days as your last vacation … and know that soon we will be going home."

We all went upstairs and our separate ways, people talking quietly or not at all. Damien and I had an unspoken agreement to come to my room.

I turned around to the sound of him shutting my door and saw what was underneath his arm.

"Well?"

"I don't know," I answered. "I have too many questions."

"Me too … this is just too messed up."

"It's obvious Mitchell is delusional," I declared. "The Mayan thing isn't true. There is just no way."

He sat in my desk chair, placing the box down and not looking at it.

"Do you think the others actually believe him?"

"Yeah," I said truthfully. "They will believe anything he says. We do too, sometimes … without really realizing it."

I walked over to the desk and put my hand on the box.

"I think we both know who to talk to."

His lips pursed, and I agreed that I didn't really want to do it, but I felt like we had to. We both took the box and sat it down as we always did, this time more delicately, carefully pulling the Ouija board out of its box like it was a live, delicate living thing.

Damien and I place our fingertips on the planchette.

"You … you go first," Damien muttered.

I took a deep breath.

"Is the spirit present one who ... died in the woods?"

The piece moved. *Yes.*

"And all of those spirits are here in The Manor?"

Yes.

"Is the world going to end on December 21st?"

Damien and I stared at the piece, our hands shaking above it, but it did not move. I tried again.

"Please tell us, is what Mitchell says true? Is the world going to end on December 21st?"

The piece slid around the board.

Maybe.

Damien and I sighed.

"What are we supposed to do?" I asked, shaking a little more.

Join us.

Before Damien and I could react, the piece started to move on its own again.

We are waiting.

Damien and I both stood up and walked out my door, but once we got to the hallway, we realized we could not go anywhere or do anything. We just threw our heads into our hands and paced, listening to our hearts throb. It became too much, and we both knew it.

"I'm done with this," Damien muttered.

I nodded. "It is no use."

After about a minute or so, we went back into my room and quietly approached the board on the floor. While we were outside, the piece had moved over to *Goodbye* and stayed there.

CHAPTER 29

Thanksgiving came, and Mitchell went to great lengths to remind us up until that day that it was going to be a big day. We were to have a big dinner, of course, and day and night activities with little free time. He told us we should think of it as a special day to be thankful for our lives on Earth. I only had time to call my mom at my grandparents' to wish everyone Happy Thanksgiving and answer the usual questions with I'm fine, and school is fine, and classes are fine, and such.

Damien and I put away the Ouija board, not consulting with it ever again. The spirits made their point clear, and from then on we needed to stay out of everyone's way— everyone's—if we were going to go through with a plan. It was starting to turn into an obsession. I couldn't shake the idea that leaving The Manor was going to be impossible.

"Thanks for putting that envelope back," I told Damien the next time I saw him.

"No problem," he answered. "You got it the first time and almost got caught. I ran in there before dinner like nothing happened."

"So…" I said, stating the obvious. "What's our other plan?"

"I don't know we have any?"

We sat in the kitchen putting away our tea cups before the first day's activity downstairs. People were around us, but not paying attention to what we were saying.

"It seems like Mitchell is keeping us all on a short leash," he muttered.

"You can say that again."

Of course, Mitchell always showed up when his name was mentioned.

"Come, my Lights!" announced Mitchell. He came out, greeting us in full GOL cloaks. "Put on your member cloaks now. As we take this day to be thankful, we can't forget to be thankful for who we are. Come into the Mess Hall!"

It was another poster project set up at all the tables, our member cloaks greeting us at the first table. Poster boards and buckets of colored pencils and markers waited as well, blank white and ready to make our visions come to life. Mitchell beamed at the front of the room as the masses trickled in.

"The next project we are going to do is a timeline of the most important milestones of your life. Start with the day you were born, of course, and fill in key milestones. Today, on Thanksgiving, we reflect on our lives and have to remember to be thankful for what we experienced and learned."

Mitchell's voice hung over all of our heads, and we took his words in. He certainly wanted us to believe so. He had a childlike joy that seemed to warm us all. I thought it might actually be a good idea to reflect on important milestones in my life ... even though some of them were not pleasant. I paused for a moment, wondering if I needed to include it. What I did was include it, but wrote how it caused me to turn inward and have more faith, have the desire for a stronger spirit. As instructed, the last thing to put on our poster timelines was joining GOL.

When we were done, we all went downstairs to the lower lounge to put them on the walls. They filled the walls like they were engulfing us, and we were surrounded by the lives that we have lived.

We had almost no free time on Thanksgiving, no surprise there, but after a while I forgot what bothered me so much earlier. The meal we had ... I couldn't even begin to describe it. It must have been two meals in one ... or maybe even all three. Mitchell and Carol went all out on this one. We had the traditional turkey and stuffing and mashed potatoes and green beans and more. It was massive.

The mess hall, already cleared of that afternoon's poster project, had been transformed into a grand banquet hall. Velvet, maroon tablecloths covered all the tables, the uneven parts hanging by the ground and covering the chair legs. They were all decked out with fancy table settings and silver wear, and even those fancy napkin holders that you only see on magazine covers. At the centerpiece of each table was, naturally, a candleholder hosting three sharp sticks of fire, looking like burning tridents.

The meal took our energy. Why wouldn't it? We feasted on turkey and wine and felt every morsel of food sliding through our bellies to find room. All along the table I could see the mellow—and yellow—faces glowing by dinner candles and the warmth of the meal.

"We are thankful for our Light," Mitchell toasted.

In unison, we all responded in one voice: "We are thankful for our Light."

And, in unison, we all lifted our glasses and drank that wine.

I woke up the next day feeling like I was floating on a cloud. I was very light-headed, and when I stepped down and my feet touched the floor, I was practically weightless. I barely felt the carpet under my walk as though I were walking on feathers. All I did was wipe my eyes as I made my way into the bathroom to brush my teeth.

Once I got downstairs, I realized the aftermath of our Thanksgiving feast didn't wear off. I didn't remember how much wine I had. I felt drugged. I stopped on the way down the staircase when I got a look at the window. It was grayish and smoky. Very smoky. There was a fog so high it reached the windows on the top floor.

I found Damien at the kitchen counter eating toast.

"Er..."

"I know."

It was the way he replied that made me sit down right away.

"Can you believe it?" he asked.

I could see the fog from the kitchen window, and the thing was, I couldn't even make out the trees through its thickness. Damien took a couple of looks over his shoulder before leaning in to me.

"I tried to leave The Manor," he started.

I felt his nerves and knew exactly that he meant he didn't make it very far.

"What happened?"

He muttered, "I couldn't."

"Why?"

"I wanted to get out today," he continued. "Just for a bit, just for a chance, and see if the rest of campus was up and running again. I felt like going to the coffee shop in the library for a breakfast sandwich, but I never made it past the fence. I couldn't see in front of me. I was lucky Iris saw me go out. She led me back in and told me it was too dangerous, that I couldn't go out. Who knows how lost I could have been?"

The fog was more than just weird. It had a presence, and it almost had a purpose. Was it surrounding us, making us float high above the world? Damien got up and got himself a mug for coffee.

"Want a cup?"

"Yeah," I said right away.

Damien fixed our mugs, cream and sugar and all, and put them at our places at the counter.

"Ah, crap," he said, looking at the coffee machine. "Anyone that uses the last of it before noon has to make a fresh pot."

I drank mine as he opened cabinets and drawers in the kitchen. As he got out a filter package, Iris strolled into the kitchen with wet hair fresh from a shower.

"Hi everyone," she said with a smile. "Careful not to go outside today. The fog is just way too thick."

As if we didn't know.

Damien looked up at her, then back down at the coffee filters and the bag of grounds. Iris and I both noticed how lost he looked.

"Need some help there, rookie?" asked Iris with a flirty smirk.

Damien only smiled sheepishly. "Yeah, you know, I had one of those Keurig things in my room with the little cups that is much easier—"

"Oh, don't worry about it."

She walked over right past me and set to helping Damien make more coffee; her backside brushed against his left leg and he started, trying to act like it was nothing. I drank my cup as she made a fresh brew.

"There ya go!" Iris proclaimed.

I leaned my head down as she left and kept it down until Damien sat down next to me.

"Sky? You okay?"

"I'm fine."

Our first gathering of the day started soon after. Everyone was comfortable in the lower lounge already as Carol fixed up the fireplace. High on the mantelpiece stood a Mayan calendar. I supposed Mitchell found one somewhere and thought it very necessary to sit there and stare at us all. It was the digital clock counting down to Judgment Day and our supposed doom. The fog that surrounded The Manor and the wooded area kept us packed in tightly. No one dared to go outside the house for fear of getting lost. You couldn't see your own feet outside. It just wasn't an option. I, of course, had my theory on the fog.

There were also two trays of banana bread on the table most of us had our eyes on.

"Don't let a little fog frighten you," Mitchell started. "Just think of it as The White Light's blanket of protection." He held a stack of napkins in his hand and passed them out, turning to the table to get a tray.

"Keep bringing leftover bananas from the caf' and you get homemade banana bread!" Mitchell said enthusiastically. "Smooth and moist with a little nut crunch."

Nuts. The ultimate bubble burster. I stole a look at Damien.

Mitchell passed the bread out to everyone and once Damien and I got ours, when the teacher wasn't looking, we stole looks again.

"What do you have?" I whispered.

"Chocolate ho-hos," he whispered back.

"Close your eyes while you are enjoying your treats," Mitchell instructed. He closed his eyes as well, while Damien quietly rummaged in his backpack. I swear, he always bought snacks from every vending machine in the school store. He was my own 7-11.

"Children, when The White Light appeared to me all those years ago, it gave me the vision of hope. The vision of The New Life and what's to come ahead. You've heard the expression 'there is light at the end of the tunnel.' Well, some like to say that light is actually the headlamp of an oncoming train ... if they were pessimists. But I say to you the real answer is that light symbolizes hope. It symbolizes the answer to all problems. You must follow the light to get out of the dark. The Light is waiting for us ... wants us to find it. Are we ready to accept the Light? Concentrate, concentrate on your Lights. Go towards the Light. Go towards it. Cast us out of the world of darkness. We are coming, White Light. Say it out loud."

"We are coming, White Light," we repeated.

I took a deep breath and relaxed, but really, I couldn't get anywhere. I didn't seem to see anything or feel anything special. When the meditation session was over, everyone got up and filed out of the lower lounge like soldiers, clearly still in touch with themselves and what they were able to reach that I somehow did not. It could have been that I had so much on my mind, I just could not relax. I went up the stairs like normal, but everyone else floated. They walked like they carried eggs on their heads ... like these eggs were a secret everyone knew about but me.

Almost everyone.

I found Damien at dinner early, alone, chin in his fists. His punctuality bugged me, but it was his stature that bugged me the most. He looked like The Thinker, and that was all he was doing, and his face said that he got nowhere so far.

"Damien?" I asked, sitting down.

"I still can't do it."

"Do what?"

"I can't ... concentrate. I think I am the only one whose ... spirit ... hasn't traveled yet."

I wouldn't have been more surprised if he levitated off the ground right then and there.

"What are you talking about?"

"Iris," he spat. "She told me I wasn't strong enough."

My jaw clenched, and I exclaimed before he was done talking.

"Why would she say that?"

"Because I wasn't tired after the meditation session. She came up to me with a disappointed look on her face and said I wasn't 'connecting.' It made me feel like a little kid."

"Okay," I said, finger-combing through my hair. "Well, I wasn't 'connecting' during that session, either. All I can think about is that fog and..."

My voice trailed off as I looked out the window.

"Did it get thicker?"

Damien looked in my direction and his look stayed there. The fog was so great it seeped through the windowsill and wood of the house.

"Maybe Iris knows about it."

"No, man! Seriously, what is with you? Do not ask her! She's a manipulator. She's probably possessed."

We heard some voices coming down the hall, and soon the others started trickling in for dinner. We were having, of course, turkey sandwiches.

I had some time the next day to do some exploring after we parted ways for free time ... and before Mitchell could put us in another group activity. I wasn't even sure there was going to be anything. The Manor was so quiet, the freezing fog outside was enough to keep everybody in and hidden. In my mind, I turned on all my senses. I thought that now I had a very keen sense, but even more so if I concentrated.

I need your help, I thought. *Guide me.*

I wasn't even sure if he could hear me. It bothered me that I was unable to see his spirit in a very long time, but I knew that beyond all that fog he still lingered, still watched over me. He probably knew all about the spirits of The Manor. Maybe it was he who tried to warn me. Either way, they were not letting him come any closer.

I passed the hallway leading to the lower lounge, the door slightly ajar. The angel statue turned away from me, its nose pointing directly down the stairs. I went down, expecting candles lining the stairs, but there were none, as there was no ceremony planned. The lower lounge was dark, a little chilly, and it surprised me no one was down there. Part of me felt uneasy, thinking I shouldn't go down there. I pressed on. I pressed on only because I heard the fireplace again.

It wheezed as usual, but I could have sworn it was also whispering. I reached the base of the stairs and tried to make it out. I didn't really hear words, but a human voice rushed in and out of the fireplace as effortless as wind. My legs pinched with cold, my socks stiff over numb toes as I walked downstairs. The Mayan calendar stared at me from the mantle, and the fireplace still huffed and puffed but did not blow down the poster board timelines from the walls. A whisper ran right past my left ear, forcing my head to turn towards the windows. Another past my right ear, turning my head again. I stared at both windows, back and forth, where both the fog and the frost worked together. Something was breathing on the windows.

The fog swirled against a mighty wind; the fireplace echoing it in a wheezy burst. I saw on the window the frost began to shift and the window cleared up, only to have fresh frost form against it. I heard voices fly by my ear, but I couldn't hear what they said. It didn't matter. The windows told me what they said.

In the fog and frost, I saw the letters swirl in cursive. First a D, then an E, and more and more. My head frantically turned at all the windows, reading the phrase as it repeated itself across the room.

DEATH IS THE ANSWER

DEATH IS THE ANSWER

DEATH IS THE ANSWER

Everywhere I turned, the phrase ran across the windows, like writing on the car window with your finger. Now I could hear it.

I went back upstairs casually and asked around if anyone saw Damien. I got mostly blank stares and shrugs. Seth was reading his braille device and Becky was helping Carol put away dishes, and no one really knew anything. The cold traveled from my legs to my heart as I rushed into the hallway to the residential floors. I had a feeling. You know the kind. When something inside you just knows that something is going on. I couldn't exactly explain how or why, but I felt that, and after seeing what happened downstairs, it was like it gave me the answer I wasn't looking for, but I thought I understood.

I ran by the hallway, soon coming up to the little library area. I paused when I saw him. I knew it was him since I recognized the back of his head, but there was something not quite right about him. Eerie, ghostlike, I saw the hair on the back of his head waving like he was swimming, like his body stood still and he was drowning in air. I moved closer, trying to see what he was looking at … if he was looking at anything at all. He moved slightly, his face turning towards me. I saw his eyes, and I knew that they saw me. They were alert and focused, but still dream-like.

"Damien," I said. "Go back to your body."

CHAPTER 30

nd he did.

He disappeared right in front of me; his entire being dissolved away among the bookcases. The last thing remaining was his eyes, still locked on mine. Then he was gone.

I remembered when I had my first out-of-body experience. I was in deep shock. I raced up the stairs.

He sat Indian style on his bed, his mouth agape and exhaling forcefully. I ran over and put my hand on his shoulder.

"Oh my God," he finally said. "That was ... incredible."

"That was your first, then..." I said.

"Yeah," he answered, looking at me. "I didn't really do it before now. I mean, I guess you could say I did before when we did meditations ... but this was all me without help. I could see everything and I could feel everything."

His eyes stayed wide open. "You saw me."

"Of course I did. I was looking for you. There is something I need to tell you."

"I felt so powerful. Like I could do anything and go anywhere. I never felt like that—"

"Damien."

"—Before and you know what? Iris helped me. She helped me do this. She made me realize my potential."

"*Damien*," I snapped. "This is great, it is, but I really need you to focus right now. The spirits gave me a message."

"They did?" he asked, unfolding his legs and letting them hang over his bed. "What? What happened?"

"They communicated with me. On the lower lounge windows. They wrote 'death is the answer' all over the window fog and frost."

Damien only answered with his face.

"Just now," I continued, pointing towards the door. "Just as I went down there. 'Death is the answer.' Everywhere. I saw it and I even heard it whispered from the fireplace. That was their message."

He looked at me. "So ... do you think they want to kill us?"

I sat down next to him. "No, not really, but I do think they believe the world is going to end on December 21st."

Damien nodded. "Yeah, moving on to The Next Life. That's all Iris ever talks about."

"What does she say?" I demanded. "What did you get out of her? When were you with her, anyway?"

He held up his hands in defense. "Whoa, it's okay. She helped my spirit go free, remember? I meditated with her and then I went to my room to try it again on my own. All she said was only the strongest spirits could go to The Next Life after time on Earth ended, and she wanted to be sure I went with. She wants me to be strong."

"Okay ... anything else?"

"No. I don't know anything else. Do you think I should hang out with her more, to try to find out?"

"No," I said. "We don't want her to get suspicious. She's probably working for the spirits, remember?"

Damien sighed. "So what does this all mean now? I am strong, I know I am, but are we strong enough?"

"Well," I admitted. "I don't know. We don't know, do we? I mean, do you really think the world is going to end in a month?"

"I ... I don't think so," he answered, although with a bit of hesitation. "I mean, do you think ... do you think we could make it happen?"

"That is what I thought," I said. "If we were capable of a tornado, then that means we are probably capable of other things ... this is completely crazy, but I think that has been at the back of our minds this whole time."

"Or it is just a prophecy Mitchell believes in."

"Or that, but again, we don't know."

"So what do we do?"

I looked at him.

"Well, I guess, nothing. Nothing. Think about it. If nothing happens on December 21st, then nothing happens."

We did think about it, even though we both knew it to be completely insane.

"Sky," Damien said. "Everyone believes it *so much*. Iris had me convinced today that it is going to happen and we are going to die—and we are all going to go to another planet and spend eternity there. Like we're the chosen ones or something."

"I know. They all do! Even Becky. Especially Becky. But, we can't show any signs we're against it or *any* rebel. Look what they did to her and Seth! The spirits know whenever someone does!"

He shifted uncomfortably. "So we wait it out?"

I looked outside the window in the room, still with hard frosted lines on the edges and fog clouding the outside view.

"We play along," I said, nodding. "Until a time comes when we can report Mitchell and this group to the school."

"Do you think they'll believe us?"

"About brainwashing students about death? Yeah, I would think so."

Damien swallowed. "Look, how about if I try to find out more from Iris? Like, she and some others are close with Mitchell. They're his trusty sidekicks or something. Maybe she can give me some evidence."

I couldn't look at him when he said this, instead stared solemnly at the cracked window frost, so detailed it could have been spray paint.

"Yeah, okay," I finally said. "You do that. I've got other plans. When other people are back on campus, while everyone is occupied, I am going to see who is around. Authority wise."

He winced. "Be careful. Mitchell doesn't want anyone to leave."

I almost smirked. "Oh, I know."

We both heard the shuffling outside the door, followed by tapping. Moments later, the door, still slightly ajar, opened and Seth's inquisitive face poked in.

"Hello, Damien? Sky?"

"Hi Seth," I said casually.

He smiled, his opaque eyes seeming to as well.

"What are you guys up to?"

"Nothing really," Damien replied almost instantly. "I was just telling her about my first out-of-body experience!"

"You had your first?" asked Seth enthusiastically.

"I did. It was the most amazing thing I've ever experienced! I really was in touch with myself and I saw the Light."

Seth's smile got bigger.

"I see the Light every day."

We were all silent, as I knew how sincere that was.

"Come on, you two," Seth said. "Game time downstairs."

After the game, which was a big game of Blind Man's Bluff, I thought it would be a good time to try to go outside. Seth, for some reason, was expected to have a leg up on the game as he was a pro now. He was—actually finding others with ease and especially finding me. I found out afterward in the hallway that Seth sought me out on purpose.

I was in the middle of putting my coat and scarf on, my keys jingling, ready with the excuse to go check my campus mailbox if anyone asked me. Sure enough, Seth passed by in the kitchen area carrying Ad Astra's food dish.

"Be careful," he said in my direction.

My hands tangled in my scarf. "Oh, well, maybe the fog's cleared up a bit."

"It might be so, Sky. But where are you going?"

"Check my mailbox," I rehearsed.

"I don't think that will be possible. Be careful."

"I will," I answered.

Opening the front door for the first time in a week felt wrong, like it was something I should not be doing. Sure enough, the door opened up to fog, fog, and more fog. I saw the path down the sidewalk and the trees in the distance and foreground, but barely. I shut the door behind me. Our solar lamps were barely alive, the faintest glow existing in their protective lanterns. They were holding out the best they could with the days and days of little to no sunlight. They were all I had to rely on.

Arms out in front of me, I descended the path. I felt the fog all around me, thick but permeable, as soft as spider webs, but I couldn't rely on what I barely felt in front of me. Instead, I relied on every stone I kicked over and every stiff, cold leaf that crunched under my shoes. It was as though the world was on mute, or that the fog traveled in my ears and turned my hearing down. I tried to concentrate on where I was going and trying to make out the path in front of me. I knew as soon as I got to the end of the dim solar lamps that I was on my own. Nothing but gray. I could barely make out the trees next to me. The atmosphere had grown thicker deeper in the woods, and as much as I frantically tried to wave it away, it stayed.

A cold gust breezed past my face. I pulled my scarf up to my nose as it repeated. This wind was so strong it set me back a little, and even as I fumbled through with my scarf ends flapping behind, I still had to catch my balance. I barely took two more steps before the wind started up again. This time, it was stronger. It was also louder, and as the wind hit me again, I heard the whistling run past my head and tingle my ears. My feet lifted—almost floated—off the ground, and I went almost a foot back. I almost cried out before I felt the ground again.

I stood still in my place, the woods quiet again. I took a few more spaces forward before the wind threw me back again, and again, my arms covering up my face. Every blow was a sting to my face and I could barely bear it. The gusts became stronger, sending me back down the path, my shoes kicking stones with me until I completely fell over on my back.

I stood up and tried to see—no, really, tried to see. Nothing was there but the fog, and the wind only blew each time I tried to walk. I got up in a half-trot only to make it not make it far at all. The next gust of wind hit me dead on, a powerful blast where I fought to keep my balance. I reached my hands out and pushed against it. The harder it pushed me, the harder I pushed back, but I was no match. The wind burst almost right through me. I couldn't take any more steps. I would lift a foot off the ground in a mid-step, only to be knocked over again. It blew me over onto my back. This time, when I got up, I turned around and walked. The woods were quiet again on my way back. Not even a gentle breeze.

CHAPTER 31

Kimberly came downstairs just as I thought to make some tea and try to relax.

"Hey," she said. "Mitchell wants to have a meeting later. He says it will be important, and we should all rest up."

She left to go play messenger to the rest of the house. I didn't even bother looking out the window that day, knowing there was nothing I could see.

We got downstairs and Mitchell was wearing a cloak. We were taken aback for a minute, because it wasn't his usual black GOL cloak. It was crisp white. He looked like a priest, or a ghost, or a ghostly priest.

"My Lights," he started, almost as monotone and robotic as a priest. "My Lights, I hope you all got adequate rest this week. It is important for you to have a rested mind and spirit. Today is Sunday, and it is officially the end of Thanksgiving Break and the end of our retreat. Tomorrow we resume classes."

A breeze whistled outside and Mitchell paused for a moment.

"The White Light appeared to me again in a dream," he continued, squeezing his eyes shut. "It said to me that the hour is upon us, and I know this, we know this, but we must start to prepare. Today is November twenty-fifth. We have twenty-six days. Got that? *Twenty-six days.* We will finish off the retreat, and this day, with another vow of silence. And also, during this time, we must learn to devalue material possessions. For when we leave Earth, once it ends, we cannot take them with us. We will not have the use of cell phones where we are going. Therefore..." Mitchell looked over at Seth, who Frankenstein-walked from the lounge stairs to Mitchell carrying a large wicker basket.

"Therefore," Mitchell continued. "You will all leave your cell phones here before you go back upstairs."

Several protested. Some even tried to stand up, but either thought the better of it or felt they couldn't.

"Silence, please."

Everyone stood still, although we were all filled with confusion and fury.

"You will leave them here. If you do not have them with you, you will get it and put it in this basket. You must learn not to rely on material possessions. You can't take it with you. You all must learn this."

And that was that. There was no more arguing. What Mitchell says, goes. I wondered just how long he would keep our phones for. Forever? Longer? Until after this December 21st Doomsday was over? What will happen after that? One by one we went up there and surrendered our cell phones to Mitchell, smiling gently, and Seth, not reacting at all. We were motioned to go upstairs, understanding that we were not to speak after this. Another day of no communication. My insides boiled, and I sweated steam. I couldn't talk to Damien. I couldn't tell him that now I had a worse feeling about Mitchell's intentions. I couldn't talk to him about anything at all. Now we couldn't even text with our heads craned in our laps during dinner like we've done so before.

We were ushered upstairs in silence, Mitchell gesturing to each one of us. Seth and the basket followed up the stairs and then stationed at the base of the residential hallway staircase. I saw more people come back from their rooms and reluctantly drop their phones in the basket, the black and silver devices making protesting clicking noises as they hit one another.

All the GOL members scattered, meant to privately reflect and journal and whatever else we were supposed to do. I couldn't concentrate. I apparently was one of the only ones still angry. Everyone else seemed to puppet-walk to their rooms submissively. I carried myself to the stairs, only because I felt forces behind me almost making me go. I struggled to think, but any and all thoughts I had were leaking out of my head and floating away. What were they? I looked up at the wooden log ceiling of The Manor to see if I could see and rescue them. Who was taking my thoughts away? So many of them were leaving my head I was starting to feel a little dizzy. I managed to make it to my room and sit on my bed. Meditation seemed like the best and only option. It had to be the thing that could get my head on straight. Easily, and almost instantly, I was taken away.

One exhale was all it took. The next thing I knew, I was floating back across green spiked fields and noisy waterfalls. I could see the masses now. We were all here together. I couldn't see them too well. I couldn't make out faces, but I knew they were there. I could feel them, too, as they brushed against me as light as spider webs, but enough to make me feel it. Enough to make me want to scratch that tiny itch. I took a breath in but did not get a chance to breathe out. Instead, those chilly spider webs got sucked down my throat. I almost gagged; I tried to gag, but, for some reason, my body let it happen as though it were normal. I drank a spirit. It froze my esophagus and stomach. I couldn't cough or make a sound. It scared me, but I also felt very peaceful. I did not know what was happening and why.

Soon I woke up. My eyes snapped open, and I was back in my room. We took the vow of silence, but this time, the vow of silence took us. I couldn't clear my throat, or cough, or even whisper...

All communication was cut off. I got off my bed to go downstairs. Everyone filtered out as apathetic as zombies, only slightly acknowledging each other. I tried to find someone—anyone—who could and would communicate. Just one look, just one glance to let me know they were in control on the inside ... but no one did this.

The day just dragged on. It was so dreamlike I could have still been in meditation. I'd open my mouth to eat, or just open it from time to time, my insides screaming out for noise and no sound forming. At one point, I did see Damien, but he barely looked at me. In fact, when he looked at me at dinner, I could have sworn his eyes were trying to tell me something. Even worse, I could tell that something was holding him back. He kept his head down like the rest of them. The only sounds we heard were the scraping of forks and knives and the spa music Mitchell kept on.

There was no one I could talk to. Not really, anyway. I thought if anything, I could try to find my dad. I tried to cough, my insides heaving, but I was still completely mute. "Where are you?" I mouthed. "Talk to me. Talk to me now."

After dinner, we were to go to our rooms to do private journaling. All Mitchell did at dinner to tell us this was stand up, motion to the crowd, and hold up a journal. He pointed upstairs and, smiling, held a finger over his lips. We filtered upstairs, and it wasn't until I got to my room that my head cleared a little bit, forming an idea of my own.

I sat down on my bed with a spiral notebook, the kind you could tear out. This part was important, as my words were not going to be private. I flipped open a blank page and began to write as though Damien were sitting right across from me, watching me with his soft and curious eyes and following everything I was saying:

> We are not going to be controlled! I don't care what Mitchell says, or whatever made up higher power says, or whatever else the spirits that haunt this place do. This cannot go on any longer! People are going to get hurt or worse, and I don't think it is a good idea for us to stick around to find out what they believe is going to happen on December 21st ... or what they are planning to make happen on December 21st. You and I are the only ones who are truly strong here, and we are strong enough to get out of here and send a different kind of message. This group is dangerous, they have dangerous abilities and are in touch with some things that should not be messed with. The school needs to know the destructive things Mitchell has been doing to control us and mess with our minds. The first chance we get, we are going to sneak the hell out of here while everyone is asleep and get to someone who can help immediately. When this day is over, and we can get our voices back, come to my room at night so we can put together a plan. We are getting out of here...

I sat back from my journal and read everything I wrote, and felt instantly rejuvenated. Now, all I had to do was get this note to Damien.

I got up and ripped that paper from its metal coils; actually, I ripped it along the dotted line as to not disturb the coils and come out smoothly. Then I folded that paper delicately so that it fit in my hoodie pocket and could easily be concealed. My next job was a simple one: Go to Damien's room for delivery, and probably some hand-written chatting.

There was only one problem: Damien was missing from his room.

I only knocked twice before I let myself in and stared at his empty, neatly made bed. I would have to wander the halls in search of him and now pass him my note without anyone seeing. Chills shot up my legs. How could I do that without anyone seeing? Especially if he wasn't alone? I did not want anyone to see that note ... I had to be extremely careful.

I went downstairs to get a glass of water, even though I really wasn't that thirsty. As I thought, the place was empty. I stalled, taking a couple more sips before finally deciding to brave the lower lounge ... going down there alone became a bad idea. I only felt better once I saw that I would not be alone. Ad Astra sat at the top of the stairs. She appeared to be very casual and blinked her eyes at me casually as I approached. The angel statue's head faced me, acknowledging me with its innocent marble face. I bent down to pet the cat, her purring as soft as her fur, listening carefully to the downstairs. The wind whistled in and out of the fireplace, heavy winds in the lungs of the chimney ... almost muffling out a quiet shuffling. Ad Astra turned her head instantly, her ears giving a little twitch. I jerked my head behind me to make sure no one was watching or even caring what I was doing. When I looked back to the stairway, I saw the statue's head was now turned in that direction. I stood up and went down.

The evening dusk spread an orange and pink glow on the lounge carpet and made it look as though there were a fire burning in the fireplace. I peered at the floor from the stairs. I could feel a strong gravitational pull from the fireplace as it wheezed in and out. The cat sat perched on one of the stairs, her ears twitching, keeping an eye out for me as I walked downstairs.

I knew it wasn't strong winds from outside breathing in and out of that fireplace. They only got stronger and louder as I approached. I stood still, captivated by the fireplace, but also recognizing some danger. I stayed back far enough to watch it, as somehow I knew something was about to happen. The next breath the fireplace took blew my hair and clothes in whiplash. I shielded my face and ran back to the steps. It continued to wheeze—now the wind was stronger in its lungs—as it helped a folded piece of paper move along the floor.

I held on to the banister while searching my pockets, confirming that thought to be true. I ran up as far as I could go, still obligated to watch the scene before me. The paper on the floor rolled in the wind. I watched and listened as the fireplace's breath brought it in closer with every inhale. The paper skidded along; possibly unaware it was going to be sucked in. One final gust of air brought that note all the way in its open jaws, and once it had its prey, I heard a loud crunching sound with the wind swirling all around it. Ad Astra hissed and ran up the stairs, and I did not wait to join her.

CHAPTER 32

No, I didn't see Damien that night. I just ran back to my room and shut the door, shutting out everyone and everything else.

I did check out the fireplace the next day. I was curious, after all, even though I was still slightly terrified. I didn't have much time before classes resumed, but it was almost like I was looking for proof that actually happened. There were ashes all right, but that could have been from the last fire. There were no traces whatsoever that a flimsy one sheet of notebook paper had burned in there ... if it burned at all. The fireplace was quiet that way, no doubt its appetite satisfied. Whoever had been watching apparently decided I wouldn't be talking to anyone. My note was destroyed, but the vow of silence day ended and we all could get back to normal. Sort of. I did not even consider following through with my plan since that had happened, knowing perfectly well that if I even attempted something, I might be the next thing to burn in that fireplace.

My stomach was in knots. My brain was in slush, and I could only go about my everyday routine in safety. On my way to class, one of the other girls ran up to me.

"I hear we're not getting our phones back ... at all."

"That's ridiculous," I replied. "That is just wrong."

"Well, that's what Kimberly said today. I heard her telling some of the others. They were pissed, but she didn't even seem to care."

"He can't do that," I tried again.

"Well, I guess he can. Kimberly said that we need to get used to it where we're going."

"We're not *going* anywhere!" I practically cried.

She shrugged, her expression making my stomach sink. "I don't know..."

I made it to class, ready to huff and puff and blow it down. I knew we were giving up our phones for the vow of silence day, but I expected we would be getting back our personal property at some point. This needed to stop. Once Mitchell's class finally arrived, I saw my opportunity.

"Mitchell," I approached him right away as I was one of the first students to arrive, anyway.

"Yes Sky, what is it?"

"You took our phones for good? You're not going to give them back?"

"Patience, my child," was his answer. "What good will it do you? You may find it hard now, but it will be for the best. It will be."

We got the power of speech back, but I was speechless. Other students began to trail in as Mitchell went on.

"This will build character and show strength. We all need willpower. We all need to prove that we are better than technology and material possessions. It is just a test of strength."

I didn't feel like he was reassuring me. I felt like he was reprimanding me, like I just got caught passing notes in class and he was calling me out on it in front of the whole class. What was his deal?

"Sky, you know better than to doubt The White Light. It knows what is best for us. It knows everything. You will see. Sit down now, my child."

And I did, being the obedient monkey I was. I suddenly thought that because of me, now Mitchell was going to have another one of his heavy recruitment classes.

"Everyone, I want to give you all an experiment," he started, and I felt like sinking lower in my seat. "You will all go a week without technology and write a journal of what changed in your life. No phone calls, internet, television, video games..."

"Mitchell, what about homework? We can't do homework if we can't check emails and type up papers, or practically anything," spoke up one student, and I cringed like someone just challenged God.

"You will use it for school work, yes. I am talking about personal reasons and leisure. This will be a social test."

The people in my class were more outraged than the GOL members at The Manor, but that was expected. It was also expected that Mitchell had more flyers to hand out.

"Consider joining us if you want to see what it's like to live in peace."

I was glad to get out of that class to avoid the strange looks. Anytime Mitchell said something weird, or anything GOL related, people avoided talking to me. I was almost used to it by now. Getting back to The Manor actually made me feel ... happy. Not content since I was done with classes at the end of the day, but happy like I was coming home from a place I did not belong. Even though we spent a week there without leaving, going back to classes almost made me feel homesick. I opened the front door and stomped off the snow clumps from my boots, not quite winter-friendly and already leaving gray stains on black suede. Some people were doing homework at the table and sofas. I noticed Becky at the table working on a drawing. I sat down by her, at once noticing the couple layers of paper under her as she drew.

"What's all this?" I asked.

She looked up at me from making strokes with a colored pencil. The drawings she had were all remotely the same. I recognized the wide green fields and splotches of mountains instantly, deeply shaded and multicolored. She had drawings of that same waterfall we have all seen and all been to, but there was something else that was not ... something that touched the very bottom of my gut. Becky had the gray pencil as she outlined them again, those long arms and legs and egg-round shaped heads.

Before I could stop myself, I blurted out, "Are those aliens?"

Becky looked at me and smiled, sort of shrugged, then pointed to herself and to me and back to the picture.

"Do you see them in the visions?" I asked.

Becky pointed to them and to us again, steady and delicate, like this girl will always just be recovering from a lobotomy. Her finger circled in the air counterclockwise and then I got it. Our future selves. Great.

"Oh ... kay," was all I said. "Um, have you seen Damien?"

She nodded and pointed above her head. It was the best news I got all day.

I barely knocked on his door. He was at his desk doing homework. Or pretending to.

"Dude."

"Oh, hey."

He swirled his desk chair to face me, and I noticed the Word application he had open was completely blank.

"So, obviously, we couldn't talk yesterday."

"Or text."

"Or text. I can't believe Mitchell just took our phones like he owns them."

"He says we will get them back."

"Right. Whatever. He is just trying to control us."

"No, I don't think so. Don't say that."

I just shook my head.

"So," I said, changing the subject. "I was just downstairs, and I saw Becky drawing. Her pictures are all the same."

"I've seen them," Damien replied. "They keep popping up all over the place."

"Well. I had the thought that that's what people think we are going to be ... next."

He seemed to think carefully about it, but brush it off a little.

"Yeah, that could be."

I jerked my head a little. "Damien. Did you hear me? Becky—and probably the others—got the idea in their heads that when we die, we're going to go be aliens on another planet."

"Of course, Sky," was his surprising answer. "It's kind of awesome if you think about it. Isn't it? A next life?"

"I don't know," I replied. "Honestly, I don't know what to believe anymore. I keep trying so hard to find the truth, and each time I think I'm getting closer to it, it drifts further away."

"You just have to have faith. They have the answers! Mitchell trusts The White Light, and so do we. They have plans for us. The spirits are on our side."

I felt that same brush at the bottom of my gut.

"Guess what?"

"What?"

"I wrote you a note the other night about ... everything that has been going on, and trying to come up with a plan. I was walking around looking for you, and then I went down to the lower lounge and the fireplace was possessed again. It kept huffing and puffing and then it actually sucked the note out of my pocket and it burned in the fireplace."

He just stared at me.

"The fireplace ate my note. On purpose."

"They didn't like what you wrote."

"Um, no," I said, shuddering a little. "I guess they did not."

Damien didn't say anything else. He stared at a spot on the carpet.

"We have to come up with something. I don't know what else to do," I blurted out. "We better figure it out fast, and if the world is going to end on December 21st, or if we're all going to *make* the world end on December 21st, then we have to figure out how to stop them and fast, otherwise, we'll all be dead. Or, something else will happen and I don't know and don't want to know what that will be. What are some of the others saying? Do you know? Did you hear anything? Did Iris say anything?"

Damien was still staring at the spot on the floor, eyes tied down without a twitch.

"Damien."

Not a blink.

"Damien!"

He jerked up and looked at me.

"Sorry," he said bashfully. "I sort of zoned out. I was thinking."

Whatever he was thinking about, it had turned his cheeks pink.

CHAPTER 33

Our next meeting was necessary, very necessary, as the clock on the mantle ticked and the countdown to Doomsday went down. The students moved both in obedience and in fear. Mitchell gathered us all downstairs for another session.

"You are doing this for yourselves," he began. "But you are also doing it for your families."

He paced the room, his cloak dragging along the floor, or so it seemed. It could not have been touching the floor at all.

"Your families do not know what the stars have in plan for us. They do not know the presence of The White Light. They have not been educated, but you have. You have, and it is up to you to guide them. You have to show your families how strong you are now, for the New World will need leaders like us once Earth is finished. Only the strong will move forward, and only the strong will survive."

The fireplace behind him wheezed, shooting out bits of ash here and there. Mitchell at once stopped and spread his arms.

"My children ... The White Light and its followers are with me. They know and understand our faith, but they also know and understand our lack of faith. Who among us does not believe? Who among us does not have faith? The White Light needs our faith."

Suddenly, his cloaks fluttered behind him, and once I looked at his face, I had to lean forward. There was something wrong with his eyes. They were stone hard and dilated, and there was also something familiar about them. He cast his look at all of us, and once his sight beam hit me, I knew exactly where I had seen them before: in his office in one of the pictures on his desk. The eyes stared at me then and they stared at me now. Fresh beams of light to outshine any sun.

Mitchell's arms continued to rise and his eyes opened wider, and before anyone could make a sound, our teacher floated above the floor. There were some gasps and cries as our leader levitated, his arms out and his cloak fluttering all around him. I recognized this phenomenon from the first time I saw it, and the first time I truly saw the power behind this group. The minute we could all see his feet pointed towards the ground, everyone became silent and still. It seemed even Seth knew what was happening, craning his head upwards and smiling. We watched Mitchell drift towards the ceiling; the wind started to pick up in the room. Our hair blew around our faces, the fireplace whistled, the pages in books in the room opened and flipped uncontrollably. The wind blew around the room, but we stayed in our places. We were secure in our places, our bodies the paper weights, watching our leader rise up all the way to the ceiling ... and then gracefully come back down again.

The wind stopped; the curtains and drapes relaxing back against the windows. Mitchell's cloak softly swirled down and hugged his sides. He lowered his head to the room, his eyes still piercing beams.

"Have faith, my Lights. Have faith."

The room touched us, all of us, and made our skin prickly. If anyone, anyone at all, had even an inkling of disbelief, it was now gone. The Guardians of Light exhaled as one, marveling at the figure at the front of the room, which now possessed some sort of power ... or was simply possessed. He smiled at us, looking at us all as though we really were his own children ... or his prey.

"My children, go on now and do some private reflecting. We will meet again for dinner later tonight. Go on now. Keep your Lights focused. The clock ticks."

In my room, I couldn't think of anything to do. I remembered Mitchell's eyes, both the time I saw them in the picture frame and just now in the lower lounge. He had a new power in him. He might even be the guardian of a spirit right now ... sent in to watch over us in the weeks to come. Sent in to keep a very close eye on us to make sure we did what we were supposed to do. I shuddered, realizing what I just thought. I just referred to Mitchell's body as a "guardian."

Dinner was mostly quiet. I was ushered in with the rest of the herd and just sat down; recognizing that this dinner was meant to be reflective instead of social. I mostly ate with my head down, fearful to meet any piercing glance, as if it could see right through me. At one point, I looked up to try to see where Damien was and if we could communicate via looks. It was no surprise to see that Iris had pulled him next to her at her table, and that was where he stayed, like an obedient puppy. I saw her whisper in his ear; he nodded quickly and took a sip of water, not saying anything else. I think I chewed the same piece of food for twenty minutes until it just dissolved itself in my mouth and I had nothing left to take my energy out on. Whatever she wanted with him, it had to stop.

No one was expecting to play any more games tonight. We were to have another sort of activity immediately after dinner. Mitchell sent us all downstairs in silence, instructing us to take a candle from a box and then take a seat on the floor cushions.

We lined up, toes to heels. When we all took candles from the last mess hall table, we held them in our right hands, connected in our own chain link. The angel statue greeted us before the lounge stairway, face turned upwards to the ceiling. No one dared to follow its glance. No one did anything else except sit down on the floor as we were instructed. Soon the upperclassmen came down with Mitchell taking up the rear. He was radiant; he was holy ... he was still under some influence. We could all see it, but most importantly, we could all feel it. Waves of recognition washed over us, but they were also waves of understanding and belief. Mitchell looked around at all of us and we saw it in his eyes. He had the power within him. What he had was real.

Mitchell's candle was the only one that was lit. In unison, we all held our flameless wick sticks in the air as a greeting.

"Good evening, my children."

"Good evening, Mitchell." Our voices sounded as melodious as a chorus. Nothing was going to take our attention away from him. It was our own little miracle.

"My children, my Lights ... the White Light within me knows we are strong. I have allowed it access to my own body so that it can become closer to us. I am the Guardian of the White Light, and now it wants to spread its power to all of us. We will all light our candles and pass it around so we all share the same flame."

Mitchell's candle flame was taller than it should be, and much lighter. It was not the usual yellow spark a flame would have, but rather it was almost a white, or a yellow so pale it could pass as white. Gently, he glided from the front of the room to the upperclassmen seated in the front row. One by one we touched wicks until we all had burning candles, all growing fires to almost the length of a finger. These flames barely moved, barely had a flicker here and there, but it held us in hypnosis. I stared at mine in awe, or fear, or a combination of both. I could make out something in the flame. Something almost ... human. Inside the flame itself, I could almost see the figure of a human ... or something that used to be human. Its body swirled in fire and opened its arms to me like in a warm embrace. I held my candle tightly, marveling at this power and this miracle. I knew that all the students now had the same burning flame once it changed again. All the candles turned the same whitish color that Mitchell held and suddenly cast a brighter light in the lounge room. The power was speaking to us, and we knew what it said. It was with us and we were one. It was real. We belonged to it.

The rituals that took place captured my attention, of course, but you could also say it was distracting. I forgot about my cell phone for a couple of days and found that I didn't care. I could not even tell you what we did in the next couple of days. It really was that uneventful; all of us moved forward in our everyday routines on autopilot and did not care. We carried ourselves egotistically. Everyone's noses turned up a bit snobbishly, for we all thought and knew that we were the Chosen Ones.

Mitchell pushed for more recruits. We were to hand out flyers and post them at random points on campus again. This time, our flyers had a picture of the Mayan calendar with the December 21st date and a message: "Join us to BE SAVED! Guardians of Light will lead you out of darkness!" We were given stacks before leaving for classes and were expected to come home empty-handed. Mitchell looked at us longingly as we would leave for classes, working to guilt-trip us … to make us feel ashamed if we did not do our part to spread the word. I managed to put up as many as possible, the back of my neck turning hot at all the stares I got from passing students. I even heard a muffled laugh or two as they read it and passed me. How were we to recruit other students if they didn't understand? How were we to make them understand our message if they were being judgmental and refused to be open-minded? At one point, standing by a bulletin board outside my classroom, I took a moment to really read the flyer. It was informative, and it was interesting. I could not understand. What was so wrong with it? I got back home to The Manor after classes, empty of flyers, hoping it would make Mitchell happy. I could tell a white lie and tell him some students were even reading it, but I would leave out the part of them giggling and walking away. Would he see that I did what I was supposed to do?

The first thing I did was check my emails, and my heart fluttered a little to see a couple from my mom and sister that I didn't get a chance to answer. I opened the most recent one quickly:

> Hey Sky! I haven't heard from you in such a long time! Did your cell phone run out of juice? I tried calling you and texting you and you never responded! Is everything all right? Please contact

me as soon as you can, so I know you're all right. You must be really busy with classes and such. I would be nice to hear from you once in a while though! How was your Thanksgiving?

Love, Mom.

I hit "reply" immediately.

Hey Mom! So sorry I couldn't call you back! We are actually having trouble with signal out here. My phone isn't working right now. I am going to look into getting this fixed. Maybe it's a network thing. Who knows? Thanksgiving was great! We all had a nice relaxing time, and it was so much fun! Classes are good. I am at a 3.5 average, which is all right, but I know I can do better! Write back soon!

Love, me.

I sat back and read it a couple of times, cringing at my stupid lie. What was I supposed to do? Tell the insane truth?

A knock at my door startled me. I hit my leg against my desk as Damien leaned in my doorway.

"Hi, what's up?"

"Nothing," I said, turning around. "Just emailing my mom back ... because you know, I can't call her."

Something dark passed over Damien's face and I knew it was the same thought I had.

"My family's been emailing me too," he admitted. "Asking me why I haven't returned calls and stuff. I didn't know what to say at first. I just said I was really busy and I would call them as soon as I got the chance. I felt horrible, you know? I never lie to my parents about that. This is so stupid. I feel like I can't tell them what's going on over here."

"Me neither. I feel like it would be wrong, like I would feel ashamed of myself or something. I just told my mom we had a network problem."

Damien shook his head.

"God, this is really messed up," I said, prompting him to say something.

He just looked at the floor, not sure what to say.

"We have to be strong, Sky. We have to be."

"I don't like lying so much. I'm worried that they want us to cut off all communication with everyone and it is freaking me out. We have to get our phones back."

"We probably will. We just have to pretend like we don't care."

"I was thinking of sneaking into Mitchell's office again. This has gone far enough. But I'm afraid he would … you know…"

"Catch us? Punish us?"

"Well, yeah. Especially now. Especially now that he's possessed." I shuddered. "That along is enough to give anyone the creeps. We don't know what sort of power he has now."

"Do you believe in it?"

"Yeah. I do. And I think that's exactly what scares me."

Damien and I sat by each other at dinner, to my joy and relief. It was pleasant and relaxing until I saw Iris from across the hall scowl at us. My stomach jumped at seeing the look on her face. I kept my head down and ate and slightly turned my face to him.

"What's with Iris?"

He didn't look. "She's probably just jealous. I don't know. Maybe she has a crush on me or something. I don't know. Don't think anything of it."

We stuck together after dinner and during our next group activity. This time, it made us all stiffen cold with fear. We didn't even need Mitchell to tell us anything. We passed the angel statue going downstairs; the head turned downward, but its gaze was not looking at anything. It was a very dismissive pose ... its carved eyes were now shut. I wondered if anyone knew it once had open eyes. Either way, we all opened ours just a bit wider as we descended the stairs and felt the chills run up and down our bodies.

Mitchell waited for us with a large poster board at the front of the room. It sat on a stand, but it was blank. Mitchell watched us all, his skin so pale and blemish-free it looked like all the blood had drained from his face. He looked on at us and seemed to speak with his eyes. Hello my children, please come in, look at all of you, I am so proud of you. He did not say these words, yet they formed in my head. We took our seats and looked up at him patiently.

"Tonight," Mitchell began. "The White Light wants more from us. It wants ... unison. We shall have a special kind of ceremony tonight. It is not lighting candles or meditating. Tonight we prove our loyalty towards The White Light in the most serious and dedicated way possible. The White Light wants a life sample, a life sacrifice. Tonight we will give it our blood."

Some people looked at one another, but we somehow knew there was nothing to fear. This was Mitchell, our fearless leader. Our lives were in his hands and we trusted him. We were not scared when he said this to us, and we were not scared when he brought out a tiny box of needles.

"On this board behind me, we will all give The White Light a couple of droplets of our blood. It is the symbol of the life we have right now, knowing we make the best of being human while we still can, and still are. It will also symbolize that we are one, we are together. We do this in its name."

Mitchell demonstrated, carefully poking his index finger and discarding the needle in the trash. He pressed his finger to the board until he painted a single stroke of deep red. "I give you human life," he said, ending it with a hard smear. One by one, we were to do the same. We were given a needle. We pricked our fingers and blotted, dripped, smeared and wiped our own personal marks on that board. I got up and did it quickly on my turn, taking a Band-Aid like the others before me once I was finished. As I was fastening the Band-Aid, I noticed that Mitchell did not take one. He instead let the tiny bloodstream flow down his finger and rest in the crevice of his nail. He moved his thumb around in it as though he enjoyed playing with it.

The board was hung up on the wall and was to be left alone. It was a strange piece of art with its crude red strokes, looking like tiny dead rose petals. As time passed, I knew those red strokes would turn brown and rust with age, and if anyone was to see it, they would have no clue what it was.

The rest of the evening was uneventful ... except for when I walked to the kitchen for a drink and saw Damien and Iris on the couch. They were huddled together talking intensively, and I couldn't tell what was going on until I got closer. My feet came to an abrupt halt, and I nearly collided with the cat—realizing they were not doing any talking at all. Iris moved her mouth around his chin and made her way down his neck passionately.

CHAPTER 34

The sun leaked through my blankets the next morning, which were still over my head. I stared at the individual lines and ridges in my pillowcase, the tiny lint balls on my sweatshirt, the freckles on my arms, and the folds and creases of my blankets. I stayed inside my tent, debating on whether I wanted to stay there or get out of bed to confront Damien. I did not like this. I did not like this at all, but my insides were boiling and I knew I had to do it eventually.

So, once I was ready, I went downstairs.

I didn't exactly rehearse what I wanted to say, because I was not even sure what to say. I suddenly realized I had an intense headache and not the kind in your forehead and temples. I am talking about the headaches that are in the back of your head, which, in my opinion, hurt much more. I kept patting that part of my head as I walked downstairs and scanned the residents. The image of them still made me shudder and the pain in the back of my head throbbed. I could not stand this anymore. I casually turned and went back upstairs, pausing hesitantly at my floor before going up to Damien's.

I felt like such a spy, the way I crouched down and sat there like a cat. The door opened, and I fell back. Sure enough, Damien himself stepped out with his T-shirt on backward and his hair out in as many angles as possible. That part was normal, but there was something else that was not: a blemish about the size, shape, and color of a raspberry appearing on his neck. My anger grew, and it only increased my headache from bad to worse, but I was too livid to care.

I jumped up and got in his face before he could come all the way down the hallway to the bathroom. Cornered, Damien's eyes widened, but he kept them on me.

"Uh, hi."

"What the hell?"

"What?" he said, acting like an innocent dope.

"Since when is Iris your girlfriend?"

His eyes darted.

"Ummm...."

"Umm what? I saw you two."

"So what? We weren't doing anything."

"You fucking *made out* with her, Damien! I can't believe it. I just cannot—"

"What is your problem, Sky?" Damien's voice turned from cool to cold in just seconds. "She likes me, okay? And I like her. She is the most amazing person I have ever met. She taught me things. She taught me ... a lot of things. She believes in the most beautiful things. She tells me I can do anything and be anything."

"No, she is not!" I cried, exasperated. "You are so blind. She is manipulative and is just trying to control you! She just wants to make you her bitch! And clearly, she succeeded!"

"There! Right there! She was right. Iris said how judgmental you are. That's all you do. If you would just wake up and see what I see. She showed me the most beautiful experience of my life. You wouldn't understand."

"I am not judgmental. You are brainwashed!"

"See? Judging. You don't even know Iris like I do. I believe in her. Okay? So stop being so jealous of what I have."

"You have nothing!" I yelled at him. "You have nothing and you're just going to be a puppet. So you know what? Have fun with that."

Damien's entire body was tense, even the nooks and crannies of his face, although I could have sworn I saw differently in his eyes. I didn't wait around for a counterattack and didn't feel the need to. Damien clearly dug his own grave, and I could not say anything else.

"I don't need you to judge me!" he called after me as I thundered down the stairs. My headache now formed a circle around my entire head.

I kept to myself for the rest of the day, evening, night, whatever. The concept of time and day never mattered to me anymore and I couldn't think straight. I mostly sat on the couch among a small to medium group of people and tried to be invisible. I did my homework in my room and answered emails, mostly from my mom and siblings, saying the same stupid response: "Hi, I'm fine, everything's fine, just busy. How are you?" The last thing that I wanted to have was a meaningless conversation that small talk usually brought, but I have often thought of what would happen if I told anyone anything. My fingers hovered over the spacebar of my computer as I stared at my response to an email. Sure, I could say that my ... friend just got seduced by this girl and is letting her control him. I could also say that spirits are haunting the house we live in, possessing the teacher and convincing him and us that the world is going to end and we are the ones who will be the leaders in a New Life. Sure, I could tell my mother that. Would you?

I instead skirted around everything, even answering that yes, of course, I would be home for Christmas and I couldn't wait to come home and go sledding and caroling and make gingerbread houses with my cousins at Uncle Freddy's house. I didn't know what Christmas would bring. I didn't even know what next week would bring. I sent the email before I could say anything else and hated myself for it.

I hated myself even more at dinnertime. I hated myself every time I looked over at Damien sitting next to her, of course. He sat there like an obedient puppy and ate casually. Once in a while, she'd pat his arm or stroke his hair. I didn't stare too long because I didn't want either of them to see me, so I ate in silence and pretended to be interested in the conversations going on at my table. After dinner, Mitchell said we would be going to the lower lounge again for a casual reflection.

This time, we were seated in half-circles, very close-knit circles, which meant this evening was supposed to be a discussion. The cushions wedged together edge by edge, leaving little to no leg room, making me almost forget how many members we had now. We arranged ourselves and watched as Mitchell sat down at the front, now turning these half-circles into a whole one.

"My children, I was watching one of those talk shows the other day and it brought up a very interesting subject. This talk show had an individual on it who considered themselves to be 'genderless' or 'gender neutral.' This person had very plain features that were very androgynous, but they still were just as human and beautiful as anybody. It was very interesting to watch, and it got me thinking. While this genderless person is different from you or me, we sort of have the same beliefs on other things. We are in a lot of ways genderless as well, figuratively speaking. Yes, the human bodies we have now identify us as male or female, but the White Light itself is genderless. The White Light is genderless, just as some believe that their God is genderless, considered to be both with names like "The Holy Father" and "Mother Nature." When we all got together as a group, we lightly discussed becoming simple beings and not relying on material possessions or beautification rituals. We have not really discussed this matter further, and I think it would be a good discussion subject for us tonight."

Mitchell looked around at all of us, many very attentive.

"The White Light is not a he or a she. It is both. It is both because higher life forms do not have the need for gender separation. What if when we go to the Next Life, we do not need gender at all? Why put labels on beings to tell them what they're supposed to be? That is only an Earth thing. Where we're going is the level that is above human, where everyone is equal and free. What are your thoughts on this? What do you believe gender assignment actually does?"

A random girl's hand went up.

"For mating, reproduction."

"That is correct," Mitchell said. "A man and a woman together reproduce to make another human."

"It gives people an identity from birth," a boy answered.

"Yes," Mitchell said again. "An identity that you can't choose. You are just given it. Did you know that I always liked long hair? Even as a boy, I insisted that I keep my hair long because I liked it better. When I was very young, I was often mistaken for a girl because I had long hair. It frustrated me. I never understood why boys *had* to have short hair and only girls could have long hair. Who decided this? Does anyone else have any 'gender-bending stories?'"

The evening went on with almost everyone participating. I said very little. Even though I was enjoying the discussion we were having, I was still not in the best of moods. I spoke up about why girls and women had to wear makeup to feel like they were attractive, and how I never understood why they didn't appreciate their natural beauty like men did. Mitchell smiled and gestured towards me.

"Yes. There are an awful lot more prejudices and social judgments on women than on men. But you at least know that you do not need fake beauty in order for someone to love you, right? Excellent point, Sky."

I felt my face redden a bit, but I did not look at Damien. I could not look at Damien. *I don't need fake love either,* I thought.

"The fact that you are all in uniforms is a fantastic step in this direction. You are blended together and part of a whole, yet still free beings. The White Light would like to receive us all as free to be who we want and free to appreciate one another without labels or physical attributes that were just chosen for us. In the next couple of weeks, I want you to look past the physical stuff. Look inside yourselves and try to see inside others. Look past the Guardians and instead, focus on the Lights inside them. Learn just how powerful you can be."

The next day I woke up, not having been sleeping well again. That went without saying. I half-dragged myself to the bathroom, not expecting anything at all. When I walked in and looked at the activity in the bathroom mirror, I stopped at the door, unsure if I should go in or not or stay behind and eavesdrop. I didn't need to as the four girls standing before the sinks, all with scissors in hand, looked back at me via reflection. Kimberly took another part of her hair and cut it off, right at the base of the ear, as though she were trimming hedges. She turned to the girl next to her and asked her to do her back.

I walked in to see the rest of them all doing the same, the girl near the end already sporting a pixie do. The scissors kept snipping, and I watched as the hairs gracefully fluttered down at their feet. The floor confetti consisted of various shades of blonde and brown and black.

"What do you think?" Kimberly asked me, the corners of her mouth turning up into what could be a smile, but didn't look like one.

I didn't know what to think.

"Do you want to join us?" she asked.

I walked in closer and looked at all of them and then looked at myself in the mirror, imagining my hair joining the mingle on the floor.

"I mean, you don't really have to," she continued. "We're doing this because we want to. Casting off our labels and becoming neutral. It would make The White Light proud. It would make Mitchell proud."

The girls next to her ran their fingers through their new short haircuts, various pieces and spikes sticking up at new angles. Their faces were beaming, and it had nothing to do with a beauty salon.

"Let me ask you something, Sky," Kimberly said, now facing me. "Do you believe in androgynous beauty? Do you believe you'll have the same form where we're going?"

"Yeah, I believe," I answered. "And I believe that someday we will just all look the same."

I looked in the mirror at myself, at my shabby form that just rolled out of bed. How wonderful to think that someday no one will have to worry so much about what they looked like ... or what others thought of them. How wonderful it would be to just be one form of beautiful forever. I took the scissors and felt my hair down. Then, I got to work.

I was really hungry by the time I got downstairs. Hungry for food since I spent most of the morning in the bathroom prepping myself, but also hungry for the right kind of attention I was going to get from my new look. I felt eyes on me as I made my way into the kitchen. People looked, but they did not say anything. I held my head up high. *Look at me now,* I thought. *Look how I am a believer.*

The next time I saw Damien, he did a double-take at me. His mouth popped open a little, but no sound came out. I did not look at him as I sat at the kitchen table and pretended to be intensely focused on my own homework. When Iris came into the room, I had to look up, because I almost did not recognize her. Her long black hair was gone, and in its place was a swirly black bowl around her face. I stared at her as she made her way across the room. She and I made eye contact for a second. She acknowledged me, took me in, and then moved on, sitting next to Damien, and then proceeded to rub his back.

Word had spread fast. Well, I almost can't say if that much word was said at all. The students kept quiet for a while, but it seemed like I was starting to see more and more people with their hair cut off. It was not just the girls. The guys were starting to show as well, some almost to the point of a buzz cut. Someone even gave Seth a hand and every once in a while, I caught him touching his head lovingly. I don't know how this happened or who actually started it, but now everyone had fallen in line. Everyone had done the same thing. I couldn't look at Damien for long, whose own buzz cut and forlorn look made him look like an Army recruit drafted into war. Iris couldn't keep her filthy hands off of him. I imagined her holding him down and coming at him with the electric razor. It disgusted me. His smiling at her while she did it disgusted me even more.

At our next gathering after dinner, I anxiously awaited Mitchell's reaction and response to the group's makeover. We sat before him, breathing in incense, while Ad Astra sat on the stairs, her tail twitching almost in tune with the ticking clock.

"My children ... you are all ... one. You are the strongest people in the world to set the example."

CHAPTER 35

My meal was interrupted by an unexpected guest. Usually, Ad Astra would weave in between my legs and scare the crap out of me, or meow at me for a piece of whatever I was eating, but this guest was not so pleasant. The first thing I noticed about her was her eyes. They used to be bright green, at least I thought they were, but now they looked almost green-hazel. They couldn't have changed, but then again, I wasn't the one who stared into them often.

"Hi Sky," she said, her words dripping with poison.

"Um hi," I replied, not really sure what else to say. Iris rounded the table until she came to sit right across from me, right where we both could see each other. I had no idea where this was going, but suddenly, I began to itch. I prayed anyone, *anyone*, would come into the kitchen.

"You know, Damien is worried about you."

I crunched that last mouthful of cereal and swallowed it right then and there. It scratched my throat all the way down, but I didn't care. I didn't even sip my tea, because I knew I wasn't going to be drinking much of it.

"What do you mean?" I asked coldly.

"Well..." Iris finger-combed her hair and folded her hands on the table, all prim and proper. "He has been telling me things about you from time to time. I know you're good friends, so that is why he tells me. You question The White Light, don't you?"

I didn't like the way she asked that. I didn't like the way her eyes looked. I was certain now they looked different. I had to compose myself.

"Why would I question a higher spiritual being?"

"Damien told me you might not believe in it. He said you were always looking for answers ... and you wanted to get away. You almost ran away to find them. Looking for answers is admirable, and I heard about you two consulting spirits through a Ouija board, which is beautiful, but you still don't truly believe in it, do you?"

I half-sat up, words spewing out of my mouth before I could think about them.

"No, no, that's not true! Why would Damien say that? We were both full of wonder, he and I, and we wanted to seek answers. We both believe in The White Light and we both put our fate in its care. I am a believer. Why would he say that?"

Iris shrugged innocently. I was angry enough to throw my cereal bowl at her, but I held back. I held back because I knew that the consequences for even thinking of doing that would be dire.

"It's a crucial time right now," she continued. "We are on a tight schedule for time left on Earth. Just trying to ... make sure we're all on the same level. That's all. See you later."

And just like that, she gave me a casual smile and took off. I was left with soggy cereal and still staring at her empty chair for a while.

When I decided it was a good time, I took off and went upstairs. He was probably in his room doing his homework. If Iris was off doing something else, trying to manipulate someone else in her free time, I could get him alone. I knocked, trying not to pound too hard.

"Yeah," he said.

I opened his door and took a deep breath. Damien sat at his desk and looked surprised to see me. I couldn't tell if it was a good surprise or a bad surprise, but I didn't wait long enough to wonder.

"Why are you telling Iris that I don't believe in anything?" I demanded.

He sat up in his chair and dropped a pencil. "What? I didn't—"

"Spare me. She just had a little talk with me about how you told her all this stuff about us seeking answers and that you told her that I was the one who questioned everything and was going to run away or something—"

"Oh calm down, Sky."

"What the hell is your problem?" I snapped. "First you're her bitch and now you spread rumors? Why would you say all that stuff?"

"Jesus, Sky."

"Answer me."

"Well, if you have to know, it's because she knows more. She has the right idea about things and you sort of ... don't. She told me it's dangerous to lose faith and I shouldn't be spending time with people who are unfocused."

"What did you just say? Just what is that supposed to mean?"

"I don't want to be left behind..." he trailed off.

I threw my hands up in the air.

"You should hear yourself talk right now! You are unbelievable."

"It's almost Judgment Day," he said. "And I would watch myself if I were you. Our actions are all on display."

"Oh, I wish all of *your* actions were on display."

I stormed out of his room and shut his door, almost slamming it, but not wanting the whole house to hear it.

We saw each other at dinner, around the house, in between classes, and at gatherings, but we didn't speak. In fact, we didn't even make eye contact. Every time I'd pass him, I'd just ignore him. I lost track of the days at times and just tried to stay focused. He didn't say anything to me, and I didn't say anything to him. This was fine with me. At our gatherings, Mitchell explained to us what made us human. It made us human to feel and our actions justified our feelings and our actions were the result of our feelings sometimes. They were like a knee-jerk reaction. I would listen wholeheartedly during these sessions. Human feelings sometimes made us do and say things. It wasn't always us; it was just our human feelings. This made a part of me very happy. Mitchell told us that in our Next Life we would not have to worry about that anymore. Our spirits, the living energies we had within us, would be in charge. No one would be controlled by human emotions anymore. We would be free of that as higher beings. I sat up straight. The level above human sounded better and better every day.

And so, we treated ourselves as higher than human more and more. Or tried to. It was hard to push personal feelings aside. I felt anger every time I saw Damien and Iris. Judgment Day, huh? Well, let him see. Let him see who gets judged and who does not.

I had a short meditation session in my room after lunch one day. I urged my spirit to travel, hoping that I could make some connections along the way. I was hoping to make any sort of connection at this point. My body fell asleep quickly, the weight of my breath leaving it lifelessly behind as I concentrated. It was cool where I soared, although I couldn't see where. In my mind, I searched and searched. *Where are you?* I called out. I flew around clouds, which morphed into a foggy meadow, missing any sort of sunlight.

I was not alone for long. A figure floated by me but did not come too close. Or it could not come too close. It lingered, camouflaging into the mist at a distance. I focused on it, trying to form an outline of the figure and see if it had a face. The more we moved, the more I saw that this figure was very much on the outside of a group of clouds and could not get in. This made my spirit sink a little as I figured out who it was.

I didn't see him anymore, and I didn't hear him anymore, but I knew he still hung around. I knew that we could still be connected. Still, I struggled with the fact that his place was not in The Manor. I struggled that I didn't even know his place at all. The more he moved around the clouds, the more I saw that he was patrolling them, like he was standing guard and protecting what was inside ... which was me. I longed to know what he knew and saw outside those clouds. I only hoped that someday I would.

My eyes snapped open at the knocking on my door. I sat up a little on my bed and moved my asleep, tingling legs.

"Yeah, come on in."

Kimberly opened the door with a concerned look on her face.

"I'm happy you're here, Sky. I just wanted to see if you were okay."

She came in and sat on my bed, all motherly.

"I'm fine," I said right away.

She shook her head like she didn't believe me.

"Look, I know that you and Damien have been having problems. Is everything all right?"

I sighed and rubbed my legs.

"We had a fight. He just—I don't know. It's complicated."

"There is a lot of tension going on between you two. People have seen it. I can sense it's awkward and hard for you, but you show that you are struggling. You have so much anger."

I didn't know what to say to that, but I couldn't make eye contact with Kimberly for long. I didn't have to say anything because the next thing that came out of her mouth made me feel worse.

"The thing is, Mitchell noticed it, too. He wants to see you in his office."

My legs tingled more than when they were folded up pretzel-style. I suddenly had a current of different thoughts that ran through my head as soon as Kimberly said our teacher's name. *Mitchell noticed it, too. He wants to see you in his office.* What did Mitchell notice, exactly? Damien and I weren't speaking. So what? What exactly did Mitchell know? What in the world did he want to talk to me about?

I tried to play it casual as I left my room and went downstairs. No matter who you are or what it is about, no one likes confrontations. The very words "we need to talk" are usually enough to put anyone on the edge. This was more than that. I would be going to Mitchell's office, this time because

I was supposed to, and no one really knew what happened beyond those doors. So I thundered down the stairs.

I almost felt like all the others were staring at me, but they were not. They were minding their own business. I was happy to see Damien was nowhere in sight. I did not want to see him. I walked down that hallway and pretended like I was going to use the bathroom. I got to Mitchell's office, my dumb nervous heart so loud I could hear it. I knocked, but my heart knocked louder.

"Come on in."

I opened that door, and the minute I did, I realized I had to act as though it was my first time seeing Mitchell's office. I stepped in hesitantly and awkwardly, noticing he sat seated business-like at his desk. He wasn't doing anything. He had his fingers laced together on top of a pile of papers.

"Hello Sky, my Light, my child. Come on in and shut the door, please."

I did as he asked, only having a millisecond to compose myself before I approached the desk and faced him. Mitchell's gaze stayed only on me, his eyes a lost hazel with a hint of gold, no doubt matching the picture that sat directly across from him.

"Have a seat, Sky. You are looking good."

I gave a weak smile as I touched my hair. So, he did notice.

"Thanks Mitchell. Kimberly said that you wanted to see me?"

"Yes, I did. I am a little worried about you. You seem to be having a bit of a rough patch with Damien, aren't you?"

I shrugged a bit. "Yeah, a little. It's complicated and personal."

He titled his head a bit so that he was now looking at me over his glasses.

"You both were arguing quite a bit. Some sources told me that Damien was, in fact, trying to save you."

"Save me?" I practically exclaimed.

"Yes," Mitchell continued. "That you were talking about leaving and he was trying to stop you."

"That's not—"

"Sky, you know this is a crucial time for us. Be a good girl now and tell me why you would want to leave, and where you think you would go."

"I did *not* try to leave," I stated. "That's not what it was about. Damien and I were just disagreeing on other things. Personal things. About his relationships and his life and such. They have nothing to do with Guardians of Light or The White Light or anything like that."

"That's not what I heard," he said, slowly shaking his head. "I've heard you questioned things. I heard you wanted to go tell the school we were doing something wrong."

"What?!"

"Why do you think something is wrong, Sky? Have you looked around you? Do you see anything wrong?"

"No, no! I don't see anything wrong. I wasn't going to tell anybody anything. Tell them what, anyway? They wouldn't understand anything. They wouldn't understand us. That was not what that was about. I questioned things, but I have found my faith. I have faith. I believe in and am dedicated to The White Light."

Although my brain was spinning and my heart was racing, I did not spew out that paragraph. I made sure to express myself delicately and confidently. I had no choice. Mitchell's gaze on me was stone hard and—well—digging. He was digging past the surface to see what was underneath, and it was scaring every part of me. Something was going on and I needed to take control of it, and fast.

"Now's the time to be true," he continued. "Now's the time to be true to yourself. The White Light will know who is true and who is not. Do you understand?"

"Absolutely. I do believe. I am true."

Mitchell smiled. "Good. Good, my Light. Be careful what you say and do. We are all under inspection. Go on now, my child. Just remember that they see everything."

I thanked Mitchell and got up, keeping the smile on my face from shaking, and frankly, keeping my whole body from shaking. He watched me get up and leave, not moving from his desk or saying another word.

I felt wobbly and weird, and the first thing I wanted was a hot cup of tea and honey. The idea itself sounded soothing and I badly needed to relax and get a hold of myself. I sat at the kitchen counter for a minute, slapping my palms down on the counter and exhaling slowly. In my mind, I replayed the scene in Mitchell's office and everything that we said, but most importantly, I tried to imagine what exactly was said about me ... and by whom. I, of course, had my suspicions. I felt the tension in my fingernails as they pressed against the counter and if I could have dug down and ripped right through it, I would have. I would have if I could pretend it was Damien and Iris. I wish I did have Damien and Iris at my mercy. They and their sharp tongues would be sorry. *What was Damien getting at by what he said about me? Did he say things on purpose, or was it pressured out of him?*

I got up and fixed that cup of tea, filling the water up so high it actually could be seen over the rim. I got it out of the microwave and dunked the tea bag in over and over, feeling just how hot I made it. Tiny drops of fire rained on my hand—and at once the activity outside began to mimic. I felt the drops on my skin and then heard the drops splatter on the window, the porch, and the roof. The faster I drowned the tea bag, the faster the rain began to fall. The evening storm made itself very clear. The first flash of lightning and small crack of thunder shot through the outside, and almost at the same time, the lights above began to weaken.

I heard voices rush in and out of the walls. The voices increased when the house lights flickered and then went out completely. The microwave time went out and flashed as people walked about The Manor, announcing there was a blackout and looking for flashlights and candles. Kimberly and Carol came in with a handful of candles and started to light them, placing them all around the kitchen and counters.

"Give us a hand, would you Sky?" asked Kimberly. "We are going to need more of these."

I got up and lit some candles while the rain and thunderstorm roared outside. People got to work lighting up the house, their voices coming from every corner of the place, and some of them I knew did not belong to students.

CHAPTER 36

That night I dreamed I was wading through a pool that came up to my waist, but it was not filled with water. It was more like mercury or molasses. It felt as thick as molasses, but it was the color and look of mercury. The pool was long and wide and silver and did not seem to have an ending point. I didn't know what this dream meant or where I was supposed to go, but I was having a hard time getting anywhere. I pushed and pushed through that substance, struggling to make it a few inches, finding that each time I tried to fight through it, my very bones were breaking. I struggled to make a step and bend my knees and instead felt like they were being crushed. I pushed against the stuff I was in, only to give up midway and sink.

I woke up instantly, seeing gold instead of silver. In the daytime sunlight, I could tell that the rainstorm had settled, and the power had come back on. My alarm clock flashed repeatedly to remind me to set it properly once I got the chance, or whenever I felt like it. As I moved around in my bed, I realized that the feelings I got from my strange dream were all still there. I moved to sit up and move the blankets around, and everything from the waist down became incredibly sore. I wiped my eyes and rubbed my head. The minute I pushed down on the bed to get up, something disturbed me.

I tried to push again, tried to move more ... only to realize that I was having a hard time moving. Confused, I pulled back my blankets to look at my body.

Everything was in place, and despite the realistic injuries I felt in my dream, I didn't have any broken bones. I didn't see anything, but the pain was there. It was there when I moved my knees, but it was there even worse when I moved my feet. Needles of various sizes stabbed every part of my left foot. It felt more than it was just asleep. My feet felt heavy, and it hurt to move them. I rubbed my legs up and down, only to see that they felt the same way. My legs ached and the more I urged them to move, the heavier they felt. My pulse started to race as I started to panic. I tried with all my might to move my legs over the side of the bed to get out, but something was going on. The entire lower half of my body felt like it was stuck in concrete and I was a living statue. I pulled and pulled and twisted and turned in my bed, until finally, I rolled over and completely fell out. I landed—hard—on the floor and screamed.

I screamed again because I landed on my hip and it did not feel like little prickles. I pulled myself up the best I could and urged my feet to move. I twisted sideways to look at my bottom half just as I heard feet thundering down the hallways.

"Sky?"

The door opened and Holly, Kimberly, Carol, Becky, and some others rushed into my room. They saw me lying on the floor and looked equal parts concerned and confused.

"My legs!" I cried. "I ... I can't move my legs!"

They came all the way in, Carol at once trying to move me.

"Someone get a chair or something," Carol said. "A desk chair."

Carol squatted down and attempted to pick me up. She scooped me up, and I put my arms around her shoulders, not realizing how strong she was.

"We'll find out what's wrong with you," Carol said. "We'll get you fixed."

The caravan brought me downstairs, and Becky found an extra desk chair from one of the study rooms. She rolled it over just as we were coming downstairs. I clung to Carol's shoulders, deathly afraid that if she were to put me down or drop me at any moment, I wouldn't be able to stand up. My feet swayed pathetically like two wet noodles as we went down the stairs. They moved lifelessly, weightlessly, but to me, they still felt concrete and hard. By this time, there was a small commotion over me and other students started to take notice.

"Bring that over here, Becky!"

I was put in the chair, and as soon as my butt hit the seat, my legs fell before me and there was where they would stay. I scrambled in the chair, pulling myself up and trying to pull at my legs. It really was no use. I really could not move them at all.

"What happened?"

"Are you okay?"

"Did you hurt yourself?"

I, of course, had a ton of questions fired at me from all directions, and I wished I had at least one answer.

Carol disappeared and left me with everyone. I thought at this point that I would be going to the nurse when Mitchell showed up.

"Sky, what's the matter?"

I looked up at him, almost thinking the rest of me had gone paralyzed as well. His eyes were steady and relaxed, showing no signs of alarm or even acknowledgment that one of his students was hurt.

"Something's wrong with my legs," I stammered. "I woke up, and I couldn't move them or get up at all and they hurt when I try to move them."

Mitchell suddenly shut his eyes. Some of the students stayed by me, putting a hand on me or on the chair as they watched Mitchell. His eyes did not shut completely. From my chair, I could tell that they barely squinted shut, and all we saw were the whites of his eyes, as they had rolled in the back of his head. Mitchell's forehead tensed as small wrinkles snaked across his eyebrows ... then they were gone. I sat up as Mitchell opened his eyes and looked at me, his entire face relaxing.

"Come, Sky. Let us assess the situation before we get you any medical attention."

Mitchell came behind me and started to roll me over to his office. I gripped the arms of the chair, knowing that I was now completely at his mercy and would have nowhere to go if something happened. But what would happen? What could happen? What exactly was wrong with me, and why did danger settle at the corners of my mind?

We got into Mitchell's office—now officially my third time in there—and he turned to face me. I kept my grip on those chair arms and addressed him.

"How and why would I lose complete feeling in my legs all of a sudden? I woke up and felt like a statue!"

"My child, I have consulted with The White Light and the spirits, who are with me. The Light watches over us, as you know and see. It seems to me that this incident of yours corresponds with the talk we were having yesterday."

"What does that mean?"

"Well, I am not completely sure, but it seems to me that the spirits felt like you needed to be grounded … literally."

Mitchell rested his hand on his chin while he addressed me and looked at my legs. He sounded almost too casual, as if my sudden paralysis didn't raise an alarm. I stared back at him, fighting to get any words processed in my head. I had to say something, but I was completely speechless.

"I wouldn't worry," was Mitchell's conclusion. "They do like to test us once in a while, don't they? Test our loyalty and test our strength. It seems to me that you might have been struggling with your proper place. This is your proper place, Skyler. "

I had been trying not to blow up or hyperventilate.

"Am I paralyzed?"

"I don't believe so. You are stronger than this. You just have to look within yourself and prove it."

I had a million questions. Of course I did. I didn't get a chance to get any more of them answered, or frankly, to get any more answers out of Mitchell. Someone knocked lightly on the door and he turned his attention away from me, chatting with someone for a second and then opening the door all the way.

Carol came into the room and approached me.

"So she's doing okay?"

Mitchell gave a brief nod. "Let us just be sure she gets plenty of rest. This little Light will not go out."

I looked to the both of them, feeling helpless and confused.

"Keep your faith, Sky," Mitchell said. "Carol, why don't you fix her something to eat?"

And just like that, I was rolled out of the office without a second thought. There was only one silver lining to this horrible situation: It was Saturday, and I did not have to worry about how I was going to get to classes. I could just relax at The Manor. For the rest of the day, I felt like a handicapped person. Technically, I was, and what frightened me the most was I didn't know for how long. I needed help to get food, get around, and be carried upstairs to the residential floor to brush my teeth and change my clothes. I didn't feel numb in only my legs; I felt numb emotionally and could not look at people. Everyone asked what happened to me, and I kept telling them that I didn't know and I woke up that way. I knew that they talked about me. I could tell by the way people would look at me and say something to one another privately, but secretly, to make sure I wasn't looking. At one point I turned my head and heard "Skyler … run away.…" Now, they thought of me as a prisoner being punished for trying to escape.

Damien and Iris saw me. I know they did. Iris acknowledged me casually, but I saw the same look on her face that I saw on Damien's. It had to be the lowest form of pity. Look at her, what a little invalid. She can't use her legs. She has to pay for not believing. Damien's face was the worst. I couldn't tell if he now looked down on me, or if he truly felt sorry for what was happening to me. Either way, it was like he believed it happened to me for a reason.

I kept to myself for the most part. I only had the company of others when I needed to be waited on. Each time someone got me a glass of water, I tried in vain to see if I could do it myself. I would grab on to the chair arms and thrust my pelvis out, but I could not get my legs to cooperate. Each attempt became harder and harder. I became a jellyfish with sprawling limbs that I could not control or even maintain. So, I spent most of my time feeling scared and sorry for myself. I eventually went into a slump for being emotionally drained, and tired for struggling so much physically and mentally. *Please,* I begged whoever was listening. *Let my body move again.*

I looked down at my feet, stretched in yellow socks with little goldfish all over them. If I could move my feet, it would look like those goldfish were swimming. I needed those goldfish to swim again. I at once thought of that scene in *Kill Bill Vol. I,* right near the beginning when the main character gets out of the hospital and steals a car. She sat in the seat with her paralyzed legs stretched out in front of her, concentrating very hard, and saying out loud to wiggle her big toe. Wiggle your big toe. She says this over and over again and concentrates, and finally we see an inch of movement that tells us everything we need to know. The main character breaks out of her confinement and is mobile again. In vain, I picture this scene and try to mimic it, focusing on those goldfish and urging them to start swimming.

Wiggle your big toe.

Wiggle your big toe.

Something moved all right, but it was not my toes. A tidal wave of a shadow washed over those fish, and I looked up. Seth stood by the armchair I was in, in the upper lounge, and I didn't even hear him come in.

"Sky?"

"Yeah?"

"How are you?"

It was an innocent question, but Seth did not put it casually. He said it as though he were looking for a specific answer.

"Well, I still can't move. I'm confused and angry and freaked out and I don't know what to do anymore."

Seth's glossy eyes stayed in one place, barely blinking.

"I understand."

"I don't think you do."

"Well, I do," he said, coming over to me. He felt his way over to an empty chair and sat in, slowly and carefully, like an emperor would. "Sky, we were chosen by the spirits to test. They recognized something in us that was not right, and they decided to fix us. We were fixed."

I could barely sit up, but I tried to.

"What in the world are you talking about? You can't possibly think..."

"Do you believe that everything happens for a reason?"

I paused, considering his face and how serious his tone was.

"No," I answered honestly. "Because I don't think I did anything to deserve to lose the ability to move my legs!"

"Sky, this is a test. Don't you see? You have to look past the physical burdens that our human bodies give us every day. The White Light is trying to teach you something. You felt like you did not want to be here, you felt like you wanted to leave. The White Light is teaching you that you did not make a good decision. It is helping you look past a physical burden to become stronger. You can become stronger."

It was taking all of my willpower not to cry, and all of my mental power to deny everything he was saying. There was no way that this was happening to me ... without a real reason. There was no way that my entire lower half just *stopped*.

Seth couldn't see the skin on my face scrunch up in agony, but he did know how I was feeling. I came to find that nobody could really hide anything from Seth. He could sense everything.

"I know this is a difficult time, Sky. But you will get through it. And you will become a stronger being, ready for The Next Life. Look at me. Look at how I overcome my burden. And the spirits took away my eyes very early on in the year."

My face froze, knowing this to be completely true.

"You remember." Seth smiled slightly. "Halloween time, I believe. I was starting to go blind and lose my vision. Mitchell knew it. He knew it because he warned me. He told me to be careful what I said to the others, because I was seeing things all wrong. Let me tell you something personal."

I waited, and he paused.

"I had questions, too. I questioned Mitchell mostly, and his intentions. He told me that I saw things through the wrong eyes, and I needed a different perspective. Then I had a vision of nothing but beauty. It was around then I went blind. And now I can see inside myself and see my Light. It is beautiful, Sky. It's the most beautiful thing in the world. Once you become grounded, it will be beautiful, too. Trust me. Trust us."

He didn't see me shake my head, but I did it anyway.

"And Becky," I said.

"Yes," Seth answered. "Becky, too. Becky had a wicked tongue. But she is better now. See how happy she is?"

I let the passing of other students break the moment's silence we had. I slumped down in my chair and stayed there, wishing nobody would see me.

To my fear, my paralysis went on. Mitchell, at one point, came to me in The Manor with the only practical solution for me to get around on my own: a wheelchair. A goddamn wheelchair. I was officially handicapped and was forced to wheel myself around campus, around all the staring eyes and pointed fingers. It was bad enough I did not have a good explanation for GOL members, who, with their wide and concerned eyes, knew that this was punishment for something. I had done something wrong, and now I had to suffer for it. Explaining myself outside The Manor would be difficult, too, even though I didn't talk to anyone else. How could I? By association with the "weird group" on campus, I was automatically labeled a pariah, and no one wanted to talk to me, anyway. It killed me inside. I didn't know what was going on with me. I didn't know how to change or control it, and I was clearly not in charge of myself.

I'd climb into that chair every day, and do my everyday tasks, silently praying in my head that I needed to get back to normal. I wanted whoever—or whatever—was listening to know that I would do anything it took to get my old body back. It was almost like I was apologizing, although I couldn't be sure what for. Apologizing for having suspicions with this group? For believing a teacher was taking things too far? But, of course, it wasn't just him, and even if I did tell anyone about the spirits that controlled the house we lived in, they would not believe anything I said, from the cat to the Ouija board to faces in soup to the writing on the windows. But this was too real, and I needed to play my cards straight. I needed to get back on the spirits' good side if I was going to survive this.

Rolling in the snow was, as expected, nearly impossible and a nightmare. Kimberly sort of became my handler at one point and would help me navigate the icy sidewalks.

In Mitchell's class, I almost knew the worst was coming. As tiny sugar specks of snow fell outside the classroom window, I knew what Mitchell was thinking about and what he was going to talk to the class about. If I could sink any lower in my chair, I would, but all I could do was sit there and pretend that everything that came out of his mouth was completely valid and sane.

"Everyone keeps bringing up those Mayans and their prophecy of the world coming to an end … in just a couple of weeks…"

When Mitchell paced this classroom, it didn't have the same effect on the other students, but it had the same effect on me.

"The question is, what will happen to all of us once it does? The world will end, we as human beings will die, and then where will we go? Many people believe that we will die and go to Heaven, but what exactly is Heaven? Better yet, what exactly is death?"

"Join us tonight," Mitchell continued. "Join us if you are looking for questions, because we have the answers. We have the answer and we know how you can be saved from floating aimlessly after the destruction of Earth. Join the Guardians of Light to have the best afterlife."

Of course, no one showed up to The Manor later. It made many people upset and disappointed, and it made many only grow to hate the human race even more.

"People are stupid, selfish and close-minded," I heard one guy say. "They don't know anything."

"I am so happy to get out of here," another girl chimed in. "I can't wait to be with more intelligent beings."

I kept my mouth shut.

That night, we had a gathering in the lower lounge. It was shocking to me that the person who was in charge of carrying me up and down the stairs was Seth. He came over to me just as we were about to go and lifted me up.

"Are you … are you sure…" I started to say.

"Not to worry," Seth answered right away. "My senses are the strongest they have ever been, and I know this house better than anything or anyone. I can get you around safely. I can feel it."

So, he scooped me up, and I was at the mercy of a blind man, shuffling his feet and walking with extreme care and confidence. The echolocation vibrated off of his skin, and he did not even brush against a wall or chair or any obstacle that got in his way. The Guardians of Light descended to the lower lounge, Seth and I among them and not missing a single step nor hesitating at the stairs. He put me down on the floor cushion and took a seat nearby. Mitchell must have told him, too. He must have told him that he was now my personal handler. I was completely dependent.

Mitchell glided down the stairs to his awaiting crowd, all of us waiting anxiously for him to start the gathering, or just anxious in general to whatever he wanted to say this time.

"We await the Judgment Day," he started. "We are only a few short weeks away. People are busy getting ready for Christmas and other holidays, and I say why do we celebrate? Why do we celebrate that which will not happen? Will it happen?"

"No," everyone said in unison.

"Will this Christmas be the same as the last?"

"No."

"No is right. We will have time to celebrate, all right. We will celebrate later, and with a much better reason. The White Light is ready to receive us in The New World. We are going home. Do you hear me? We are going home."

"We are going home," we all said in unison. I could actually hear the excitement in some people's voices. Very soon, we were to believe we were leaving all of our problems behind.

"I have something else to tell you," Mitchell said, pacing the room. Behind him, the candles on the mantle flickered uncontrollably. "Something that will no doubt make you all very happy. Since we are scheduled to leave on December 21st, then, well, what use do you have for final exams?"

The entire room was quiet as Mitchell looked around with a sly smile. He wanted to see everyone's reactions before saying any more.

"Oh my children, as a teacher, usually this idea is preposterous. But think about it: What use is it to study or do any work for exams if *we will not be having any?* I encourage you to make better use of your time. I encourage you to instead continue to reflect and meditate on the New World."

The candles flickered again, no doubt showing their approval of Mitchell's announcement.

"Your other teachers do not know, of course, and they will carry on and talk to you about all the classwork you need to do. You, of course, know better. You know better, but your teachers and other classmates do not. That puts us ahead of everyone, doesn't it?"

Mitchell's eyes mimicked the candle flames for a minute as he paced. I could tell those beams behind them reflected out at every person he looked at.

"You don't have other teachers anymore. I am your only one now. I am your only leader."

It was easy to say that the atmosphere around The Manor became ... blissful. Students almost became arrogant to the fact that they no longer needed classes, and began to do half-assed work just for the sake of doing work and appearing productive. I let myself slide as well. I accredited it to my traumatic event of becoming paralyzed, which was only half of a lie. Ever since I lost the use of my legs, teachers and other students just plain felt sorry for me. I didn't do a few papers. I bombed a couple of tests and quizzes. They confronted me about it. They asked what a smart student like myself was doing. I mainly shrugged and said I didn't feel like myself. It was the truth. Now that I thought about it, I really did believe that I no longer needed classes. Why should I? The world was going to end and we all were going to die ... and spend eternity on some space paradise. I of course, left that part out. I was at the point where I was letting the current take me wherever it wanted to go. I was not in control anymore.

The atmosphere around The Manor also became clouded. Literally. As the winter set in, the fog returned in the highest depths and smoked up the pathways leading to the woods. I would wheel myself over the path and as soon as I got to the woods, the sidewalk gradually disappeared. It was replaced by miles of heavy smoke, smoke that seemed to have no beginning and no end. Now that I was in a chair, it made me closer to the ground. As I wheeled through the path, the fog consumed me. It rose up as high as my chest, and at one point, I was certain it went over my head. I looked up above me, looked up to the lines of trees which were now a couple feet higher than they used to be. I had to stretch my neck back to look all around me. It made me feel smaller. I felt as though I had shrunk and the world now loomed above me and was ready to devour me up at any moment.

The fog surrounded The Manor, swallowing everything in its path and barely leaving room for the solar lanterns. Those fought through the fog to light the way, but they didn't need to light the way because by now we were all supposed to know exactly where The Manor was. There just was no question.

Inside, bits of the fog made their way through to make the whole house a little gloomy. I saw candles lining up the kitchen counter already, and it was not even sunset. As I wheeled myself in, I saw Holly finishing up some candles on the kitchen table.

"Spirits are here, you know," she said without even turning around.

"I know."

"They like to remind us they're here once in a while, you know? We have friends waiting for us. That is kind of nice."

Right. Nice.

I carried on with my new usual routine: waiting for someone to carry me up to my room (which was usually Carol) so I could hide in there and do my homework and just be alone until someone came to get me. That night, Seth knocked on my door and announced we were having another meeting downstairs. Seth's carrying me around sort of became a routine as well, more for him as well as me. He scooped me up like an empty potato sack, and never once struggled with his own handicap. He led me downstairs almost effortlessly now.

Mitchell had a different kind of activity in store for us that evening. Once I saw it, I was confused and maybe even a little nervous. He paced in front of the camera, sitting on top of the tripod proudly, and waited until everyone was downstairs and seated to begin. He looked almost anxious.

"Everyone, look at this camera here. Relax, it's not on right now, but it will be of use to you in the next couple of days. We will be doing a new project, and it is something I want you to take very seriously, because you might just consider this to be your last project. You all will have some personal time with the cameras to get a chance to do a video reflection. You will take turns and sit down in one of our study rooms for a private recording. There is where you will film your Exit Video."

My nails dug into my ankles, but I couldn't feel anything, anyway. I didn't even know if I drew blood. I didn't even know if I had any blood in my legs anymore, but Mitchell's words made me just want to tear through them.

"Your Exit Video will be your personal reflection of your life. Your ups, your downs, your milestones and more. You will talk about the most meaningful times in your life, and what were the most important things you learned. These are the most important things we can accomplish right now as our time becomes near. These videos will be something that we are going to need to take with us. We won't be leaving anything behind on Earth, because Earth is going to perish! What was it? It was doomed to begin with, and the ancient peoples knew that. It is a stepping stone, it is training grounds. And when we leave, we need to bring with us some sort of proof that we were, in fact, here and trained for the level above human. Right?"

We all nodded and said yes. Mitchell then took the tripod and gestured to Iris for help.

"Why don't you set this up in the back? I would like to record a little of tonight's gathering to show us all as a whole, as a group. I think The White Light and spirits would appreciate seeing us all together, and that I am carrying our message the way it is intended."

Mitchell went on with his usual great speeches while that camera recorded a part of history that will probably never be seen again. This scene, this very one, will never be seen either. I had my own visions of the whole "found footage" motif found in many horror movies. Our film would be found after the apocalypse, after the world blew up or whatever and whoever survived it would search among the rubble and come across something from a school. They would watch it and witness all of Mitchell's prophecy ramblings and know at once who was responsible for the world coming to an end. That is, if there were any survivors. If there were, that is probably what would happen.

"It is during our last days on Earth that the spirits that have passed before us continue to watch over us," Mitchell continued. "You all know about the students from many years ago who followed the teachings of The White Light. They chose to end their time on Earth. They chose to go before their time as humans was actually up, no doubt when they were still young and pure of heart, which is admirable in its own way. But, instead of passing on to the Next Life, they have fallen behind and need guidance. The right guidance. Now, through the protection of The White Light and the strengths that they possessed, they can go to a better place with our help. Do we know where for certain? We do not. We only know that we must put our fate in the hands of The White Light. It is here to remind us of what lies beyond. We can all help each other once the Day is upon us and guide us through this rough yet beautiful transition. Let us all cross over in peace!"

"In peace," we all echoed confidently. The camera recorded all of us nodding our heads in unison at Mitchell at the things he was saying.

"We are going to set this camera up in this study room back here," Mitchell indicated. "For all of you to do your Exit Videos. They do not have to be long at all, just a few minutes of your time to highlight the most important things. There will be a sign-up sheet outside this room so we can keep track of who did it and who has still to go. Do it during your free time, take your time, but do so quickly."

Mitchell made big gestures as he spoke, no doubt turning on the dramatics. Instead of being cheesy and amusing, they scared me a little, knowing that Mitchell could control anything and anyone with the wave of his hand.

"I know this may seem frightening. I know you might be scared. But I say to you, do not be afraid of the glorious future we have ahead of us. Do not be afraid of the paradise that awaits us in our Next Life."

I didn't do this video right away. A couple times I'd ask Seth or Carol to take me downstairs, and then I would see the study room door closed with the clipboard sitting idly on a chair next to it. Every time more and more names appeared on it, and I would have to go to class and not wait around for it. My time came eventually. The door opened while idly sitting there in Seth's arms and the camera was ready. Seth walked me in and set me down on the chair, close enough so I could reach the camera and work it on my own.

"I will take my turn after you," Seth said as-a-matter-of-factly and shut the door behind him. I shuffled a bit in the chair, manually moving my legs out so they wouldn't twist around themselves. Then I looked at the camera lens near the desk, the mysterious eye of the New World watching me and what I had to say about my life. I took a moment to think about exactly what I wanted to say, and I struggled quite a bit. This was basically a suicide note in person. A final farewell to the world that nobody will probably ever see. I might have been alone, but I knew I was not. The camera lens was not the only eye on me, and I had to think fast. No doubt Mitchell would also view the student film segments all together … just to make sure we did it justice. I heard papers shuffling outside the study room door and I knew that was Seth moving some things around to sit down and wait for me. I took that as my cue to reach over on the desk to turn on the camera, and just get it over with.

The little red light went on and it was like a little red light went on inside me as well. I faced the camera and sat up straight.

"My name is Skyler Monroe and I am thirteen years old and in 7th grade. I found out about Guardians of Light when I came to this school and joined them with no hesitation. Their sense of wonder and awe and how they are so in touch with themselves really spoke to me, since I was in a very difficult place when I first came here. In the past year, I lost my dad due to gang-related violence and my family was and is still recovering from it. I joined Guardians of Light knowing that they would be the ones to help me heal properly and accept his passing with an optimistic faith. And I have. I have learned so much and have grown as a person. I have personally had contacts with not only his spirit, but others as well, and it really opened my eyes to 'the other side' and I am a true believer. I believe that now, on my own journey to 'the other side,' my dad is personally there and he will help guide the way for me."

I started to get a little choked up, but I forced myself to stay with it. It never occurred to me that I believed my dad really was trying to guide me down the right path until that moment, and I was trying hard not to react.

"He has seen the Light," I continued, staring seriously at the camera, my voice cracking a little. "I will see the Light … we will all see it very soon. In my journey to find the right path, I have suffered another travesty. I woke up one day to find that I completely lost the use of my legs. I was paralyzed, I was completely helpless, and now I am in a wheelchair."

I paused here, shuffling a bit in the chair uncomfortably.

"I still don't know exactly why I lost the use of my legs. I suppose ... somewhere down the line and recently I had a moment of weakness. I suppose the spirits that are here relying on us found that I wanted to steer away from the path, that I tried to run away from my destiny, and they have bestowed this onto me to teach me a lesson. They are teaching me to stay where I belong. They are also teaching me that my body is only temporary ... soon I won't suffer anymore. Soon I will be free. And I will be headed down that right path..."

I took a deep breath, and before anything else could happen, I reached up and hit the stop button. I sank back in the chair, finally relaxing, and processed everything that I said. The bit about my dad shocked me. Was that really what I thought this whole time, and I was completely oblivious to it? I did believe he was still around, but I did not believe that he was in the same place as these other spirits... In fact, I almost knew that he wasn't.

I cocked my head to the side, listening for Seth outside the door, even though I knew he was the whole time. I knew he heard every word I said. I leaned over towards the door and called for him.

Once Seth got me up and carried me up the stairs and to my wheelchair, I asked if he would bring me up to my room. I wanted to have a private meditation. Nodding, Seth understood. Or, he didn't question. He put me on my bed and shut the door, telling me that he will be sure that I could come back downstairs for food.

I got into that pretzel yoga position on my bed and shut my eyes. I had to concentrate well on this and hope with all my might that it would take me to where I wanted to go. I could make the right connection if I tried hard enough, and the way that I was feeling, I was going to get it. I had to get it.

The fog came back. It was calmer this time, but still too thick to make anything out. I floated in my vision, at once deeply surprised by the cool air that I felt—I felt it all over me—my legs rejoicing in the comfort of the fog. The gray figures that floated with me stayed their distance and did not reveal themselves. They could have been anyone's spirits, really, the way they were all just lumped together aimlessly. I at once noticed the one spirit that lingered outside of the fog, the very one that I was following previously. Its shape became more humanlike as I approached it, and as I approached, it separated itself from the fog and became an actual shape.

He was still too far away. I knew instantly that he could not get into the fog I was in—and I could not get out. I drifted as far as I could, trying to make out a face to see if he could see me. Of course, I knew he could, and I knew he knew my presence because I saw an arm and hand wave. He waved at me, trying to tell me something, and I pushed forward. By this time, I could see the shape of his head more clearly, and it was funny. I almost swore he was forever going to wear his favorite Windsor hat. I pushed against the fog; I pushed through the other spirits that were there with mine until I came to the edge of a dark circle. I stopped short, realizing I had never seen before in any of my visions, and was completely set back when I saw ahead. My dad was here, all right, but I was in one circle and I saw that he was in another one. We were in two rings, separated from one another and barely touching. He waved at me again, waved in the direction of the path he was in. He waved at me to follow him, at first slowly, and then his last wave was a little more urgent. He moved a little, as though he were trying to break through into the area I was in, but he could not move. I stayed still as the fog and other spirits brushed through me. Before I could say or do anything, I woke up from my vision as someone called my name.

My eyes popped open, and I shivered. Standing in my doorway were Kimberly and Seth.

"Time for dinner, Sky," Kimberly announced.

"Okay, sure," I said, getting back to reality as Seth scooped me up. They brought me down silently. I thought about just how isolated we really were.

All around campus, snakes of evergreen and holly coiled around the lampposts, candy-rainbow lights strung around trees and even some lit-up Santa and Frosty figures were put up by the library. It was like I had to visit the rest of campus to remember what time of the year it was, because, on our end, it did not exist. Everyone did a very good job ignoring it because we believed—knew—Christmas would not come. Whenever I would go to classes or to the coffee shop, I would get to see, up close and personal, exactly what I was missing. I saw cheer. I saw excitement and fun. The coffee shop proudly served peppermint hot chocolates and eggnog lattes and didn't hold back on the decorative decals on the windows, slightly obscured by frost. It made my stomach hard. There were just different rings of existence all around. On our own little island at The Manor, we were to have different thoughts about the time of the year. Students at The

Manor decorated by just putting up candles here and there. As far as we were concerned, we were having our own O Holy Night.

I got back home one day, after what seemed like the worst day to navigate the icy sidewalks with freezing wind stinging my face. My arms throbbed, and I already wore out the fingers in my gloves, tiny holes forming at the tips and loose threads threatening to unravel at any minute. I wanted nothing more than to park myself on the couch and not have to wheel anywhere. Once I got inside, the cold didn't leave me. I immediately spotted Iris and her boy toy all snuggled up on the couch. I avoided eye contact, trying to sink my face down into my scarf as though I could disappear in it, but Damien actually looked up. I saw him eye me curiously. At once, Iris brushed the side of his face to turn him away from me. She leaned in and said something to him. To me, it sounded like she said, "You are better than that." His expression changed from soft to stone, and he looked away.

They resumed cuddling in front of the TV and I got out of there as fast as I could. I wheeled over to Carol's room, wanting to get back to my bed to pay another visit to the mysterious planes. I awkwardly went around corners but stopped abruptly at the hushed voices coming from Carol's room. I held on to my wheels to stop them from making any noise and stood as still as possible. The door was open a little, and I was able to see Carol inside talking with someone. There was tension in her back as she leaned towards the person she was talking to, and I didn't need to see inside to know it was Mitchell. His voice came through loud and clear no matter what, even in whispers. His voice was always heard.

"And how do you know this?" Carol demanded. "Is this what The White Light is telling you?"

"My dear, it is what we knew all along," Mitchell answered very calmly. "We weren't going to go out the same way. Certainly not. We're going first."

At that moment, my left wheel betrayed me, a small movement let out a squeak so loud that it would have been a miracle if they didn't hear. Sure enough, the door opened all the way and the two of them came out, acting like they were discussing sports or the weather.

"Sky, I'm sorry I didn't mean to forget you," Carol said. "Would you like me to take you up to your room now?"

"Yeah," I said. "Sure."

I put on a fake smile and tried not to look directly at Mitchell, who was eyeing me suspiciously.

"Were you waiting ... long, my child?" he asked me.

"No," I answered right away. "Just got here. I didn't even see you there."

He smiled a little and blinked a nod.

Before anything else could happen, Carol scooped me up from my chair and carried on.

She was quiet as we went upstairs. Quiet even for her. I saw her lips pressed a little and actually wished I was waiting outside that door longer. She sighed once she noticed me staring at her.

"Mitchell and I were having a bit of a discussion."

I didn't say anything.

"What did you hear, exactly?"

"Nothing, really. Just Mitchell saying something about how he wanted to go first at something. That's all."

"Okay," she answered.

"I didn't hear your private discussion, I swear."

"I believe you," she said.

"Is everything all right?"

"Of course. Everything is as it should be, of course. We just have to remember to keep the faith. Right?"

"Yeah."

She dropped me off on my bed and turned to leave, then looked at me again.

"Continue to meditate, Sky. We need to be in as close touch to the spirits as possible. We all need to be in on this together so we can go home."

Dinner was awkward for many reasons. One reason was that I had no clue what was brewing with Mitchell and Carol. Another reason was just the students themselves, who at one point decided just to quiet down. The mess hall was no longer the boisterous social gathering that any normal cafeteria full of students would bring. No one talked or laughed or goofed around. People chatted casually but mostly kept quiet, mostly kept their heads down as though in prayer. Who could tell for sure? Were people really praying at this point? And what were they praying for?

Another reason dinner was awkward was Damien. He kept trying to casually steal a glance at me. The more he did, the more it annoyed me. I had no clue what was going on with him anymore, and I had no clue what Iris was saying to him. A couple of times I tried to catch him in his stare and return it with a stare of my own, to see how he would react, and he mostly just pretended not to see me and continue eating. I saw Iris look my way once, scowl, then turn back to him. I almost wanted to roll over there and ask them what their problem was, had it been anyone but Iris. Anyone approaching Iris had to do so delicately. But was there any way that Damien would ever be alone? It never seemed like it.

They say be careful what you wish for, and I was thinking exactly that after dinner. I was bored and restless roaming around the upper lounge and kitchen area. Lo-and-behold, my knight in shining denim came out of nowhere carrying his empty hot chocolate mug. He went over to the sink, ignoring me, or just trying to ignore me. I wanted to roll right up to his face and confront him, but I didn't. Part of me didn't even want to talk to him. He turned cautiously, almost nervously.

"What, Damien?" I demanded.

He completely turned around now.

"Nothing Sky, I was just looking for Iris."

"Well, she's not here, so you can stop acting like a timid dog."

I noticed that Damien still did not look at me, at least not directly.

"I just..." he started. "I've thought about you a lot. I mean, I was concerned."

I sighed. "Well, I am doing fine, I guess."

"I mean, I was really concerned about ... what happened to you. Or ... what the spirits decided was best for you. I just hope you learned from it."

Just when I thought he would come around again.

"*Learned* from it? Oh Jesus Christ, Damien, I didn't do a god damn thing to deserve to be paralyzed and you know it! Or is that it? Is that why you are avoiding me?"

He looked at the floor, rubbing down his hair.

"No, I just ... I just want to be strong. I don't want that to happen to me."

"You think I am contagious or something?!"

"We just … we just need to be strong. We can't be weak and then become deformed because of it. It's wrong, and it's a punishment." He still refused to look at me, and even as he said that last sentence, I could tell he was holding back on something. "We all need to be strong," he said again.

"Yeah, well, let me tell you something," I said. "One of us is strong, while the other one is a weak and brainless sheep. And it's *not* the girl in the wheelchair."

I just rolled away, fed up. There was no way I could get through to him, and I wanted to be done trying. Trying to reach Damien was becoming exhausting.

Mitchell requested—well—ordered another meeting to be held one evening. I got this email in between classes at the library. I almost felt like I needed to shield my computer screen from neighboring students. While most students were studying for finals and working on projects, we were journaling in our rooms and filming our Exit videos. No one knew what happened inside The Manor but us, and no one could find out. Even if I actually had any friends outside of GOL, it was something I could never talk about. I felt like I needed to be protective and keep everything and anything GOL-related to myself. It was selfish, in a way, like I felt I was harboring this big secret from the rest of the world that they were unworthy of. This was exactly what we all were supposed to think.

The countdown on the fireplace mantle was getting closer and closer. It was the elephant in the room no one directly talked about, but there it was all the same. Mitchell looked at it almost adoringly as he waited for the entire ensemble to—assemble—in our places on the floor.

"I know you've all noticed this," Mitchell said, gesturing to the elephant. "So you all know just how closer we are getting! And I know you all must be just as excited as I am, as you should be. Pretty soon, we will leave life on Earth and go to where we are supposed to go. We're going home!"

Everyone nodded in approval, some had grins spreading ear to ear and some actually had glistening, teary eyes. "The spirits and I spent a lot of time talking. You could even say I spend most of my time turning inward to listen to what they have to say. Do not be afraid."

"Mitchell?" some girl's hand went up. "Mitchell, has The White Light said exactly how we are going to go?"

"Have no fear, my child," Mitchell answered. "Or do you fear that you will feel pain on Judgment Day?"

"No," the girl answered.

"Do you have fear and doubt inside of you?"

"No, no," the girl answered immediately. "No, I have no fear! I have no doubt!"

"The White Light," continued Mitchell, "Assures us that we all will go peacefully. Which brings me to the subject matter of this evening."

Mitchell paced the room, taking the time to look at each and every one of us. No one asked any more questions or even stirred. He moved slowly, carefully, as though carrying an enormous weight in his body.

"The White Light tells me that Earth will end when it is scheduled to, of course, but why should we wait?"

I sat up a little bit, the sinking feeling in my gut coming back, remembering his and Carol's conversation. I did not like where this was going.

"We are going to be leaders in The New World. We have been trained already to become that level above human, so we're ready. Did you all hear me? We are ready. So why shouldn't we go sooner?"

There were some murmurs, but no one spoke out.

"We have the right to see this New World sooner than the rest of Earth, or for whoever is deemed worthy to live in it. We are the leaders, so it is our duty to go first and lead the way for the rest. It is our duty that our families have us as leaders, otherwise where would they be? They would be lost. So, naturally, that is why we have to go first. Listen carefully, my Lights … we have only a couple days left on Earth, don't we? You have all completed your Exit Videos, right? If you have not done so, I strongly advise you to do it right away, as that will be one of the most important things we can take with us. Because we will be going a day earlier. Mark your calendars for a different kind of 'Eve' and shoot for December 20th. That is The White Light's final decision."

It was so quiet I could hear my own breathing: scattered and uneven.

"We have put together a plan of how we will go. It will be a very peaceful, relaxing and enjoyable way, for we deserve that and much more. We will go by means of personal meditation that will start out as any ordinary vision, but the only difference is we will finally just be our Lights, and we will no longer have need for our Guardians. We shall finally be free. It will be our final meditation here, all done from the privacy and comfort of our own rooms. Then … we will be reunited again in paradise."

It didn't take a genius to figure out what Mitchell was really telling us. No, the world wasn't just going to blow up on December 21st, we all were getting the magical privilege of dying a day sooner. And how? I didn't exactly know. What, we were going to go to sleep or have a vision and just have our souls to be whisked away? Did they really think that was going to happen?

Was that really going to happen?

Well, of course, that wasn't possible. How could that be possible? No. There was no way that we were going to all just permanently leave our bodies ... and die. That could not happen! Even if it weren't voluntary, how were they going to make us? Mitchell may have been possessed, but the rest of us were not. At least, I certainly was not. I was still in control of my own brain and I could decide whether I lived or died and that was it! It was all in everyone's heads, anyway. Why does everyone believe a stupid ancient Mayan prophecy, anyway? What the hell did they know then, and what the hell did that have to do with anything now? Nothing, that's what. The whole December 21st thing was stupid, and it wasn't going to happen, and we were not going to have our souls be sucked out by spirits.

I paced my room for the most part of the evening, and when I say "paced," I mean I jerked the wheels at every sharp corner and turn, so this was my way of pacing. I put all my energy into those turns and had to be careful not to crash into the walls. I even did a few times and did not care. My head raced more than my chair.

I thought back to the beginning of school, and how stupid and naïve I was. Look, a group of people with paranormal connections! Sure, how about I go and join this group I know nothing about? There's no *way* anything could go horribly wrong! I turned so hard and so fast I knocked into my dresser and knocked some papers on the floor, but I didn't care. I wasn't going to pick that up. What did it matter, anyway? Nothing mattered. My thoughts turned to my visions and the spiritual encounters and seeing … my dad. I suddenly threw my face up to the ceiling.

"Yeah, nice going!" I cried. "Do you think you could have straight out told me what I was getting into? You think if I knew this was a death cult, I would have joined in the first place? No, now I'm here and stuck with it and whatever happens! Why me, huh? Why did I have to get involved in this? I didn't even do anything wrong!"

I brought my wheels to an abrupt halt, tangling up the rug.

"Did I deserve *this?*" I gestured to my noble steed. "Did I really do something to deserve losing my legs?"

I had my journal out, but I couldn't write that much. I had ideas that I couldn't put in the right words. I wrote a few sentences as they came to me.

Call the school and tell them everything.

Instantly, I scratched this out. They wouldn't believe me. Either that, or Mitchell and the spirits would find out and I would be severely punished again. I didn't know what was worse than becoming paralyzed. Could they do something worse at this point?

Okay, what if I wrote them an anonymous letter and dropped it off sometime in between classes? Yes, this one I would take extra care of to make sure—you know—fireplaces didn't eat it or anything. Yes, what if I went for help right away? Then the school would shut down the group and the meditation sessions won't happen and then we would all be saved. And I could call my mom to get me out of this place.

Or I could just stop freaking out and finally let go. I could believe in it completely and put my entire fate on the line, because maybe that is what "being saved" actually means. Maybe that is all I need to do in order to save my life. I will believe in the Next Life so that I can actually *have* a next life! Yes, all I needed to do was to put up a front, even if it was an act. Or, once they see me going along with everything, maybe I can find a way to stop it.

I sobbed quietly, if that were even possible. I muffled my cries so no one could hear. Even as I stared at the letter I wrote, I knew it would never get out. It would never get out because I would never get out. They were watching us all too closely, and I could jeopardize everything and make it worse. My short life was going to be over, and there was nothing I could do about it. First my dad, and now me. The emotions drained out of me as I thought about my family. I thought about my mom, brother and sister, who at first had to lose my dad and now they were going to lose me. Or we were going to join him, whether we wanted to or not. Life was going to be over. It was over and it didn't even start. I didn't even get my driver's license yet. I will forever be a young teenage girl who didn't even get to the good parts. I would never know love, and what it was like to be in love and be happily married. Life was short, but it was too short, and it was going to be over.

I'm so sorry, Mom.

I cried harder because I knew somehow this was all my fault. I saw all of this happening and I just went along with it. I was wrong, so very wrong. I should have gone with my gut feeling about this group that something was not quite right, and now I was paying for my mistake. It just all sounded so *good*.

I stretched out on my bed as tiny snow sprinkles fell down my window. All my emotions were drained out of me, and I felt peaceful. I thought about the Peter Pan quote: "To die ... would be an awfully big adventure." That's what it was. It was an adventure, and it was something we were all going to face at some point. It was inevitable. Maybe the spirits and the higher power we put our faith in we trying to protect us after all. They knew that this was going to happen, so this is why they isolated us like this, this is why they started appearing to Mitchell in dreams to tell him the truths they knew. Life was going to end, but we still had something ahead of us. We had the mystical mystery of the afterlife. My cheeks, stiff with dry tears, hurt a bit as I smiled.

CHAPTER 37

December 19th, 2012. Two days remained on Earth, and only one day for the Guardians of Light to make their special exit. The halls were somber on this day. Everyone walked around light-paced and quiet, focused. We put on brave faces as we acknowledged each other, and the atmosphere around us … for it had also changed. We could not see them, but we could feel them. There was a presence in every room, every hallway, and almost every corner. They drifted up to the ceiling and tampered with the overhead lighting. They dashed down the halls to create bursts of cold air as a constant reminder. At one point, sitting in the kitchen, I saw that they started to create a snowstorm. I heard miniature snow cyclones rush in between the trees in the woods, saw the trees themselves disappear behind a gray sky, and watched snow fall in clumps too large to be snowflakes. We were supposed to be snowed in, after all.

The rest of the campus went home for Christmas break. We, however, would not be leaving campus, but we would be going home...

Mitchell wanted us to spend every waking moment together, and his enforced schedule was nothing to sneer at. He at one point put up a bulletin board in the upper lounge and would write inspiring messages on it. Sometimes there were even special orders or rules to follow. From time to time, we all started to notice different things change on the bulletin board. Some words were taken away and added, but no one said anything, and no one even blinked at the changes. I noticed right away that we were not to go any-where alone, especially today. It said, clear as day, "All Lights are to be in groups or pairs, never separated, and no one is permitted to leave The Manor unattended." To separate ourselves from the group meant that we were breaking the bond, and this was a big offense. It was so big that Mitchell decided to enforce it a little more.

After breakfast in the mess hall, Mitchell brought us back to the bulletin board. This was the only time that he actu-ally acknowledged a change made on there as opposed to pretending not to notice it.

Mitchell stood before the board now, his face almost as white as it.

"Children, today we must continue to enforce the unbreakable bond we all have together. We must preserve it and keep it strong."

Without breaking his eye contact with the group, Mitchell pulled a ball of yarn from his pocket, bright and festive red good enough for any Christmas wrapping ... if that was what it was for.

"We tie that bond together today to remember so. Like the double helix of DNA, we will form our own linkage. We will spend time physically connected to one another. This will help us grow our bond strong and preserve us as a group once we leave Earth. We will assemble starting now, and you may only leave to take care of personal matters. Pretty soon, we will not have to confine ourselves to the burdens of human bodily functions at all. We can no longer stand the weakness of our bodies. Come together, my Lights!"

We lined up—almost perfectly—in a similar Jacob's ladder fashion. The yarn that held us together acted as a belt tied around one waist and then across to another.

I couldn't decide if this was more awkward for me or more convenient. I would be surrounded by other people for the whole day. I could even get pushed around today, but that meant I needed to be extra careful not to run anyone over. I was across from a girl I didn't know that well, which was fine because no one felt like having lengthy discussions like this.

There was apparently one person who wanted to have a discussion with me because I caught him looking at me.

He was attached to Iris, of course, as she probably wouldn't have it any other way. I first noticed he was acting funny for at least a few days, but today it was finally getting to him. Today it was like it was finally hitting him, but that couldn't have been it. It seemed like it was something else, and for the first time in a long time, I saw some of the old Damien I came to miss. One time, in passing, I could have sworn he almost smiled at me, like his eyes were waving a white flag. He had so much pain in them when he looked at me, but I saw something else. It wasn't cruelty, it wasn't fearful, it was just ... Damien. Damien with his old self again.

After a drowsy meditation session, we were sent to bed. I obviously did not intend to fall right to sleep as soon as Carol plopped me down on my blankets. I only slept for a little while when I heard a knock on my door, and I knew it was not coming from a dream.

I sat up and squinted in the dark. The knock was faint at first, but then pounded again a little louder. My door opened with a slow creek.

"Sky?" I heard my name whispered.

"Damien?" I said loudly.

He came in and shut the door, and I heard him feel his way around for my desk lamp.

I reacted the way anyone would and shielded my eyes.

"I'm ... so sorry..."

I opened my eyes and looked at him. His eyes were tired and his hair was disheveled. He looked like he slept very little, or not at all. He sat down on my bed and looked me in the eye. I didn't need much to tell me that he was officially snapped out of it. Before I could say anything, his face scrunched up in sorrow.

"I am so, so sorry."

For the first time, I saw Damien cry, the awkward way guys do with their fists at their foreheads in shame.

He struggled with his words in between little hiccups.

"I was wrong. It was wrong of me to be so shitty to you after everything that happened, but it was because I was so scared something was going to happen and you didn't deserve it and Iris—"

I hugged him.

"Shut up, it's okay."

"No, it's not! Iris said all that crap and made me believe it, but I don't even like her, anyway. She's so controlling and—"

"Don't worry about it."

"*NO, you have to listen to me.*"

Damien looked at me at direct eye level, his face so stern and serious it made my expression fall.

"I found out some stuff. From Iris. About what is going on and what has been going on. They've been drugging us."

"What?"

"They've been drugging everyone *but* us! Remember when we weren't involved with the tornado and how everyone else seemed to be completely brainwashed but us? It's the cookies and the banana bread and stuff. They have been putting something in all the baked goods and feeding them to everybody—"

"But we didn't eat them!" I interrupted.

"Exactly," Damien spat. "Any time we ate our snacks and not theirs, we weren't drugged up."

I sat there and let this sink in. It was so sneaky, so under-the-table manipulative. I wanted to scream. They were drugging kids. We were screwed up mentally as well as physically. Only Damien and I were the only ones who still had part of our consciences. At least part of them.

"Oh my God," I answered. "So that's what Iris said? She told you all of that?"

"Yeah, but she wasn't supposed to. No one is supposed to know about it, but she wanted me to be in on it, and I had to tell you. She is super serious about it. All the members are, especially the older high school kids. I just ... I just felt really weird. I don't know what the hell I was thinking, or what she made me think these past couple of days, and I am so sorry for being such a jerk to you, but I'm glad it made me think ... and now we can focus on what to do. Or what not to do."

I looked at him. "So we watch what we eat from now on. What about the food? The spaghetti? I won't even eat that."

"No, it's not the food. Whatever Mitchell is making Carol put in, it's in the baked stuff. It's easier to hide, I guess, and just enough to make everybody more stupid and weak."

"Well, *we're* not stupid and weak," I said, my eyes hardening. "As long as we can keep them from drugging *us* and messing with our heads, we can get out of here."

"That's what I want to believe ... but you and I both know the things that Mitchell, this group, and the ghosts are capable of if we don't play along."

I shuddered a bit as I looked out the window, knowing the isolated cloud of fog we were in the middle of.

"Well, what are they going to do? Blow up the world?"

"Oh jeez, Sky, don't say it like that!"

"We're past this now, Damien."

For the first time in what felt like eons, I sat up a little straighter. It was like my backbone woke up.

"We have to go along with everything like we know nothing, and you see if Iris says anything else about what Mitchell says about December 21st. Whatever he's planning, we need to be on top of it. And we will be. You know what else you need to do? Stock up on more supplies."

He smiled a little, but only a little. The weight of the situation before us could not be lifted.

We both paused, listening for anything outside the door or anything within the walls. Our conversation stayed private.

CHAPTER 38

December 20th, 2012.

We woke up almost simultaneously, getting out of bed and lightly pulling our sheets over our pillows. We moved as one; we worked as one, dressing and trickling downstairs to the mess hall. Even though it was Christmas Break, Mitchell ordered us to all be in uniform. We had to look our best for our grand exit, of course. We felt solemn and silent but at the same time, peaceful. Everyone had a creepy smile on their faces. "It's going to happen tonight," I heard some whisper.

Damien and I didn't act out of the ordinary. We couldn't. We blended in and showed no signs of rebel. We were afraid to step one toe out of line and show any difference. We could not show any signs of hesitation. Our faces became stone and stayed that way, but on the inside, we were screaming. Each member wore the special occasion cloaks that day ... these white ones covering us from head to toe, head and all. It was crucial that The White Light see us in our attire. We were white Lights on our own. The Manor was filled with these individual white lights, all spread out but together. It was also filled with candles on every windowsill and table. It had to have been the entire collection.

It became a silent day, that day. It flowed together in an almost dream sequence of eating and meditating with very little talking or activities. Whenever we meditated, Damien and I sat side by side. Everywhere we went, he carried me. In a way, I carried him too.

At night, we gathered in the lower lounge for what would be our final meditation session. Mitchell's eyes swam and glazed over, but no tears fell. He kept those in, almost afraid of letting any part of his soul out. It was not time for that yet.

"My children ... all my children..." he announced, standing before the fireplace and addressing us, all of us. He even looked to the ceiling and to the walls, no doubt addressing those others. "Judgment Day is the day of peace and reflection. Soon we will be casting off our shells, these guardian bodies of ours. We don't need them anymore. We are strong enough to stand on our own. We have left our bodies several times. Soon it will be time to leave them for good."

A gust of wind blew through the fireplace, a coughing, painful gasp that turned into a weak whisper.

"Yes," Mitchell answered it. "We are coming."

Damien and I held our breath as Mitchell walked over to a table, where we saw a tray of neatly lined up pudding glasses. They were staring at us in the face, twisted into distorted smiles in each cup.

"Come up and get yours ... and then proceed to your bedrooms. I want you all to relax and take your time if needed. Reflect in a journal if you wish. But do not linger too long. The sooner we can all meet together again is crucial. We need to leave Earth before it is no more. Enjoy your bedtime snack but make sure to eat all of it, as we will need some sustenance when we travel, then lie in your beds and allow your souls to finally escape."

Mitchell might not have allowed his tears to fall, but some of the others did. I couldn't tell if it was out of fear, or belief, but some of the others could not hide their emotions. Some sniffed and wiped their faces with their cloaks but did not say anything.

"Come, my Lights," Mitchell said, holding out the tray.

And so we went. One by one, we took our glasses. And then we left. We left Mitchell standing there, watching us all leave, saving the very last pudding on the tray for himself. He stayed until we all got to our rooms first, but I was never sure if he waited. I was not sure if he absolutely wanted to be the first, or the last.

As usual, Damien lifted me up to take me to my room. I held our two pudding glasses while he carried me down the floor. "Trade you for a swirl?" I whispered.

He nodded and dropped me on my bed.

"Now what?" he whispered.

"We wait for a minute until the others settle down ... then come back here. We need to stay awake this time. We need to watch to see what happens. If weird shit starts to happen, then we can stop everybody. We can wake them up."

Damien agreed and left my room for the moment. I sat as straight up as I could, knowing perfectly well that Damien and I would probably not be sleeping that night. The others would eat that drugged up pudding and then ... something.

I put my pudding glass on my dresser, as far away to the wall as I could. Nothing was going to touch me anymore. I was not going to do that meditation ... at least not the same one as the others. Instead, I steadied my breathing pattern and closed my eyes.

Stay with me, Dad. I know you're around here somewhere. Stay with me and give me the strength I need. Please. Give me strength. I am not with them anymore. I am not with them anymore.

My own spirit was intact, and that was exactly how it should be.

I listened, listened for everything and anything that would happen in these walls. I listened for spirits creaking under the floorboards, but the only thing I heard was Damien making his way back, carefully. He came into my room without the slightest squeak, and in his arms were blankets and a bag of food with two Pepsi cans. He spread the blankets on the floor and opened the bag, taking out some chips and popcorn and two cups of chocolate and vanilla swirl pudding.

I got down off the bed, Damien and I fueling on our little picnic but careful not to make noise—any noise—as our ears strained for house activity. I watched him tilt his head towards the window, afraid that if he chewed too loudly, he would miss something. I then started to smooth the blanket around me, taking things to line the edges with such as the Little Debbie snack cakes he brought.

"What are you doing?"

"Forming a circle," I answered. "A protective circle. Help me. We're going to try something."

We got the blanket all lined around the edges, like we were at the beach and preventing our towel from blowing away. Damien and I sat in the center facing each other and squeezed hands, squeezing our eyes shut as well.

"Just breathe and concentrate," I instructed. "Let's see if we can ... do something."

I am not sure exactly what Damien meditated on, but I know I wanted to make a protective barrier ... around us and the house and the whole world, if I could. I knew I didn't need the Guardians of Light—or Mitchell—anymore and from that point on I was going to be working free of them. I concentrated on that circle, imagining we were sitting on clouds that took us out of The Manor and out of school.

We peeked an eye open once in a while, training our ears towards the walls and door for anything out of the ordinary—or anything at all. I don't know what we were expecting that we were equally terrified of. A rumbling that would be the beginning of a hideous earthquake? I did not feel any rumbling, but just the opposite. In what seemed like the later hours of the night, I started to let go of my tension and breathe it all out, because it seemed like the house did the same. It was as though it had breath it held this whole time, air stuck behind the walls in one upright inhale that finally just let go. Damien and I let go of our tension along with our expectation.

After I while I checked the clock: 4:12 A.M

"It's December 21st," I remarked.

We looked at each other, then out the window, where all we could see was the darkness that was our only company.

"Do you think it was just another meditation?" he asked.

"It has to be," I answered, looking up at the ceiling. "It might just be that."

"Nothing happened ... at least not yet."

"No."

We had some blankets wrapped around ourselves—for warmth or protection, I don't know.

"Nothing is going to happen," I finally said, not sure how I knew this.

"So now what?"

"I can't wait to see what Mitchell has to say about this when everybody wakes up. Let him explain it. And watch everyone lose their faith in all this crap. No believers mean no power."

Damien and I did not want to go to sleep yet, still wary of the quiet. It was the longest and most excruciating night of our lives. We struggled to stay awake at times, but the heaviness in our heads traveled down to the rest of our bodies and made it hard to sit upright. I started to doze first, and I know this because Damien scooped me up without a word and put me in my bed. Then, he laid back down on his blanket spread, using his sweatshirt as a pillow.

I worked all my mental power to connect with my dad's spirit, to ask for his protection, and I felt him. I felt him watching over me as I went to sleep, drug-free, but still vulnerable in ways I did not want to be.

December 21st, 2012

I woke up to the sound of silence ... It was the loudest silence I had ever heard. There were no wind gusts outside, there were no creaks in the floorboards, no whispering voices in the halls ... or in the walls. My eyes adjusted and I saw my room. I blinked once, twice, and saw that it looked exactly the same as when I went to bed. My room was still in one piece and didn't change. Damien was on his side and still wheezing gently. I sat up. I threw back my covers at once—because I did feel one change. To my utter shock, my knee moved.

I jumped and gasped, and at once my other knee moved. I slowly started to move more and sure enough my heels dragged down my sheets until my legs closed in completely.

And then I jumped up. My legs and feet reacted and instantly fell back into place; fell back into blood circulation and life. Not only was I alive, but I was completely alive. The parts of me that were dead had been restored. I got up and stood on those legs of mine.

It did not take long for me to wake up completely as I remembered what it was like to walk. My legs carried me around my room, old friends awakened from a coma and picking up stamina and speed. It was my focus and my pride, I was so euphoric I barely noticed Damien sitting upright and gawking at my miracle.

His eyes bulged.

"Oh my God."

"I'm ... cured."

"I can't believe it," he said again, getting up and approaching me. We had a million words between us but we didn't say them ... because we both knew we needed to see what else had changed.

Damien and I left my room and started to make our way downstairs. We first noticed the candles, the way they had burnt all the way down until there was no more wick left. We noticed them in the way that we knew that no one tended to them. The flame ghosts lingered a bit that gave me a funny tingling feeling. Damien stared next to me. There was definitely something wrong here. We almost felt like we were in a different place. There was something wrong, but we did not know what it was. The kitchen and the upper lounge were all empty.

We walked down the stairs to the lower lounge to find that empty as well. Not a sound, not a soul.

I turned to Damien.

"Everyone should be up by now. Shouldn't they?"

"Let's go check on them..." he said.

Normally we would not feel so alone, but we did and with good reason. Damien and I were nervous about what we had to do next. I led the way back up the residential stairs towards the first room, which was Iris's. I gently knocked, unable to make anything louder than a tap, before I finally pushed the door open.

What we saw almost sent my entire body to paralysis.

Iris's body was still ... still and paler than the chalky wallpaper in her room. We rushed to her bed to touch her, and found her ice cold and unresponsive. Crusts of leftover pudding stuck at the ends of her lips, a cruel paste to fasten them permanently shut.

"Oh my God..."

"Is she?..."

"She's ... dead."

Our eyes trailed to the pudding glass on the dresser next to her bed, which had its own leftovers. Along with pudding looked like some traces of brownish powder.

"Poison. It was poison this time, Damien."

Everyone else was all the same.

Their bodies were, anyway.

They looked so fake and unrecognizable, like displays in a wax museum. They all lay on their backs in bed, still wearing their full school uniforms—and GOL white cloaks. They all had uniforms for burial as well, all empty shells cast off in the same way.

Damien and I left each room in sickly, horrified panic.

There was one more room to check...

We walked down stairs to his office, opening that fateful door and turning into the section that was his room. Mitchell's bed lay hidden in an alcove darker than the desk and I found the lamp. As expected, we found his body just like the others; his empty pudding glass scraped the cleanest of them all. The spoon sat on the table licked completely clean of any evidence that it served as a deathly weapon … a weapon still fresh from activity just shy of a few hours. Mitchell's face, unlike the others, still looked awake. His eyes were open and stared at nothing and looked at nothing, no more, like he was a stoic portrait hanging over a fireplace. His hands were also clasped together under his covers, and we bravely pulled it back to glimpse what it was: He was holding—very closely—one of the newspaper articles from the folder he kept. His fingers were interwoven...like he was using his last few seconds of life to pray...for something, someone, or even to someone.

I couldn't breathe. We left immediately and threw ourselves on a couch in the upper lounge. I heard Damien choke on his breath as we had our emotional release with shaky sobs. We held each other tightly, and as our tears fell, I looked outside to see that a light snow fell, too. The flakes were softer than snow and almost looked like the cotton clumps that escaped on a windy day ... free falling and trusting wherever the wind was taking them.

CHAPTER 39

It was suicide and murder at the same time.

That was what we concluded, anyway. Maybe no one knew the pudding was poisoned but we knew everyone was convinced they were going to die and were willing to. It was scary—and it didn't help at all Damien and I were expected to have all the answers.

I would say from that moment we called 911 and on, and many moments after that, everything just blurred by. I don't even remember how things happened from the bodies being taken away to the millions of confrontations and questions Damien and I were asked. With our help, the authorities got the understanding of what happened by the other activities the group had done. Kids were drugged and brainwashed by a sick, tormented man who led them to kill themselves while he did the same.

The only thing about this ordeal that was any good at all was that it was Christmas break, and school wasn't in session, which meant Damien and I went home that day and got to stay there. From then we were under multiple layers of protection. No doubt if the rest of the school were there, we wouldn't be able to handle the intense media circus that took place around campus. The Manor became internet and TV famous overnight, and of course the school tried everything to protect its precious reputation. It was considered a crime scene, and they needed to search through The Manor for evidence. It was sickening seeing the yellow tape surrounding the house. Before The Manor was doing everything to bring people in, and now it was doing everything to keep people out. I suppose there were no more secrets anymore, nor were there suspicions. As of then all rumors and suspicions were confirmed: The Guardians of Light were freaks after all, and now they were all dead. All except for the two lone survivors. And these two survivors would be going to therapy for a while. I was an expert by then so it just added to my personal track record. It was a first for Damien and he did not take it so well at first—but our phone calls to each other helped. We promised to have our own holiday and get together to exchange, what else, Christmas cookies. I knew we would be there for each other.

It was obvious to say that it did not feel like Christmas at all and the incident involving me meant my family tip-toed around me and tried to comfort me in little ways, all while subtly trying to ask about that boarding school that had a cult.

Damien and I arranged to meet one day. There was something that we needed to do ... when we felt up for it. After talking about it with the police, they agreed to let us have the item we needed ... they wanted some confirmation from it as well. He came over and I already had the TV set up in a room where we could be alone. I popped the first disk in.

It was weird to see all of their faces and hear their voices again. I didn't even recognize myself or the words that I was saying. Was that even me talking? Did I even believe all those things? I wasn't too surprised that many of the other students were saying the same things about The Next Life. Damien and I huddled together. The very last person to make their Exit Video was, of course, Mitchell Brooks himself.

He turned the camera on and sat down in the chair, making sure to take his time with it. He took a breath and acknowledged the camera right away, or rather allowing whoever was watching to acknowledge him. He gazed into the lens very intimately and I felt a shudder. Mitchell almost knew immediately that he had control, even on the other side of a video clip.

"My brush with The White Light was immaculate, to say the least. To say that I have been touched by such a powerful source of life and saved from the very things that make human beings bad is a miracle. The White Light knows of higher power and life, The White Light is the one whose job it is to lead us to this higher power and life. We are not meant to live on Earth forever as human beings, as creatures with so much fault and very little abilities. Our time on Earth is merely the 'training grounds,' or stepping stones for the lives we are supposed to live. It was a test, really, all one big test to determine the strongest points of our character so that we can take those with us. When we leave Earth in the afterlife to the Next Life is when we truly live.

The White Light appeared to me in a dream many years ago, when I was working as an announcer and public speaker. I was touched by its beautiful message … and since then I have dedicated the rest of my life to living it as fulfilled as possible. I started to spread my message, but with very little success. I soon gathered a group of followers who understood me. They, too, began to take the message of The White Light into their lives. We were a small group, but we were a start. These young people were so dedicated and so inspiring, but not inspiring enough to inspire others to join us in our charade. We meditated on our own and concentrated on self-reflection. I lived alone at the time; being married with no family. I considered these people to be my family and I was theirs. We moved in together, finding an apartment complex that was by a heavily wooded area. We were very happy there and enriched. Our time together was intense and their Lights were strong. Very strong. They were so strong that one night when we met together, I asked them if they were strong enough to go to The Next Life. Without hesitation, they all said that they were. Without hesitation, they all said that they were ready. It was then we decided my family would not wait until their time on Earth was over. They would go now. They would go as the leaders of The Next Life. It was what The White Light wanted. We all knew this to be true. I meditated on my own and found that these strong little Lights of mine needed to shine. I was scared to lose them, I was sad to be left alone, but The White Light told me to be strong. It told me it was the right time to let go. So, I had another meeting with my children, my Lights. I told them how The Next Life needed them to go and become leaders, and pave the way for other Lights once their time had come. I told them that they were to go alone. I was to stay behind and spread the message and recruit more followers. So, we arranged a ceremony.

We donned our cloaks, our special garments with the symbol of our family and went to a secluded area in the woods. It was to be a clean act and a painless one, of course. I had the very important job of supervising this task to make sure it was executed properly and then taking care of their bodies afterwards. It was all as simple as adding something to their favorite iced tea bottles. It was fast, and then, it was over. I felt something very deep that night. I felt something so powerful that I could not describe, and it was because of me that this power was moving forward. I knew that I had plenty of work to do to spread this message and gain more recruits. So, I did the best thing I thought I could do: I became a teacher at a prestigious school.

Soon, the Guardians of Light found another home, and this time it was at a prep school that was built, very coincidentally, near our old apartment complex. But, it could not have been a coincidence. It was The White Light who made that happen so I could finish my work. It had to have been it, so that was what motivated me in everything that I did. I started slow and easy and started to gather some young and fresh new followers. There was a house built in the wooded area where my old home used to be, meant to be another form of student housing that no one wanted, and I knew right then and there that it was meant to be mine again. It was meant to be ours. Not long after I moved into that house that I learned that my other children, my first Lights, did not exactly leave it..."

It was here Damien and I saw something dark cross Mitchell's face, something neither of us had seen before: Fear. Mitchell's brave guard went down and we saw his vulnerability.

"They were still here ... in the very same site they were before. They had not moved on to the Next Life. They were still here and they were unhappy. They were not strong enough to go on to The Next Life. It was too soon ... their Lights were not ready yet and they were trapped in between planes. I learned this spending time in the house and recognizing signs that they were there with me ... and that they desperately needed my help. They were not going to go unless I went with them, and took some more recruits with me. Their voices echo in the walls and they floated everywhere. I felt their spirits. I became scared... I admit that I had my own moments of weakness. I felt like I was not ready to go yet and neither were my new students. But still, the spirits persisted and came to me almost every night in dreams. I meditated and meditated to The White Light for help. Soon, the answer came to me as the year 2012 was approaching. There was a prophecy from long ago from the Mayans describing the end of Earth. I knew this was a sign. I knew this seemed to be the perfect solution. Now, now we have found the opportunity to go. I have trained my new Lights and we are setting off for the New World and the Next Life. Do not worry my children, my family. I am coming. I am coming and I am bringing more family with me!"

By the time Mitchell's speech commenced, Damien and I held each other in cold sweat. Did we think Mitchell was closely connected to the spirits? Yes, but not this close. It was his plan all along. The emotion we witnessed was raw and real. We looked at his eyes, almost believing he could see us from the other side of the camera. He was gone now, and we were to believe that the power that went with him was gone too. *Where are you now, Mitchell?* I thought. *Where are you now?*

CHAPTER 40

Christmas Eve arrived without my even paying attention to it, since in the past few days they let Damien and I go back to The Manor with our families to get our stuff. We got it out quickly not wanting to spend a lot of time there at all, and the last time I was there I rushed and did not notice nor care if I forgot anything.

Early that day while my mother and aunts were in the kitchen getting things ready, I sat staring at the Christmas tree in the living room. It was filled with ornaments we either bought or the ones my siblings and I made. I stared at a snowflake that I made out of white pipe cleaners and then I called my mom.

"Yeah, honey?"

"Do you think you can take me back to The Manor real quick? I forgot something."

She came in to the living room, considering me for a while, wiping her hands on a towel.

"You did? Well, it's early enough … so of course I can take you."

And my mom and I took off, the thought in the back of my head pushing itself to the front the closer and closer we got. We pulled in to the deserted campus and kept going to the even more deserted part where The Manor resided in the woods.

"I'll just be a minute," I promised my mom and I got out alone.

I walked along that path, the same one I used to take not too long ago in the woods. Nothing changed or felt too different. It was eerie in the way that it was more isolated than before; I felt a comfort in this privacy but a resourcefulness at my courage to face it head-on. The Manor greeted me, large and empty. I approached that front step and just looked at it for a while. Since the Incident, it wasn't left open for anyone to just waltz on in. I looked at the door and looked at the windows ... wanting to see if anything was around. I looked around the trees and the grounds in general. I did not hear any voices in the wind, did not see any stray shapes between trees. The place did not seem to have the same hold on it as it did before. It was quiet. In my head I played back a montage of my time there and how I could not make any sense of it. Everything that had happened there was clear to me now and why... and it still gave me a little shock that I managed to survive it all. I did in fact feel a presence, and it was the very thing I suspected. When I looked around The Manor again, I knew that Damien and I were, in fact, not the only survivors.

The movement came around the side of the house, first slowly and then quickly. She and I made eye contact right away, acknowledging each other with both respect—and relief. She took a moment before she ran to me rather quickly. As soon as she got to my feet I bent down and picked her up, all white fur soft as a first snowfall. I petted her head and looked into her eyes again. She blinked them at me, golden and alert, yet trusting and at peace. I hugged her close, and she purred quietly. I turned to leave, carrying her at my shoulder. As I walked back down the path Ad Astra suddenly turned her head and watched behind me—just as she always had—for everything and anything that might be there.

1. A common trope for the beginning of a story is the main character attending a new school. From your impression of Sky's point of view, do you think that Sky has a positive or negative viewpoint of going to a new school? Why?

2. Isolation is a main theme in this book and Sky becomes isolated in one way or another throughout the book events. Describe instances when she was isolated that was beneficial to her character and decisions she made and ways when it was not.

3. Animal companions and familiars are a recurring theme the author uses in her books, in this case the cat Ad Astra. It is also a recurring theme in culture and literature where cats have a "sixth sense" and can sense paranormal activity. In what other stories does the main character get aid from an animal companion that can sense the paranormal?

4. Power is an important theme in the book, from characters to events to places and to activities. Which

characters have the most power and why? Which activities have power behind them and what is the outcome?

5. In an original draft, MY SOUL TO KEEP was written with older characters and it took place on a college campus instead of a boarding school. In your opinion how would the story be different with older characters? Do you think the outcome would be the same? Do you think the characters' interactions with one another would be the same? What are the benefits of changing it to younger characters?

6. As terrifying as they are, cults are real and have been real and have done many of the things the Guardians of Light do. Discuss how cults come to power, what they have in common and who they prey on and why.

AUTHOR BIO

Jackie Sonnenberg has a background in journalism and theatre. She lives in Orlando, Florida where she is surrounded by creativity and imagination. Jackie is known for creating all her original characters from her stories in costumes and attending events in character, bringing her love of character development, costuming, and acting from being an avid member of the haunted house industry.

Follow her at www.jackiesonnenberg.com

AUTHOR'S NOTE

The Guardians of Light is based, loosely, on a real cult called Heaven's Gate. Heaven's Gate members believed in reaching a level above human ... and that Earth was going to be wiped out. On March 26, 1997 the group ultimately committed a mass suicide with the idea that they would be taken away to the next life. They planned it specifically during the HaleBopp comet believing it would be their mode of transportation, just as the Guardians of Light planned their ritual around a current event. Many characteristics of GOL come from Heaven's Gate such as this core belief, the group suicide, the Exit Videos, and Applewhite Prep is named after the Heaven's Gate leader himself: Marshall Applewhite.

All these references to Heaven's Gate were done so to pay homage to a real-life event, to tell a story with highlights of the horrors and mysteries that come from real life. I, as the author, only used this information as inspiration and do not condone the beliefs of this cult. The story is fiction: but there is truth down to the bone. And, speaking of truths—I would like to thank the people I interviewed who have had real paranormal encounters and out-of-body experiences. This is something I DO believe in and it has been such a profound discovery to hear about traces of spirits ... especially loved ones that want us to know they are still here. Lastly, duh, my family (and extended family) for knowing and accepting how weird I am, and knowing and accepting that they don't know what in the world I am going to do next.

Discover more at
4HorsemenPublications.com

10% off using HORSEMEN10